Addicted to daydream   age, **Angela Bissell**   become a writer althou   career path on her way to authordom. Like many an intrepid Kiwi she also travelled the world, backpacking through Europe, Egypt, Israel, Turkey and the Greek Islands before settling for a time in London. Now she lives back home in New Zealand, never taking a day in her beautiful country for granted and loving the challenge of pursuing her writerly dreams.

Lynne Graham lives in Northern Ireland and has been a keen romance reader since her teens. Happily married, Lynne has five children. Her eldest is her only natural child. Her other children, who are every bit as dear to her heart, are adopted. The family has a variety of pets, and Lynne loves gardening, cooking, collecting allsorts and is crazy about every aspect of Christmas.

Michelle Smart is a *Publishers Weekly* bestselling author with a slight-to-severe coffee addiction. A book worm since birth, Michelle can usually be found hiding behind a paperback, or if it's an author she really loves, a hardback. Michelle lives in rural Northamptonshire in England with her husband and two young Smarties. When not reading or pretending to do the housework she loves nothing more than creating worlds of her own. Preferably with lots of coffee on tap. michelle-smart.com

Italian Summers

Italian Summers The Ultimate Revenge

ANGELA BISSELL

LYNNE GRAHAM

MICHELLE SMART

MILLS & BOON

First Published in Great Britain 2022
By Mills & Boon, an imprint of HarperCollins*Publishers*
1 London Bridge Street, London, SE1 9GF

www.harpercollins.co.uk

HarperCollins*Publishers*
1st Floor, Watermarque Building,
Ringsend Road, Dublin 4, Ireland

ITALIAN SUMMERS: THE ULTIMATE REVENGE © 2022
Harlequin Enterprises ULC.

Surrendering to the Vengeful Italian © 2016 Angela Bissell
The Italian's One-Night Baby © 2017 Lynne Graham
Wedded, Bedded, Betrayed © 2016 Michelle Smart

ISBN 978-0-263-30562-3

MIX
Paper from responsible sources
FSC
www.fsc.org
FSC™ C007454

SURRENDERING TO THE VENGEFUL ITALIAN

ANGELA BISSELL

For Tony. Because you never stopped believing.
And you never let me quit.
Love you to infinity, Mr B.

And for Mum.
The memories have left you but our love never will.
You are, and always will be, our real-life heroine.

CHAPTER ONE

HELENA SHAW HAD been sitting in the elegant marble foyer for the best part of two hours when the man she had trekked halfway across London to see finally strode into the exclusive Mayfair hotel.

She had almost given up. After all the effort she had devoted to tracking him down, she had almost lost her nerve. Had almost let cowardice—and the voice in her head crying *insanity*—drive her out of the plush upholstered chair and back into the blessed obscurity of the crowded rush-hour streets.

But she had not fled. She had sat and waited—and waited some more.

And now he was here.

Her stomach dropped, weightless for a moment as though she had stepped from a great height into nothingness, and then the fluttering started—a violent sensation that made her belly feel like a cage full of canaries into which a half-starved tomcat had been loosed.

Breathe, she instructed herself, and watched him stride across the foyer, tall and dark and striking in a charcoal-grey two-piece that screamed *power suit* even without the requisite tie around his bronzed throat.

Women stared.

Men stepped out of his way.

And he ignored them all, his big body moving with an air of intent until, for one heart-stopping moment, his footsteps slowed on the polished marble and he half turned in her direction, eyes narrowed under a sharp frown as he surveyed the hotel's expansive interior.

Helena froze. Shrouded in shadows cast by soft lighting and half hidden behind a giant spray of exotic honey-scented blooms, she was certain he couldn't see her, yet for one crazy moment she had the unnerving impression he could somehow sense her scrutiny. Her very presence. As if, after all these years, they were still tethered by an invisible thread of awareness.

A crack of thunder, courtesy of the storm the weathermen had been promising Londoners since yesterday, made Helena jump. She blinked, pulled in a sharp breath and let the air out with a derisive hiss. She had no connection with this man. Whatever bond had existed between them was long gone, destroyed by her father and buried for ever in the ashes of bitterness and hurt.

A hurt Leonardo Vincenti would soon revisit on her family if she failed to stop him seizing her father's company.

She grabbed her handbag and stood, her pulse picking up speed as she wondered if he would see her. But he had already resumed his long strides towards the bank of elevators. She hurried after him, craning her neck to keep his dark head and broad shoulders in her line of sight. Not that she'd easily lose him in a crowd. He stood out from the pack—that much hadn't changed—though he seemed even taller than she remembered, darker somehow, the aura he projected now one of command and power.

Her stomach muscles wound a little tighter.

Europe's business commentators had dubbed him the success of the decade: an entrepreneurial genius who'd turned a software start-up into a multi-million-dollar enterprise in less than ten years and earned a coveted spot on the rich list. The more reputable media sources called him single-minded and driven. Others dished up less flattering labels like hard-nosed and cut-throat.

Words that reminded Helena too much of her father. Yet even *hard-nosed* and *cut-throat* seemed too mild, too charitable, for a man like Douglas Shaw.

She shouldered her bag, clutched the strap over her chest.

Her father was a formidable man, but if the word *regret* existed in his vocabulary he must surely rue the day he'd aimed his crosshairs at Leonardo Vincenti. Now the young Italian he'd once decreed unsuitable for his daughter was back, seven years older, considerably wealthier and, by all accounts, still mad as hell at the man who'd run him out of town.

He stopped, pushed the button for an elevator and shoved his hands in his trouser pockets. Behind him, Helena hovered so close she could see the fine weave in the fabric of his jacket, the individual strands of black hair curling above his collar.

She sucked in a deep breath. 'Leo.'

He turned, his dark brows rising into an arch of enquiry that froze along with the rest of his face the instant their gazes collided. His hands jerked out of his pockets. His brows plunged back down.

'What the hell…?'

Those three words, issued in a low, guttural growl, raised the tiny hairs on her forearms and across her nape.

He'd recognised her, then.

She tilted her head back. In her modest two-inch heels she stood almost five foot ten, but still she had to hike her chin to lock her gaze with his.

And oh, sweet mercy, what a gaze it was.

Dark. Hard. Glittering. Like polished obsidian and just as impenetrable. How had she forgotten the mind-numbing effect those midnight eyes could have on her?

Concentrate.

'I'd like to talk,' she said.

A muscle moved in his jaw, flexing twice before he spoke. 'You do not own a phone?'

'Would you have taken my call?

He met her challenge with a smile—if the tight, humourless twist of his lips could be called a smile. 'Probably not. But then you and I have nothing to discuss. On the phone *or* in person.'

An elevator pinged and opened behind him. He inclined his head in a gesture she might have construed as polite if not for the arctic chill in his eyes.

'I am sorry you have wasted your time.' And with that he swung away and stepped into the elevator.

Helena hesitated, then quickly rallied and dashed in after him. 'You've turned up after seven years of silence and come after my father's company. I hardly think that qualifies as *nothing*.'

'Get out of the elevator, Helena.'

The soft warning made the skin across her scalp prickle. Or maybe it was hearing her name spoken in that deep, accented baritone that drove a wave of discomforting heat through her?

The elevator doors whispered closed, cocooning them in a space that felt too small and intimate despite the effect of mirrors on three walls.

She planted her feet. 'No.'

Colour slashed his cheekbones and his dark eyes locked with hers in a staring match that quickly tested the limits of her bravado. Just as she feared that lethal gaze would reduce her to a pile of cinders, he reached into the breast pocket of his jacket and pulled out an access card.

'As you wish,' he said, his tone mild—*too mild*, a voice warned. He flashed the card across a sensor and jabbed the button labelled 'Penthouse Suite'. With a soft whir, the elevator began its stomach-dropping ascent.

Helena groped for the steel handrail behind her, the rapid rising motion—or maybe the butterflies in her belly she couldn't quell—making her head swim.

It seemed her ex-lover could not only afford the finest digs in London…he could afford to stay in the hotel's most exclusive suite.

The knowledge made her heart beat faster.

The Leo she'd known had been a man of understated tastes, stylish in that effortless way of most Italian men but never flashy or overt. She'd liked that about him. Liked his grit and drive and passion. Liked that he was different from the lazy, spoilt rich set her parents wanted her to run with.

And now...?

Her hand tightened on the railing. Now it didn't matter what she felt about him. All that mattered was the havoc he'd soon unleash on her family. If he and her father went head to head in a corporate war and Douglas Shaw lost control of his precious empire the fallout for his wife and son would be dire. Her father didn't take kindly to losing; when he did, those closest to him suffered.

'Has your father sent you?' The way he ground out the word *father* conveyed a wealth of hatred—a sentiment Helena, too, wrestled with when it came to Daddy Dearest.

She studied Leo's face, leaner now, his features sharper, more angular than she remembered, but still incredibly handsome. Her fingers twitched with the memory of tracing those features while he slept, of familiarising herself with that long, proud nose and strong jaw, those sculpted male lips. Lips that once could have stopped her heart with a simple smile—or a kiss.

Emotion rose and swirled, unexpected, a poignant mix of regret and longing that made her chest ache and her breath hitch.

Did Leo smile much these days? Or did those lines either side of his mouth stem from harsher emotions like anger and hatred?

Instinctively Helena's hand went to her stomach. The void inside where life had once flourished was a stark reminder that she, too, had suffered. Leo, at least, had been spared that pain, and no good would come now of sharing hers.

Some burdens, she had decided, were better borne alone. She let her hand fall back to her side.

'I'm not my father's puppet, Leo. Whatever your misguided opinion of me.'

A harsh sound shot from his throat. 'The only one misguided is you, Helena. What part of "I never wish to see you again" did you not understand?'

She smothered the flash of hurt his words evoked. 'That was a long time ago. And I only want an opportunity to talk. Is that asking too much?'

A soft ping signalled the elevator's arrival. Before he could answer with a resounding *yes*, she stepped through the parting doors into a spacious vestibule. She stopped, the sensible heels of her court shoes sinking into thick carpet the colour of rich chocolate. Before her loomed an enormous set of double doors. It was private up here, she realised. Secluded. *Isolated.*

Her mouth went dry. 'Perhaps we should talk in the bar downstairs?'

He brushed past her and pushed open the heavy doors, his lips twisting into a tight smile that only made her heart pound harder.

'Afraid to be alone with me?'

Helena paused on the threshold. *Should* she be afraid of him? In spite of her jitters she balked at the idea. Leonardo Vincenti wasn't thrilled to see her—that was painfully clear—but she knew this man. Had spent time with him. Been intimate with him in ways that marked her soul like no other man ever had.

Yes, she could sense the anger vibrating beneath his cloak of civility, but he would never lose control and lash out at her. He would never hurt her the way her father hurt her mother.

She smoothed her palm down the leg of her black trouser suit and assumed a lofty air. 'Don't be ridiculous,' she said, and strode into the room.

Leo closed the penthouse doors, strode to the wet bar and splashed a large measure of whisky into a crystal tumbler. He knocked back the potent liquid, snapped the empty glass onto the bar and looked at the woman whose presence was like a blowtorch to his veneer of calm.

'Drink?'

'No.' She reinforced her refusal with a shake of her head that made her auburn curls bounce and sway. 'But... thank you.'

Shorter, he noted. Her hair was shorter, the dark silky ribbons that had once tumbled to her waist now cropped into a sophisticated cut above her shoulders. Her face, too, had changed—thinner like her body and more striking somehow, her cheekbones strong and elegant, her jaw line firm. Bluish crescents underscored her eyes, but the rest of her skin was toned and smooth and free of imperfections. It was a face no man, unless blind, would pass by without stopping for a second appreciative look.

Helena Shaw, he reluctantly acknowledged, was no longer a pretty girl. Helena Shaw was a stunningly attractive woman.

Scowling, he reminded himself he had no interest in this woman's attributes, physical or otherwise. He'd been blindsided by her beauty and guise of innocence once before—a grave error that had cost him infinitely more than his injured pride—and he'd vowed his mistake would not be repeated.

Not with any woman.

And especially not this one.

'So, you want to talk.' The *last* thing he wanted to do with this woman. *Dio.* He should have bodily removed her from the elevator downstairs and to hell with causing a scene. He banked the flare of anger in his gut and gestured towards a duo of deep leather sofas. 'Sit,' he instructed, then glanced at his watch. 'You have ten minutes.'

She frowned—a delicate pinch of that smooth brow—then put her bag on the glass coffee table and perched on the edge of a sofa. She drew an audible breath.

'The papers say you've launched a hostile takeover bid for my father's company.'

He dropped onto the opposite sofa. 'An accurate summary.' He paused. 'And...?'

She puffed out a sigh. 'You're not going to make this easy for me, are you?'

Easy? That simple four-letter word made him grind his molars. This girl's entire life had been easy. Her family's excessive wealth, her father's connections, had ensured she wanted for nothing. Unlike Leo and his sister who, after their mother's death, had survived childhood in a murky world of poverty and neglect. For them, nothing came easy.

'You want me to make this easy for you?'

Like hell he would.

She shook her head. 'I want to understand why you're doing this.'

So she could talk him out of it? Not a chance. He'd waited too many years to settle this score with her father. He returned her gaze for an extended beat. 'It's business.'

She laughed then: a short brittle sound, not the soft, sexy laughter that resided in his memory. 'Please—this isn't business. It's...payback.'

Her voice conveniently wobbled on that last word, but her ploy for sympathy, if that was her angle, failed to move him.

'And if I said this *is* payback, what would you say?'

'I'd say two wrongs don't make a right.'

He barked out a laugh. 'A quaint sentiment. Personally, I think "an eye for an eye" has a more appealing ring.'

She dropped her gaze to where her fingers fidgeted in her lap. Her voice was husky when she spoke again. 'People aren't perfect, Leo. Sometimes they make mistakes.'

His gut twisted. Was she talking about her father? Or herself? 'So you're here to apologise for your mistakes?'

She glanced up. 'I tried that once. You didn't want to listen. Would it make any difference now?'

'No.'

'I was trying to protect you.'

He bit back another laugh. By driving a blade through his heart? Leaving him no choice but to watch her walk away? A bitter lump rose in his throat and he swallowed back the acrid taste.

Seven years ago he'd come to London to collaborate with a young software whiz on a project that, if successful, would have guaranteed his business unprecedented success.

As always, he was focused, dedicated, disciplined.

And then he met a girl.

A girl so beautiful, so captivating, she might have been one of the sculptures on display at the art gallery opening they were both attending in the West End.

He tried to resist, of course. She was too young for him, too inexperienced. Too distracting when he should be focused on work.

But he was weak and temptation won out. And he fell—faster than he'd ever thought possible—for a girl who, five weeks later, tossed him aside as if he were a tiresome toy she no longer wanted or needed.

He curled his lip. 'Remind me not to come looking for you if I ever need protection.'

She had the good grace to squirm. 'I had no choice. You don't understand—'

'Then explain it to me.' Anger snapped in his gut, making him fight to stay calm. 'Explain why you walked away from our relationship instead of telling me the truth. Explain why you never bothered to mention that your father disapproved of us. Explain why, if ditching me was your idea of *protection*, I spent the next forty-eight hours watching every investor I'd painstakingly courted pull their backing from my project.'

He curled his fingers into his palms, tension arcing through his muscles. Douglas Shaw had dealt Leo's business a significant blow, yet his own losses had barely registered in comparison to the impact on his younger sister. Marietta's life, his hopes and dreams for her future, had suffered a setback the likes of which Helena could never appreciate.

Sorry didn't cut it.

'Perhaps you wanted an easy out all along—'

'No.'

'And Daddy simply gave you the perfect excuse.'

'No!'

There was more vehemence behind that second denial than he'd expected. She threw him a wounded look and he shifted slightly, an unexpected stab of remorse lancing through him. *Hell*. This was precisely why he'd had no desire to see her. Business demanded a cool head, a razor-sharp mind at all times. Distractions like the beautiful long-legged one sitting opposite him he could do without.

A lightning flash snapped his gaze towards the private terrace overlooking Hyde Park and the exclusive properties of Knightsbridge beyond. His right leg twitched with an urge to rise and test the French doors, check they were secure. He didn't fear nature's storms—on occasion could appreciate their power—but he didn't like them either.

Didn't like the ghosts they stirred from his childhood.

A burst of heavy rain lashed the glass, drowning out the city sounds far below. Distorting his view of the night. He waited for the rumble of thunder to pass, then turned his attention from the storm. 'How much has your father told you about the takeover?'

'Nothing. I only know what I've read in the papers.'

Another lie, probably. He let it slide. 'Then you are missing one important detail.'

Her fidgeting stilled. 'Which is…?'

'The word "successful". In fact…' He hooked back his shirt-cuff and consulted his watch. 'As of two hours and forty-five minutes ago my company is the official registered owner of seventy-five percent of ShawCorp.' He offered her a bland smile. 'Which means I am now the controlling shareholder of your father's company.'

He watched dispassionately as the colour receded from her cheeks, leaving her flawless skin as white as the thick-pile rug at her feet. She pressed her palm to her forehead, her upper body swaying slightly, and closed her eyes.

A little theatrical, he thought, the muscles around his mouth twitching. He shifted forward, planted his elbows on his knees. 'You look a touch pale, Helena. Would you like that drink now? A glass of water, perhaps. Some aspirin?'

Her lids snapped up and a spark of something—anger?—leapt in her eyes, causing them to shimmer at him like a pair of brilliant sapphires.

Leo sucked in his breath. The years might have wrought subtle differences in her face and figure, but those eyes… those eyes had not changed. They were still beautiful. Still captivating.

Still dangerous.

Eyes, he reminded himself, that could strip a man of his senses.

They glittered at him as she raised her chin.

'Water, please.' She gave him a tight smile. 'You can hold the aspirin.'

Helena reached for the glass Leo had placed on the table in front of her and sipped, focusing on the cold tickle of the carbonated water on her tongue and throat and nothing else. She would not faint. Not in front of this man. Shock on top of an empty stomach had left her woozy, that was all. She simply needed a moment to compose herself.

After a third careful sip she put the glass down and folded her hands in her lap. She mustn't reveal her turmoil. Mustn't show any hint of anxiety as her mind darted from one nauseating scenario to the next. Had her father hit the bottle in the wake of this news? Was her mother playing the devoted wife, trying to console him? And how long before the lethal combination of rage and drink turned him from man to monster? To a vile bully who could lavish his wife with expensive trinkets and luxuries one minute and victimise her the next?

Helena's insides trembled, but it wasn't only worry for her mother making her belly quiver. Making her pulse-rate kick up a notch. It was an acute awareness of the man sitting opposite. An unsettling realisation that, no matter how many days, weeks or years came between them, she would never be immune to this tall, breathtaking Italian. She would never look at him and not feel her blood surge. Her lungs seize. Her belly tighten.

No. Time had *not* rendered her immune to his particular potent brand of masculinity. But she would not let her body betray her awareness of him. If her father's endless criticisms and lack of compassion had taught her anything as a child it was never to appear weak.

She laced her fingers to keep them from fidgeting. 'What are your plans for my father's company?'

A muscle in his jaw bunched and released. Bunched again. He lounged back, stretched out his long legs, draped one arm across the top of the sofa. 'I haven't yet decided.'

She fought the urge to scowl. 'But you must have some idea.'

'Of course. Many, in fact. All of which I'll discuss with your father, once he overcomes his aversion to meeting with me.' He paused. 'Perhaps he's hoping his daughter will offer his new shareholder some…incentive to play nice?'

Heat rushed her cheeks, much to her annoyance. 'I don't know what you mean.'

'Oh, come now. There's no need to play the innocent for me.'

Leo's hand moved absently over the back of the sofa, his fingers stroking the soft black leather in slow, rhythmic patterns. Helena stared, transfixed, then hastily averted her eyes. Those long, tanned fingers had once stroked her flesh in a strikingly similar fashion, unleashing in her a passion no man had unleashed before or since.

She pulled in a breath, tried to focus on his voice.

'You needn't look so worried, Helena. You won't have to dirty your hands with the likes of me again.' His fingers stilled. 'I have no interest in anything you could offer.'

As though emphasising his point, his gaze travelled her length, from the summit of her blushing hairline to the tips of her inexpensive shoes. 'As for the company,' he went on, before she could muster an indignant response, 'if your father continues to decline my invitations to meet, my board will vote to sell off the company's subsidiaries and amalgamate the core business with my own. A merger will mean layoffs, of course, but your father's people will find I'm not an unreasonable man. Those without jobs can expect a fair severance settlement.'

Her jaw slackened. 'Dismantle the company?' The one thing guaranteed to bring her father to his knees. 'You would tear down everything my father has worked his entire life to build?'

He shrugged. 'As a minority shareholder he'll benefit financially from any asset sales. He'll lose his position at the head of the company, of course, but then your father's no longer a man in his prime. Perhaps he'll welcome the opportunity to retire?'

She shook her head. For Douglas Shaw it wasn't about the money. Or retirement. It was about pride and respect and status. About winning. *Control.*

'You don't understand.' Her voice trembled. 'This won't hurt only my father. It will hurt others, too—my family. Is that what you want, Leo? To see innocent people suffer?'

His eyes narrowed, his gaze hardening under his dark slanted brows. 'Do not talk to *me* about suffering. You and your family don't know the first meaning of the word.'

Not true! she wanted to shout, but she held her tongue. Another habit deeply ingrained from childhood, when she'd been taught to avoid such indiscretions—to lie, if necessary, about her less than perfect home life.

She stifled a frustrated sigh.

Why did people think growing up with money meant a life filled with sunshine and roses? That might have been the case for some of her friends, but for Helena it had been nothing more than a grand, sugar-coated illusion. An illusion her mother, the ever-dutiful society wife, still chose to hide behind.

Leo lunged his powerful shoulders forward, planted both feet firmly on the floor. 'This is business. Your father knows that. Better than most.'

He rose to his full impressive height: six feet four inches of lean, muscled Italian.

'I could have made things much worse for him. You might remind him of that fact.'

For a moment Helena considered telling him the truth—that she'd not seen or spoken with her father in years. That she worked as a secretary and lived in a rundown flat in North London and visited her family only when her father was absent on business. That Douglas Shaw was a domineering bully and she didn't care a jot for the man, but she did care for those who would suffer most from his downfall. That she held no sway with her father and could offer Leo nothing in return for leniency except her eternal gratitude.

But caution stopped her. The man who stood before her now was not the Leo she'd once known. He was a tough, shrewd businessman, bent on revenge, and he would use every weapon in his arsenal to achieve it. Knowledge was power, and he had plenty of that without her gifting him extra ammunition.

Besides, he'd already accused her of lying—why should he believe the truth?

She unlaced her hands and stood.

'There must be other options,' she blurted. 'Other possibilities that would satisfy your board and keep the company intact?'

'My board will make their decisions based on the best

interests of my business. Not your father's interests and not his family's.' He looked at his watch. 'Now, if you have nothing else to discuss, there are more important matters requiring my attention.'

She stared at him.

More important matters?

A bitter laugh rose and died in her throat.

Really, what had she expected? Understanding? Forgiveness? A friendly chat over a cup of tea?

Humiliation raged through her. She was a fool, wasting her time on a fool's errand. She snatched up her handbag. 'Next time you look in the mirror, Leo, remind yourself why you despise my father so much.' She returned his stony stare. 'Then take a hard look at your reflection. Because you might just find you have more in common with him than you think.'

His head snapped back, an indication that she'd hit her mark, but the knowledge did nothing to ease the pain knifing through her chest. Head high, she strode to the door.

The handle was only inches from her grasp when a large hand closed on her upper arm, swinging her around. She let out a yelp of surprise.

'I am *nothing* like your father,' he said, his jaw thrusting belligerently.

'Then prove it,' she fired back, conscious all at once of his vice-like grip, the arrows of heat penetrating her thin jacket-sleeve, the faint, woodsy tang of an expensive cologne that made her nostrils flare involuntarily. 'Give my father time to come to the table. Before your board makes any decisions.'

Leo released her, stepped back, and the tiny spark of hope in her chest fizzed like a dampened wick. God. She needed to get out. *Now.* Before she did something pathetic and weak—like cry. She pivoted and seized the door handle. At the same instant his palm landed on the door above her head, barring her escape.

'On one condition.'

His voice at her back was low, laced with something she couldn't decipher. She turned, pressed her back to the door and looked up. 'Yes?'

'Have dinner with me.'

She blinked, twice. Three times.

'Dinner?' she echoed stupidly.

'*Si.*' His hand dropped from the door. 'Tomorrow night.'

Her stomach did a funny little somersault. Was he fooling with her now? She narrowed her eyes at him. 'Is that an invitation or a demand?'

The shrug he gave was at once casual and arrogant. 'Call it what you like. That is my condition.'

'Tomorrow's Friday,' she said, as if that fact bore some vital significance. In truth, it was all she could think to say while her brain grappled with his proposition.

His nostrils flared. 'You have other plans?'

'Uh…no. *Brilliant.* Now he'd think she had no social life. She levelled her shoulders. 'A minute ago you couldn't wait to get rid of me. Now you want us to have dinner?'

His lips pressed into a thin line. Impatience? Or, like most men, did he simply dislike having his motives questioned?

He jammed his hands in his trouser pockets. 'You wanted an opportunity to talk, Helena. Take it or leave it. It is my final offer. I return to Rome on Saturday.'

Helena hesitated, her mind spinning. This could be her one and only chance for a calm, rational conversation with him. An opportunity to appeal to his sense of reason and compassion—if either still existed. The takeover was beyond her control and, if he spoke the truth, a *fait accompli,* but if she had even a slim chance of dissuading him from stripping the company's assets, convincing him to settle on a strategy more palatable to her father, she had to take it. Had to try, no matter how daunting the prospect.

She nodded. 'All right. Dinner. Tomorrow night. Where shall I meet you?'

'I will send a car.'

Her stomach nose-dived. The thought of Leo or anyone in his employ seeing where she lived mortified her. Her neighbourhood was the best she could afford right now, but the area was far from salubrious.

She fished in her handbag for pen and paper, jotted down her work address and her mobile number. 'You can pick me up from here.' She handed him the slip of paper. 'And my number's there if you need to contact me.'

'Very well.' With scarcely a glance at it, he slipped the note into his trouser pocket and pulled open the door. 'Be ready for six-thirty.'

With a nod, she stepped into the vestibule and pressed the elevator call button, having briefly considered then dismissed the stairs.

She would *not* bolt like an intimidated child.

The man who'd stolen her heart and left behind a precious gift she'd treasured and lost might be gone, the stranger in his place more formidable than she'd imagined, but she would *not* be cowed.

Ignoring the compulsion to glance over her shoulder, she willed the elevator to hurry up and arrive. When it did, her knees almost buckled with relief. She started forward.

'Helena.'

Leo's voice snapped her to an involuntary halt. Without turning, she braced her arm against the elevator's door jamb and tilted her head fractionally. 'Yes?'

Silence yawned behind her, turning the air so thick it felt like treacle in her lungs.

'Wear something dressy,' he said at last.

And then he shut the door.

CHAPTER TWO

LEO PICKED UP the half-empty water glass and studied the smudge of pink on its rim. *Had Douglas Shaw sent his daughter as a honey trap?* The idea was abhorrent, yet he wouldn't put it past the man. What Shaw lacked in scruples he more than made up for with sheer, bloody-minded gall.

He crossed to the bar, tossed out the water and shoved the glass out of sight along with the whisky bottle. Then he smashed his palms down on the counter and let out a curse.

He should have let her go. Should have let her walk out of here and slammed the door—physically and figuratively—on their brief, discomfiting reunion.

But standing there watching her strut away, after she'd stared him down with those cool sapphire eyes and likened him to her father; seeing the haughty defiance in every provocative line of her body...

Something inside him had snapped and he was twenty-five again, standing in a different room in a different hotel. Watching the girl who'd carved out a piece of his heart turn her back and walk out of his life.

Bitterness coated his mouth. He opened the bar fridge, reached past a black-labelled bottle of Dom Perignon and a selection of fine wines and beers and grabbed a can of soda.

At twenty-five he'd considered himself a good judge of character—a skill honed during his teens, when looking out for his sister, taking on the role of parent during their father's drink-fuelled absences, meant learning who he could trust and who he couldn't. Over the years he developed strong instincts, avoided his father's mistakes and weaknesses, but Helena remained his one glaring failure. For the first and last time in his life he'd let his feelings for a woman cloud his judgement.

He would not make the same mistake twice.

Just as he would not be swayed from his purpose.

Douglas Shaw was a bully who thought nothing of destroying people's lives and he deserved a lesson in humility. Leo didn't trust the man and he didn't trust his daughter.

He drained the soda and crumpled the can in his fist.

Shaw wanted to play games? Leo was ready. He'd been ready for seven years. And if the man chose to use his daughter as a pawn, so be it. Two could play at that game.

He threw the can in the wastebin, a slow smile curving his lips.

Si. This might be fun.

'Go home, Helena.'

Helena looked up from the papers on her desk. Her boss stood holding his briefcase, his suit jacket folded over one arm, a look of mock severity on his face. It was after six on Friday and their floor of the corporate bank was largely deserted.

'I'm leaving soon,' she assured him. 'I'm meeting someone at six-thirty.'

David gave an approving nod. 'Good. Enjoy your weekend.'

He started off, but paused after a step and turned back. 'Have you thought any more about taking some leave?' he said. 'HR is on the use-it-or-lose-it warpath again. And if you don't mind me saying…' he paused, his grey eyes intent '…you look like you could do with a break.'

She smiled, deflecting his concern. David might be one of the bank's longest-serving executives and knocking sixty, but the man rarely missed a beat. He was sharp, observant, and he cared about his staff.

She made a mental note to apply more concealer beneath

her eyes. 'I'm fine. It's been a long week. And the rain kept me awake last night.'

Partly true.

'Well, think about it. See you Monday.'

'Goodnight, David.'

She watched him go, then glanced at her watch.

She had to move.

The car Leo was sending was due in less than twenty minutes, and earning a black mark for running late was not the way she wanted to start the evening.

Shutting herself in David's office, she whipped off her trouser suit and slipped on the little black dress she'd pulled from the bowels of her wardrobe that morning, then turned to the full-length mirror on the back of the door and scanned her appearance.

She frowned at her cleavage.

Good grief.

Had the dress always been so revealing?

She couldn't remember—but then neither could she recall the last time she'd worn it. She seldom dressed up these days, even on the rare occasions she dated. She tugged the bodice up, yanked the sides of the V-neck together and grimaced at the marginal improvement.

It would have to do.

There was no time for a wardrobe-change—and besides, this was the dressiest thing she owned. She'd sold the last of her designer gowns years ago, when she'd had to stump up a deposit and a month's advance rent on her flat. Keeping the black dress had been a practical decision, though she could count on one hand the number of times it had ventured from her wardrobe.

She turned side-on to the mirror.

The dress hugged her from shoulder to mid-thigh, accentuating every dip and curve—including the gentle swell of her tummy. Holding her breath, she pulled in her stomach and smoothed her hand over the bump that no number of sit-ups and crunches could flatten.

Not that she resented the changes pregnancy had wrought on her body. They were a bittersweet reminder of joy and loss. Of lessons learnt and mistakes she would never make again.

She snatched her hand down and released her breath. Tonight she needed to focus on the present, not the past, and for that she would need every ounce of wit she could muster.

Outside the bank a sleek silver Mercedes waited in a 'No Parking' zone, its uniformed driver standing on the pavement. 'Ms Shaw?' he enquired, then opened a rear door so she could climb in.

Minutes later the car was slicing through London's chaotic evening traffic, the endless layers of city noise muted by tinted windows that transformed the plush, leather-lined interior into a private mini-oasis. Like the luxury suite at the hotel, the car's sumptuous interior epitomised the kind of lifestyle Helena had grown unused to in recent years—unlike her mother, who still enjoyed the baubles of wealth and couldn't understand her daughter's wish to live a modest life, independent of her family's money and influence.

She dropped her head back against the soft leather.

She loved her mother. Miriam Shaw was a classic blonde beauty who had moulded herself into the perfect society wife, but she was neither stupid nor selfish. She loved her children. Had raised them with all the luxuries her own upbringing in an overcrowded foster home had denied her. And when they'd been packed off to boarding school, at her husband's insistence, she'd filled her days by giving time and support to a long list of charities and fundraisers.

Yet where her husband was concerned Miriam was inexplicably weak. Too quick to forgive and too ready to offer excuses.

Like today, when she'd called to cancel their prearranged

lunch date. A migraine, she'd claimed, but Helena knew better. Knew her mother's excuse was nothing more than a flimsy veil for the truth, as ineffectual and see-through as the make-up she would use to try to hide the bruises.

Denial.

Her mother's greatest skill. Her greatest weakness. The impregnable wall Helena slammed into any time she dared to suggest that Miriam consider leaving her husband.

A burning sensation crawled from Helena's stomach into her throat—the same anger and despair she always felt when confronted by the grim reality of her parents' marriage.

She massaged the bridge of her nose. Over the years she'd read everything she could on domestic abuse, trying to understand why her mother stayed. Why she put up with the drinking, the vitriol, the occasional black eye. Invariably, when the latter occurred, a peace offering would ensue—usually some priceless piece of jewellery—and then Miriam would pretend everything was fine.

Until the next time.

Helena had seen it more times than she cared to count, but now the stakes were higher. Now her father stood to lose everything he held dear: his company, his reputation, his pride.

If Leo got his way the ShawCorp empire would be carved up like twigs beneath a chainsaw, and Helena had no doubt that if—*when*—her father went down, he would take her mother with him.

'Miss Shaw?'

She jolted out of her thoughts. The car had stopped in front of Leo's hotel and a young man in a porter's uniform had opened her door. Lanky and fresh-faced, he reminded Helena of her brother, prompting a silent prayer of gratitude that James was in boarding school, well away from all this ugly drama.

She slid out and the porter escorted her through the hotel

to a grand reception room with a high vaulted ceiling and decorative walls. The room was crowded, filled with tray-laden waiters and dozens of patrons in tailored tuxedos and long, elegant evening gowns.

'Have a good evening, miss.'

The young man turned to leave.

'Wait!' She clasped his arm, confusion descending. 'I think there's been some mistake.'

He shook his head, his smile polite. 'No mistake, miss. Mr Vincenti asked that you be brought here.'

Leo stood at the edge of the milling crowd, his gaze bouncing off one brunette after another until he spied the one he wanted, standing next to a wide marble pillar just inside the entrance. Weaving waiters, clusters of glittering guests and some twenty feet of floor space separated them, but still he saw the flicker of uncertainty in her eyes. The twin furrows of consternation marring her brow.

Satisfaction stirred. Last night the element of surprise had been hers. How would the minx cope when the tables were turned?

He lifted two champagne flutes from a passing silver tray and carved a path to her side.

'*Buona sera*, Helena.'

She spun, her startled gaze landing on the flutes in his hands, then the bow tie at his throat, before narrowed eyes snapped to his.

'*This* is dinner?'

Score.

He smiled. 'You look very…elegant.'

The look she gave him might have sliced a lesser man in half. 'I look underdressed.'

She smoothed an invisible wrinkle from the front of her short and exquisitely low-cut black dress.

'The other women are wearing ball gowns.'

'Your dress is fine,' he said—an understatement if ever

he'd uttered one. The dress wasn't fine. It was stunning. No eye-catching bling or fancy designer frills, but its simple lines showcased her lithe curves and long, toned legs better than any overblown creation could.

She stole his breath. As easily as she'd stolen his breath the first night he'd laid eyes on her. Her dress that night, however, aside from being a daring purple instead of black, had been less revealing, more…demure. By comparison, tonight's figure-hugging sheath was sultry, seductive, the tantalising flash of ivory breasts inside that V of black fabric enough to tempt any man into secret, lustful imaginings.

'It's a plain cocktail dress,' she said, fretting over her appearance as only a woman could. 'Not a gown for an event like this.' She pressed a hand to the neat chignon at her nape. 'And you're sidestepping the question.'

He extended a champagne flute, which she ignored. 'This—' he gestured with the glass at their lavish surroundings '—is not to your liking?'

'A charity dinner with five hundred other guests? No.'

He feigned surprise. 'You don't like charity?'

She glanced at a wall banner promoting the largest spinal injury association in Europe and its twentieth annual fundraiser. 'Of course I do.' Her eyebrows knitted. 'But I thought we'd be dining in a restaurant. Or at least somewhere…I don't know…a little more…'

'Intimate?'

Her eyes flashed. 'Private.'

'There's a difference?'

She glared at the flute in his hand, then took it from him. 'Do you make a habit of attending charity dinners at the hotels where you stay?'

'*Si*. When I'm invited to support a worthy cause.' He watched her eyebrows arch. 'There are better ways to spend an evening, admittedly, but this event has been a longstanding commitment in my diary. And it coincides with my need to do business in London.'

'Ah, well…' She paused and sipped her champagne. 'That's convenient for you. You get to mark off your social calendar *and* wreak revenge on my family—all in a week's work.' Her mouth curled into a little smile. 'There's nothing more satisfying than killing two birds with one stone. How eminently sensible for a busy man such as yourself.'

Leo tasted his bubbles, took his time considering his next words. Exert enough pressure, he mused, and a person's true colours would eventually surface. 'Revenge is a very strong word,' he said mildly.

Her eyes widened. 'Oh, I'm sorry. Do you have a different name for what you're doing?' She raised her palm. 'No, wait. I remember—"an eye for an eye", wasn't it?'

He studied the churlish set of her mouth, the dainty jut of her chin. 'I had not remembered your tongue being so sharp, Helena.'

Twin spots of colour bloomed on her cheekbones, but the glint of battle stayed in her eyes. 'This is retaliation for last night, isn't it? I turned up unannounced at the hotel and you didn't like it. Now you get to spring the surprise.' She raised her glass in a mock toast. 'Well-played, Leo. So… what now? You parade me on your arm at some high-profile fundraiser and hope it gets back to my father?'

He smiled—which only irritated her further if the flattening of her mouth was any indication. Her gaze darted towards the exit and the idea that she might bolt swiftly curbed his amusement.

Helena would *not* run from him.

Not this time.

Not until he was good and ready to let her go.

'Thinking of reneging on our deal?'

Her gaze narrowed. 'How do I know you'll keep your side of the bargain?'

'I've already spoken with your father's solicitor.'

'And?

'He has until Tuesday to get your father to the table.'

Her mouth fell open. 'My God…that's four days from now. Can you not give him longer?'

'Time is a commodity in business, not a luxury.' He didn't add that the solicitor's chance of success was slim, no matter the time allowed. Both men knew the invitation would be rejected. A great pity, in Leo's mind. He'd hoped to see for himself the look on Douglas Shaw's face when the man learnt the fate of his company. But Shaw's repeated refusals to turn up had denied Leo the final spoils of victory.

'He won't show.'

Her voice was so small he wasn't sure he'd heard correctly. '*Scusi*?'

'My father. He won't show. He won't meet with you, will he?'

He schooled his expression. Had she divined his thoughts? *Absurd.* He shook off the notion. 'You tell me. He's *your* father.'

'Leo, I haven't—'

'Leonardo!'

Leo heard his name boomed at the same time as Helena stopped talking and darted a startled look over his shoulder. He turned and saw a lanky, sandy-haired man striding forward with a petite blonde by his side.

Leo grinned. 'Hans.' He gripped the man's outstretched hand. 'I didn't know you'd be here. How are you? And Sabine.' He raised the woman's slender hand, planted a kiss on her knuckles. 'Beautiful, as always.'

She issued a throaty laugh. 'And you, my dear, are still the charmer.' Rising on tiptoes, she kissed him on both cheeks, then turned her sparkling eyes on Helena. 'Please, introduce us to your lovely companion.'

Leo shifted his weight, fielded a sidelong glance from Helena and sliced her a warning look. *Do not embarrass me.*

'Helena, this is Dr Hans Hetterich and his wife, Sabine. Hans, when he is not winning golf tournaments or sailing a yacht on the high seas, is one of the most prominent spinal surgeons in the world.'

'Nice to meet you, Helena.' Hans took her hand. 'And please pay my friend no attention. I am not nearly as impressive as he makes me sound.'

An unladylike snort came from beside him. 'I think my husband is not himself tonight.' Sabine commandeered Helena's hand. 'Normally he is not so modest.'

Hans guffawed and clutched his chest, earning him an eye-roll and a poke in the ribs from his wife. He winked at her, then turned a more sober face to Leo. 'Our new research unit in Berlin is exceptional, thanks to your support. Our stem cell procedures are attracting interest from some of the best surgeons in the world. You must come soon and see for yourself. And you are most welcome too, Helena. Have you visited Germany?'

Her hesitation was fleeting. 'Once, a long time ago. On a school trip.'

'Perhaps in a few months,' Leo intervened. 'When I get a break in my schedule.'

'How is Marietta?' Sabine said. 'We haven't seen her since her last surgery.'

His fingers tightened on his glass. 'She's fine,' he said, keeping his answer intentionally brief. He had no wish to discuss his sister in front of Helena. Proffering a smile, he gestured at the dwindling number of people around them. 'It appears the waiting staff would like us to be seated. Shall we…?'

With a promise to catch them later in the evening, Hans and Sabine joined the trail of diners drifting through to the ballroom. Leo turned to follow, but Helena hung back.

He stopped, raised an eyebrow. 'Are you coming?'

After a pause, she jammed her evening purse beneath her arm and shot him a baleful look. 'Do I have a choice?'

He gave her a silky smile—one designed to leave her in

no doubt as to his answer. But just to ensure she couldn't mistake his meaning he leaned in and said softly, 'You don't.'

Gorgeous. Devastating. *Lethal*.

Those were three of a dozen words Helena could think of to describe Leonardo Vincenti in a tuxedo. And, judging by the lascivious looks he was pulling from every corner of the ballroom, she wasn't the only female whose hormones had clocked into overdrive at the mere sight of all that dark, brooding masculinity.

He spoke from beside her. 'The fish is not to your taste?'

She cast him a look from under her lashes. 'It's fine. I'm not very hungry.'

The treacle-cured smoked salmon served as a starter was, in fact, superb, but the knots twisting her stomach made the food impossible to enjoy. Which really was a shame, some part of her brain registered, because she rarely had the opportunity these days to sample such exquisite cuisine.

She laid her fork alongside her abandoned knife and leaned back in her chair. So much for a quiet dinner *à deux* and the chance for a serious talk. She almost rubbed her forehead to see if the word *gullible* was carved there.

Surreptitiously she watched Leo speak with an older woman seated on his left. His tux jacket, removed prior to appetisers being served, hung from his chair, leaving his wide shoulders and lean torso sheathed in a white wing tip shirt that contrasted with his olive skin and black hair. He bowed his head, murmuring something that elicited a bright tinkle of laughter from the woman, and the sound scraped across Helena's nerves.

Age, evidently, was no barrier to his charms.

She averted her gaze, smothered the impulse to get up and flee. Like it or not, she'd agreed to be here and she would not scarper like a coward. If she was smart, bided her time, she might still persuade Leo to hold his plans for her father's company. A few weeks…that was all she needed. Time to make her mother see sense before—

'Bored?'

Leo's deep voice sliced across her thoughts.

She drummed up a smile. 'Of course not.'

'Good.' His long fingers toyed with the stem of his wine-glass. 'I would hate to bore you for a second time in your life.'

Helena's smile faltered. His casually delivered words carried a meaning she couldn't fail to comprehend. Not when her own words—words she'd bet every hard-earned penny in her bank account had hurt her more than they'd hurt him—were embedded like thorns in her memory. *I'm bored, Leo. Really. This relationship just isn't working for me.*

She shifted in her seat, her face heating. 'That's unfair.' She glanced around the table, pitching her voice for his ears alone. 'I tried once to explain why I said those things.'

After he'd left that awful message on her phone—telling her what her father had done, accusing her of betrayal and complicity—she'd gone to his hotel room and banged on his door until her hand throbbed and a man from a neighbouring room stepped out and shot her a filthy look.

'You didn't want to listen.'

He shrugged. 'I was angry,' he stated, as if he need offer no further excuse.

'You still are.'

'Perhaps. But now I'm listening.'

'I doubt that.'

'Try me.'

She arched an eyebrow. He wanted to do this *now*? *Here?* She cast another furtive glance around the table. *Fine.*

'I needed you to let me go without a fight,' she said, her voice a decibel above a whisper. 'And we both know you wouldn't have. Not without questions. Not unless I—' She stopped, a hot lump of regret lodging in her throat.

'Stamped on my pride?' he finished for her.

Her face flamed hotter. *Must* he make her sound so cruel? So heartless? She'd been nineteen, for pity's sake, staring down the barrel of her father's ultimatum. *Get rid of the damned foreigner, girl—or I will.* Naive. That was what she'd been. And unforgivably stupid, thinking she could live beyond the reach of her father's iron control.

She smoothed her napkin over her knees. 'I did what I thought was best at the time.'

'For you or for me?'

'For us both.'

'Ah. So you were being...how do you English like to say it...cruel to be kind?'

His eyes drilled into hers, but she refused to flinch from his cutting glare. She didn't need his bitter accusations. She, too, had paid a price, and however much she longed to turn back the clock, undo the damage, she could not relieve the pain of her past. Not when she'd worked so hard, sacrificed so much, to leave it behind.

She mustered another smile, this one urbane and slightly aloof—the kind her mother often wore in public. 'Hans and Sabine seem like a nice couple. Have you known them long?'

The change of subject earned her a piercing stare. She held her breath. Would he roll with it?

Then, 'Nine years.'

He spoke curtly, but still she breathed again, relaxed a little. Perhaps a normal conversation wasn't impossible? 'You never talked much about your sister,' she ventured. 'Sabine mentioned surgery. Is Marietta unwell?'

Long, silent seconds passed and Helena's stomach plunged as the dots she should have connected earlier—Leo's choice of fundraiser, Hans's reputation as a leading spinal surgeon, talk of the Berlin research unit followed by the mention of Marietta and surgery—belatedly joined in her head to create a complete picture.

A muscle jumped in Leo's cheek. 'My sister is a paraplegic.'

The blood that had heated Helena's cheeks minutes earlier rapidly fled. 'Oh, Leo. I'm… I'm so sorry.' She reached out—an impulsive gesture of comfort—but he shifted his arm before her hand could make contact. She withdrew, pretending his rebuff hadn't stung. 'I had no idea. How… how long?'

'Eleven years.'

Her throat constricted with sympathy and, though she knew it was silly, a tiny stab of hurt. Seven years ago they'd spent five intense, heady weeks together, and though he'd mentioned a sister, talked briefly about their difficult childhood, he'd omitted that significant piece of information.

Still, was that cause to feel miffed? She, too, had been selective in what she'd shared about *her* family.

'Did she have an…an accident?'

'Yes.' His tone was clipped.

'I'm sorry,' she said. 'I didn't mean to pry. I can see you don't want to talk about this.'

She lifted a pitcher of iced water in an effort to do something—anything—to dispel the growing tension. She'd half filled her glass when he spoke again.

'It was a car accident.'

Startled, she put the pitcher down and looked at him, but his head was angled down, his gaze fastened on the wineglass in his hand.

'She was seventeen and angry because we'd argued about her going to a party.' His black brows tugged into a deep frown. 'I didn't like the neighbourhood or the crowd, but she was stubborn. Headstrong. So she went anyway. Later, instead of calling me for a ride home, she climbed into a car with a drunk driver.' He drained his wine, dropped the glass on the table. 'The doctors said she was lucky to survive—if you can call a broken back "lucky". The driver and two other passengers weren't so fortunate.'

Helena tried to imagine the horror. Teenagers made bad decisions all the time, but few suffered such devastating, life-altering consequences. Few paid such an unimaginable price.

She struggled to keep her expression neutral, devoid of the wrenching pity it was impossible not to feel. 'Sabine mentioned surgery. Is there a chance…?'

Leo's gaze connected with hers, something harsh, almost hostile, flashing at the centre of those near-black irises. 'Let's drop it.'

Slightly taken aback, Helena opened her mouth to point out she *had* tried to drop the subject, but his dark expression killed that pert response. 'Fine,' she said, and for the next hour ignored him—which wasn't difficult because over the rest of their dinner another guest drew him into a lengthy debate on European politics, while the American couple to Helena's right quizzed her about the best places to visit during their six-month sabbatical in England.

When desserts began to arrive at the tables the compère tapped his microphone, waited for eyes to focus and chatter to cease, then invited one of the organisation's patrons, Leonardo Vincenti, to present the grand auction prize. After a brief hesitation Helena joined in the applause. In light of his sister's condition Leo's patronage came as no real surprise.

His mouth brushed her ear as he rose. 'Don't run away.'

And then he was striding to the podium, a tall, compelling figure that drew the attention of every person—male and female—in the room. On stage, he delivered a short but pertinent speech before presenting a gold envelope to the evening's highest bidder. People clapped again, finished their desserts, then got up to mingle while coffee was served.

Twenty minutes later Helena still sat alone.

Irritation sent a wave of prickly heat down her spine. *Don't run away.*

Ha! The man had a nerve.

She dumped sugar into her tea. Gave it a vigorous stir. Was he playing some kind of cat-and-mouse game? Or had he cut his losses and gone in search of a more agreeable companion for the evening?

Another ten minutes and finally he deigned to show. He dropped into his chair but she refused to look at him, concentrating instead on topping up her tea.

'You have no boyfriend to spend your Friday nights with, Helena?'

Her pulse skipped a beat. No apology, then. No excuse for his absence. Had his desertion been some kind of test? An experiment to see if she'd slink away the minute his back was turned? The idea did nothing to lessen her pique.

She piled more sugar in her tea. 'He's busy tonight.'

'Really?' His tone said he knew damn well she was lying. He lifted his hand and trailed a fingertip over the exposed curve of her shoulder. 'If you were mine I would not let you spend an evening with another man.' He paused a beat. 'Especially not in that dress.'

Carefully, she stirred her tea and laid the spoon in the saucer. He was trying to unsettle her, nothing more. She steeled herself not to flinch from his touch or, worse, tremble beneath it.

His hand dropped and she forced herself to meet his eye. 'You said my dress was fine.'

His gaze raked her. 'Oh, it's fine. Very fine, indeed. And I am sure not a man here tonight would disagree.'

Did she detect a note of censure in his voice? She stopped herself glancing down. She'd been conscious of her plunging neckline all evening, but there were dozens of cleavages here more exposed than her own. And, though the dress was more suited to a cocktail party or a private dinner than a glittering gala affair—cause at first for discomfort—there was nothing cheap or trashy about it.

She crossed her legs, allowing her hem to ride up, until

another inch of pale thigh defiantly showed. 'And you?' She watched his gaze flicker down. 'I wouldn't have thought a man like you would need a last-minute dinner date. Where's your regular plus-one tonight?'

His lips, far too sensual for a man's, twitched into a smile. 'A man like me?'

'Successful,' she said, inwardly cursing her choice of words. 'Money attracts, does it not? The world is full of women who find wealth and status powerful aphrodisiacs.'

One eyebrow quirked. 'When did you become a cynic?'

'Oh, I don't know.' She pursed her lips. 'Maybe around the time you were getting rich.'

He lounged back in his chair, the glint in his eye unmissable. 'In answer to your question, I'm between mistresses.'

'Oh…' She fiddled with the handle on her teacup.

Not girlfriends or partners. *Mistresses.* Why did that word make her heart shrink? So he enjoyed casual relationships. So what? His sex life was no business of hers.

She sat back, forced herself to focus. She couldn't afford to waste time. The evening was slipping away. If she didn't speak soon her chance would be lost. 'Leo, my father and I are estranged.'

In a flash, the teasing light was gone from his eyes. Her stomach pitched. Should she have blurted the words so abruptly? *Too bad.* They were out there now.

A vein pulsed in his right temple. 'Define "estranged".'

She hitched a shoulder, let it drop. 'We don't talk. We don't see each other. We're estranged in every sense of the word, if that's what you're asking.'

'Why?'

She hesitated. How much to tell? The bitter memory of that final violent confrontation with her father was too disturbing to recount even now.

'We fell out,' she said, her tongue dry despite the gallon of tea she'd consumed. 'Over you and what he did after we—after *I* broke things off. I walked out seven years ago and we haven't spoken since.' She paused and glanced down. Her hands were shaking. She lifted her gaze back to his. 'I dropped out of university and went to live in a rented flat. Father cut off my allowance, froze my trust, so I work at a full-time job. As a...a secretary. In a bank.'

Leo stared at her, his face so blank she wondered if he'd heard a single word she said. Her insides churned as if the tea had suddenly curdled in her belly. She wished she could read him better. Wished she could interpret the emotion in those dark, fathomless eyes.

And still the silence stretched.

God, why didn't he say something?

'You gave up your design studies?'

She blinked. *That* was his first question? 'Yes,' she said, frowning. 'I couldn't study full-time and support myself. The materials I needed were too expensive.'

Other students on her textile design course had juggled part-time jobs along with their studies, but they'd had only themselves to think about. They hadn't been facing the same dilemmas, the same fears. They hadn't been in Helena's position. Alone and pregnant.

Careful.

She shrugged. 'I might go back one day. But that's not important. Leo, what I'm trying to tell you is that I'm not here for my father.'

'Then why *are* you here?'

She leaned forward. 'Because what you're doing will hurt the people I *do* love. And before you remind me that my father—and thus his family—stands to gain financially from having his company torn apart, it's not about the money.'

Helena hesitated. She had to choose her words with care. Miriam Shaw might be too proud to admit to herself, let alone the world, that she was a victim, but she was none the less entitled to her privacy. Her dignity. She wouldn't

want the painful truth about her marriage shared with a
stranger. Who knew what Leo might do with such sensitive information?

'My father can be…difficult to live with,' she said. 'At
the best of times.'

Leo sat so still he barely blinked. Seemed barely to
breathe. 'So what exactly do you want?'

'I want you to reconsider your plans for ShawCorp.'
The words tumbled out so fast her tongue almost tripped
on them. 'At the very least give my father more time to
come to the table. Offer him a chance to have a say in the
company's future. Maybe keep his position on the board.'

He gave her a long, hard look. 'That's a lot of want, Helena. You do realise my company is overseen by a board of
directors? I am not the sole decision-maker.'

'But you have influence, surely?'

'Of course. But I need good reason. Your concern for
your family is admirable, but this is business. I cannot let
a little family dysfunction dictate corporate strategy.'

'Can't you at least delay Tuesday's deadline by a few
weeks?'

His eyebrows slammed down and he muttered something under his breath. Something not especially nice.

He rose. 'We will finish this talk later.'

Warmth leached from her face. Her hands. Had she
pushed too hard? Said too much? 'Why can't we finish
it now?'

He moved behind her chair, lowered his head to hers.
The subtle scent of spice twined around her senses. 'Because we're about to have company.' His hot breath fanned
her cheek. 'Important company. And if you want me to
consider your request you will be very, *very* well behaved.'

CHAPTER THREE

Leo straightened and quelled the urge to mutter another oath.

Of all the damnable luck. This night was going from bad to worse. First a call on his mobile from a board member whose angst over a minor matter had required twenty minutes of placation, followed by his relief at finding Helena hadn't done a runner in his absence turning into stunned disbelief over her staggering revelations—revelations his reeling brain had yet to fully process.

And now Carlos Santino. Here in London. At this hotel. At *this* function.

Tension coiled in his gut as the older Italian approached. Santino stood a full head shorter than Leo, but the man's stocky build and confident gait more than made up for his lack of stature. Add to that hard, intelligent eyes above a beaked nose and a straight mouth, and you had the impression of a man who tolerated weakness in neither himself nor others.

Leo liked him. Respected him. Santino Shipping dominated the world's waterways, and in the last three years its cyber security needs had generated sizable revenue for Leo's company. The two men shared a business relationship based on mutual trust and respect.

But Leo had not seen Carlos Santino for several months. Not since he'd rejected the man's daughter.

'Carlos.' He gripped Santino's hand. 'This is unexpected. What brings you to London? I thought few things could prise you away from Rome.'

His client grunted. 'Shopping. Shows. Anything my wife and daughter can spend my money on.' A chunky gold watch and a heavy signet ring flashed in the air. 'Nothing they cannot get in Rome, or Milan, but you know women—' he shrugged expressively '—they are easily bored.'

Leo fired a loaded glance at Helena, but she was already rising, gifting the newcomer a million-dollar smile that drove a spike of irrational jealousy through his chest because *he* wasn't the recipient.

'Helena, this is Carlos Santino, head of Santino Shipping.' A deliberate pause gave his next words emphasis. 'One of my company's largest clients.'

She extended a slim hand. 'A pleasure to meet you, Mr. Santino.'

'The pleasure is mine.' Santino's hand engulfed hers. 'And, please, call me Carlos.' For a long moment he studied her face in a frank appraisal that nearly but not quite overstepped the bounds of propriety. By the time he released her hand, her cheeks glowed a delicate pink. He turned to Leo. 'Business is not your only good reason for visiting London, *si*?'

Leo forced a smile that almost made his eyes water. 'This is a coincidence, running into you here.' He pulled out a vacated chair for his client. 'Maria and Anna are with you?'

Carlos waited for Helena to resume her seat before taking the proffered chair. 'This was Anna's idea. She remembered you were patron of this organisation and…well—' another very Italian shrug '—when my wife planned the weekend Anna called your office and asked if you would be in London.' His smile offered only the vaguest apology. 'You know my daughter. She is resourceful and persistent. And furious with her *papà* right now. She woke with a bad cold this morning and I forbade her to come out. The tickets were already purchased and Maria insisted she and I still come.' He waved his hand. 'My wife is here somewhere—no doubt talking with someone more interesting than her husband.'

Some of Leo's tension eased. The young, voluptuous Anna Santino was an irritation he'd spent several months trying hard to avoid. Running into her this evening, or rather running *from* her, would have turned the night into a complete disaster.

Carlos switched his attention to Helena. 'It is fortunate, I think, that my daughter could not be here tonight. I fear she would be jealous of such a beauty at Leo's side.'

The provocative compliment heightened her colour but her hesitation was brief. 'I'm so sorry to hear your daughter is too ill to come out, Mr San— Carlos. That really is most unfortunate.' Her voice sang with sympathy. 'I do hope she'll be back on her feet again soon. You must tell her she has missed a wonderful, wonderful evening.'

Leo fought back a smirk. She might blush like a novice in a convent, but there was backbone beneath that pseudo-innocent charm. He noted a quirk at the corner of Santino's mouth. A flash of approval in his eyes.

Carlos inclined his head. 'I will, my dear.' To Leo, he said, 'I owe you an apology, my friend. When you told my daughter you had someone special in your life I assumed you were letting her down gently with a lie. I see now I was mistaken. You do have a special lady, indeed. And I am pleased to make her acquaintance at last.'

Leo felt the flesh at his nape tighten. He'd known that small white lie would come back one day and bite him. But flat-out rejecting the daughter of a client as powerful as Santino had seemed as sensible as cementing his feet and jumping into the Tiber. Claiming he was committed to another woman had seemed a kinder, more effective solution.

Carlos's focus returned to Helena. 'How often are you in Rome, Helena?'

Her lips parted and Leo shot her a hard, silencing look. She closed her mouth and frowned at him.

'Not often,' he interceded. 'Business brings me to London on a regular basis.'

'Ah, shame. In that case you need a reason to bring her to our great city.' Carlos's sudden smile drove a shaft of alarm straight to the centre of Leo's gut. 'My wife and I are celebrating our twenty-fifth wedding anniversary next weekend. Maria has organised a party—something large and extravagant, knowing my wife. Please join us. We'd be delighted to welcome you both.'

In the fleeting moment of silence that followed Leo caught a movement from the corner of his eye, but not until he felt the press of her palm on his thigh did he get his first inkling of what Helena intended.

Too late, his brain flashed a warning.

'Thank you, Carlos,' she said, her voice as smooth and sweet as liquid honey. 'That's very kind of you. We'd love to come.' She turned her head and flashed him a dazzling smile. 'Wouldn't we, darling?'

She squeezed his leg and heat exploded in the muscle under her hand. He tensed, biting back an exclamation, the fire shooting straight from his thigh to his groin. *Madre di Dio.* If the vixen inched her fingers any higher he would not be responsible for his body's reaction. He gritted his teeth until pain arced through his jaw—a welcome distraction from the killer sensations stirring south of his waist.

'I will need to check my schedule.' He forced the words past the hot, viscous anger building in his throat. *What the hell was she doing?* 'I may have another commitment.'

'Of course.'

Carlos stood and Leo rose with him, unseating the hand that was dangerously close to setting his pants alight.

'My assistant will contact your office on Monday with the details.' Carlos inclined his head. 'I look forward to seeing you again, Helena. And now I must find my wife before my absence is noted. Leo—good to see you. It has been too long.'

Leo nodded and watched his client's retreating back, the

tension in his chest climbing into his throat until it threatened to choke off his air supply.

He turned, glared at her. 'Get your bag.'

'What?' She stared up at him, wide-eyed. 'Why?'

'Just do it.'

When she hesitated, he grabbed her bag and wrapped a hand around her upper arm, hauled her to her feet.

She snatched her bag from him. 'Where are we going?'

'Somewhere private. To talk. Is that not what you wanted?'

She didn't utter a single word as he marched her out of the ballroom.

The instant the elevator doors closed Helena jerked her arm out of Leo's grasp. 'There's no need to manhandle me.'

He punched the button for the top floor of the hotel and threw her a look so thunderous a sliver of fear lodged in her spine. She edged away, reminded herself with a hard swallow that not all men were physically abusive. But if he was planning to shout she wished to God he'd get on with it. Anything had to be better than this...this tense, oppressive silence.

Moments later he slammed the door of his suite closed and rounded on her. 'What the *hell* was that?' His roar rose to the ceiling, echoed off the walls and reverberated through her chest like a boom of thunder.

She stood calm even as her insides quaked. 'I don't know why you're so angry. I thought you'd be grateful.'

'*Grateful?*' The word barely escaped his clenched teeth.

'Yes.' She pulled her brows into a delicate frown. Ignored the jelly-like quiver in her knees. 'You were in a sticky situation and I was being helpful.' Not to mention reckless and impulsive and out of her mind crazy. *Lord help her.* Whatever she'd done, it was either very clever or very, *very* stupid. 'Or would you have preferred I set Carlos straight about us?'

'*Dio*.' He threw his tuxedo jacket over a lounge chair, ripped his bow tie from around his neck. 'I should have known you'd have another stunt up your sleeve.'

Oh, now, *that* was rich. 'You brought me here tonight,' she reminded him. 'Not the other way around. I couldn't have foreseen your client turning up.'

'But you didn't waste a second in twisting it to your advantage, did you?'

She let out a clipped laugh. 'And *you* made no effort to correct his notion that we're a couple. I'm not a mind-reader, Leo. How was I to know I shouldn't play along?'

'It was simple, Helena.' He enunciated each syllable as if she were missing a few critical brain cells. 'All you had to do was keep your mouth shut. Oh, but wait—' he flung his arms wide '—you're a woman. That would have been impossible!'

He tossed down the tie, tore loose the buttons at his throat, raked lean fingers through his thick black hair. Gone was the cool, suave businessman from the charity dinner. In his place stood a man who looked hard. Fierce. *Dangerous.*

Helena drew a calming breath. She couldn't bottle now. Not when she could see the future looming with such frightening clarity. The takeover was only the beginning. If her mother thought things were bad now, they were only going to get worse. Leo didn't want to own ShawCorp; he wanted to destroy it. And when he succeeded her father's rage would need an outlet. A victim. Helena could not sit on the sidelines. She couldn't stand idle while her mother became that victim.

'Look, I…I'm sorry if I made things worse.' She tried for a softer, more apologetic tone. 'But maybe we could turn this to our advantage? Come to some…arrangement that would benefit us both?'

He stalked towards her and stopped inches short of their bodies touching—so close she could feel the heat emanating from him. In sharp contrast, his dark eyes carried a chill that needled into her flesh like icy midwinter sleet.

'Newsflash, Helena. Mutual benefit works best when each party has something the other needs. And, like I told you last night, you don't have anything I want—or need.' He spun on his heel and strode to the bar, pulled a large bottle from a black lacquered cabinet.

For her own benefit, not his, she straightened her spine. 'You need a girlfriend for your client's party next weekend.'

'Wrong.' He fired the word over his shoulder as he uncapped the bottle. 'On Monday my assistant will advise Santino's office that I am, regrettably, unable to attend.'

'Carlos will be disappointed.'

Amber liquid sloshed into a crystal tumbler. 'He'll get over it.'

'And next time you see him? What if he asks about me? Will you pretend there's still *someone special* in your life?'

'That is not your concern.'

'It is if you pretend that someone is me.'

He turned, the whisky untouched on the counter beside him. 'I will tell him our relationship ended.'

She dropped her purse on the arm of a sofa and sauntered over. 'I'm sure his daughter—Anna, was it?—will be delighted by that news.'

Was that a growl in his throat? She lifted the tumbler of whisky, inhaled the eye-watering fumes and, before she could think twice, helped herself to a generous swallow. The fiery liquid shot down her throat and extinguished the air in her lungs, but the molten heat spreading through her innards fired her courage.

Frowning, he snatched the glass back. 'What exactly are you proposing?'

Hope flared. 'That I attend the party with you in Rome—at your expense, of course—and help you prove to Carlos and his daughter that you're a happily attached man.'

His brows sank lower. 'And in return?'

'In return you defer your divestment of ShawCorp's assets and keep any announcements under wraps until my father agrees to meet you. In the meantime the company operates as normal and my father retains his position on the board.' It would give her father a sense of security. A belief, albeit false, that he still wielded some control.

Leo fell silent for long seconds and she imagined his brain ticking through the options.

'What makes you think your father will come around?'

She hesitated. Chances were he wouldn't. He was too arrogant, too proud, and that was what she was counting on. Because she didn't want to *prevent* her father's downfall. She only wanted to delay it—long enough for Miriam Shaw to accept some hard truths, come to her senses.

'We can agree a time limit. Say…four weeks.'

In two smooth motions he downed the remaining whisky and set the glass on the counter. 'Let me get this straight. You want to play-act at being my mistress—'

'Girlfriend.'

He flicked a hand in the air. 'Same thing—in return for granting your father a grace period?'

'Of sorts. Yes.'

He closed his eyes. Ran a wide palm over his jaw. 'That's insane.'

Totally.

She hiked her chin, swatted away the inclination to agree with him. 'Why? We'd each be doing the other a favour. What's so insane about that?'

'Because I don't need—'

'I know. I know.' Her turn to flick a hand. 'You don't need or want anything from me.' She let that hang a moment. 'But Carlos has met me now, and you said yourself he's an important client. Why decline his invitation if you don't need to? And, assuming you do want Anna to get the message loud and clear that you're unavailable, why not make use of the opportunity?'

He folded his arms, his shirt stretching over biceps that bunched and flexed with what she guessed was a surge of testosterone-fuelled pride. 'I can handle Santino's daughter without your help.'

She let a knowing smile curve her mouth. 'I'm sure you can. And, let's face it, you've done a stellar job so far. So stellar, in fact, that she went to all the trouble of tracking your whereabouts and arranging to be at the same event as you—in a different city. A different *country*.' She shook her head, turned her smile into a pitying grimace. 'I hate to say this, Leo, but that's not a girl who's accepted no for an answer. That's a woman still hot for the chase.'

His muscles deflated slightly, though the arrogant set of his jaw remained. 'That's quite some proposition, Helena. You and I pretending to be lovers. How do you think your father would feel about that?'

Helena swallowed, or tried to, but her mouth had gone suddenly dry. *Lovers.* The word had skimmed off his tongue with such ease and yet it drove home the reality of what she'd suggested. Of precisely the kind of role-playing required to convince a crowd of partygoers that she and Leo were a committed couple. Her belly quivered with something much more unsettling than nerves, but she couldn't back down now.

She moistened her lips. 'I don't mix in my father's circles. Not any more. Few people of note would recognise me, and certainly not in Rome. And if they did, well…why would you care? Isn't that the reason I'm here tonight? Because you like the idea of getting under his skin?'

He frowned at that, eyes narrowed, his fingers yanking loose another button at his throat. He tugged at the collar and the shirt gaped, exposing the base of his strong neck and a triangle of chest deeply bronzed and dusted with fine whorls of dark hair.

Helena jerked her gaze north of his chin. *Focus.*

'There's no reason this can't work. If people in Rome

question why they haven't seen us together before we'll say we wanted to keep our relationship private until we'd figured out the long-distance thing. If we're convincing, Anna will back off and lose interest, and once she's moved on you can tell Carlos we broke up. That way he won't ever have to know you lied to his daughter—' she paused for a significant beat '—or to him.'

His jaw ground from side to side. 'You really think you could pull that off? Convince the Santinos and their hundreds of guests—and there *will* be hundreds—that we're a couple?'

'Sure.' She shrugged, strove for nonchalance. 'Why not? We were lovers once.'

Briefly, admittedly, and then only after she'd convinced him that at nineteen, besides being a legally consenting adult, she was a level-headed young woman who knew her own mind. He had been older, yes, but six years was hardly cradle-snatcher territory. She'd wanted it, wanted *him*, as she'd never wanted anything before. And not once had she regretted what they'd shared—even in the days and months of heartache that followed. Sex with Leo had been the most intense, most beautiful and physically liberating experience of her life.

Nothing, and no one, had come close since.

Drawing courage from the alcohol warming her blood, she stepped forward and cupped a hand around his jaw. 'It wouldn't be so difficult, would it? Pretending we're lovers? Pretending we're enamoured of each other?'

She swayed her hips—a gentle, seductive grind that bumped their bodies and sparked a slow blossoming of heat low in her pelvis.

Bone and muscle shifted under her palm. He ground out an oath, seized her wrist. 'What are you doing?'

'Proving I can play the part. I *can*, Leo, if that's what you're worried about.'

There was no mistaking the growl in his throat this time.

Or the sudden flash of heat in his eyes. His grip tightened and she thought for one heart-stopping moment he was going to kiss her—haul her against him, crash that harsh, beautiful mouth down on hers and kiss her. Her breath stalled. Her heartbeat hitched. A tiny, forbidden thrill of anticipation skimmed her spine.

Then his head was snapping back, his hand thrusting hers away as if he found her touch, her very proximity, repugnant. 'How do I know your father didn't put you up to this? That everything you've told me tonight isn't more lies? Tell me why I should trust you.'

Heat seared Helena's face even as the flare of desire in her belly iced over.

Because I loved you once! she almost shouted. *Broke my heart in two for you. And, by God, doesn't that make me the world's biggest fool?*

She bit the lining of her cheek. Distrust was written all over his face. In the hard, narrowed eyes, the implacable jaw. The contemptuous twist of his mouth.

She looked him in the eye and spoke with a quiet dignity that camouflaged the turmoil inside her. 'I lied to you once, Leo. I don't deny it and I'm not proud of it. I made up a weak, hurtful excuse to end our relationship because that was what my father wanted. *Demanded.*'

She passed a hand over her eyes, the strain of recent days coupled with sleepless nights taking its toll.

'My greatest mistake was believing that if I obeyed him, did what he wanted, that would be the end of it. Why he went after you I'll never know. Maybe he was punishing me. Maybe he did it simply because he *could*. Whatever his reasons, I can assure you this—I did *not* tell him anything about you or your project. Wherever he got his information, it wasn't from me.' She exhaled on a heavy sigh, the last of her energy rapidly waning. 'Is it really so hard for you to believe me now?'

His gaze held hers, no softening visible in those midnight depths. 'After the stunt you just pulled, what do you think?'

She backed up a step, the ice in her belly trickling into her veins. Astonishing that a man could nurse his anger, his resentment, his need for retribution for so many years. Pride, rage, distrust—whatever the emotions that drove him, they were too strong, too ingrained for her to fight against and win.

She collected her purse, turned to face him one last time. 'You really want to know what I think? I think you're right. This is insane, and I'm sorry I suggested it. Manipulation might be my father's forte, maybe even yours, but it's not mine.' She walked to the door and glanced back, her smile brittle. 'Good luck with taking my father down a peg or two.' She inclined her head. 'I believe he might have met his match.'

She opened the door and paused a moment, half expecting a presence to loom at her back, a hand to fall on her shoulder. But she heard no footfalls, no rustle of movement behind her. She stepped out, closed the door and rode the elevator down to the foyer.

Minutes later, striding through the brisk evening air to the nearest tube station, she angrily dashed the tears from her eyes.

She would *not* let them fall.

Leo didn't deserve her anguish.

Not seven years ago, and not now.

Leo stopped pacing just long enough to glare at the whisky bottle and dismiss the notion of refilling his glass.

Getting tanked so he could obliterate this evening from his memory held a certain appeal, but he'd cleaned up his father's drunken messes too often as a kid to condone such mindless excess. Not to mention he'd have one hell of a hangover. Besides, his pilot had scheduled an early-morning return to Rome, and a flight-change was out of the question. If he turned up to Marietta's first ever art exhibition a dishevelled, ill-tempered wreck he'd spend days, if not weeks, earning his little sister's forgiveness.

He flung his restless frame into a chair, his muscles stiff after the effort of holding his body in check. Of stopping himself from charging after Helena like some raging Neanderthal and forcing her to press those sultry curves against him one more time.

Scowling at the flash of heat in his groin, he got up to pace again. He was too wired to sit, his head too full of questions clamouring for answers. Answers he needed if he were to make any sense of Helena's actions. The idea that she'd come to him without her father's knowledge, that she and Shaw were estranged and had been for years, that she'd abandoned her studies, now lived alone in the city, worked nine-to-five as a secretary in a bank...

He shook his head as if he could clear the overload from his brain.

Truths, half-truths, or carefully constructed lies?

Whatever the answer, there were more layers to this situation than met the eye. And if his years of dealing with wily competitors and cut-throat corporates had hammered home any lessons, they were never to accept anything at face value, never to underestimate your opponent, and never to assume he'd go down without a fight.

Turning on his heel, he retrieved his tux jacket and pulled out his mobile. He placed a call and his friend Nicolas answered within two rings. Leo skipped the pleasantries—Nico didn't do small talk—and launched into his request.

'I need this ASAP,' he finished.

A short silence came down the line, then Nico's deep voice. 'No problem, *mon ami*. I will have something for you in forty-eight hours.'

Gratitude surged, even though Leo had known his friend would do him this favour, no questions asked. Nicolas

César ran a global security firm with an investigative arm reputed for its reach and discretion. He was a man with the resources to uncover the secrets of the world's most powerful and influential people. Confirming a few basic facts about an Englishwoman would amount to little more than child's play.

Leo tossed aside his phone, stripped off his clothes and headed for the en suite bathroom. He turned on the shower and let the steaming jets of water ease the tension from his muscles.

If Nico delivered with his trademark efficiency Leo would soon know if there was any truth to Helena's claims. And whatever his friend's probing unearthed, whatever truths—or lies—were revealed, she would soon discover this was far from over.

Whether she had planned to or not she'd started something tonight, and Leo intended to finish it.

The next time Helena Shaw walked out of his life it would be on *his* terms.

On Monday morning Helena stepped out of the elevator on the forty-second floor of the bank and knew at once something wasn't right. For a start the receptionist grinned at her, and prim, efficient, fifty-something Jill didn't grin. She smiled. Professionally. No grinning allowed.

'You're late,' Jill announced.

'I know,' Helena said, flustered enough without Jill stating the obvious. 'The Underground was a nightmare this morning.' And the last thing she'd needed on the heels of a long, sleepless weekend. All she wanted was to get to her desk and bury herself in work. 'Any mail for David?'

'He collected it ten minutes ago—along with your visitor.'

Helena stopped. 'My visitor?'

'A man.'

And there it was again. Not a smile. A *grin*. Helena

couldn't recall ever before seeing so many of her colleague's teeth.

'He said he was a friend, so once Security cleared him I had them send him up. When David arrived and I mentioned you had a visitor he took him through to your office. His name was…' She picked up a piece of notepaper. 'Yes, that's right. Mr Vincenz—no, Vincenti.'

Helena blinked. She wasn't at the office at all. She was still tucked up in bed. Dreaming about the infernal man who had single-handedly ruined her weekend.

Jill frowned. 'Helena? Are you okay?'

No. 'Yes,' she said, forcing herself to rally. To *think.* She managed a smile. 'Thanks.'

Before Jill could probe further, she pushed through the glass security doors and followed the executive corridor down to her workspace. With every step the tremor in her knees threatened to escalate into a full-blown quake.

At her desk, she dumped her bag, removed her blazer—the temperature in the office had soared suddenly—and glanced around. No tall, dark, brooding Italian in sight. She could, however, hear voices in David's office, and when a burst of laughter carried through the half-open door any lingering doubts were swiftly dispelled.

She clutched the edge of her desk, her stomach clenching in response to that rich, full-bodied sound and the confirmation that Leo was not only here, at her office, *in her boss's office,* he was having a nice little one-on-one with David while he waited for her to arrive.

Confusion followed by a spurt of alarm jolted her into action. Without knocking, she pushed open David's door and two heads swung in her direction. In a matter of seconds her brain registered two things.

First, David was not behind his desk but seated out front, beside his guest—a relaxed approach he only ever adopted with her or with people he especially liked. And second, though by no means less noteworthy, was the simple fact that Leonardo Vincenti looked just as mind-blowingly sexy in a silver suit, pale blue shirt and striped tie than he did in any formal tuxedo.

Helena's mouth went dry. No wonder Jill had been grinning like a schoolgirl.

'Ah, here she is,' said David, and then both men were on their feet, greeting her with smiles, the megawatt force of Leo's almost knocking her back on her heels.

He walked over, slipped his arm around her waist and dropped a featherlight kiss on her temple. Her knees nearly gave out.

'Morning, *cara*.' The firm press of his hand in her side sent a message—or was it a warning? 'My meeting was cancelled at the last minute and, since I was nearby, I thought I'd take the opportunity to see your offices.' He drew her into the room. 'And to meet David, of course.'

Her gaze darted to the older man, who now wore a grin to rival Jill's. She opened her mouth, but the dryness had crawled down her throat and no sound came out aside from a slight wheeze.

She gave herself a mental kick. 'Sorry I'm late, David. Problems on the tube…'

He waved off the apology. 'It's a nice change to beat you into the office for once. And I must say it's been an unexpected pleasure to chat with your man, here.'

Her man. The floor lurched and it was only Leo's grip that kept her steady, despite the unsettling effect his touch had on her insides. She wanted to swat his hand away, sink into a nearby chair. She forced herself to concentrate on David's voice.

'I was just telling Leo how seldom you take any leave, and he mentioned how keen he is to get you to Italy.'

He paused, rocked on his heels, looking immensely chuffed with himself all of a sudden. Helena felt faint.

'He also tells me you're off to Rome at the weekend and it would be the perfect chance for you to stay longer.' The men exchanged a glance. 'I think it's an excellent idea. Why don't you take a week?'

Helena couldn't help herself; she gaped at her boss. 'A…a *week*?'

Leo's fingers dug into her side but she refused to look at him. If he flashed her another of those devastating smiles she'd lose her ability to think, let alone remain upright.

She stared at David. 'I…I couldn't. Things are much too busy.'

'Nonsense. The office won't grind to a halt in your absence and neither will I. Hire me a temp who's half as efficient as you and I'll survive the week just fine.'

'Perhaps you should listen to your boss, *cara*,' came a silky voice in her ear, and she stifled the adolescent urge to stamp her heel onto his foot.

'I'll think about it,' she said to David. 'I promise. But right now we should get back to work. I'm sure Leo's taken enough of your time.'

A slight shift in her stance dislodged his hand from her hip. She turned, forced a smile onto her stiff lips.

'Shall we grab a quick coffee before you go?'

CHAPTER FOUR

HELENA OPENED THE door to a vacant meeting room, stood to one side and waited for Leo to enter. He paused, gave the room a cursory once-over, then crossed to a large bank of windows overlooking the River Thames and the City of London's eclectic skyline of spires and towers.

'Not bad, Helena.' He turned his back to the view. 'You were a little stiff, but we can work on that.'

She closed the door, sucked in a deep breath and counted to twelve before the urge to shout had safely passed.

She expelled the air from her lungs. 'Why?'

'Why do we need to work on it?'

She made a ticking sound in her throat. 'Please don't play games with me.'

One eyebrow hooked up, as did one corner of his mouth—a subtle shift of facial muscles that barely qualified as a smile, yet Helena had the distinct impression he was enjoying himself.

'The only game I'm playing is the one you wanted to play, *cara.*'

'Stop calling me that.' She crossed her arms over her chest. 'And stop avoiding the question. I assume you've changed your mind about things since Friday? Why?'

Moving with more grace than a man of his height and size should possess, he propped his hip on the long conference table dominating the room. 'You're assuming my mind was made up.'

'Wasn't it?'

'No.'

'Then why did you let me leave?'

He shrugged. 'I wanted time to consider your proposal.'

She huffed out a breath. The possibility that in the interim *she* might change *her* mind clearly hadn't occurred to him. She changed tack. 'Why are you here?'

His brow furrowed. 'Did we not just establish that?'

'No, I mean why are you *here*? At my office. Talking to my boss.' She narrowed her eyes at him. 'How did you know where I work?'

'You gave me the address yourself.'

She thought about that, then bit her lip. He was right. She'd jotted down the address so he could send a car to collect her on Friday. A simple enquiry at the downstairs security desk would have filled in the rest. Still, it didn't excuse his turning up here with no warning. He had her mobile number. He could have phoned.

Like you could have phoned him before turning up at the hotel?

She slammed a lid on that voice. 'And your little *tête-à-tête* with David? What was that all about?'

His mouth quirked again. 'He invited me into his office. Refusing would have been rude, no?' The quirk lingered a few seconds more. 'Your boss seems a pleasant man—he speaks very highly of you, by the way. But tell me...' He paused, all trace of levity leaving his face. 'Why are you wasting your time in a job like this?'

His question stung. It shouldn't have, but it did. It reminded her of her father and all the hurtful criticisms she'd endured as a child. The small, painful barbs that pierced the protective wall her mother tried to erect between father and daughter. Her list of faults was exhaustive. And while being born a girl surely drove the first of many nails into her coffin, opting for design school over a law degree and dating a man not of her father's choosing certainly hammered in the last.

She lifted her chin. 'You're belittling my job now?'

'Not at all. I appreciate the value of a skilled assistant. I have an excellent one myself, and she is an asset to my office. But this—' he lifted a hand to indicate their surroundings '—is not the career you were planning seven years ago.'

Not the answer she'd expected. Still, she didn't need to justify her choices. Her job was *not* the dream career in design she'd once envisaged, but hopes and dreams, just like people—just like tiny, innocent, unborn babies—could unexpectedly die.

She dismissed his censure with a shrug. She worked hard, made an honest independent living, and no one— not her father and certainly not this man—had any right to judge her. 'Plans change. People change. And how I make a living is no business of yours.'

His black-lashed eyes treated her to a long, intense regard that made her tummy muscles tighten. 'You are right—it's not my business,' he said at last, though his tone wasn't in the least contrite. 'What you do in the coming weeks, however, *is*. Assuming you want to proceed with this little plan of yours?'

She stared at him, a prickle of unease tiptoeing down her spine. *Weeks?* Her arms fell to her sides. 'You're not serious about me spending a whole week in Italy?' Her stunned gaze met his cool, unwavering stare. She shook her head. 'Oh, no. That…that wasn't the agreement.'

His brows snapped together. 'We had no agreement, as I recall. You chose instead to put me in a difficult position with my client and then used it as a means of blackmail.'

Blackmail? 'I did no such thing!' Her face flamed. With indignation, she told herself. Not with guilt. Definitely not guilt. '*You* chose not to correct Carlos's assumption about us. I simply played along and then suggested we might come to some…some mutually beneficial arrangement.'

'Ah. Yes. The "mutually beneficial arrangement" in which I grant your father a grace period of four weeks, and in return you give me the pleasure of your company for—' his eyebrows rose '—one night?'

She smoothed her palms down the front of her black knee-length skirt. 'One *evening*,' she corrected, keeping her chin elevated. 'And, yes, that would be the arrangement to which I'm referring.'

He laughed—a deep, mellifluous sound that seemed to reach out and brush her skin like the rub of raw silk.

Her anger spiked. 'Is something amusing?'

'Only your ability to play naive when it suits you.'

'What is that supposed to mean?'

'It means you are well aware those terms are weighted in your favour and not mine.' He took his time adjusting a silver cufflink on his left sleeve. When he looked up, his expression had hardened. 'Did you think I would simply roll over for you, Helena?'

The undercurrent of menace in his voice made her knees quiver again. 'But why?' she blurted. 'What could you possibly want with me for a week?'

One side of his mouth kicked up. 'What, indeed?' he murmured, his gaze sweeping her length in an unhurried appraisal that set her teeth on edge—more so because she knew her clumsy question had invited it. 'Let's call it a balancing of the odds.' His eyes flicked back to hers. 'It would be a crime, would it not, if one of us were to feel…cheated?'

An enigmatic response at best. A deflection of her question as skilful as it was irritating.

She crossed to a window, leaned her hip against the metal sill and attempted nonchalance. 'So our pretence of being a couple—you're suggesting we keep that up for the entire week?'

'*Si.*'

'Why?'

'People will want to see us.'

'What people?'

'The people who have heard about you.' He tilted his head and smiled. 'Do not look so puzzled, Helena. You know how it is among the rich and privileged—the gossip mill is a voracious beast. And Rome is no different from London. Worse, in fact. We Italians love our drama.'

Her temples started to throb. 'But I met Carlos only three nights ago.'

He gave another of his maddening shrugs. 'Carlos tells his wife. His wife tells their daughter. Anna tells a friend… or twenty. News travels. You know how it works.'

Yes. She knew how it worked—that brittle, superficial world of the social elite. It had been her world once and she rarely missed it. Scratch the surface of gloss and glamour and every time you'd find a bitter core of hypocrisy and backstabbing.

She massaged the growing pressure in her temples. What madness had she started? 'What if we don't convince them?'

'That we are lovers?'

'Yes.' The word came out slightly strangled.

He straightened from the table. 'You assured me you could handle it. Are you getting cold feet already, Helena?'

She almost laughed at his choice of expression. Cold? Oh, no. No part of her felt cold right now. Not even close. Not when the prospect of their playing lovers for an entire week had her blood racing so hot and crazy she feared her veins might explode.

He stepped towards her. 'There *is* one way to ensure we're convincing.'

'Oh?' She tamped down the urge to scurry to the other side of the room. 'How?'

'Drop the pretence.'

Her brain took several seconds to register his meaning. She blinked, a bubble of incredulous laughter climbing her throat. 'You're kidding, right?'

'You find the prospect of sex with me abhorrent?'

The question—so explicit and yet so casually delivered—triggered a fresh wave of heat that burned from her hairline all the way down to the valley between her breasts. Abhorrent? No. Dangerous? Yes. Terrifying? *Utterly.* Though not for any reason she was fool enough to admit.

Her brain scrambled for a foothold. 'I don't understand.' That sounded lame. 'You said you didn't—that you weren't—that you no longer...' *Wanted me.* Were those the words he'd used? She squeezed her eyes shut. No. His exact words had been, *I'm not interested in anything you could offer.*

A shard of pain in the vicinity of her heart made her wince.

'What is there to understand?'

She opened her eyes to find him standing in front of her. Startled, she stepped back, the windowsill's sharp edge biting into her thighs.

'We know we're compatible in bed,' he said, his voice so calm, so matter-of-fact she wanted to scream. 'Why not make the most of our arrangement—throw some pleasure into the mix?'

Lightheaded suddenly, she gripped the ledge behind her, its hard metal surface cool and reassuringly solid beneath her palms. She breathed in. Out again. Summoned calm. He was toying with her...having fun at her expense. Needling for a reaction he wasn't going to get.

She tightened her fingers on the sill. 'I still don't believe you're serious.'

'And you still haven't answered my question.'

'What question?'

'Do you find the prospect of sleeping with me abhorrent?'

She looked him in the eye. She wouldn't lie.

'Of course not.'

But neither would she pander to his ego.

'But that doesn't mean I have any great desire to jump into your bed.'

He shifted closer and she shrank back—away from the

wall of masculine heat threatening to envelop her. A tell-tale pulse galloped at the base of her throat and she cursed her body's irrepressible responses. Why, oh, why could she not control her reactions to him?

'Is that so?' He lifted a finger and traced a fiery line from her jaw down to that delicate pulse-point in her neck. 'Then why do I make you nervous? Or is there another reason your heart is beating so wildly right now?'

She smacked his hand away and tried to straighten, barely daring to breathe. If she swayed the tiniest fraction their bodies would connect. Just the thought made her nipples peak hard and sensitive under the cotton layers of her bra and blouse.

'Don't flatter yourself,' she snapped, but his gaze was already dipping, taking in the evidence of her body's swift, mortifying arousal.

When his eyes reclaimed hers, the naked hunger in those inky depths nearly took her knees from under her.

'Your body betrays you, Helena.'

Before she could utter a denial his hands spanned her waist, his palms searing like hot iron through thin cotton as they slid upwards, coming to rest beneath the swell of her breasts. He dragged his thumbs up and outward, gliding them over taut, sensitive peaks. Her breath locked in her throat, a combination of panic and unbidden craving making her blood pulse at a dizzying speed.

'I think you are not as immune to me as you would like to believe,' he crooned in her ear.

And then he was setting her away from him. Stepping back. Giving her room to breathe.

Leaving her hot and flustered and confused.

He straightened his silver tiepin. 'Those are my terms.'

His tone had turned crisp, businesslike, his face impassive, and she wondered with a touch of hysteria if the lust she'd seen in his eyes had been imagined or real.

'Take it or leave it, Helena. But I need your answer—*now*.'

She hesitated, her thoughts splintering, scattering in too many directions. *Too unexpected...too overwhelming... too crazy...*

She drew a shaky breath and expelled it. 'I...I don't know...'

'In that case we have no deal.'

And just like that he turned to go.

Stunned, she stared after him, motionless at first, then with teeth clenched, hands fisting by her sides. She closed her eyes, the throb in her temples building to a painful crescendo. *What was she doing?* Was she really going to stand here and watch him leave? After he had, in essence, offered her what she wanted? He'd asked for one week in return—one week out of her life. Was that sacrifice so unthinkable?

For her mother?

She snapped open her eyes. 'Wait!'

He stopped, glanced back, one hand raised to the door. *'Si?'*

'Five days,' she croaked.

His arm lowered. *'Scusi?'*

She cleared her throat. 'Five days,' she repeated, certain he'd heard her well enough the first time. 'And my own room.'

'Seven.' He turned, his dark eyes glinting. 'And I can guarantee you'll find more satisfaction in my room.'

Cocky bastard. She smiled thinly. 'My own room.'

He shrugged, unconcerned. As if, for all his baiting, where she slept mattered to him not one way or the other.

'And my father gets six weeks.'

A mirthless laugh rumbled in his chest. 'Nice try.'

'Five, then.'

'Four.'

They stared at one another, eyes locked in challenge, each waiting for the other to concede. He wouldn't, she knew, but she needed this final moment of defiance.

Needed to savour these last precious seconds of sanity before she plunged off the edge into madness.

The prospect alone had fear clawing her insides, but it wasn't the promise of night-time pleasures with the man who had once owned her heart that frightened her beyond measure. It was the hot, delicious, burgeoning spark of desire in her belly she could neither extinguish nor control.

She squared her shoulders. Hiked up her chin. *Please don't let me regret this.*

'We have a deal.'

On Thursday, close to noon, Helena's mobile phone rang. She answered on the run, dashing out to collect a sandwich for David and a salad for herself prior to a lunch meeting.

'You're panting.'

Leo.

'I'm running.'

Well, almost. Walking briskly. She dodged a flying cycle courier, who in turn dodged a double-decker bus.

'Contrary to popular belief, secretaries don't spend all day sitting on their backsides.'

An unexpected chortle came down the line. A deep, sexy, gravel and velvet laugh that reminded her, fleetingly, of the old Leo. Her stomach flip-flopped.

'A car will pick you up tomorrow, at six p.m., to take you to the airport. Where do you wish to be collected?'

She jostled her way into a popular sandwich bar, wondered if he was still in London or back in Rome, then wondered why she cared.

She mimicked his cool, no-nonsense tone. 'From the office.'

'Fine. Six o'clock. Don't be late.' He ended the call as abruptly as he'd commenced it.

Helena frowned at her phone, then shoved it back in her blazer pocket and smothered a flash of annoyance. Letting his lack of geniality irritate her was silly—a waste of mental energy when she had none to spare. They weren't a couple, and nor were they friends. Out of the public eye there was no need for pleasantries or false sentiment. And as for his taunts about her sleeping in his room, sharing his bed—turning their ruse into reality—they had been nothing more than that.

Taunts.

Unfortunately that thought didn't placate her nerves later that evening as she stared at the neatly packed contents of her suitcase. Stomach churning, she ran through the list in her head one last time, confident she hadn't overlooked any essential items. Tomorrow the compact roller case would wheel easily on and off the train to work and her canvas carry-on, holding her passport, purse, and the jeans and tee she would change into for travelling, was light enough to hitch over one shoulder should she need a hand free.

Satisfied, she made some peppermint tea to pacify her tummy and settled on her sofa. It was late now—well after eleven—and her flat was silent, the tenants upstairs and the neighbourhood streets finally, blissfully quiet. She sipped her tea, let the fragrant brew circulate and soothe, then put down her cup and picked up the envelope she'd pulled from her nightstand drawer earlier in the evening.

She lifted the flap and pulled out a photograph—a picture of a tiny baby swaddled in the soft folds of a hospital-issue blanket. For long moments she studied the image, noting every detail even though she could close her eyes and still know every individual feature by heart. From the adorable tufts of jet-black hair to the miniature half-moons of delicate lashes and the sweetest little Cupid's bow mouth she'd ever seen on a child.

She'd named her son Lucas, and he would have been six now had he lived. She had other mementos of him, too. Small treasures. Keepsakes. Stored in the beautiful wooden memory box her mother had bought. But this image of her son—so tiny and precious, cradled in her arms as if he simply slept—was by far her favourite.

She swallowed and breathed through the dull, familiar ache that settled in her chest whenever she thought of her stillborn son.

Carefully, she slipped the photo back into the envelope.

Leo had been long gone by the time she had learnt she was pregnant, and though she'd known in her heart she had to tell him she hadn't found the courage to do so. He'd been so angry the last time they'd spoken, his declaration that he never wanted to see her again so adamant and final. Far easier, she had discovered, to let fear and hurt rule her head than to step back into the firing line.

And yet the day she gave birth to their son—the moment she cradled his tiny, silent, still warm body in her arms—all that fear and hurt became trivial. Irrelevant. Because she knew. Knew that if Lucas had been gifted life she could never have kept him from his father. Could never have denied Leo the chance to know he had created such a beautiful, perfect little boy.

She rose, went to her bedroom and slid the envelope back into her nightstand drawer.

Months of counselling had helped her to move on with her life, overcome her feelings of anger and guilt, but those dark, endless days of soul-destroying grief—she wouldn't wish those on anyone. Not her worst enemy and not Leo. What could be gained now by dredging up all that heartache and sorrow? Nothing. It was history. Water under the bridge. Whatever cliché one wanted to assign it.

Some burdens, she reminded herself, were better borne alone.

Leo stood at the head of the steps that scaled the private jet and checked his watch for the fifth time in as many minutes.

Damn it. Why did his shoulders feel as if they were

roped into knots the size of fists? And why couldn't he shake this weird, jittery feeling from the pit of his stomach?

Granted, he'd expected the car he'd sent for Helena to have arrived by now, but it was Friday rush hour and this was London. Traffic would be hitting its peak and a fifteen-minute delay was negligible. If the driver had encountered any serious hold-ups, or if Helena had failed to show, he'd have heard by now.

All of which meant he needed to kill this obsession with his watch and *relax*.

This arrangement of theirs might top the scale of hare-brained ideas, but his impromptu return to London on Monday had at least gained him an edge. In less than an hour he'd blindsided Helena at her office—fair payback for ambushing him at the hotel—tossed her firmly on to the back foot and enjoyed their verbal sparring to boot.

Though not nearly as much as he'd enjoyed putting his hands on her.

His fingers curled at the memory of her skin's heat penetrating his palms through her thin blouse and the way her nipples had pebbled in response to his touch. At some point the vibrant girl with her bold colours and creative ambitions had given way to a woman too content with mediocrity, yet he'd seen a spark of fire in her blue eyes that convinced him some remnant of that passionate, captivating girl still existed.

A flash of reflected sunlight at the edge of the Tarmac caught his eye and he squinted into the lowering sun. A silver SUV with tinted windows approached, cruising to a stop in the traffic safety zone alongside the aircraft hangar. The driver sprang from the vehicle and made for the other side, but his passenger had already climbed out. Smiling at the man, her loose curls tossed by the evening breeze, she spoke a few words Leo strained to hear but couldn't catch from where he stood.

He sucked in his breath, the edgy, irritable mood that

had plagued him all day dissipating beneath an entirely different kind of tension.

Dio.

Even casually attired, the woman was a breathtaking vision. A perfect combination of long, slender limbs and feminine curves in all the right places. An ache stirred deep in his groin as he watched her cross the Tarmac, her rounded breasts clearly outlined beneath her figure-hugging tee, the denim of her jeans stretched over shapely hips and slender thighs. In one hand she carried a jacket, in the other a small holdall.

He descended the steps. When she neared he took her bag, slipped an arm around her waist and pulled her flush against him. Her eyes widened, her mouth forming a perfect O of surprise.

'*Ciao*, Helena.' He lowered his head, intending to drop an experimental kiss on those sweet, inviting lips, but she averted her face and his mouth collided instead with her cheek.

Her body stiffened. 'People are watching,' she hissed.

He glanced at the men in overalls working around them, some engrossed in their tasks, others paused and openly staring.

'So they are.' He dragged her closer, some deep, primal instinct urging him to send a clear message to the onlookers. *Mine.* He turned his attention back to her mouth. 'Perhaps we should not disappoint them?'

Her eyes narrowed to pinpricks of sapphire and she pulled in a breath, but whatever retort hovered on that pretty pink tongue she chose not to share it. Instead she twisted from his grasp and started up the steps, the mesmerising roll and sway of her hips holding his gaze captive. He tightened his grip on her bag, his amusement tempered by a sting of annoyance.

Was this how she planned to fulfil her role as his mistress? By tolerating his touch only when it suited her?

Think again, cara.

'Drink?' he offered after he'd stashed her bag in an overhead locker and snapped the cover closed. For a woman she travelled exceptionally light. The carry-on he'd just stowed was small and compact, the single piece of luggage the driver had removed from the SUV not much larger.

The observation gave him pause. A week ago he'd have shrugged it off, assumed she planned to hit the shops in Rome and buy an extra case to carry home her purchases. Now, after Nico's report, he knew that scenario was unlikely. Despite her family's enviable wealth, Helena's lifestyle appeared modest, even frugal. A revelation he found oddly disturbing.

She tossed her jacket over a seat. 'Yes, please.'

He moved to a built-in bar where a bottle of champagne sat chilling on ice. He filled two long-stemmed flutes, handed one to Helena and raised the other in a toast. 'To our arrangement.'

She hesitated before touching her glass to his. The crystal sang sweetly as the rims clinked. 'To our arrangement.'

Her head arched back on her graceful neck as she took a surprisingly long swig of the effervescent liquid. She lowered the glass, gestured a hand at the cabin's interior.

'You travel in style.'

He considered the gleaming mahogany fixtures, fine Italian leather and thick cut pile carpet. The expansion of his business into Asia and North America over the last few years had demanded extensive travel, and his board had deemed the corporate jet a justifiable expense.

'You sound surprised.'

She shrugged. 'It's more luxurious than I'd expected.'

'And you disapprove?'

For a second the question seemed to throw her, then her features morphed back into an aloof, dignified mask. 'No. Of course not. It's just…not what I'm used to these days.'

'And what *are* you used to?'

Her eyebrows tugged together. 'I don't know. Things more…ordinary, I suppose.'

'In that case—' he took her glass, placed both flutes on the bar '—you will need to reacquaint yourself with things less…ordinary.'

He moved closer, enjoying the way her eyes flared wide, the titillating glimpse of her tongue as it darted across her lower lip. She was nervous, despite her cool, controlled demeanour. The skittering pulse at the base of her throat gave her away.

'And there is one more thing you must become accustomed to.'

She notched her chin. Quietly defiant. Utterly beautiful. 'And that is…?'

He captured her jaw between thumb and forefinger. 'Me.'

CHAPTER FIVE

HELENA SWALLOWED. THE generous mouthful of bubbles she'd foolishly imbibed on an empty stomach was meant to give her sass and courage. Instead she felt lightheaded and shaky on her feet. She wanted to turn her head, tear her gaze from those mesmerising eyes, but his fingers held her captive.

'I don't know what you mean.'

'Then I will demonstrate.'

The instant his head lowered, panic seized her. 'Wait!' Her hands flew to his chest. 'What are you doing?'

He halted, his lips mere inches from hers, his black-fringed eyes glittering like a star-studded night. *With what? Amusement? Desire?*

'Demonstrating my point.'

She pushed harder, her fingers tingling, his warmth— his vitality—seeping through the fabric of his shirt and into her nerve-endings. 'What point?'

'That you seem to have developed an untimely aversion to me.'

He grasped her wrists, the latent strength in his long fingers making her bones feel small. Fragile.

'No one will believe we are lovers if you balk at my touch.'

She tried to free herself but he held fast, keeping her hands anchored to his chest. Under her palms his heart beat strong and steady, unlike hers, which had launched into the cardiac equivalent of a Fred and Ginger tap routine.

'We agreed to play lovers in public.' *Why did her voice sound so high and breathless?* 'Not in private. And I've proved to you I can do this.'

'Yet you stiffen in my arms like an innocent.'

He pulled her hands upward, linking them behind his neck. Dragging her body into agonising contact with his.

'It will not do, Helena. Carlos Santino is an astute man, his daughter no fool. If we are to convince them you must learn to relax with me.' His big hands circled her waist. 'And now is the perfect time for a lesson.'

Heat spiralled through her, but she fought the shiver of desire gathering momentum in her muscles. He was testing her boundaries, pushing her limits, and she would not give him the satisfaction of seeing her quiver. She dropped her arms and willed her body to go lax. Unresponsive. She could struggle, make it difficult for him, but he was strong. He'd kiss her anyway. Better to play it cool and aloof and retain at least some scrap of dignity.

She closed her eyes, pressed her lips together and waited, but the expected pressure of his mouth didn't come.

His hot breath skimmed her lips as he spoke. 'Your little martyr act doesn't wash with me, *cara*. Admit it. You want my kiss. My touch. Your body craves it—' his hand rose to the back of her head and closed around a fistful of curls '—just as mine does.'

She opened her eyes and shook her head—or tried to. Moving was difficult with his long fingers tangled in her hair. 'You're wrong.'

'Are you sure about that?' His teeth flashed, his quick smile too sharp. Too knowing. 'I remember the nights you begged for my touch…the nights you lay naked beneath me, panting and pleading—'

'Stop!' His brazen words evoked a hot rush of erotic memories. Fresh panic spurted in her chest. 'Maybe this was a…a mistake.'

His eyebrows hiked. 'This was your idea, remember? What are you afraid of?'

Myself.

'Nothing.'

Amusement rumbled deep in his chest. 'Liar.'

He tugged her head back, tilted her face to his, and she knew in the span of a single panicked heartbeat she was headed for trouble. Knew the instant his mouth covered hers this kiss would not be the hard, demanding, alpha-take-charge kiss she'd expected. No. This kiss was something altogether different. Something far more calculated and disturbing. A skilled, sensual assault that sent his mouth and tongue moving in long, lazy strokes over her tightly clamped lips.

Helena's nostrils flared, her sharp inhalation drawing in the heady spice of his cologne, and a whimper of protest caught in her throat. Or was it a moan? Either way, Leo showed no sign of relenting. His lips coaxed, his tongue teased, his teeth lightly grazed. And with every stroke, every nip and tug, her resolve to refuse him access suffered another crippling blow.

Ruthless, she thought, the floor tilting under her, the bones in her legs melting like heated wax. He was ruthless and she was drowning, oblivious to everything except the hard male body imprisoning hers and the sweet, blistering assault of his mouth.

Belatedly she registered a tugging at her waistband, a whisper of cool air on her midriff—and then the explosive charge of flesh against heated flesh. She jerked with surprise, but the hand behind her head held firm while the other rose to cup her breast. Deft fingers hooked aside cotton and lace and closed around one hard, almost painfully taut peak.

Helena arched her back and groaned. She couldn't help it. Her body was on fire and she couldn't douse the flames. Her lips parted, her lungs desperate for air, and she did nothing to resist when Leo's tongue swept in and tangled with her own. He growled—with satisfaction or triumph?—and then she was lost, unable to remember why she didn't want this. Didn't want *him*. With a moan of surrender, she wound her arms around his neck. Arched into his touch. Opened herself to his kiss.

'Ahem…'

Helena froze.

Oh, no, no, no.

That could *not* be the sound of a man clearing his throat inside the cabin. Heat of a different kind crawled up her neck as she realised that Leo, too, was motionless, his mouth locked on hers, one hand twined in her hair while the other cradled her breast beneath her tee.

Horrified, she wriggled to snap whatever spell held him frozen. Slowly his head lifted, his gaze blazing into hers with momentary intensity before shifting to the uniformed man standing near the entry to the cockpit. Her cheeks flamed. Why didn't Leo release her? Remove his hand from her breast? She squirmed, mortified.

'Five minutes to take-off, sir,' the attendant said, his voice neutral, his face devoid of expression.

Leo nodded. '*Grazie.*'

The man retreated behind a floor-length curtain and she dragged in a breath, waited for the curtain to fall, then shoved at Leo's chest. Her trembling arms possessed just enough strength to break his hold. Hastily she rearranged her bra and tee, conscious of her smarting cheeks. Her tingling lips.

One kiss.

And she'd lost herself completely. Been ready to give him whatever he wanted. Whatever he demanded. How could she be so weak? So pathetic?

Was this what her mother did every time she kissed and made up with her husband? Did she let herself get played? Sucked in by some practised seduction routine that made her forget all the hurt that had gone before? All the ugliness that would surely follow?

Anger flared, at herself. At him. 'Is this part of our

deal?' She yanked the hem of her tee into her jeans. 'That you get to maul me whenever you feel like it?'

He had the nerve to smile. A cool, sardonic smile that made her want to throw something—preferably at his head.

'You call that being mauled?'

'What would *you* call it when a man forces himself on a woman?'

His soft laugh jarred her nerves. 'Force?'

She would have spun away if his hand hadn't risen with startling speed to capture her jaw. Her pulse skittered.

'Don't fool yourself, *cara*.' He dragged his thumb over her mouth, parted her lips. Ran his tongue over his own as if recalling how she tasted. 'You enjoyed that as much as I did.'

A sharp denial danced on her tongue but she choked it back. His heated appraisal, the glitter in those dark eyes, told her he felt the pull of their physical attraction as surely and inexorably as she. Refusing to acknowledge what they both knew existed was futile. Dangerous. Instinct warned he'd take great pleasure in proving her wrong—again.

She jerked free of his grasp, moved to a window seat and strapped herself in. Outside, the ground crew completed their final safety checks and she stared out the window, feigned interest in their activity.

Leo made her feel vulnerable, exposed, and she hated it. Hated that her desire for him was so plain to see. Hated the ease with which he zeroed in on it, ruthlessly exploiting her weakness for him.

Her father did the same thing—found people's weaknesses, their soft spots and vulnerabilities. Was that why her mother stayed? Did he wield her fears and weaknesses against her? Use them as leverage so she didn't leave?

Helena blinked away the burn of tears. She'd never make her mother's mistake. She'd rather die a dried-up old spinster than tolerate a man who didn't treat her with respect.

If only Leo's kiss hadn't made her blood sing. Hadn't fired every dormant cell in her body to glorious life.

With a ragged sigh, she closed her eyes and let her head fall back against the seat.

So much for cool and aloof.

Leo closed his laptop as the pilot announced their descent into Rome's Fiumicino Airport. The flight had been uneventful and he'd passed the time with work, sifting through emails and reports while Helena had mostly slept. Or pretended to. He wasn't sure which. Either way, she'd avoided engaging with him, stirring only once in two hours to visit the restroom and accept refreshments.

He studied her in the seat opposite. Her eyes were closed, long lashes the same dark auburn as her hair fanned over ivory skin, and the slopes of her breasts rose and fell in time with the steady, hypnotic rhythm of her breathing. Her hair was shiny and tousled and the thick, lustrous curls he'd enjoyed twining his fingers through tumbled in soft waves to her shoulders.

His groin stirred, unbidden. She was a temptress. Beautiful as a mythical siren and twice as dangerous with those sweet, alluring lips that could test the restraint of any man with a libido and a heartbeat.

They had certainly tested his.

He let his gaze linger a few seconds longer, then dragged his focus to the window and the vast sprawl of lights in the blackness beyond.

This version of Helena was a mystery to him and he didn't like mysteries—or secrets. He liked staying one step ahead of the game. The takeover was a done deal, but writing off his opponent would be premature. Douglas Shaw would be seeking ways to retaliate, and the man had a reputation for playing dirty. The possibility that he'd reached out to his estranged daughter, manipulated her in an effort to undermine his adversary, was one Leo couldn't afford to ignore.

The jet's wheels hit the Tarmac and Helena stirred. She straightened, blinked, looked out the window, then peered at her watch.

'One hour,' he said.

She glanced up. 'Sorry?'

'Turn your watch forward one hour. It's just after ten.'

The plane taxied to a stop near a large hangar. Fifteen minutes later customs formalities had been completed and their luggage transferred to the trunk of a black Maserati convertible. He guided Helena into the front passenger seat, then slid behind the wheel, anticipating at once the dichotomous feelings of control and freedom he enjoyed whenever he took charge of the sleek, powerful machine.

'The Eternal City,' Helena murmured when, a short time later, he manoeuvred them into busier, more densely populated streets. She stared out her side window at the illuminated façades of elegant old buildings, towering columns and ancient timeworn structures.

'You've never visited Rome?'

She shook her head. 'I never got around to it.'

He glanced at her. Was that a wistful note in her voice? Seven years ago she had bubbled with excitement when he'd suggested bringing her to Rome. He didn't know why the fact she hadn't come with a boyfriend or lover in the years since should give him a small kick of satisfaction—but it did.

'I'd love to explore while I'm here.'

'You can sightsee during the days, while I'm working. I will arrange a driver and a guide.'

He sensed rather than saw her sharp look. 'I don't need a babysitter.'

'I am not suggesting you do.'

'But you'd be happier if someone kept an eye on me,

right?' Her sigh was loud. 'You really *do* have trust issues, don't you?'

A young couple on a red scooter swerved in front of the car, forcing him to brake. 'Meaning…?'

'Meaning I'm not going to run off the minute your back's turned. We made a deal and I don't plan to renege on it. I'm here, aren't I?'

The scooter sped off down an alley and he hit the accelerator again. 'Rome is a vast city, Helena. An experienced guide can ensure you see the best sights. Go to the right places. There are areas I would not like to see you, or any woman unfamiliar with the city, go to alone.'

'I can take care of myself.'

He smiled. Briefly. 'I have no doubt. But if you wish to sightsee you will have a guide. I will not debate with you on this,' he ended, injecting a note of finality into his voice.

Helena averted her face and he wondered if she would sulk. He didn't recall her being the petulant type, but then neither did he remember her being so argumentative. Perversely, he liked it.

'Are you always so over-protective?'

Her voice was soft, laced with curiosity rather than the irritation that had spiked her earlier words. He frowned, a ripple of discomfort sliding through him. The question felt intrusive, too personal, and for several awkward moments an answer eluded him.

'I do not consider the use of good sense to be over-protective,' he said at last.

Silence met his statement, and when he glanced over she was studying him intently. He tightened his grip on the steering wheel. Marietta, too, had accused him of being over-protective at times, but taking care of his sister was a responsibility he would never shirk—no matter how vociferously she objected. He knew the consequences of failing in that duty and he never wanted to feel the devastation of such failure again. Loving someone, being responsible for them, was no trifling task. Most days it scared the hell out of him.

Setting his jaw, he crunched the Maserati's gears and turned into the narrow lane that ran down the side of his apartment building. He pressed a key fob on his visor and a wrought-iron gate rattled open, granting access to the secure courtyard he shared with his tenants. He nosed the car past two others and stopped in a reserved space beneath the leafy branches of a mature orange tree.

Helena peered up at the building's ornate façade. 'You live right in the city?'

He shut off the engine. 'Apartments in central Rome with private parking are rare. When one of my clients put the building on the market last year I considered it a good investment.'

She gaped at him. 'You bought the entire building?'

He shrugged. 'It's convenient. My office is a few blocks from here.'

She shook her head and climbed out of the car, completely absorbed, it seemed, in her surroundings. Leo retrieved their luggage from the boot and hoped their previous discussion was over and forgotten. With any luck she'd realise the futility of defying him and accept his edict about the sightseeing.

If she didn't…?

Well, he could think of several ways to silence her arguments. And he wasn't above a few dirty tactics of his own.

Leo's penthouse apartment was spectacular.

Stylish modern furniture, richly textured rugs and great expanses of glass created a slick, contemporary oasis that floated in peaceful isolation above the heart of the ancient city.

Helena tried hard not to look impressed.

Tried harder still to calm the flutter in her belly as he took her to a bedroom with stunning views from a floor-to-ceiling window and an en suite bathroom so massive she could have swung a tiger. She slipped her holdall off her shoulder, her gaze landing on the gigantic bed with its big, plump pillows and soft ivory comforter.

A steady flush crept up her neck.

'Hungry?'

She darted him a look. 'A bit.' On the plane she'd snacked on biscuits and fruit between bouts of sleep. Now her stomach craved something more substantial. Not to mention her mouth. Dry as a sandpit. 'Thirsty more than anything.'

He laid her case on the upholstered ottoman at the end of the bed. 'Settle in, then come and find me in the kitchen when you're done. Back down the hall on the right.'

Left alone, and with a burst of energy born of nervous tension, Helena made short work of unpacking. Not that the task required much effort. Even with all her clothes arranged on individual hangers she'd utilised only a fraction of the gargantuan wardrobe. She straightened the skirt of the long black gown she'd bought on impulse from a store selling pre-loved designer fashion, stashed her case in the rear of the wardrobe, then checked her phone.

No messages, but she hadn't expected any. She'd told her mother she was going out of town, visiting a girlfriend in Devon and then attending a team-building course with colleagues during the week. Small, innocuous lies that had caused a pang of guilt, but there was no reason her mother should know about her arrangement with Leo.

She tucked her phone away. Recent conversations with her mother had been stilted, tense, but Miriam *had* agreed to meet and talk the following weekend, and that, if nothing else, was progress. In the meantime Douglas had run off to Scotland to shoot deer and no doubt seek solace in a bottle or two of single malt: typical behaviour for a man who thought himself untouchable. But on the upside her mother was safe. For now, at least. The coward couldn't lay hands on his wife while he wallowed in denial four hundred miles away.

Expelling her father from her thoughts, Helena ventured into the hall and followed the faint aroma of garlic and basil until she came to a big, stainless steel and black granite kitchen.

Leo stood behind a large central island, his hand wrapped around the handle of a sharp knife, a partially sliced tomato on the thick wooden board in front of him. An open can of soda sat on the granite. He appeared relaxed. At ease. And more achingly handsome than any man had a right to look, standing at a bench chopping vegetables.

She raised her eyebrows. 'You cook?'

He glanced up. 'Bruschetta is hardly cooking. But, yes, when I have the time. My housekeeper stocks the kitchen for me.'

A housekeeper. That explained the spotless floors and gleaming surfaces everywhere she looked.

'You said you were thirsty. Wine, juice or soda?'

Wine was tempting, but her lack of control after the bubbles on the plane made her shy away from that idea. 'Juice, thanks.' She raised a hand when he paused his work. 'I can help myself.' Better that than stand there gawking at him. She crossed to a stainless steel double-door refrigerator, surveyed its impressive contents, and selected a carton of apple juice. 'Glasses?'

'Cabinet on your left.'

After filling a tall glass and savouring her first thirst-quenching swallow, she hovered awkwardly. 'Anything I can do?'

He scooped the cut tomato onto a platter with thin strips of prosciutto, sliced mozzarella, fresh basil leaves and fat cloves of garlic. 'If you still like Cerignola olives, there's a jar in the fridge door. Small bowls are in the same cabinet as the glasses.'

Her mouth watered. Years ago he'd introduced her to the

large, sweet-flavoured Italian olives and she'd loved them. Still did. The fact he remembered that tiny detail made her heart clench in an unexpected way.

What else did he remember?

She found the jar and grabbed two ceramic bowls—one for the olives and one for discarded stones.

It didn't matter what he remembered. Or what he didn't. She wasn't here for a waltz down memory lane.

She hunted out a spoon and fished out the olives, putting them into a bowl, careful not to transfer too much of the oily brine.

She couldn't resist. The olives were plump and juicy and she was ravenous. She popped one straight from the jar into her mouth, paused a second to anticipate the burst of flavour on her tongue—then nearly inhaled the olive whole when two large hands circled her waist from behind. Her hand jerked and the spoon slipped, catapulting an olive over the benchtop like a miniature green missile. Helplessly she watched it shoot off the end and roll, leaving a wet, glistening trail over the limestone floor.

Leo pulled her against him. 'Relax,' he murmured in her ear, and she bit through the flesh of the olive.

The temptation to do exactly that—relax into him, let her shoulders and buttocks mould to his hard, muscular contours—was too strong. Too dangerous.

She gripped the edge of the bench.

Oh, God.

She wasn't ready for him to touch her like this, hold her like this, whisper in her ear like a sweet, familiar lover. No more than she'd been ready for the mind-blowing impact of his kiss. Yet in less than twenty-four hours she had to be ready. Tomorrow people would watch them closely. Especially the Santinos. And Italians were demonstrative people, unafraid to express themselves in front of others. She and Leo couldn't simply claim to be lovers. They must *behave* like lovers.

She forced her grip on the bench to loosen.

'I'm just getting in some practice.' His warm lips brushed the sensitive skin below her earlobe, inciting an involuntary shiver in her muscles. His arms tightened around her. 'You are cold?'

Damn him. She wasn't cold and he knew it. The evening was humid and sultry. She shook her head, not trusting herself to speak.

'So quiet, Helena…' His mouth trailed to the ultra-sensitive spot between her neck and shoulder. 'What are you thinking?'

That I want this. I want you. I want you to stop and I want you never to stop.

She removed the olive stone from her mouth and very carefully placed it in the empty bowl. 'I'm thinking I'd quite like that glass of wine now.'

He straightened. And chuckled? Yes, she could hear the gravelly purr in his throat. Feel the vibrations in his chest. His hands slid off her waist and she returned to her task. Focused on her breathing in an effort to slow her heartbeat.

He placed a glass of wine beside her.

'Thanks.' Somehow she managed to sound normal rather than breathless. Lifting the glass to her nose, she inhaled the spicy, berry-scented aroma. Did he also remember her preference for red wine?

Eager to avoid the onset of a tense, awkward silence, she sipped and said, 'Mmm…nice.'

'Vino Nobile di Montepulciano.'

She blinked. 'Pardon?'

'Noble Wine from Montepulciano. Not to be confused with the more commonly known wine derived from the Montepulciano grape in Abruzzo.' He extracted a tray of rustic-style bread slices from the oven's grill. 'Montepulciano is a hill town surrounded by vineyards in southern Tuscany. Vino Nobile di Montepulciano is one of Italy's oldest wines.'

'Tuscany?' Was he trying to put her at ease now with idle chitchat? Okay. Fine. It was safe ground—safer than where they were before. She'd go with it. She had to. She wouldn't survive the week if she couldn't handle a harmless conversation with him. 'I hear that part of Italy is beautiful.'

'*Si*. Very.' He transferred the platters to a slab of granite extending from the island and pulled out two high leather stools. 'I have a villa in the province of Siena, not far from Montepulciano.'

She sipped her wine, quietly digested that snippet of information. A villa in Tuscany. A penthouse in Rome. Exclusive hotel rooms in London. Not forgetting the house-keeper and, of course, his company jet. However severe his setback at the hands of her father, it hadn't stopped his meteoric rise to success.

She perched on a stool, decided that now was not the time to challenge him on that, and focused on the food. 'I'm hungry.' She studied the platters. 'Where do I start?'

'Here. Like this.' He rubbed a garlic clove on a piece of grilled bread, drizzled over olive oil, piled on tomato and mozzarella and topped it with basil leaves and a grind of salt and pepper. He handed it to her. 'Bruschetta—*tradizionale*.'

'Looks wonderful.'

And it tasted just as good.

They ate and drank and she asked him about Rome and Tuscany, quizzing him on the culture, history and climate of each region. He seemed content to keep their conversation light, the topics neutral, and gradually the pretence of normality eased her tension. Or was that thanks to the wine she'd consumed?

When Leo picked up the bottle again she covered her glass and shook her head. The wine had helped her relax, but too much would lull her into a false sense of comfort.

'We need a story about where and when we met,' he said,

his gaze fastening on her mouth as she fired in another olive. 'I suggest we use a version of the truth.'

Conscious of his scrutiny, she removed the olive stone as daintily as she could and washed the pulp down with a gulp of wine. 'The truth?'

'That we met at an art gallery in London some years ago and have recently become reacquainted.'

She nodded slowly. 'How recently?'

He sipped his wine, considered. 'Five months.'

Five months? Did that account for the time since he'd rejected Anna Santino and then some? Or had it been five months since his last mistress? Abruptly, she killed that line of thought. She didn't need to know. Didn't want to know.

'Okay. Five months.'

'Good.' He put his glass down, reached for an olive, the movement bringing his arm into contact with hers. The touch was fleeting, inadvertent, yet instant heat flared beneath her skin.

Without meaning to, she flinched.

His brows slammed down. '*Damn* it, Helena.'

'I'm sorry.'

'I don't bite.'

'I know.'

'Then why leap like a scalded cat every time I touch you?' Lines bracketed his mouth—deep grooves of displeasure that made her stomach lurch. 'Do you find my touch so repellent?'

Her eyes flared. 'No—'

'Perhaps you were right to have second thoughts.' He balled up his paper napkin and tossed it over the benchtop. 'We'll never pull this off. The whole thing is crazy. *Pazzo.*'

Panic surged up her throat. 'It's not. I *can* do this.'

'Can you?'

She pushed off her stool. 'Yes,' she said, her tone low and fierce, and before she could stifle the impulse she fisted her hands in his shirt, shoved him against the granite and slammed her mouth over his.

Reckless! a voice in her head screamed, but she silenced it. What better way to prove her ability to play his mistress than with a kiss? A kiss that had to knock him dead, she told herself, letting instinct and boldness take over as she flicked her tongue into his surprise-slackened mouth.

Heat combined with the taste of salt and red wine exploded on her tongue, and when he grunted she thrust deeper, a second time and a third, until his grunt became a low growl against her lips.

Leo moved, shifting his weight on the stool, and she felt the hot imprint of his big hands curving around her buttocks. Then he hauled her in close, his powerful thighs parting to accommodate her, and angled his head to give their mouths a better fit.

And, Lord, the man knew how to kiss. Knew how to use those sensual lips and that wicked tongue to devastating effect. He stroked into her mouth, his tongue hot, demanding, and she almost lost her grip on his shirt. Almost lost her grip on *herself.*

A warning shivered through her.

How easy it would be for her to let hunger overcome sense and give in to the hot need pulsing at her core. But this kiss wasn't about sating her needs, or his. It was about taking control. Proving a point. To herself as much as to him.

She wrenched her mouth away, stepped back and watched a range of expressions roll over his chiselled features. Her heart slammed against her ribs and she balled her hands, concentrated hard on calming her breathing.

Leo made no such effort. His breath fired from his chest in short, harsh bursts and a dark flush rode high on his cheekbones. She took in his bunched shirt, wet lips, stunned gaze. He looked like a man who had been thoroughly kissed.

Please, voice, don't tremble. 'I can handle this, Leo.'

She leaned in and rubbed her thumb over his mouth, wiping away the moisture from their kiss. His eyes darkened and his hands reached for her, but she backed off before he could touch her.

'Thanks for supper,' she said lightly. 'If you don't mind, I think I'll turn in. It's been a long day and I'm rather tired.' She paused in the doorway, forced a smile onto her lips. 'Goodnight.'

By the time Helena closed the door of the guest bedroom her heart was pounding so hard she felt short of breath and dizzy.

With swift, robotic movements that required blessedly little co-ordination, she brushed her teeth, shed her clothes and pulled on pyjama shorts and a matching cami. Then she crawled under the covers of the huge bed and groaned into a pillow.

These seven nights in Rome were going to be agony.

CHAPTER SIX

LEO PUNCHED HIS pillow three times, and when that failed to appease him he sat up and hurled it across the room. The pillow sailed through the air, hit the far wall with a dull, satisfying thud, and slumped to the bedroom floor.

Juvenile behaviour, but it felt good.

He swung his legs off the bed, glanced at the digital clock telling him it was five minutes past six a.m.—ten minutes since he'd last glared at it—and pulled on some sweats. He needed to expend some energy, and since bed-wrecking sex with his house guest wasn't an option—not a wise one, at any rate—he'd have to settle for exercise.

Hard, punishing, sweat-drenching exercise.

Damn the minx.

He slung a towel over his shoulder, padded down his hallway to the small, well-equipped gym at the far end and set himself a gruelling pace on the treadmill.

Forty minutes later every muscle from his groin to his Achilles tendons strained and burned. Without slowing he swigged from his water bottle, yanked his tee shirt over his head and threw the sweat-soaked garment to the floor.

Perhaps if he'd made time for a mistress in recent months he wouldn't be struggling now to harness his libido. But his work in the lead-up to the takeover had consumed him day and night, leaving scant time for distractions of the female variety no matter how tempting or willing. A blonde, career-driven attorney in New York had been his one indulgence—a brief bedroom-only affair that ended by mutual agreement after his last visit eight, maybe nine weeks ago.

Nine weeks.

He cranked up the speed on the treadmill. No wonder he

was fit to explode after Helena's little sexpot performance in the kitchen last night. His memories of their lovemaking had remained vivid over the years—more so than he cared to admit—but he couldn't recall her ever having kissed him so senseless. Even now he could feel the imprint of her mouth, her tongue driving him wild, firing his body into a state of near-painful arousal.

With a grunt he stopped the treadmill, grabbed his towel and tee shirt and headed back to his room for a cold shower.

Helena was a paradox…a hotbed of unpredictability. Cool and flighty one minute, scorching the next. Estranged from her father yet willing to do almost anything, it seemed, to delay his day of reckoning. What game was she playing? So far nothing about her actions made sense. Nothing sat quite straight in his mind. And wasn't that the reason he'd brought her here? To keep her close until her true motives were revealed?

He snapped off the water, towelled himself dry and dressed in jeans and a button-down shirt. Feeling rejuvenated, he glanced at the clock. Still early, but he had emails to sift through, a mountain of paperwork to sort. He'd allow her another hour of beauty sleep. Two at the most.

And then, cara mia, *it's game on.*

'Morning, *cara.*'

Helena opened her eyes. Scowled. Shut them. She was dreaming again. Except this time Leo wasn't hot and naked and tangled in her sheets. He was sitting on the bed, fully clothed.

She threw her arm over her eyes.

Get lost, Mr Sandman.

'Your coffee is going cold.'

She snatched her arm down, blinked three times, then bolted upright so fast a galaxy of tiny stars danced in front of her eyes. 'Oh, my God!' *Not dreaming.* 'Wh…what are you doing here?'

'Breakfast.' He inclined his head towards a tray on the nightstand. 'Orange juice, *cornetti* and coffee. Unless you prefer tea in the morning?'

'I prefer *privacy* in the morning,' she snapped, to which he simply responded with a bone-melting smile.

Her heart tripped and fell and she swallowed a groan. Why must he look so crisp and gorgeous? She yanked the sheet to her chin, pushed a hand through her jungle of curls. 'What time is it?'

'Nine o'clock.'

'Oh…' She frowned, dismayed. 'I don't normally sleep so late.'

The tantalising smells of strong coffee and warm pastry wafted from the nightstand. She eyed the *cornetti*, all fresh and fluffy and tempting. Had he gone out especially for them?

She tried for a conciliatory smile. 'If you give me a few minutes I'll get up and dressed.' *In other words, get out. I can't breathe with you here.*

'Take your time.' He stood, and her shoulders sloped with relief—only to inch up again when he sauntered to the wardrobe. He flung open the doors. 'What are you wearing tonight?'

She blinked. 'I beg your pardon?'

He started riffling through her clothes and she leapt forward, one foot hitting the floor before she remembered her skimpy pyjama shorts. She sank back, frowning when he pulled out the long black dress.

He held it up. 'This?'

Her hands fisted in the sheet gathered against her chest. 'Yes. Does that meet with your approval?'

'It is black.'

'You're very observant.'

'And boring.'

She gritted her teeth. Okay, the high neckline and long

sleeves *were* a little conservative. But it was elegant and practical. 'I think the term you're looking for is classic.'

He tossed the dress onto the bed, flicked an imperious hand at the rest of her clothing. 'Where is the colour?'

She shrugged, but the tension in her shoulders made the gesture jerky. Where was he taking this? 'I'm a working girl now. Neutrals are more practical.'

He studied her intently. 'You used to like colour.'

His observation was hardly profound, yet all the same her insides twisted. 'Well, now I don't.' She reached for the orange juice, her throat suddenly parched, but her hand trembled and she put the glass down again.

She'd rather die of thirst than admit it, but he was right. Colour had been her passion. Her talent. Her joy. And her textile design degree, had she graduated, would have turned that passion into a career. But the day she buried her son—*their* son—the colour vanished from her world, and though she looked for it, tried desperately to reconnect with her passion, all she saw for the longest time were lifeless shades of grey. Bright colours had felt wrong. Artificial. Like painting the outside of a house to make it pretty while the inside remained neglected and rotten.

'I want to see you in something eye-catching tonight,' he said. 'Something more befitting my mistress.'

She stiffened. 'I don't measure up to your standards now?' An old familiar ache sparked in her chest. How many childhood years had she wasted, trying to live up to her father's impossible standards, knowing that no matter what she did it would never be good enough?

Leo's eyes narrowed. 'I'm talking about the dress. Not you.'

'Well.' She hiked her chin, tamped down her old insecurities. 'It will just have to do. It's the only gown I've brought.'

'Then we will shop today and buy you another.'

She shook her head. 'I can't afford anything new.'

'We agreed I would take care of expenses, *si*?'

'Travel costs. Not clothes. I don't need your charity.' *Or to be told what to wear.*

His eyebrows plunged into a dark V. 'Do not mistake my intent for charity, Helena. Outside of these walls you are my mistress, and tonight many eyes will be upon us. I will not have you fade into the background like an insipid wallflower.' He walked to the door, paused and glanced back. 'Enjoy your breakfast. We will leave as soon as you are ready.'

Helena sucked in her breath to hurl a refusal, but he was gone before the words could form on her tongue.

Insipid?

She glared at the closed door, seething for long minutes until a loud, insistent grumble from her stomach dragged her attention back to the pastries. Huffing out a resigned sigh, she picked up a fat *cornetto* and studied its golden crust. If she couldn't avoid the excursion, she could at least take her time getting ready.

Slightly mollified by the thought, she slouched against the pillows, bit off a chunk of pastry and chewed very, very slowly.

'Not this one.'

Helena dug her heels into the cobbled stones outside yet another exclusive boutique. She eyed the name etched in discreet letters above the door. If the prices in the last three stores had been outrageous—and they had—here they would surely qualify as scandalous.

Leo's grip on her hand firmed. 'It is not to your liking, *cara*?'

For what seemed like the hundredth time that day she let his endearment slide over her, forced a blithe smile and suppressed the inevitable shiver that single, huskily spoken word evoked. Like everything else, it was all part of their ruse—a ruse he had evidently decided to embrace today with unrestrained relish. Indeed, from the time they'd left his apartment scarcely a moment had passed without him touching her in some way: a hand at her waist, his thigh brushing hers, a random kiss on her mouth or temple.

And when, sitting at a quaint sidewalk café for lunch, he'd wiped a dash of cream from the corner of her mouth and sucked it off his thumb, her body had damn near dissolved into a puddle of liquid heat.

Worse—he *knew*. Knew that every touch, every lazy, lingering look from his hooded eyes, was making her quiver and burn.

She kept her voice low. 'It looks too expensive.'

His lips curved into the same tolerant smile he'd worn for much of the day, fuelling her suspicion that this exercise was less about buying a gown and more about some underlying battle of wills.

'I will decide what is too expensive.' He tugged her forward. 'Come.'

Inside, the routine was much the same as it had been at the other boutiques, only here the saleswoman was twice as elegant, the gowns four times more exquisite, and the proffered beverage not espresso or latte or tea, but sparkling wine served in tall, silver-rimmed flutes.

Helena pasted on a smile, as determined now as when they'd started out to find nothing she liked.

'I'm sorry,' she said to the tireless saleswoman four gowns later. 'It's just not my style.'

'Ah, pity…' The woman smiled, too professional to exhibit more than a glimmer of disappointment. 'The blue is perfect with your eyes.'

Helena carefully peeled away the layers of beaded chiffon and offered up an apologetic smile. 'It's beautiful, really, but the detailing is too fussy for me. I'd prefer something…plainer.'

A male cough, loud and lacking any kind of subtlety, came from beyond the mirrored screen.

Helena ground her teeth, then raised her voice. 'But nothing in black, please.'

Undeterred, the saleswoman tapped a red fingernail to her lips, then set off with a look of renewed focus.

As soon as she'd gone Helena pulled a silk robe over her bra and knickers, yanked the sash into a knot and stepped out from behind the screen. 'This is ridiculous.'

Leo sat—or rather, lounged—in a blue and gold brocade chair in the private sitting room, a half-consumed glass of champagne at his elbow, his long legs stretched out over a plush velvet rug.

He didn't bother glancing up from his phone. '*Scusi?*'

She scored her palms with the tips of her nails. 'Don't *scusi* me. You heard me perfectly well. This is pointless.'

He pocketed the phone and raised his head, his gaze travelling with a discernible lack of haste from her feet to her face. She squirmed, heat trailing over her skin in the wake of his indolent scrutiny. Teeth gritted, she fought the urge to adjust the robe over her breasts.

'Pointless only because you are being stubborn.'

She snorted. 'I'm not stubborn. I'm just…selective. I haven't seen anything I like, that's all.'

'You have tried on fourteen dresses.'

He was counting? She crossed her arms. 'And I told you—I haven't seen anything I like.'

'Then I suggest you find something you do.'

'And if I don't?'

'I will choose for you.'

The desire to stamp her foot was overwhelming. But no doubt he would enjoy her loss of composure. She settled for raising her chin. 'I don't know what type of relationships you have with the women in your life, and frankly I don't care. But I, for one, do *not* like to be bullied.'

In a single fluid movement of his powerful frame Leo surged off his chair. He prowled towards her and her nerves skittered, but she held her ground. He stopped just short of their bodies touching and locked his gaze on hers.

'My mother gave me three pieces of advice before she died.'

It wasn't remotely what she'd expected him to say. She frowned, uncertain. 'Did she?'

'*Si.*' His right index finger appeared in front of her face. 'One, to take my schooling seriously.' His middle finger rose beside the first. 'Two, to learn English and learn it well.' His third finger snapped up to join the others. 'And three, always to choose my battles wisely.'

Her frown deepened—a convulsive tug of the tiny muscles between her brows. During their brief time together he'd not spoken of his mother except to say that she'd died when he was eleven. Her heart squeezed now at the thought of a young boy grieving for his mother and it stirred a ridiculous urge to comfort him—this proud, infuriating man who wouldn't accept her comfort if they were the last two people on Earth.

'Your mother was a sensible woman,' she ventured, unsure how else to respond.

'*Si.*' He hooked his fingers under her chin. 'And her advice has served me well. As it will you, if you have the sense to heed it.'

She gave him a blank look. 'I was a straight A student, thank you very much. And I think you'll find my English is perfect.'

His teeth bared in a sharp smile that mocked her attempt to miss the point. 'Then you will have no trouble understanding this.' He lowered his mouth to her ear, his breath feathering over her skin in a hot, too-intimate caress. 'Wisdom is not only in choosing your battles with care, *cara*. It is knowing when to concede defeat. We will stay here until you choose a dress or I will choose one for you. Those are your options. Accept and decide.'

'I—'

He planted a brief, hard kiss on her mouth, stealing her breath along with any further attempt at protest, then held her gaze in mute challenge until she gave a grunt of anger and whirled away.

'Bully,' she muttered, but he either didn't hear or chose to ignore the slur, and by the time the saleswoman reappeared he was seated again, dark head bowed, his attention back on his phone.

With mammoth effort she mustered a smile and cast a critical eye over the two latest gowns, both backless halternecks with ankle-length skirts, one a bright turquoise, the other a deep, stunning claret. She ran an appreciative hand over the latter.

The saleswoman removed the dress from its hanger. 'Beautiful, *si*?'

Helena had to agree. 'How much?' she asked quietly.

The Italian woman quoted a number in euros that dropped the bottom out of Helena's stomach. The equivalent in pounds would pay the rent on her flat not for weeks, but for months.

She slipped into the gown and it was even more beautiful on, its weightless silk gliding like cool air over her body, the shimmering claret a striking contrast against her pale ivory skin. She performed a little pirouette in front of the mirror, her stomach fluttering with a burst of unexpected pleasure.

The saleswoman smiled. 'This is the one?'

Helena hesitated. Could she *really* allow Leo to buy her this dress? She studied her reflection. A lot of skin was exposed, and the style called for going braless, but he *had* said he wanted her in something more eye-catching. Something more *befitting his mistress*.

She chewed her lip. She could go out there, parade for his approval, but pride and some residual anger over his high-handedness stopped her. Maybe she lacked the glamour of his usual mistresses, and maybe her wardrobe was a little staid, but she still had enough feminine savvy to know when she looked good.

Confidence swelled. *Yes.* She could do this. She could play her part and convince the world—or at least the Santinos and their guests—that she and Leo were lovers. She had to. If she wanted to honour her end of their bargain—if she wanted Leo to honour *his*—there could be no half-hearted performances. She either did this properly or not at all.

She gave the ever-patient saleswoman a beatific smile. 'This is the one.'

Leo eased the Maserati to a stop in the gravel courtyard outside the Santinos' palatial mountainside villa. Behind him a long queue of taxis, luxury cars and black-windowed limousines stretched into the distance. Valets swarmed like worker ants on a sugar trail, keeping the line moving as guests poured from the vehicles and watchful dark-suited security men oversaw the hustle of activity.

He glanced at Helena, sitting silent in the passenger seat, but her face was angled away and he couldn't gauge her reaction.

He liked the way she'd styled her hair tonight, her glossy curls piled high on her head, a few random ringlets left loose to float around her face. He *didn't* like that all he could think about was how it would feel to pull out the pins and watch those silky tresses spill over his hands... his sheets...*his thighs*...

He killed the engine. 'Are you ready for this?'

Her head swung around, her blue eyes inscrutable under their canopy of dark lashes. 'Yes. Are you?'

He smiled at the challenge in her voice. 'Always.' He fired off a wink that earned him a frown, then climbed out, grabbed his suit jacket from the back seat and shrugged it on.

On the other side a valet opened Helena's door and she stepped out, a swathe of rich burgundy silk cascading like wine-infused water down her body. She smiled, and the kid's face split into a goofy grin that lasted all of three seconds—until he met Leo's dark stare.

'One scratch,' he warned in Italian, handing over his key, 'and I will find you.'

The young man nodded, his Adam's apple bobbing as if jerked by an unseen string, and Leo eyeballed him until he disappeared into the driver's seat.

The vehicle purred to life and Helena froze, her eyes widening. 'The gift!' She whirled and tapped on the side window as the car started to move. When it stopped she pulled open the back door and reached into the footwell.

Behind her Leo dug his fingers into his palms. Did his damnedest not to notice how the sheer dress clung to her hips and buttocks below her naked back. An exercise in futility, no less. He'd have to be blind not to notice all that smooth ivory skin. Those beautiful curves.

Dio.

He should have let her wear the black dress. It might remind him of a nun's habit, but at least his thoughts wouldn't be steeped in sin.

She turned and stilled, the gift-wrapped antique silver Tiffany bowl clutched in her hands. 'You can stop looking at me like that.'

Like what? Like he wanted to slide her dress up her thighs and bend her over the hood of his Maserati? He unfurled his hands. Tried to blank his expression. Hell, was he that transparent?

'I'm not going to screw this up, so you can wipe that frown off your face,' she said, her voice tinged with exasperation. 'Here—' she thrust the gift at him '—you take this. It's your gift.'

And a detail he'd have overlooked if she hadn't asked him earlier in the day what he'd bought the Santinos. Normally his PA took care of such things, but Gina had had a family emergency on Tuesday and he'd told her to take the rest of the week off work. He'd cursed at the over-sight, but Helena had promptly set about finding some-thing suitable—and pricey, he'd noted when handing over his credit card. Funny… Once she'd overcome her reluctance to choosing a dress she'd warmed noticeably to the idea of spending his money.

Inside, a waiter took the gift, offered them wine and guided them through a long piano hall doubling as a ball-room and outside to the uppermost of three sprawling ter-races. A floodlit swimming pool dominated the middle tier and in the distance, beyond the landscaped grounds, the lights of Rome winked like fallen stars under a purpling sky, painting a view of the ancient city that might have been impressive—breathtaking, even—had the flash and dazzle of the party guests crowding the travertine terraces not eclipsed the panorama beyond.

'Oh, my.' Helena stood beside him, one hand resting in the crook of his arm, the other cradling a glass of ruby-red wine. 'It's very…um…'

Leo dragged his gaze from the landscape back to the glittering assemblage before them. 'Flamboyant?' He didn't bother hushing his voice. The music piped into every corner of the grounds, mixed with the babble of a hundred con-versations and the chiming of crystal and laughter, made discretion unnecessary.

'That's one description.'

'You can think of others?'

'Mmm… Nothing as polite. You should have told me I'd need my sunglasses.'

Her wry humour extracted a grin from him. 'We Ital-ians know how to do bling, *si*?'

After a short silence she squeezed his arm. 'Thank you.'

He looked down at her. 'For what?'

'For not letting me wear that "boring" black dress.'

He shrugged. 'It wasn't—'

'Charity.' She looked him in the eye. 'Yes. I know. But thank you all the same.'

Her gratitude caused a ripple of guilt to radiate through him. The truth was she could have worn a sack and still outclassed every woman here—a fact he'd been confident of long before they'd arrived—but he had wanted to see her in something other than the nondescript black that seemed to have become her standard default. Had wanted, for reasons he refused to examine too closely, to see a glimpse of the old Helena.

She turned, lifted her face and broke into a smile that struck him square in the chest. 'Whisper in my ear and kiss me,' she said, her voice urgent, breathy. 'Carlos is on his way over. And he has company.'

Well, hell... That was an invitation he didn't need to hear twice. Without a beat of hesitation he put his lips to her ear, murmured a few words in Italian, then angled his mouth over hers.

And tried not to groan at the feel of her soft lips parting under his.

Just for show, he reminded himself, as the temptation to run his tongue into those warm, honeyed depths proved a true test of his restraint. Even knowing that his host approached and others looked on, he wanted to prolong the kiss into something far less chaste and fit for public display.

Helena, by contrast, appeared in full control, and by the time Carlos—and his daughter—reached their side she was rubbing the gloss off his lips and giggling as if they'd just shared some private joke.

Anna Santino glowered at them.

'Good to see you again, my friend.' Grinning, Carlos took Leo's hand in a strong grip. 'And Helena.' He turned, clasped her hands and kissed her on both cheeks. 'You look radiant, my dear. I am delighted you could make it.'

'Thank you, Carlos.'

Her voice was husky, her cheeks tinged a delicate shade

of pink. From the compliment? Or their kiss? The latter, he hoped.

'And congratulations on your wedding anniversary. What a wonderful party your wife has thrown. Thank you again for inviting us both.'

Carlos inclined his head towards the dark-haired girl by his side. 'May I introduce my daughter, Anna?'

Helena extended her hand, smiled warmly. 'It's a pleasure to meet you, Anna.'

'Likewise,' the younger woman said, her pretty face barely cracking a smile.

Had Leo been a betting man he'd have wagered that Carlos had dragged her over, told her to be polite, but the young socialite's pout said she was in no mood to be gracious.

She dropped Helena's hand and nodded at Leo, her brown eyes dark. Petulant. 'Leo.'

'Anna,' he said, and felt Helena's slender hand slide into his.

She pressed close and he caught a drift of the light, summery scent she wore on her skin. He tightened his hand over hers and she squeezed back, the contact spreading a peculiar warmth up his arm.

Smiling, she addressed Carlos. 'Leo has persuaded me to stay in Rome for an entire week. I'm planning to sightsee while he's working, but it's hard to know where to start. There's so much of your fabulous city to see.'

Smart girl. A safe, neutral topic and an irresistible opening to a man passionate about his city. Asking questions, listening intently, she kept the conversation alive until finally Carlos excused himself, invited them to a Sunday luncheon for their out-of-town guests, and moved on with his hosting duties. His sullen-faced daughter, who'd uttered not a word since the introductions, trailed away with him into the crowd.

Helena stared after them. 'She looks so miserable I almost feel sorry for her.'

He snorted. 'Don't.'

'Why not?'

'She's a pampered party girl with three priorities in life. Money, attention, and getting what she wants.'

Helena's expression was contemplative. 'She didn't get *you*.'

Thank God. He almost shuddered with relief. 'And see how she sulks.'

'Yes.' Helena sighed. 'A tragedy in the making, no doubt.' She hooked her arm through his. 'I dare say the poor girl's heart is ruined. You do realise she may never get over you?'

He narrowed his eyes. 'Are you mocking me, Helena?'

Her lashes swept down, but not before he'd caught the bright glitter of amusement in her eyes. He felt a thump under his ribs. A stirring of recognition in his blood. *There. That's her. That's the girl you remember.*

She signalled a passing waiter, swapped her empty wine-glass for a full one and turned her mischievous eyes back to him. 'Darling…' she cooed, loud enough for those nearby to overhear. 'Make fun of *you*?' She pursed her lips in mock reproach. 'Never. You're too sensitive. It's one of the things I adore about you. Come on.' She grabbed his hand. 'The night is young. Let's mingle.'

Letting her lead him into the crowd, Leo filed a mental note to teach her later about the perils of overacting. He could think of any number of activities he'd enjoy performing with her right now. Mingling wasn't one of them.

Yet mingle they did. For two endless hours. Hours during which his eyes glazed over and he repeatedly fought the urge to glance at his watch. Small talk was an art he'd mastered over the years out of necessity, not preference. Business dinners and charity events—the select few he supported—at least had a deeper purpose. But the kind of meaningless prattle that typified gatherings like this invariably wore at his patience.

'*Signor?*'

Assuming it was a waiter who had spoken behind him, Leo turned to say that he didn't want a drink or another damned canapé. What he wanted, he thought moodily, was Helena back by his side. How long did a woman need to powder her nose?

He frowned. The waiter was not bearing the usual tray of decadent offerings.

'Signor Vincenti?'

His frown sharpened. '*Si.*'

'Signorina Shaw would like you to know she is resting in the salon off the piano hall.'

Resting? 'Is she all right?'

The man hesitated. '*Si.* But there has been a small incident—'

Leo didn't wait for the man to finish. He powered up the steps of the terrace and into the hall, skirting the edge of the surging, overcrowded dance floor until he found the salon. He paused in the doorway. In the far corner Helena sat on a red velvet divan, and a kneeling waiter held a compress to the top of her left foot. Off to the side, a middle-aged couple hovered. As if intuiting his arrival, Helena glanced up and smiled and his chest flooded with relief.

He strode over.

'I'm fine, darling,' she said, her game face firmly in place. 'I just had a minor mishap.'

The middle-aged woman stepped forward. '*Je suis vraiment désolée*—I am so sorry,' she added in heavily French-accented English. 'I was clumsy. We were dancing and I did not see her walk past behind me.'

Leo took in the woman's solid frame and six-inch stilettos, then glanced at Helena's foot with renewed concern. '*Scusami,*' he said to the waiter, indicating that he should lift the compress, and then knelt on one knee to examine the damage.

'It's not serious,' Helena said quickly. She looked up to the woman. 'Please don't feel bad. It's just a scratch.'

More like a gouge and the promise of a decent bruise, but, no, it wasn't serious. He stood, picked up her purse and the high-heeled sandal she had removed and put them in her hands. Then he bent and hooked one arm around her back, the other under her knees, and lifted her against his chest.

'Oh!' Her exclamation came out on a gush of air. She frowned at him even as her arms looped around his neck. 'Really, darling.' She gave a little laugh. 'This isn't necessary. I can walk.'

He ignored her protest. 'Thank you for your concern,' he said to the couple. 'Please enjoy the rest of your evening.' He nodded to the waiter. '*Grazie.*'

Then he strode from the room and made for the nearest exit.

'We're leaving?' She stared at him, wide-eyed, her cheeks flushed, Her lips soft and pink. She looked sexy. Adorable. *Beddable.*

'*Si.*'

'But it's only ten-thirty.'

'You want to stay?'

She shook her head so quickly, so adamantly, a long auburn curl slipped its binding and bounced against her cheek.

His answering smile was swift. Satisfied.

'Good. Neither do I.'

CHAPTER SEVEN

LEO CONTROLLED THE urge to floor the Maserati's accelerator until they'd cleared the mountain roads and had hit the expressway back to the city. Without traffic delays the journey time was forty minutes. He reckoned he could do it in thirty.

Helena leaned forward in the passenger seat, removed her other sandal and massaged her ankles. 'I swear high heels were invented by men as instruments of torture.'

She sighed—a soft, breathy sound that coiled through his insides like a ribbon of smoky heat.

'Could we have the air-con up a bit, please? It's awfully warm.'

Happy to oblige, he adjusted the controls and glanced over as she settled back in her seat. Her eyes were closed, her features smooth apart from a slight frown, and for a moment he was reminded of his sister. Of that intriguing combination of strength and vulnerability some women seemed naturally to possess.

A sudden tightness invaded his chest—the same suffocating sensation he always felt when he thought of Marietta and the battles she'd had to face. He gripped the steering wheel, his knuckles whitening. He had no business comparing Helena with his sister. They were poles apart. He loved Marietta. She was his blood, and he'd give his life for hers in a heartbeat. The feelings Helena stirred in him were rudimentary, nothing more than lust—a lust he intended to sate before this evening was out.

Thirty minutes later, in the courtyard of his apartment building, he pulled open the passenger door.

Helena glanced up. 'I can walk,' she said, gathering her shoes and purse before climbing out.

'We should see to that foot.'

She shook her head. 'It's fine. Really. It doesn't hurt all that much.'

Inside, he ushered her into the building's single elevator and watched her back into a corner, her belongings clutched in front of her like some sort of shield. Against what? Him? He thought of their too-fleeting kiss and all the little intimate touches and quips that had driven him slowly insane tonight. Anticipation spiralled in his blood.

'The skin's broken,' he said, looking at her foot. 'We should at least clean and dress the wound.'

They entered the apartment and he cupped her elbow, steered her towards the living room. Ignoring her mumbled protest, he sat her on the sofa and went to fetch the first aid kit from the kitchen. When he knelt in front of her she lifted her dress, obediently stuck out her foot and allowed him to clean the shallow gash. He finished by applying a neat dressing.

She offered up a smile. 'Thanks.'

He nodded, but didn't rise. Didn't speak. He held her gaze until her lashes fell and she shifted slightly.

'Leo…'

Liking the husky little catch in her voice, he sat back and hooked his hands behind her knees. Her teeth captured her lower lip and he held back a groan. The sight of her gently biting her own soft flesh was inordinately sexy. He pulled her to the edge of the sofa, spread her legs and moved between them.

Slim, toned muscles trembled under his hands. 'Leo, please… Don't do this.'

Undeterred by her soft plea, he cupped his hand under her left breast, cradling its fullness and weight in his palm. Only a sheer layer of silk separated his fingers from her flesh.

'This…?' He slid his thumb back and forth over the slippery fabric, teasing her nipple to a hard nub beneath the burgundy silk.

A tiny groan escaped her lips—a groan he might have mistaken for protest had she not arched into his touch.

'Yes.'

Her throat convulsed around that single word, drawing his gaze to the base of her neck where the skin looked so soft, so delicate, it begged to be kissed.

He leaned in and pressed his lips to the fluttering pulse there. *Oh, yes.* Soft. Warm. Sweet. He breathed in her summery scent, used the tip of his tongue to taste her skin.

'And this...?'

No words this time. No protest. Only a silent shudder that rode her body like the crest of a powerful fever. Satisfaction rippled through him. The message her body conveyed was unequivocal: she wanted him, hungered for him as fiercely as he hungered for her.

He shifted to cover her mouth with his, but she pulled back. Desire roughened his voice. 'Do not tell me you don't want this.'

'You know I do.'

Her candid, husky confession kicked his pulse up another notch.

'But that doesn't mean we should.'

'Tell me why not.'

'It will only complicate things.'

His laugh was short. '*Cara*, our physical attraction is the only thing between us that is *not* complicated. What could be more simple, more natural, than desire between a man and a woman?'

She shook her head. 'I didn't come here to sleep with you.'

'Yet you just admitted you want to.' More than anything else that frank admission fired his blood. Drowned out the rational part of his brain urging him to concede this was a bad idea.

She wedged her palms against his chest, shoved with surprising strength. Caught off guard, he rocked back on his heels.

'Is this how it works, Leo?' She shot to her feet and glared down at him, arms akimbo. 'You buy me a dress and expect me to demonstrate my gratitude with sex?'

For a second he stared at her. Then, as her words sank in, he launched himself up, his blood roaring in his ears like the bellow of a wounded bull. The idea that he would use material gifts as leverage for sex was galling. Distasteful. He balled his hands lest he do something foolish like grab her and shake her. Demand an apology.

She collected her purse and shoes. 'I'm tired,' she said, her gaze avoiding his. 'I'm going to bed.' *Alone.* She didn't need to say the word; it was implicit in her tone.

Hands fisted, heart thumping furiously, Leo stood silent and watched her stalk from the room. When he heard the closing snick of the guest room door he snatched up the first aid kit, strode into the kitchen and rammed it in a drawer.

He shoved his fingers through his hair.

Air. That was what he needed. And lots of it.

He shed his jacket, stepped onto the terrace and stared out over the endless tiled rooftops and church domes of Rome. He closed his eyes and breathed deeply, forcing his chest to expand and contract with each lungful of air. His anger slackened in a matter of minutes but his body stayed tense, trapped in a state of aching arousal he was powerless to quell.

Powerless.

He clenched his jaw. No. That wasn't right.

'Powerless' was holding on to his mother while the skies thundered and raged and the cancer stole the last of the light from her eyes. 'Powerless' was watching his father drown in the murky waters of addiction that had blinded him to his children and finally taken his life. 'Powerless' was walking into an ICU and seeing his sister's broken body, then turning around and walking out so she wouldn't see her big brother cry.

'Powerless' was *not*, by any stretch of its definition, some pathetic inability to bring his libido under control.

And yet this burning need Helena aroused in him, this inferno in his belly, would not be doused.

Turning on his heel, he marched inside and headed down the hall.

This night was not over.

Not by a long shot.

Helena stood barefoot in the en suite bathroom and stared at herself in the mirror. 'Congratulations,' her reflection sneered. 'You just earned the rank of first-class bitch.'

She laid her palms on the cold marble vanity unit and closed her eyes. Her body hummed with a current of sexual energy, her nipples felt exquisitely sensitive, and the wet heat of arousal lingered between her thighs.

Dammit. Why had he pushed? Why had she panicked? And why had she let that awful accusation fly from her mouth? His shocked face flashed into her mind and another burst of regret soured her tongue. She'd expected him to get angry with her; she hadn't expected him to look *hurt*.

She straightened and ran her hand over her stomach. If she and Leo *had* made love would he have noticed any changes in her body? Any subtle post-pregnancy differences?

She had no stretch marks, thanks to the diligent use of hydrating oils and the benefit of youth. And, while her mid-section was slightly more curvaceous than before, overall her body was thinner. No. She would not have needed to worry, she thought with an odd mix of certainty and regret. Her body would not have given up her secrets.

Heaving a sigh, she pulled the pins from her hair, undid the gown's halter neck and let the seamless fabric glide down her body. With a tiny pang of regret she went to the wardrobe and hung up the dress, well away from her own clothes. The stunning silk creation had made her feel sexy and confident, more feminine than she had in years, but she could not accept it as a gift.

Just as she could not fall into Leo's bed.

Oh, she would find a night in his arms explosive and unforgettable, of that she had no doubt. But they had a history of heartache and hurt, a past they couldn't erase, and there was no escaping the fact he still didn't trust her. Why would he? She was Douglas Shaw's daughter, guilty by association in Leo's eyes.

Perhaps seducing her and bedding her would have been no more than an opportune means of revenge?

Suppressing a shiver at the idea of such a callous motive, she closed the wardrobe door, pivoted on her heel—and screamed.

Leo.

Not inside the room, but standing in the doorway, his large frame silhouetted by the lighting from the hall. His hand rested on the handle of the door she knew she'd closed behind her. Had she been so lost in thought she hadn't heard the latch click? Or had he worked the handle with deliberate stealth?

He stared at her—silent, unsmiling—then stepped into the room and quietly closed the door.

Fright galvanised her. 'Get out!'

She hugged her arms over her breasts, glanced at the bed and considered diving for the safety of the covers. But he was already advancing.

'Leo, stop.' She was naked except for a thong! 'This isn't fair.' She backed up, felt the wardrobe door colliding with her bare buttocks and back. 'Get out,' she repeated, but this time her demand sounded weak. Unconvincing.

He stopped in front of her, leaned the underside of one forearm on the wood above her head. The suit jacket was gone, the black silk shirt unbuttoned to a point midway down his chest. She dropped her gaze and caught an eyeful of hard muscle under a dusting of fine hair. Before she could stop it, a groan rose in her throat. She wanted so very badly to slide her hands inside that shirt. To run her palms over his wide shoulders and thickly muscled chest.

'Tell me you are not a liar.'

She blinked up at him. 'Wh…what?'

'Tell me,' he barked, making her jump.

She scowled to let him know she didn't appreciate being shouted at—or being backed against a wardrobe naked, for that matter—but the set of his jaw told her he didn't give a damn what she did or didn't appreciate.

She found her voice. 'I'm not a liar.'

'Tell me I can trust you.'

She hesitated. *Test or trap?* Both, probably. She licked her dry lips. 'You can trust me.'

His gaze held hers. 'Now look me in the eye and tell me you do not want me, do not want *this*—' The fingers of his right hand skimmed down her stomach, slipped inside her thong and, before she could fully realise his intent, pushed into her slick folds. 'And then I will leave.'

Heat erupted between her thighs, flared like wild-fire through her pelvis. Gasping, modesty forgotten, she dropped her arms and wrapped her hands around his wrist. 'Don't!' she croaked.

He thrust one finger upward, straight into her hot, moist core, then withdrew and circled his wet fingertip around her sensitised nub. Her legs nearly collapsed.

'Tell me, Helena.'

His rough command sent a hot shiver racing over her skin.

'Tell me exactly what you *don't* want.'

Convulsively her hands tightened on his wrist, his strong tendons flexing in her grip as his fingers stroked and teased. She bit her lip to keep from crying out, tensed her muscles to stop her body trembling. God help her. How could she tell him *no* when every inch of her flesh screamed *yes*?

'So wet,' he murmured, his other hand cupping the back of her head, his fingers tangling in her hair. 'So ready for me.'

He kissed her until her bottom lip came free of her teeth,

then sucked the tender flesh into his mouth. His tongue explored, invaded, as bold and shameless as his fingers— a dual assault that spun her senses until she couldn't tell which way was up.

He eased back enough to speak. 'Soon I won't be able to stop, so if you want me to leave—if you do not want this—you need to tell me now.'

She squeezed her eyes closed and prayed for sanity even as a part of her scoffed. *Sanity?* She'd forfeited that the moment she'd agreed to spend seven days with him in Rome. And no matter how many reasons she gave herself for why they shouldn't do this, why she shouldn't give in—why everything about this was wrong—one incontrovertible truth remained. She wanted this man, burned for him, and it really was that simple. That natural. Just as he'd said.

She let go of his wrist. 'Please…' she whispered, not caring how breathless and needy she sounded. 'Don't stop.'

He did stop, and she groaned, opened her eyes and frowned her dismay.

He gave a throaty laugh. 'Do not fret, *cara.*' He cupped his hands under her bottom, lifted her off her feet and headed for the bed. 'We are going somewhere more comfortable.' He started to walk and pressed an open-mouthed kiss to the base of her throat, his tongue dipping into the delicate hollow there.

She shivered with delight. If she came to her senses, told him to stop, would he honour his word and leave? She wrapped her legs around his torso, hooked her ankles behind his back. She didn't want the answer to that question. Didn't want to contemplate anything, *feel* anything, beyond the hot rush of anticipation in her veins. Surging her hands into his hair, she pushed his head back and covered his mouth with hers. He shuddered, growled something against her lips, and she sensed his control, like hers, was starting to slip.

When they reached the bed, her reluctance to unwrap

her legs had him overbalancing. He crashed down on top of her, crushing her breasts, spreading her thighs wide beneath his hips. Their mouths jerked apart and the air left Helena's lungs with a *whoomph*.

'*Dio!*' He levered his weight from her with one elbow. 'Are you hurt?'

She shook her head, too breathless for words, too aroused to care about anything other than getting her hands inside his shirt. His skin next to hers. She reached for a button, her fingers fumbling, shaking, until he closed a fist over her hands and stilled them.

'Soon,' he murmured, dropping a long, wet kiss on her mouth that made her forget what she was doing. 'First, I have something to finish.'

He lowered his head, closed his lips over one erect nipple and sucked the aching peak deep into his mouth. Then, when a shudder racked her body and she moaned, he turned his attention to the other.

Helena arched her back and dug her nails into the bedding. She couldn't decide which was more exquisite. More erotic. The graze of his teeth or the flick of his tongue. She writhed. 'Leo…'

As if responding to her strangled plea, he surged up, knelt between her thighs and slid his palms behind her knees. Their gazes locked and her breath hitched in her throat. She could see the intent in his smouldering eyes, knew that what he had in mind would drive her over the edge in seconds.

He spread her legs and stared down at her. 'I want to know if you taste the same, *cara*. If you are still sweet and hot.'

She rolled her head, tried to grasp his wrists. 'No… Wait…' *Too soon.* She would come apart too soon. And she wanted this to last. Wanted to savour every spark, every touch, every spine-tingling sensation. Wanted him to ride the swells of pleasure with her. *Inside* her. 'Not yet…'

He wasn't listening. Hands braced on her thighs, he

dropped to his stomach, hooked aside her thong, and used his mouth and tongue to take her to the crest of a swift, shattering climax. She bucked against his hands, cried out something—his name?—and then she was arching up, her thighs clenched, her fingers plunging into his hair, holding tight as each powerful wave of her orgasm rocketed through her.

Her blood pulsed. Her breath came in ragged little bursts. And through a dizzying haze of sensation she felt his hands release her thighs. Felt wet, searing kisses trailing across her hips and tummy, over her breasts and up her neck.

'Like honey,' he rasped. 'Hot liquid honey.'

He slid his mouth over hers, his kiss scorching, possessive, then pushed to his feet, tore off his shirt and tossed it to the floor. Shoes and socks next, then belt, trousers—a short pause to extract something from a pocket—and lastly his briefs. All removed in seconds.

He leaned down, hooked a finger in her thong. 'As sexy as this is, it needs to come off.' And with one yank it too was gone.

Her mouth dried. He was magnificent. Like a modern-day centurion with his wide shoulders and deep chest, his hard, flat stomach. A line of dark hair tapered south, drawing her gaze down until her eyes stopped at the sight of his impressive arousal. For a second she thought about reaching out, wrapping her hand around him, but a surge of belated shyness kept her hands by her sides, made her contemplate sliding under the covers so she didn't feel so exposed.

Leo didn't suffer the same affliction. He stood proud, unashamed of his arousal, his eyes trailing over her body like a starved man surveying a banquet, unsure which delicacy to devour first. The fierce glow in his eyes, the strength of his physical desire, told her he hadn't begun to sate his appetite.

He ripped open a condom packet, sheathed himself, and stretched out beside her on the bed.

'Beautiful.' His teeth nipped her earlobe, grazed her jaw, tugged at her lower lip. 'You are more beautiful than I remember.'

And as he kissed and nibbled and murmured words in Italian she didn't understand, his hands roamed and explored, rediscovering all the secret places from the backs of her knees to the delicate tips of her ears that he knew would drive her wild.

'And responsive,' he added, drawing one of her moans into his mouth. 'Still so responsive.'

'Leo?'

He nuzzled her neck. *'Si?'*

'Please shut up and make love to me.'

A brief moment of stillness, then a smile against her skin, a low, husky laugh that made her heart skip a beat. He moved over her, pushed his knee between hers, the chafe of his hair-roughened thigh exquisite on her sensitive skin.

He cupped her jaw with one hand, forced her to look at him. 'No regrets.'

She frowned. 'What—?'

'Say it,' he insisted.

'Okay.' *Whatever.* Whatever he wanted to hear. She needed him inside her. Now. She held his gaze. 'No regrets.'

The words had barely left her lips and he was poised for entry, braced above her, his hot tip pressed against her opening. She knew she was slick, ready to take him, yet still that first powerful thrust had her gasping aloud. She reached up and curled her fingers into his rippling shoulders. When it seemed he'd filled every inch of her he pulled out, the movement slow, torturous, then slid back in, setting a rhythm that started to build once more into that hot, sweet pressure deep inside her pelvis.

She closed her eyes, tipped her head back, let the feel of him, the scent of him, overtake her senses. For so long she'd gone without luxuries, denied herself pleasures, but tonight she would not deprive herself. Tonight she would indulge. Tonight she would take everything Leo wanted to give her and more. And tomorrow—or the next day, or the next—she would deal with the consequences.

'No regrets...' she whispered, and she moved her hips, matched his rhythm, urged him on faster and harder, until she flew apart a second time and Leo threw his head back and roared.

Leo kicked the sheets off his body, stared at the ceiling and listened to the sound of running water through the closed bathroom door.

After a long night of incredible sex he should be lying here feeling sated and spent. Instead he wanted more. More of the woman he was right now picturing in the shower, her long limbs and lush curves all soft and slippery and wet. His body stirred and yet as much as he ached to join her under the water, hoist her against the marble tiles and lose himself once more in her velvety heat, he needed to employ some restraint. Needed to bank his lust and make sure his head—the one on his shoulders, at least—was still on straight.

Anyway, she'd be too sore to take him a fourth time, and he already felt caddish on that front. Not that he hadn't tried to be the gentleman when, in the faint light of dawn, she'd winced as he'd entered her and clung to him when he'd tried to withdraw. He hadn't wanted to hurt her— had told her as much—but she'd wrapped her endless legs around him, sunk her fingernails into his buttocks and pulled him in deep, driving all thoughts of chivalry straight out of his head.

He expelled a breath, aimed another kick at the sheets.

Did her soreness mean she hadn't been sexually active for a while? In London she'd alluded to a boyfriend but he'd seen through that lie and he couldn't believe she'd be here now if she were in a relationship.

He scrubbed a hand over his bristled jaw.

Seven years ago he had taken her virginity, and though he'd been furious with her afterwards for not warning him, secretly he'd been flattered, his ego pumped by the fact she'd chosen *him* to be her first lover. In a primitive and yet deeply satisfying way he'd stamped his mark on her, and for the first time in his life he'd known the powerful pull of possessiveness—the fierce, unsettling desire to know that a woman was exclusively his.

He craned his head off the pillow and glared at the bathroom door. How many lovers had she taken since? One or two? A handful? Too many to keep count? A dark curiosity snaked through him. He should have given Nico a broader remit. Should have told him to look beyond her finances and living arrangements and dig a little deeper into her personal life: her friendships, her relationships. *Her lovers*.

He dropped his head back down and scowled.

Dio. What was wrong with him? Her liaisons with other men were no concern of his. Last night they'd indulged their mutual desire for one another—nothing more. A few hours of mind-blowing sex didn't change their past, and it sure as hell wouldn't change their future.

He swung off the bed, scooped his clothes off the floor and fired another look at the bathroom door. Either she'd managed to drown herself in three millimetres of water or she was taking her sweet time, hoping he'd give up waiting and leave.

Did she already regret their lovemaking?

The possibility turned his stomach to lead. He'd seen regret and something too much like pity in her eyes once before, the night she'd ended their relationship. He'd vowed he'd never let a woman look at him like that again.

As if he was a mistake she wanted to undo.

Naked, his chest tight, his shoes and clothes bunched in his fists, Leo turned on his heel and strode from the room.

CHAPTER EIGHT

HELENA FLICKED A speck of lint off her black trousers and cast a sideways look at Leo. 'Lunch was nice,' she ventured, adjusting the car's seatbelt over her blouse. 'The hotel gardens were beautiful.'

His gaze remained on the road. '*Si.*'

Silence fell. She waited a moment. 'Anna was conspicuous by her absence, don't you think?'

He spared her a fleeting glance. '*Si.*'

'I didn't expect her mother to be so pleasant. We had a lovely chat over dessert. Do you know Maria well?'

'No.'

Helena sighed. *Excellent.* Three monosyllabic answers in a row. She sank down in her seat. This was not the man who'd sat by her side at the long luncheon table in the sun-drenched gardens of the Hotel de Russie. That man had been charming and attentive, playing the role of affectionate lover with such consummate ease she had, for a time, confused pretence with reality. Had actually indulged the notion their lovemaking might have meant something more to him than just a convenient lust-quenching tryst.

A wave of melancholy threatened but she fought it back. *No regrets.* Wasn't that what she'd promised Leo? Promised herself?

She touched her mouth, tender still from his kisses, and conceded she'd allow herself one regret—that Leo hadn't joined her in the shower this morning. Her fault, she supposed, for being a coward. For letting her fear of what the morning might unveil in his eyes send her scurrying for the bathroom. What she'd really wanted to do was run her tongue over his salty skin, straddle his hips and take brazen advantage of his desire for her in spite of her body's tenderness.

When she'd finally emerged from the bathroom, her skin waterlogged from too long in the shower, Leo had been gone, the tangled sheets and the lingering smell of hot bodies and sex the only signs he'd been there.

She shifted in her seat, a sudden shiver cooling the warmth in her veins. Their lovemaking had been exquisite, everything she had expected, but in the sobering light of day nothing about their situation had changed. He was still a man driven by vengeance and she was still the daughter of the enemy he loathed.

Nothing would alter those facts.

Nothing.

Ten long, silent minutes later, they walked into Leo's apartment. Helena didn't bother opening her mouth. She turned down the hall and headed straight for the guest room.

'Where are you going?'

The question brought her up short. She whirled around. 'To my room. Is that all right with you?' She couldn't keep the pithiness out of her voice. His taciturn behaviour had bugged her and, dammit, it hurt. 'I'm going to change and go for a walk. Or do I need your permission for that, too?'

'Don't push my buttons, Helena.'

His deeply growled warning only fuelled her pique. 'And what buttons would they be? Clearly not the ones that control your power of speech, or I might have got more than three words out of you in the car.'

A deep frown puckered his brow. 'Why are you angry?'

She gave him an incredulous look. 'Why am *I* angry? That's a joke question, right?'

'I am not laughing.'

No, he wasn't. And neither was she. She stepped back, took a deep breath and tried for calm. Maybe they both needed some space. Maybe, after last night, she wasn't the only one feeling awkward and confused.

She retreated another step. 'I think we both need some breathing space,' she said, and turned.

'Do not walk away from me, Helena.'

Ignoring his grated command, she strode down the hall. She needed the refuge of her room. Needed to break the spell his presence cast over her. He looked so big and dark and formidable, and yet her pulse quickened not with anxiety or fear but with the vivid memory of all the ways his hands and mouth had explored her body last night.

She reached the bedroom doorway but he was right behind her, his arm bracing against the door before she could close it. 'Please go away,' she said, her voice steady even as her insides trembled.

He followed her into the room. 'Why? So you can have your "breathing space"? Is that what you need after a night in bed with me, Helena?'

She frowned at him, perplexed. 'I think *you* need some space, given your present mood.' Heart pounding, she put her purse on the dresser and removed the earrings that were starting to pinch. 'What is *wrong* with you, anyway?'

'I don't like being dismissed.'

She paused to stare at him. He looked utterly gorgeous in a light blue open-necked shirt and navy trousers, even with his features drawn into hard, intractable lines.

She put the earrings down. 'I have no idea what you're talking about.'

'No regrets. That is what we agreed, *si*? And yet this morning you could not face me. You hid in the bathroom until I gave up waiting and left.' He stalked forward. 'Why, Helena? Was the idea of waking up beside me so unpalatable?'

'Of course not!'

Her heart climbed into her throat. *Oh, God.* Had her act of cowardice unwittingly hurt him? As swiftly as the idea entered her head she rejected it. Leo wasn't the vulnerable type. Men like him were thick-skinned. Impervious. More likely his pride had suffered a blow. He probably wasn't used to women deserting his bed. Anyway, it wasn't even *his* bed she'd deserted.

'What is this really about, Leo?' She shored up her courage with a flash of anger. 'Your ego?'

Before he could answer she spun away, but he caught her wrist and swung her back to face him. The action was firm, not rough, and his grip didn't hurt, but still an ugly memory snapped in her mind. Reflexively she ducked her head, instinct driving her forearm up to protect her face.

A sharp, indistinct sound came from Leo's throat. He released her and she glanced up, saw the colour drain from his face.

'*Mio Dio.* Did you think I would strike you?'

Her chest squeezed. 'No, I… Of course I…I mean, you would never…' She bit her tongue and mentally cursed. Her babbled response had only worsened his pallor. She pulled in a deep breath. 'No,' she repeated, firmly this time. 'Of course I didn't.'

She reached out to touch him, to show she wasn't afraid, but this time he was the one who spun away.

'Leo, wait…'

But he didn't. And before she could find the right words to stop him, to erase that bleak look from his face, he was gone.

Leo stood on the terrace in the sultry afternoon heat and raked his fingers through his hair. His insides churned. The idea of Helena believing he would physically hurt her—despite her claim to the contrary—turned his stomach.

'Leo?'

He gripped the railing, loath to turn. Loath to look at her lest he see that flicker of fear on her face again.

'Leo, I…I'm sorry.' She appeared at the railing beside him. 'It was just a stupid reflex, that's all.'

He stared across the rows of tiled rooftops baking under the brilliant Roman sun. 'I would never harm you. I would never harm *any* woman.'

Her hand covered his, squeezed lightly, then slid away. 'Of course. I know that.'

Did she? Or was she offering words she thought would mollify him? The need to test that theory overtook him and he turned, lifted his hand and brushed the backs of his fingers down her cheek. She didn't flinch, and his relief was a balm more powerful than he could have imagined.

He dropped his hand. 'I am sorry. I scared you and that was not my intent.'

'I wasn't scared. Like I said, it was just a reflex.'

Leo studied her for a long moment. 'You assumed I would hit you, Helena.' Just saying the words made his stomach roil again. 'For most people that is *not* a natural reflex.'

'So I'm not "most people".' She shrugged, a smile flickering briefly on her lips. 'Really, it's no big deal. Let's forget about it.'

He wasn't fooled. Not by her dismissive tone nor by that brave attempt at a smile. Her determination to downplay the matter only sharpened his interest. He moved, putting Helena between him and the view and gripping the railing either side of her, hemming her in. He wouldn't touch her or frighten her again—not intentionally—but he would have the truth.

'Was it a boyfriend?' His gut burned, outrage simmering like a vat of hot oil beneath his calm.

Her lashes lowered. 'No.'

His hands flexed on the railing. 'Your father?'

She hesitated and the burn in his gut grew hotter. Thicker.

'You said he was difficult to live with,' he prompted, when the silence stretched.

Finally she looked up, her face pale even as a hint of defiance shimmered in her blue eyes. 'Must we have this conversation now?'

'*Si*,' he said. 'We must.'

Her gaze tangled with his for a long, taut moment, then she pulled in a deep breath and puffed it out. 'In that case I think I need to sit.'

Leo set two glass tumblers on the coffee table in the living room and poured a finger of whisky into each. He recapped the decanter, sat on the brown leather sofa and faced Helena. Inside him acid churned, along with a hefty dose of impatience, but pushing her would have the reverse effect. So he waited.

'My father's a consummate Jekyll and Hyde,' she said finally. She picked up her glass and stared into the pale bronze liquid. 'Charming when he chooses to be, lethal when he doesn't.'

'And he has struck you?'

Helena swirled the whisky, then sipped, grimacing a little as she swallowed. 'Twice.' She put the glass down, slipped off her shoes and curled her legs beneath her, favouring her bruised foot. 'The first time I was thirteen. My mother was good at running interference between Father and me, but I provoked him one day when she wasn't around. He backhanded me across the face.'

The acid rose into Leo's throat. A man could inflict pain on a woman or a child with an open-handed slap, but a backhand was a whole different level of vicious. He clenched his jaw.

'It hurt,' she went on, her gaze focused inward now, presumably on the past and whatever unpleasant images her memory had conjured. 'But the pain didn't make me cry nearly as much as the argument my parents had afterwards.'

Her chin quivered. The tiny movement was barely visible, yet still a deep-rooted instinct urged him to fold her in his arms.

He resisted.

Not only because he had told himself he wouldn't touch her unless invited, but because the compulsion stirred a dark, remembered sense of futility and loss. Of how he'd felt as a child, wanting to protect his mother, then his father, only to face the bitter reality that loving them, believing he could save them, had not been enough.

Loving them had only made his sense of inadequacy, of life's unfairness, more unbearable when they were gone.

Leo swallowed, tightened his jaw. He wouldn't let emotion distort his thoughts. Not now, in front of Helena—the woman for whom he'd once lowered his guard, opened himself to the possibility of love, only to have life serve him yet another reminder that love only ever led to disappointment and loss.

He dragged his hand over his face. Pieces of past conversations were slotting together, crystallising into a picture he didn't much like. *This won't hurt only my father. It will hurt others, too—my family.*

He refocused. 'This grace period for your father and his company—who are you really buying time for?'

She blinked, but didn't prevaricate. 'My mother.'

'Why?' He knew the answer—it had already settled like a cold, hard mass in his belly—but he wanted to hear her say it.

'When my father is angry or drunk or upset about something he can't control—like losing his company...' She paused, and the brief silence practically crackled with accusation. 'He lashes out at her.'

Leo pushed to his feet, his blood pounding too hard now for him to sit. He stared down at her. 'So you're telling me the takeover has put your mother at a greater risk of abuse?'

'Yes.'

He scraped his fingers through his hair. Frustration,

along with another, more disturbing emotion he didn't want to identify, sharpened his tone. 'Why did you not tell me this a week and a half ago?'

Her chin snapped up. 'I told you I was worried for my family.'

'But you didn't give me the whole story.' He paced away and back again. '*Dio*, Helena!'

Her posture stiffened, cords of tension visible in her slender neck. 'This is my mother's private life we're talking about—an issue that's sensitive and painful. Not to mention perfect fodder for the gossipmongers. I couldn't trust what you might do with the information.'

He bit back a mirthless laugh. *She* didn't trust *him*? He let his disbelief at that feed his anger, because the other emotion—the one that was feeling a lot like guilt—was burning a crater in his gut he'd prefer to ignore.

'Besides…' Accusation blazed in her eyes. 'Would you have reconsidered your plans if I'd told you everything then? Are you reconsidering them now?'

Dammit. Did he have an answer for that? He dragged in a deep breath, reminded himself that Douglas Shaw was the villain in all this. Not himself. 'Violent men can have many triggers, Helena. The takeover has clearly upset him—' *as intended* '—but any number of things could set him off. Changing my plans will not change the fact that your mother is in a volatile relationship and constantly at risk of abuse.'

'I understand that. But when my father learns that you plan to dismantle the company it isn't going to "trigger" a bad mood. It's going to trigger a major meltdown. I need more time before that happens—time to convince my mother to get out.'

'And our arrangement gives you that time, does it not?' Time he could extend, if he so chose. But not by much. Convincing his board to back the takeover hadn't been easy.

The buyout of shares had been costly, and divesting the company's assets would be critical for balancing the books.

Helena's shoulders suddenly lost their starch. Her gaze slid from his. 'Yes. It does. And hopefully it'll be enough.'

The resignation in her voice, the slope of her shoulders as she stared down at her hands, undid him.

His anger drained and he sat down.

'Your mother's never considered leaving?' He strove for neutrality but still the censure crept into his voice. He knew domestic violence was a complicated issue. Understood that fear and circumstance could deprive victims of freedom and choice. But surely Helena's mother had resources? Options? Why would she tolerate abuse?

'It's easy to judge from the outside looking in, Leo.'

The reproach in her tone made the tips of his ears uncomfortably warm.

'There's a hundred reasons women stay trapped in abusive relationships. Fear of reprisal. Fear of isolation from loved ones. Fear of being alone. Believe me, I've tried talking to her, but she shuts me down every time.'

He heard the tremor in her voice, saw the quiver in her lip she tried to suppress, and cursed.

To hell with not touching.

He shifted over and lifted her into his lap. She stiffened, surprise flitting over her pale features. But as he wrapped his arms around her, her body softened, acquiesced, and she dropped her head on his shoulder.

'I am sorry, *cara*,' he murmured against her hair. 'I know how painful it is to watch someone you love suffer.'

Everyone *he'd* loved had suffered. His mother with cancer. His father from grief and addiction. Marietta, whose life had been irreversibly altered by that one fateful decision.

Helena turned her face into his neck and he buried his fingers in her hair, the soft, peachy scent reminding him of the organic fruit orchards surrounding his villa in Tuscany.

He closed his eyes.

Five weeks they'd had together in London.

Five short, intense weeks. Barely enough time to get to know one another, and yet he'd fallen like a teenager on his first romantic crush.

Hell.

Had he really thought he could bring Helena to Rome for seven nights, keep her in his home, his bed, and not risk a return of the insanity that had proved his downfall the first time around? It was a colossal mistake—one he would no doubt regret. But not today. Not yet. Not until he had all the answers he needed.

'You said your father hit you twice.'

Instantly her body tensed. He waited until she relaxed, her breath warm on his neck as she released a pent-up breath.

'After that first time I'd never seen my mother more furious—or more willing to stand up to my father. It was the most violent argument I'd ever heard them have—and I'd heard a few.' She paused. 'I was in my room and couldn't hear it all, so I don't know everything she said to him, but I do know he didn't lay a hand on me again for six years.'

Swiftly Leo calculated that she'd have been nineteen when Shaw had next assaulted her. His brows sank. *Nineteen.* Her age when he'd met her. Coincidence? A sick feeling in his gut told him it wasn't.

'The night you wouldn't see me…after you sent me away from your hotel,' she said, her words segueing from his thoughts with uncanny accuracy, 'I went to confront him. I knew Mum was out at some charity thing but I was too angry for caution. Too upset to notice he'd been drinking.' A faint quiver undermined her voice. 'One minute he was cool and condescending, the next…he lashed out so quickly I never saw it coming.'

Leo gritted his teeth.

'My lip split,' she said before he could speak, 'and I fell, hit my head on the fireplace. When he came at me a second time I picked up the first thing within reach—an iron poker—and swung it at him.'

'Dio!' She'd fought back? Gutsy, but unwise if she'd had the safer option of fleeing. He smoothed her hair back, pulled her chin up so he could look at her. 'That could have been dangerous, *cara*.' He ran his thumb over the soft skin of her cheek, made the mistake of imagining that cheek bruised, her mouth bloodied. Tension coiled in his muscles. 'What happened?'

'I struck him,' she whispered, emotion creeping in now, her shoulders hunching forward. 'And he…he went down. I was horrified. I felt sick. There was a gash on his head and…and a lot of blood. I ran to help him, but he was already staggering to his feet and he shoved me away—so hard I fell again.' She shook her head, as if trying to dispel the ugly images. 'I got out as fast as I could and… Well, you know the rest. I haven't seen or spoken to him since.'

'And he cut you off?'

'He cut off my allowance, stopped paying my college fees, but *I* chose to make it on my own. As long as he supported me financially I was bound by his rules. His dictates. I wanted freedom, for myself and—' She stopped suddenly.

'Helena?'

She pulled her chin from his grasp, looked down. 'I… I wanted to live free of his control.'

Her fingers plucked at a button on his shirtfront and he covered her hand, stilled her fidgeting. 'Your father never met me, yet he took exception to our relationship. To me.' Even now, years later, that rankled deep. 'Why?'

Her hand curled into a delicate fist under his. 'Father had rules for everything—including who I dated. Boys who were wealthy, British and well-connected were the only ones deemed acceptable.' She emitted a soft snort. 'He never tried to hide his disappointment that his first-born wasn't a son. He once said my greatest worth was as marriage material, so I should at least choose someone he could benefit from.'

Leo's stomach clenched. He'd thought his loathing for the man couldn't deepen. He'd been wrong.

Helena shifted and he tensed. The glide of her soft, rounded buttocks over his groin was doing nothing to quell the desire he'd been struggling to subdue from the moment her backside had landed in his lap.

Her eyes rounded with comprehension. 'Sorry—'

'Sorry,' he said at the same time.

They both stopped, and half-laughed, half-groaned.

Before lust could incinerate his restraint, he gently moved her off him. Then rose and pulled her to her feet.

'Thank you.' He tipped up her chin. 'I know those weren't easy things to talk about.' He tucked a curl behind her ear, something tender, perplexing, moving inside him. 'Do you still want that walk?'

She stared up at him 'No,' she said.

And then she leaned in and pressed her lips to his—a move so entirely unexpected that for a moment he simply stood there, inert, caught by the sweetness of her breath and the subtle sizzle of promise in that tentative kiss.

Then her tongue darted out, stroked over his lips, and in one red-hot second her kiss had escalated from sweet to incendiary.

Leo groaned, hauled her against him and thrust into her mouth, needing to feel her, taste her, unable to get enough even when her fingers stabbed into his hair and pulled his head down for a deeper kiss. His clothes felt too tight, chafing his skin.

Too many layers.

Too much fabric between them.

He wanted the barriers gone.

Wanted her naked, laid bare—just for him.

His pulse firing with a flammable mix of impatience

and lust, he scooped her up, enjoying the warm nuzzle of her lips on his neck as he carried her to his bedroom. He lowered her feet to the rug beside his four-poster bed, satisfaction roaring when she tore at his shirt with an urgency that matched his own frantic need to get naked.

In seconds their clothes were shed and Helena was spreadeagled on his bed, her slender limbs pale against the dark cotton coverlet. He kissed her jaw, her collarbone, then sucked the hard, rosy peak of one breast into his mouth.

A low moan vibrated in her throat. When he slid his finger along her hot, wet seam her legs widened in a brazen invitation. Her fingers scraped over his scalp, her hips writhing as he circled her clitoris with his thumb and slid one finger, then two, deep inside her.

'Oh, yes…' Her moan fractured into soft little cries that stoked his desire. 'Please…I want you… Don't make me wait.'

I want you.

The words snapped his restraint. Shredded his intent to touch and taste and savour before burying himself inside her.

Hands unsteady, he pulled a condom from his nightstand and tore into the packet. Helena rose on her elbows and watched him roll on the sheath, her eyes glazed, her lips moist and slightly parted.

Leo moved between her thighs, positioned himself at her entry and began to nudge in. But she raised her knees, wedged her heels into his buttocks and tilted her hips so he slammed full-length into her searing heat.

'Dio!'

Stars exploded in front of his eyes and he squeezed them shut, opening them again when her hands framed his face and he heard his name whispered over her lips. He held himself rigid above her.

'You don't need to be gentle with me,' she said, and rocked her pelvis.

The sensual rhythm created an exquisite friction that forced another rough exclamation up his throat. He searched her face for any hint of the fear he'd seen earlier but saw only the flush of desire. The stark look of hunger in her eyes that mirrored his own.

He surrendered control and started to move, stroking his hard length in and out, building to a frenzied rhythm that she matched thrust for thrust until, a second before he climaxed, she sank her teeth into his shoulder and arched in violent orgasm beneath him.

A feral, utterly alien sound was torn from his throat, the intense pleasure of release amplified by the erotic pain of her bite and the feel of her internal muscles convulsing around him.

Moments later his strength gave out and he rolled onto his back, dragging Helena with him. Sensations came and went. Rapture. Languor. Satisfaction. But they were all fleeting. And as his heartbeat slowed and his breathing returned to normal Leo had the disquieting sense that *he*, not Helena, was the one laid bare by their lovemaking.

CHAPTER NINE

THE TINY *TRATTORIA* tucked down a cobbled lane a few blocks from Leo's building was not what Helena had expected when, after a steamy afternoon in bed, he had declared they would go out to eat. From the moment the owner had greeted them with a broad smile and a back-slap for Leo, then ushered them into a cosy booth, however, everything about the place had charmed her.

She chased down her last bite of crispy Roman pizza with a large sip of Chianti. 'You were right.' She wiped the corners of her mouth with a red-and-white-checked napkin. 'That is quite possibly the best pizza in the world.'

He smiled, and her heart missed a beat even though she tried to be unaffected. Tried to wedge a solid wall between her head and her heart. Sitting here sharing a casual meal felt too...*ordinary*—and nothing about their contrived relationship or the things she had told him this afternoon was ordinary. Letting a few hours of phenomenal sex, a little easy talk over pizza and a disarming grin convince her otherwise was naive...and yet there was no harm in relaxing for a bit, surely?

She sipped her wine, savoured the intense flavour of ripe cherries on her tongue. She was pleasantly full, but the warm, contented feeling inside her wasn't only thanks to good food and wine. It was a carryover from earlier, when Leo had held her in his arms. When he'd listened to her talk about things she'd never talked about with anyone and made her feel safer, more secure, than she ever had in her life.

'You seem to know the owner well,' she remarked. 'Are you a regular?'

He leaned back, extended his long jean-clad legs under

the table. 'I worked here as a delivery boy during my first few semesters at university—one of three jobs that supported us while I studied.'

She couldn't hide her surprise. The man who ran a multi-million-dollar global business had delivered pizzas?

'Us?' she said.

'Marietta and me. My father was still alive then, but he was drunk most days and the people he mixed with were undesirable. My sister needed a better environment, so as soon as I could afford the rent I took her with me to a bed-sit in a safer neighbourhood. It was cramped, but clean—and secure.'

Helena frowned. 'Your father was an alcoholic?'

'He turned to drink after my mother's death. He never got over her loss.'

Sympathy bloomed. Leo and his sister had had such a traumatic childhood and then, as if they hadn't dealt with enough, Marietta's paralysing accident had happened. By contrast Helena's childhood, though far from perfect, had at least afforded material comforts, her father's wealth ensuring she'd wanted for nothing except the one thing money couldn't buy. The one thing she'd constantly craved as a child. His love.

'I'm so sorry,' she said, meaning it. 'I can't imagine the hardships you and your sister endured.'

He shrugged. 'We survived.'

She twirled the stem of her wineglass. They'd survived because Leo had made sacrifices, worked hard to keep his sister safe and create a better life for them both. Leo didn't trust or forgive easily, but he looked after his own. It was a quality in a man impossible not to admire.

'Does Marietta live in Rome?'

'*Si*. She has her own apartment and she's largely independent—both at home and at work.'

'What does she do?'

'She's curator at a contemporary art gallery—and an

artist in her own right. She recently had her first exhibition.' His voice resonated with pride. 'The landscape in my entry hall is her work.'

Helena's eyebrows shot up. 'Wow! I was admiring that just this morning. It's fabulous.'

'The accident quashed her ambition for a time, but with encouragement from her physical therapist she resumed painting a few years ago.'

'It would have been a shame if she hadn't. Talent like that shouldn't be wasted.'

'No,' he agreed, watching her intently. 'It shouldn't.'

Something in his tone made Helena's hand still on her glass. He wasn't talking about his sister now and they both knew it. She dropped her gaze, a flicker of unease chasing the warmth from her insides. She couldn't let the conversation go down this road. Couldn't explain the real reason she'd abandoned her textile design degree.

Desperately she cast around for a diversion, but only one sure-fire tactic sprang to mind.

Stifling a twinge of guilt, she reached under the table and slipped her palm over one muscle-packed thigh. 'So, are we staying for dessert...?' She glided her hand higher until, under cover of the table, she found the impressive bulge in his snug-fitting jeans. 'Or should we indulge at home?'

She ran the tip of her tongue over her lips and watched his pupils dilate, his throat muscles work around a deep, convulsive swallow.

He clamped his hand over her wandering fingers and leaned close, eyes glittering darkly. His voice, when he spoke, was a low, sexy rumble. 'You, *tesoro mio*, are insatiable.'

A breathless little laugh escaped her. The flash of raw hunger in his gaze—the knowledge that he wanted her even now, after hours of lovemaking—was a potent aphrodisiac in her blood.

Keeping pace with him on the walk back proved a challenge. By the time they tumbled through the front door of his apartment—hot, gasping for breath—his roving hands had already driven her mindless with need. He toed the door shut, backed her up against the hallway wall. For a long moment they stood panting, gazes locked, the heat of desire a living, pulsing thing in the air around them. Then his head came down, and his possession of her mouth was swift, almost brutal.

Helena's body responded with a powerful throb and she wrapped her arms around his neck, hungry for the crush of his mouth, the hot slide of his tongue against hers.

Lord.

He was right.

Her need for him was insatiable. Beyond her control.

Somehow they reached his bedroom, a haphazard trail of shoes, clothes and undergarments strewn in their wake. And then he was sheathed and inside her, filling her to the hilt with the hard, powerful thrusts of his possession.

Taking her to a place where there was only him.

Only her.

Only pleasure.

And then, too quickly, she was climaxing, her body arching wildly under him, multiple waves of pleasure radiating from her core as her internal muscles milked his simultaneous release. Her orgasm was so swift, the sensations flooding her so intense, she had to bury her face in his neck and hold back a sob of some inexplicable emotion as he rolled onto his side and cradled her into his chest.

When, a short while later, he carried her into his massive marble shower and started soaping the sweat from their bodies, she didn't have the energy to talk or move. She simply closed her eyes, clung to his wide shoulders and let the hot soapy water and his gentle touch prolong her bliss.

Back in bed, dry and cosy, snuggled into his side, she

drifted towards sleep. She was teetering on the edge of that sweet abyss when his fingers tilted up her chin. She kept her eyes closed, muttered a protest.

'Promise me something, *cara*.'

She frowned. They were doing *this* again? 'No regrets…' she mumbled, and tried to drop her head back onto his chest.

His grip firmed. 'A different promise.'

Sighing, she fluttered open her eyelids. 'Hmm…?'

'Promise me you'll never let your father—never let *anyone*—tell you you're worthless.'

She hesitated, her throat growing painfully tight. 'I promise,' she whispered, and *damn* if that warm glow from earlier hadn't flared back to life.

Leo emerged from the tendrils of a deep, dreamless sleep and sensed he was being watched. He opened his eyes and blinked, adjusting to the pale morning light slanting through the gaps in the blinds. Helena lay half atop him, her naked body warm and soft, her chin propped on the slim hand splayed over his chest.

His groin stirred.

'Morning, *cara*.'

Her smile held a hint of mischief, as if she knew how easily she aroused him and revelled in the knowledge.

'Morning.' She ran the tip of one finger down his jaw, her nail scraping through a thick layer of bristly stubble. 'Are you properly awake?'

He moved slightly, his erection nudging her hip. 'One hundred per cent.'

A pretty blush stole over her cheeks.

'Can I ask you a question?'

He crooked an eyebrow. An early morning Q&A session was not quite what he'd had in mind. *'Si,'* he said, gliding his hand over her satiny shoulder, down the back of her ribs to the dip of her waist and lower.

'Leo.' She smacked the fingers that had grabbed a hand-ful of soft, delectable buttock. 'I'm serious.'

Reluctantly, he moved his hand to her waist. Helena chewed her lip, her expression growing pensive, and a sud-den stab of instinct warned that he wouldn't like her ques-tion.

'Why do you need to do it?' Her voice was soft, curi-ous rather than accusatory. 'Why do you need to ruin my father after all these years?'

The heat of arousal in his veins instantly cooled. It was a candid question, one he had failed completely to antici-pate, and had she asked it twenty-four hours earlier he'd have refused to be drawn.

But that had been yesterday. Before she had opened up to him. Before she'd answered a few equally tough ques-tions with the kind of honesty his conscience was telling him he owed her in return.

Hell.

He expelled the air from his lungs. Gently he shifted her from him and climbed out of bed. 'Wait here.'

He scooped his briefs off the floor and pulled them on. Then he pushed a button on the wall to raise the blinds, padded down the hall to his study and riffled through a drawer till he found what he wanted.

When he returned Helena was sitting cross-legged on the bed, the top sheet tucked around her middle. The morn-ing sun fell across her bare shoulders and created a halo of rich amber in her tousled hair.

Her gaze went to the items in his hand. 'Photos?'

She took the two six-by-four snapshots he held out and studied the top one, an old shot of a tall, leggy girl mess-ing around on rollerblades.

'Your sister?' She glanced up for affirmation, then down again. 'Taken before her accident, obviously. She's abso-lutely stunning.' She studied the other photo, this one more recent. Her brow furrowed. When she looked up, her eyes were solemn. 'Still beautiful.'

'*Si*. Still beautiful.'

A familiar weight dragged at his insides. Even seated in a wheelchair, the lower half of her body visibly frail, Marietta Vincenti was a striking young woman. Nevertheless, the contrast between the photos was sobering.

Leo sat on the bed. 'Do you remember the Hetterichs from that charity dinner in London?'

'Of course.'

'Sabine mentioned Marietta and you asked me about her afterwards.' And he'd shut her down—hadn't wanted to discuss it.

'I remember.'

'For the last decade Hans has led the field in experimental stem cell surgery for spinal cord injuries and patients with varying degrees of paralysis.'

'Oh…I've read about that.' She sat forward, eyes bright with interest. 'It's a bit controversial, isn't it?'

'It's *very* controversial.' For a time he'd waged his own internal war over the ethics of it, but watching a loved one suffer did wonders for liberalising one's attitudes. 'After Marietta's accident I took an interest in Hans's work. I followed the early trials and eventually I contacted him. After reviewing Marietta's case he believed she'd be a good candidate for surgery.'

Helena frowned again. 'It wasn't successful?'

He took the photos and placed them on the nightstand. 'There is a window of time following the initial trauma during which the procedure has a greater chance of success. Marietta was already on the outer cusp of that time period.'

'So…it was too late?'

'*Si*. In the end.'

'In the end?'

'The surgery was delayed—by a year.'

Confusion clouded Helena's face. 'But…why?'

The old tightness invaded Leo's chest. Talking about this wasn't easy. The anger, the guilt, the gut-wrenching disappointment and the dark emotions he'd wrestled with had nearly destroyed him, and he had no desire to bring them to the fore again. Yet for some reason he couldn't define he felt it was important to make Helena understand.

'The surgery was only available privately, and it was expensive—beyond the means of most ordinary people. I had taken some aggressive risks to grow my business, tying up most of my assets and capital, but I had investors in the wings who were interested in a project with enormous potential. I knew if I could secure those investors I would be able to free up some of my own funds for the surgery.'

A stillness crept over Helena. 'How long ago was that?'

'Seven years.'

Her comprehension was instantaneous, the paling of her features swift. She placed her hand over her mouth and closed her eyes. When she opened them her lashes glistened with something he hadn't expected—tears.

'It was the project my father derailed?'

He nodded, his chest growing tighter. One by one his potential investors had backed off, suddenly claiming his project was too high-risk, too pie-in-the-sky for a young entrepreneur whose start-up was a tiny David in an industry full of Goliaths. When cornered and pressed, two of those men had let slip the name of Douglas Shaw. Somehow the man had used his power, his influence and connections, to identify Leo's investors and scatter them to the winds.

'Eventually I resurrected that project, but my business had taken a serious hit, and it was many months before I could reverse the damage—over a year before it was stable enough financially for me to reconsider the surgery.'

For that he'd wanted to hunt Shaw down and rip his head clean off. Instead he'd bided his time. Nursed his anger. Planned every detail of his retribution.

'Hans warned us that the chance of success was severely diminished, but I encouraged Marietta to have the procedure anyway.'

'And it was a failure?'

'She has some increased sensation and movement in her leg muscles, but nothing more significant. Barring a miracle, she will never walk again.'

Helena swiped a hand across damp cheeks. 'I…I had no idea,' she croaked. 'I'm so very sorry.'

He swore under his breath. 'Don't,' he said gruffly.

'Don't what?'

'Apologise for something that's not your fault.'

Her mouth twisted. 'But it *is* my fault, isn't it? I knew my father wouldn't approve of our relationship and I took the risk anyway. And in the end you paid the price for my stupidity. You…and Marietta.' She grimaced. 'No wonder you hate me.'

Leo rubbed a hand over his jaw. Of all the disturbing emotions that had churned through him these last forty-eight hours, hate had not been among them. 'I do not hate you, Helena.'

She gave him a look. 'You don't have to humour me. I know you think I walked away from you fully aware of what my father intended.'

An accusation he couldn't refute. Not with any degree of honesty. Seven years ago he had judged and condemned her, too blinded by ego to consider that her role in Shaw's machinations might have been as victim, not conspirator.

He tipped her chin up. 'Where you are concerned, *tesoro*, I am fast learning that what I think I know is more often than not incorrect.'

He leaned in and pressed a soft, lingering kiss to her lips. When he pulled back he noted the pulse beating at the base of her throat, the flush of colour down her neck and chest—sure signs he wasn't the only one so easily aroused. His body stirred again, his blood heating. Pool-

ing. He trailed a fingertip over her collarbone down to the
sheet covering her breasts.

Enough talking.

'We have one hour before I leave for work and your
guide is due.'

She jerked back, frowning. 'My guide?'

'Si.' He curled his fingers into the sheet and yanked it
down, exposing her lush breasts to his unabashed scrutiny.
'The guide who is taking you sightseeing today.'

Her mouth opened, no doubt to voice a protest, but Leo
was already moving. With easy strength he tumbled her
beneath him, pinned her to the mattress and smothered her
squeal of outrage with a hard, ravenous kiss.

Six hours later, sitting on the Spanish Steps awaiting the
return of the five-foot-two bundle of feminine energy that
was her tour guide, Helena admitted that she'd have to eat
every ungracious word of protest she had mumbled that
morning.

She'd had fun—an absolute blast, in fact—and her
guide, Pia, had been a delight: smart, funny, full of knowledge and, thanks to her local connections, able to leap even
the longest tourist queue in a single bound.

In just a few hours Helena had counted the great marble
columns of the Pantheon, shivered in the dungeons of the
Colosseum, stood next to the towering four-thousand-year-
old Egyptian obelisk in St Peter's Square, gazed in awe at
Michelangelo's famous frescoes on the Sistine Chapel's
ceiling, and performed the traditional right-handed coin-
toss over her left shoulder into the beautiful Trevi Fountain.

Phew!

Now she basked in the sunshine of yet another glorious
Roman afternoon, watching crowds of people mill about the
Piazza di Spagna while she waited for Pia, who'd vanished
on a one-woman mission for fresh lemon *gelato*.

She pushed her sunglasses up on her nose and smiled

at the antics of two young boys playing at the foot of the centuries-old steps. Both had dark hair and olive skin and didn't look dissimilar to how she imagined her son would have looked as an energetic boy of five or six.

Just like that her meandering thoughts caught her like a sucker punch, and she hugged her knees into her chest.

It had been impossible to sleep with Leo these last two nights and not think at least once about the life they'd inadvertently conceived. About the child she'd carried in her womb with such deep maternal love and the tiny grave where every year, on a frigid February morning, she would kneel on the cold, damp ground and mourn the loss of their son.

But she wasn't ready to tell Leo about Lucas. To inflict pain where so much hurt had gone before. Not when this truce between them was so new. So fragile.

Their revelations—hers yesterday and Leo's this morning—had caused a subtle shift in their understanding of each other. A sense of growing mutual respect. She couldn't bear it if they slipped backwards. Not now. Not when she had a tiny bubble of hope inside her. A blossoming belief that maybe—just maybe—once the dust had settled from the takeover, they could have something more. Something *real*.

'Helena!'

Pia called out from the foot of the steps and Helena rose, shelving her thoughts. This was not the time to sit and ruminate. Leo had no doubt paid good money for Pia's services. The best way Helena could show her gratitude was to enjoy the day.

Aware that eating on the steps was forbidden, she descended to the bottom. A minute later, around a mouthful of cold, creamy *gelato*, she said, 'Oh, Pia, this is divine!' And then muttered, 'Darn it…' when a muffled ringtone came from her bag.

'Here—let me.' Her ebullient, ever-present smile in

place, Pia relieved Helena of her cone so she could rummage for her mobile.

She checked the display and frowned. 'Mum?'

But it wasn't her mother on the line; it was her mother's housekeeper. And as the woman started to speak, her words rushed, the line scratchy in places, a chill that bore no relation to the cold *gelato* she'd eaten slid down Helena's spine.

She gripped the phone and stared at Pia, thinking dimly that the look on her face must be quite a sight. Because suddenly Pia's smile was gone.

Leo slouched in his office chair, threw his pen across his desk and scowled at the strategy paper he'd been attempting to red-pen for the last ninety minutes.

Buono dio! Had he ever had a day at the office this unproductive? And since when had a weekend of sex so completely annihilated his ability to focus?

He rolled his shoulders, twisted his head and felt a small pop of release in his neck.

Better. *Marginally.*

He blew out a heavy breath. Blaming his lack of concentration on the sex—no matter how spectacular—was a cop-out. It was the hot tangle of emotion in his gut that he couldn't unravel that had him distracted and on edge. He glared again at the papers on his desk and conceded he'd have to open his laptop and start from scratch.

He rubbed his eyelids, not thrilled by the prospect. His board of directors was expecting a detailed plan for divesting ShawCorp's assets. Instead he was drafting a recommendation for keeping the company intact—at least in the short term.

No doubt they'd all think he'd lost his mind.

Chances were they'd be right.

Aware of a dull ache taking root in his temples, he hit the button labelled 'Gina' on his phone and waited impatiently for his PA to pick up.

When she burst into his office moments later, a stricken-faced Helena hot on her heels, a jolt of surprise drove him to his feet. He strode around his desk, the pain in his head forgotten.

'*Cara*?'

She walked into his arms, her body trembling, her eyes enormous saucers of blue in a face as pale as porcelain.

'I need to go home,' she said, her grip on his arms verging on painful. 'My mother's had a fall. She's in Intensive Care—in an induced coma.'

CHAPTER TEN

MIRIAM SHAW REMAINED in a medically induced coma for two days.

Though her recollection of the incident was hazy, it was apparent she'd suffered a severe knock to the head that caused a swelling on her brain. Her sprained wrist, the bruising along her left hip and thigh, the presence of alcohol in her blood and the location in which the housekeeper had found her all pointed to an unfortunate and—though Helena balked at the idea—drunken tumble down the stairs.

'Helena?'

She jerked awake, lurched forward in her chair and reached on autopilot for the guardrail of the hospital bed. A second later her overtired mind registered the deep, rich timbre of the voice that had spoken.

She twisted round as Leo placed a plastic cup filled with black watery coffee on the small table beside her.

He grimaced. 'The best I could find, I'm afraid.'

She settled back in her chair—one of several in her mother's private room on the ward. 'It's fine. I'm used to it after four days.' She managed a smile. 'Thanks.'

He dropped into the seat beside her and reached for her hand, lacing his fingers through hers, his other hand loosening the tie at his throat. He'd swapped his jeans for a designer suit today, having gone to a business meeting in London, but the look of unease he wore every time he came to the hospital remained.

She met his gaze and her breath caught, her belly tugging with a deep awareness of him that was inappropriate for the time and place. *Incredible.* Even dulled by worry and fatigue, her senses reeled from his impact.

'Don't say it,' he said, his brows descending, his jaw, clean-shaven for the first time in three days, clenched in sudden warning.

'I wasn't going to say anything,' she lied, unnerved by his ability to read her. Somehow he'd known she was on the brink of telling him—for the hundredth time since they'd left Rome—that he didn't need to be here. That he shouldn't have come to London. That her mother's welfare wasn't his concern.

He felt responsible in some way. He hadn't said so—not in so many words—but every time Helena looked at him she sensed a storm of dark emotions swirling beneath his veneer of control.

'Has she been lucid today?'

She shifted her attention to her mother, restful in sleep and less fragile-looking now, without all the tubes and wires that had been attached to her in the ICU. She'd been brought out of her induced coma two nights ago. So far the doctors were pleased with her recovery.

'We've had a few brief chats. And she talked with James before he returned to boarding school this afternoon.'

The chance to spend a few hours with her brother had been bittersweet, in the circumstances. By contrast, coming face to face with her father in a packed ICU waiting room had just been...*bitter*. She was surprised he'd bothered returning from Scotland. Thank God he'd turned up when Leo wasn't there.

'Have you seen your father again?'

Helena shook her head. She didn't want to discuss her father with Leo. Not when she had the sneaking suspicion he was secretly hankering for an outright confrontation with the other man.

His hand squeezed hers. 'He cannot hurt you, *cara*. I won't let him.'

A lump rose in her throat. When he said things like that, looked at her the way he was looking at her now, she was filled with confusion. Torn between the cynical voice that said he was using the situation—using *her*—to get to her father, and the whisper of hope urging her to believe he truly cared.

'Helena?'

She started. The voice uttering her name this time was not deep and manly but soft and feminine. Her mother's. Pulling her hand free, she jumped to her feet.

Leo rose beside her. 'I'll take a walk,' he murmured, turning to go. 'Call me when you're ready to leave.'

'Or you could stay.' She touched his arm. 'You barely said more than hello to her yesterday.'

He rubbed the back of his neck. 'Another time. I have some calls to make.'

Helena didn't push. She understood his unease. Her mother was the wife of the man whose company he'd set out to destroy.

She dropped her hand and waited for the door to close behind him before moving to the bed. She pulled up a chair, took her mother's hand. 'How do you feel, Mum?'

'Fine, apart from this awful headache.' A weak smile formed on her pale lips. 'He's very handsome, isn't he?'

Helena looked down, frowned at the mottled purpling on the back of her mother's hand where an IV catheter—now gone—had ruptured a vein. Yesterday she had stretched the truth. Told her mother she and Leo were seeing each other, trying to work some things out. In reality she didn't have a clue *what* they were doing—and she didn't think he did either.

'I'm sorry he didn't stay.'

Miriam's smile vanished. 'You mustn't apologise, darling. For anything.' She closed her eyes, frowning, as if the pain in her head was suddenly too much to bear.

Alarmed, Helena sat forward. 'Mum?'

Miriam's eyes opened again. 'I've made choices,' she said, her blue eyes latching on to her daughter's. 'Choices

I know you don't understand. But I only wanted the best for you, darling. And for James. Douglas is a difficult man, a proud man, but he gave us the best of everything. You can't argue with that.'

Damned if she couldn't. But she swallowed the bitter retort. Now was not the time to catalogue Douglas Shaw's many failings as a husband and father.

Miriam gripped Helena's hand. 'It wasn't all bad, was it? We had some good times. After James came along things were better, weren't they? Douglas was happy for a while.'

'Yes,' Helena agreed, reluctantly. 'I suppose he was.'

In fact the years following her brother's birth had been the most harmonious she could remember, her father seemingly content for once—because, she supposed, he'd finally got what he wanted. A son.

'But, Mum, that was a long time ago. And things…well, they aren't fine now, are they?'

The proud, resolute look she knew so well came into her mother's eyes. 'I can *make* them fine.'

Helena donned a dogged look of her own. 'For how long? Until the next time he's angry and drunk?'

She reached out, gently touched the faint discoloration under Miriam's left eye. Last week's bruise had faded, but in time there'd be another. And another.

'Things are only going to get worse. *He's* only going to get worse. You do see that, don't you?'

Miriam's mouth quivered, just for a second, before firming. 'I have to think of James.'

'Who's nearly sixteen,' Helena pointed out. 'Old enough to understand that marriages can fail. Parents can separate. I love him, too, but you can't wrap him in cotton wool for ever.'

Most of the year her brother was at boarding school, limiting his exposure to the tensions at home. But he was a smart boy, perceptive, and Helena suspected he already knew more than he let on. To her knowledge their father had never laid a hand on his precious son, but that could change. Violent men were unpredictable—especially when fuelled by rage and drink. She would sit James down and talk with him, make sure he understood his options. Ensure he was safe.

'It's a few weeks yet till the summer break,' she said. 'When he comes home he can decide who he stays with. Who he sees.'

A tiny tremor ran through her mother's hand. 'No. Your father won't let go that easily. He'll force James to choose between us.'

That was a possibility. One Helena couldn't deny. 'You're his mother,' she said gently. 'That will never change. He loves you.'

Miriam's throat worked for long seconds, then she whispered, 'I'm proud of you, darling. Do you know that? You had the courage to walk away when I didn't.' Her grip tightened on Helena's hand. 'I don't think I can be as brave.'

'Oh, Mum.' Helena hugged her, hiding the rush of moisture in her eyes.

Brave? The word seemed to hover in the air and mock her. Brave was not how she'd felt these last few nights, lying in Leo's arms as she searched in vain for the courage to talk about their son.

Cowardly was a more fitting word.

Maybe even *selfish*.

She pulled back and gave her mother a steady look. 'You can,' she said, the conviction in her voice as much for herself as for her mother.

She mightn't have a clue where she and Leo were headed but one thing she did know—she loved him now just as she had seven years ago. If they were to have any shot at a second chance she had to overcome her fear. Do the right thing and tell him about his son.

She squeezed her mother's hand. 'You *can*,' she repeated.

Miriam's eyes filled with tears. 'Your father will never agree to a divorce. And if he does where will I go? What will I do? I grew up with nothing, Helena. I can't go back to that. And I'm too old to start over on my own.'

'Mum, you're not even fifty! And you'll be entitled to a divorce settlement. We can find you a good lawyer.'

Somewhere in the distance a man raised his voice, the strident sound out of place in the quiet of the ward.

Helena tuned out the disturbance, her mind already too full of noise. 'Please, Mum,' she said. 'Let me help you.'

Miriam's tears spilled down her cheeks. She nodded and pulled her daughter into a tight hug.

'Miss Shaw?'

Helena straightened and turned. A nurse stood in the doorway.

'I'm sorry to interrupt,' the woman said, her tone brisk, her face serious. 'But could you come with me, please?'

Leo stood in the empty visitors' room at the end of the ward and stared out of the rain-spattered window. Outside, London was gearing up for another five o'clock rush hour and the frenzy of people and traffic on the wet streets below matched his edgy, restive mood. He swayed forward, letting his forehead bump the cool glass.

Why was he still here?

It was Thursday and he should be back in Rome, presenting his report on the ShawCorp takeover to his board—a task he had, until recently, anticipated with relish.

Now, not so much.

And wasn't that one hell of a kicker?

Seven years he'd planned this victory—*seven years*—and in a matter of days the taste of triumph had turned to ash in his mouth.

Footfalls echoed in the room and he straightened, pulled his hands from his pockets. Time to get some air, stretch his legs. Then he'd wait in the limo and clear his emails.

The hospital's sterile surroundings were closing in on him and, as mean-spirited as it sounded, he was in no mood for polite chitchat with the relative of a sick person.

The roar that rent the air before Leo had fully turned from the window gave him a split second to react. Even so, the fist flying towards him caught the left side of his jaw and sent a shard of pain ricocheting through his skull.

'Bastard!'

Douglas Shaw spat the word before lunging again, but Leo was ready this time. He dodged the blow and with a swift, well-timed manoeuvre seized Shaw's wrist and twisted his arm up his back.

'Calm down, you old fool,' he grated into the man's ear.

'Don't give me orders, Vincenti.'

Shaw struggled and Leo firmed his grip, inching the man's wrist higher up his back.

In a second, Shaw's voice went from gruff to reedy. 'You're breaking my arm.'

Making a noise of disgust, Leo let go with a shove, giving himself room to counter another attack if Shaw was stupid enough to try.

The older man wisely calmed down. He rubbed his arm. 'What the hell are *you* doing here?'

Leo returned his hands to his pockets, adopting a casual stance that belied the tension in his muscles, his readiness to act. He studied Shaw's hostile face—a face he had, until now, seen only in media clippings and corporate profiles. Hollows in the man's cheeks and a grey tinge to his skin made him look older in the flesh. Strong cologne and the waft of alcohol tainted the air.

Leo suppressed a grimace. 'I'm surprised you recognise me, Shaw. After all those declined invitations to meet I was beginning to think you had no interest in your new majority shareholder.'

'Is that why you're here?' Shaw snarled the question. 'Looking for a chance to gloat?'

Leo threw his head back and laughed. 'Don't flatter yourself, old man. I have better ways to spend my time.'

Shaw stepped forward, his sore arm and Leo's superiority in the strength department clearly forgotten. 'Maybe I should teach you another lesson—like the one I taught you seven years ago.'

Leo freed his fists, leaned his face close to Shaw's. 'You can try, but we both know your threats are empty. The truth is you're a coward and a bully. I know it. Your wife knows it. And your daughter knows it.'

A deep purple suffused Shaw's face. 'By God, I should—'

'Stop it! Both of you!'

A female voice sliced across the room, silencing whatever puerile threat Shaw had been about to deliver.

'This is not the time or place.'

Helena glared at each man before turning to murmur something to the nurse hovering in the doorway behind her. The woman muttered a reply, levelled a stern look at the men, then disappeared. Helena came into the room, her movements short, stiff, and stood shoulder to shoulder with Leo.

This time Shaw threw his head back and laughed. 'Of course!' he exclaimed to the ceiling. 'I should have guessed.' He snapped his chin down, pinned his daughter with a contemptuous stare. 'Some things never change— you're still a disloyal slut.'

Rage exploded in Leo's chest. Before his brain could intervene his muscles jolted into action. Within seconds his hands were twisted in the front of Shaw's shirt and he had the man pinned to a wall.

'Leo—stop!'

Helena's voice barely registered over the roar in his ears, but her firm touch on his arm dragged him back to his senses. Sucking in a deep breath, he dropped his hands, appalled by how swiftly the urge to do violence had overtaken him. That was Shaw's MO, he reminded himself with a flare of disgust, not his.

He stepped back and Shaw eyed him with a supercilious sneer that made Leo, for one tenth of a second, want to wipe the look off his face and to hell with being the better man.

Shaw straightened his attire and brushed himself off as if Leo's touch had left him soiled.

Pompous ass.

Helena turned to her father, her pale features set in the cool, dignified mask Leo had learnt to recognise as her protective armour. A week ago that very mask had bugged the hell out of him. Now her poise under pressure drew his unbridled respect.

'Leo's right,' she said, her voice as cold and sharp as a blade of ice. 'You're nothing but a coward and a bully.'

Shaw's face darkened, but Helena showed no fear. She stepped closer, and Leo braced himself to intervene if Shaw made any sudden moves.

'You tried so often to make me feel like a failure as a child. To make me feel worthless. But the truth is there's only one failure in this family and it's not me or Mum.' Her chin jutted up. 'It's *you*. It's *always* been you.' She pulled the strap of her handbag higher up her shoulder. 'Go home, Douglas,' she said, her voice quieter, weary now. 'My mother doesn't want to see you.'

And then she stepped back, looked at Leo.

'I'm ready to go whenever you are.'

Stiff and proud, she strode out of the room and Leo bolted after her, ignoring the man whose bluster had withered to a hard, brittle silence. A few days ago Leo would have sold his soul for a chance to face off with the man. Now there Shaw stood and Leo couldn't care less. The only face he wanted to see was Helena's.

He caught her in the corridor, pulled her gently to a stop. The tears on her cheeks caused a sharp burning sensation in his chest.

She swiped at her face with the heel of her hand. 'Please, just take me home.'

He frowned, picturing the cramped flat he'd cast an appalled eye over four days ago. He had announced with unequivocal authority that she would stay with him at the hotel.

'Home?' he echoed, his stomach pitching at the idea of taking her back there.

'I mean the hotel. Just anywhere that's not here.'

His innards levelled out. '*Si.* Of course.' He cradled her damp face in his hands, pressed a kiss to her forehead. 'Will you wait here one minute for me?'

She nodded and he kissed her again—on the mouth this time—then released her and headed back to the visitors' room.

Shaw hadn't gone far. He stood by the window, much as Leo had earlier, staring down at the rain-soaked streets.

He glanced over his shoulder, his top lip curling. 'What do you want now, Vincenti?'

'To give you some advice.'

Shaw snorted. 'This should be good.'

Leo stood a few paces shy of the older man. 'Next time you feel the need to lash out,' he said, undaunted by the sudden fierce glower on Shaw's face, 'stay away from your wife. If you do not, and I hear that you have harmed her, know that I will come after you and do everything in my power to see you prosecuted in a court of law.'

He eyeballed Shaw just long enough to assure the man his threat was genuine, then started to leave, his thoughts already shifting back to Helena.

'Let me give *you* a piece of advice, son.'

Leo stopped, certain that whatever gem Shaw intended to impart wouldn't be worth a dime. He turned. 'What?'

'There are two kinds of women in this world. Those who understand their place and those who don't. Miriam always knew how to toe the line, but she coddled that girl far too much. If you want obedience in a woman you won't find it in Helena. She'll bring you nothing but trouble.'

Dio. The man was a raving misogynist. 'You don't know Helena.'

Shaw sneered. 'And you *do*?'

'Better than you.'

The sneer stretched into a bloodless smile that raised the hairs on Leo's forearms.

'In that case, since the two of you are so close, I assume you know about the baby?'

At that moment a grey-haired woman entered the room and headed for the kitchenette in the far corner.

Shaw stepped forward and Leo tensed, but the other man's hands remained by his sides.

He leaned in to deliver his parting shot. 'The one she buried nine months after you scarpered back to Italy.'

For a suspended moment Shaw's words hung in the air, devoid of meaning, and then, like guided missiles striking their target, they slammed into Leo's brain one after the other. His lungs locked. The skin at his nape tightened. And when Shaw walked away, his expression smug, Leo couldn't do a damn thing to stop him. Because his muscles—the ones that had been so swift to react earlier—had completely frozen.

Through a dark, suffocating mist, he registered a touch on his arm. He looked down.

'Are you all right, my dear?' The elderly woman peered up at him through round, wire-rimmed spectacles. 'You're as white as a ghost.'

'Tell me about the child.'

Helena stared at Leo's implacable face. 'Stop standing over me.'

She wished she hadn't sat down as soon as they'd entered the suite. She fought back a shiver. She'd thought his silence during the limo ride from the hospital had been unbearable. Having him tower over her now, like some big, surly interrogator, while she cowered on the sofa was ten times worse.

He gritted his teeth—she could tell by the way his jaw flexed—then visibly flinched.

'You should ice that,' she blurted, eyeing the livid bruise beneath his five o'clock shadow. She still couldn't believe her father had punched him.

'So help me, Helena, if you do not—'

'I wanted to tell you.' She jumped to her feet, unable to sit there a moment longer while he glowered down at her. She circled around the sofa, gripped the back for support. 'I was just…waiting for the right time.'

Oh, God. How weak that sounded—how very convenient and trite. He'd never believe it. Not now. Not in a million years.

She searched his face, desperate for a glimpse of the warmth and tenderness she'd grown accustomed to in recent days. But all she saw was anger. Disbelief. Hurt. She thought of her father and his smug expression as he'd passed her in the hospital corridor. A flash of hatred burned in her chest. He'd ruined everything. *Again.*

'You were waiting for *the right time*?' Leo plunged his fingers into his hair. 'Did you not think seven years ago that it was "the right time"?'

Her legs shook and she dug her nails into the sofa. 'You left,' she reminded him. 'You went back to Italy.'

'Because I had nothing to stay for. Your father had seen to that.'

'You said you never wanted to see me again.'

'I had no idea you were carrying my child.'

'Neither did I.'

Only once had they burst a condom, and she'd sensibly taken a morning-after pill. And since her cycle had always been erratic her overdue period hadn't, at first, been cause for concern.

'And when you *did* find out? Did it not occur to you *then* to find me and tell me I was going to be a father?'

'No—I mean…' She shook her head. '*Yes*. But I was confused. Frightened.'

'So you were thinking about yourself? Not me? Or what was best for our child?'

His words cut like the vicious lash of a whip. Smarting, she prised her hands from the back of the sofa then walked around it, her insides trembling.

'Be angry with me, Leo,' she said, stalking into his space. 'But don't judge me. Don't pretend you have *any* idea what it's like to be pregnant and scared and alone. I made some foolish decisions—some *bad* decisions—but don't think for a moment I didn't realise that. Don't think I didn't hold our son in my arms and regret, to the very bottom of my soul, that I had denied you that privilege.'

Leo's face suddenly paled and the flash of anguish in his eyes sliced through her heart.

'A son?' He dropped onto the sofa and bowed his head for a long moment. 'How…?'

He didn't finish the question. He didn't need to.

She sat beside him, close but not touching, and pulled in a deep breath. She spoke quietly. 'He was stillborn. He died in my womb two days before he was due.'

She stared at her hands, pale against the dark denim of her jeans. She didn't need to look at Leo to know his reaction. His shock was palpable.

'I knew something was wrong because I could no longer feel him kicking. I went straight to the hospital and they confirmed that he didn't have a heartbeat. The doctors couldn't tell me why it had happened. Apparently it just does sometimes.'

She curled her nails into her palms. Her memory of that day was still vivid: the horror, the pain. It was a dark stain on her soul she would never be able to erase.

'They offered an autopsy but I…I turned it down. I

didn't want our little boy cut open,' she said hurriedly, feeling she had to justify that decision. 'The results weren't guaranteed to be conclusive. And it wasn't going to bring him back.'

She looked up and Leo's expression was so stark she wanted to reach out and touch him. But there was no comfort she could offer him. No words of solace. Pain, she knew, eased with time. Nothing else.

'I'm so sorry,' she whispered.

Abruptly he stood, grabbed his jacket off the chair where he'd tossed it earlier and shrugged it on.

She swallowed, her heart plummeting. 'Where are you going?'

He looked at her, the emotion in those dark eyes impossible to fathom.

'Out. I need a drink.'

'You have a bar here.'

Ignoring that, he strode to the door.

Disbelief drove Helena to her feet. 'So you're just going to walk out? You don't even want to talk about it?' She blinked back tears.

Damn him. He was hurting. In shock. She got that. But he wasn't the only one who'd been through an emotional grinder today.

He stopped and turned. Several beats of silence pulsed between them, each one long and unbearably tense. For a moment she thought he would say something. He didn't. He spun on his heel and walked out through the door.

CHAPTER ELEVEN

DARKNESS SHROUDED THE suite when Leo returned.

Had she gone? he wondered. Back to that grim flat of hers? Back to whatever bland, colourless life she'd consigned herself to since the death of their son?

He flicked on a light and blinked. He wasn't drunk. In fact he'd nursed a single Scotch in the hotel bar for over an hour before the need to move had overtaken him. And then he'd walked. From the streets of Mayfair to the teeming pavements of Soho and Piccadilly Circus and back to the tree-lined greens of Hyde Park. He'd walked until his feet burned and fatigue stripped away his anger, leaving in its wake the galling knowledge that he'd behaved appallingly.

He dumped his jacket and looked at his watch. Nine-thirty p.m. Three hours since he'd left—plenty of time for her to pack up and flee. But had she? He moved through the suite, a hard knot forming in his chest at the prospect that she really had gone.

But, no. Her clothes were still in the bedroom, her toiletries sitting in a neat row on the bathroom vanity.

So where the hell was she?

He went back to the lounge and found his phone. He'd switched it off earlier. Maybe she'd left a message? He powered it on and had his code half entered when he heard a noise at the door. A few seconds later it swung open and Helena walked in, carrying a bag and wearing a grey hooded jacket with damp patches on the shoulders.

He frowned, disguising his relief. 'You're wet,' he said. Inanely. Because it was better than shouting, *Where the hell have you been?*

'It's just started raining again.' She glanced at him, put

down the bag and took off her jacket. Her face was flushed, her breathing a little uneven. 'I only caught a few drops.'

'Where have you been?' He surprised himself with how reasonable he sounded. How *not* angry.

'I went home.'

He raised his eyebrows. 'How?'

'On the tube. You know…that thing called public transport—for common folk who can't afford limos.' Her sarcasm lacked any genuine bite.

He put his phone down. 'Why?'

'I needed to get something.'

She knelt by the bag and lifted out a wooden box, roughly the size of a document-carrier. It looked handcrafted, its golden wood polished to a beautiful sheen, the lock and key and silver side-handles dainty and ornate. She placed it on the coffee table by the sofa and straightened, holding out her hand to him.

'I named our little boy Lucas,' she said, a smile trembling on her lips. 'And he was the most beautiful thing I had ever seen.'

Helena watched Leo's expression crumple in a way she'd never have imagined it could. He closed his eyes and turned away, his shoulders hunched, his head bowed.

'No. I can't.'

She walked over and touched his shoulder. 'You can,' she said, as firmly as she'd spoken those very same words to her mother. 'Our son was *real*, Leo. He didn't cry or open his eyes or take a breath, but he had ten fingers and ten toes and everything else a perfect baby should have.' She squeezed his shoulder, felt a tremor run through the hard muscle under her hand. 'Please,' she said, willing him to look at her. Willing him to trust her. 'Let me show you our little boy. I promise it will help.'

Endless seconds ticked by. Taut, silent seconds that stretched her nerves and amplified each painful beat of her heart. At the very moment her shoulders started to slump, weighted by defeat, he turned.

'*Si.*' He dragged a hand over his face. 'Show me, then.'

Relief—and a glimmer of hope—trickled through Helena's veins. She took his hand and led him to the sofa. He sat and she kicked off her shoes, knelt on the floor and opened the box. The first item made her heart give a painful squeeze.

Hands shaking, she passed it to him. 'I knitted it myself.'

Leo's big, masculine hands dwarfed the tiny purple beanie. He turned it over several times, his eyebrows inching up as he fingered the multi-coloured pompom. 'It is very…bright.'

She waggled a pair of fire-engine-red booties. 'I liked colour, remember? Pastels didn't get a look-in, I'm afraid.'

His soft grunt might or might not have been approval. Sitting forward, he peered into the box. 'Is this…?' He lifted out a small white plaster mould. '*Mio Dio.*' He ran his thumb over the tiny indentations created by his son's hand. His voice deepened. Thickened. 'So small…and perfect…'

'There are moulds of his feet, too,' she said, blinking away the sudden prickle of tears. 'And a lock of hair. Some outfits.' She delved into the box, removed more items, including an envelope. 'And I…I have photos.'

Leo shifted suddenly, sinking to the floor beside her, so close his warm, muscled thigh pressed against hers. He reached for the miniature mould of Lucas's foot, handling the tiny object with infinite care.

Helena watched, her throat growing hot, tight. Perhaps this hadn't been a crazy idea after all? If everything fell apart from here—if *they* fell apart—at least they would have shared this.

He put down the mould and turned his attention to the other items she'd laid out, taking his time to handle and examine each one in turn. When he eventually came to the photos he studied them for a long time in silence.

'He looks like he's sleeping,' he said at last.

'Yes.' The ache in her throat became a powerful throb. 'He does.'

She sat back on her heels. She could weep right now. For the son she had lost. For the strong, proud man sitting beside her. For the future for which she had dared to hope.

Instead she climbed to her feet and looked down on Leo's bowed head. 'I'm tired, and cold. I think I'll grab a shower before bed.' She hovered a moment, but his focus remained on the photo in his hand. 'Will you…be coming to bed?'

As she waited for his answer, her muscles tense, her body shivery from tiredness, she realised how much she wanted him to say yes. How badly she needed his arms around her tonight. How desperately she ached for his warmth, his touch, *his love.*

'Soon,' he said, and his eyes, when he glanced up, revealed nothing.

But when Leo finally came to bed, over two hours later, he didn't put his arms around her. He didn't touch her. He didn't even turn in her direction. And though it was only a matter of inches that separated their bodies, the gap might as well have been a chasm. A chasm Helena feared was too wide, too dark and too deep for either of them to bridge.

Leo stood at the French doors and watched lightning fork across the night sky, the jagged streaks of white light searing his retinas.

Or was it the tears making his eyes burn?

Dammit.

He hadn't cried since the night of Marietta's accident, but that box had been his undoing. Unravelling him in ways he hadn't thought possible. Flaying his emotions until his insides felt raw. And yet his pain must be nothing compared to what Helena had suffered. Helena had borne her loss alone, grieved for their son without him because she had been too afraid to tell him she was carrying their child. Too afraid because the last words he'd spoken to her—shouted through a closed hotel door, no less—had been hard, unforgiving words, fired without a care for how deeply they'd wound.

Thunder boomed, closer now, and he stepped back from the glass. *Idiota*, standing here watching the storm. Inviting memories of the night his mother had died.

As a child he'd thought thunder was a sign of God's anger. Had thought losing his mother was his punishment for boyhood sins: avoiding homework, skipping chores, cornering the big bully who'd pulled Marietta's hair and punching him in the nose—twice.

Since then he'd hated thunderstorms. Hated the idea of something so powerful and beyond his control.

Maybe God was punishing him now?

For his pride. His anger. His failure to forgive.

He had targeted one man with single-minded purpose and spared not a thought for collateral damage. Now a woman lay in hospital. Another in his bed.

And what of her? his conscience demanded. Would Helena, too, become collateral damage when all this was over? Or would the only damage where she was concerned be to his heart?

'Leo?'

He started, the soft voice behind him catching him by surprise. When he had thrown off the sheets and padded, naked, through to the lounge he had thought Helena asleep—undisturbed, it seemed, by the storm.

'What are you doing?' she said, drowsy. 'It's three a.m.'

He didn't turn. Didn't know what to say to her. What *could* he say? *I'm sorry?* No. Useless. Mere words couldn't express his regret for his behaviour today. His behaviour seven years ago.

He'd stormed back to Italy like an angry bear, licking

his wounds when he should have been here looking after her, sharing the burden of responsibility.

Of loss.

He glanced over his shoulder. Her form was a willowy outline in the glow of the single lamp he'd switched on in the corner of the room.

'I couldn't sleep,' he said.

'The storm?'

'I don't like them.' The words just spilled out. He didn't know why. He didn't make a habit of highlighting his weaknesses to people. But then, Helena wasn't *people*. She was... Hell, she was so many things—none of which he was in any mood to contemplate.

'Why?' She was right behind him now.

He shrugged. 'Bad memories.'

He could feel her breath on his shoulder, and the tantalising scent of warm, sleepy woman enveloped him. He scrunched his eyes closed, the rush of blood to his groin turning him hard against his will.

He wanted her.

Even with his gut in turmoil, tears drying on his cheeks, he wanted her.

He heard a rustling behind him and then her arms were slipping around his middle, her slender fingers splaying over his abs. Her heavy breasts pushed into his back, her hips against his buttocks, and his desire surged with the realisation that she'd shed her pyjamas and was now, like him, completely naked.

He groaned. 'Helena...'

'Shh.' She ducked under his arm and took his face in her hands.

When he drew breath to speak again she tugged his head down and silenced him with a long, drugging kiss.

Her taste exploded in his mouth, hot and sweet and undeniably erotic. He shuddered, closed his arms around her and surrendered to the burning need only she could assuage. The solace only she could offer. He hoisted her up and her legs hooked around his waist, their mouths continuing to meld and devour—until he started for the bedroom.

She wrenched her mouth away. 'No,' she whispered, lowering her legs, pulling him back to the French doors. She sank to her knees at his feet. 'Here. Take me here.'

He stared down at her, his blood pounding, his heart pumping so hard he feared it might punch from his chest.

This woman stripped him bare. Of his pride. His anger. His guilt. Everything but this deep, compelling need for her.

'Why?' he said, his throat raw.

She reached for his hands and dragged him down to the carpet, pushed him onto his back. 'To replace your bad memories with new ones,' she said, and mounted him so quickly he almost came the moment her slippery heat encased him.

He dug his heels into the carpet, seized her hips in an urgent bid to slow her. He wasn't wearing protection and she was hot and slick, her internal muscles a tight velvet sheath pulsing around him.

The sensation was exquisite.

'Condom…' he rasped.

'I'm on the pill.' She grabbed his wrists, guided his hands to her breasts and arched her back, taking him deeper. Her dark curls tumbled around her shoulders and her features were illuminated as another bright bolt of lightning tore the sky.

Leo stared up, captivated by the sight of her riding him, by the bold, sensual grind of her pelvis driving him to the brink faster than he'd have liked. Thunder rolled down from the heavens, loud and near, a boom so powerful it slammed into his body with an almighty thud.

'Come with me,' he ground out, grasping her waist, forcing her to still so he could satisfy his need to drive up into her.

'I…I'm close.' Her body flexed, her thighs squeezing his sides, a taut O of ecstasy shaping her mouth. 'Oh, yes… Now, Leo… *Now…*'

He plunged upward, penetrating deep, and she screamed at the same instant another flash lit up the sky. Her cry of release was all he needed and he let himself go, his orgasm thundering through him in a climax so intense it bordered the line between pleasure and pain and racked his entire body with a series of long, powerful shudders.

With a whimper Helena slumped onto his chest. She buried her face in his shoulder, made a soft mewling sound against his skin, and he stroked his hands up and down the graceful lines of her back.

He didn't deserve her compassion—didn't deserve *her*—but she felt so good nestled in his arms he didn't want to let her go.

He cradled her close.

He *would* let her go. It was the right thing to do. The only thing to do. And the sooner he did, the better.

Helena navigated the bedroom on autopilot as she packed up her things. The painkillers she'd forced down earlier hadn't worked and her temples throbbed, her eyes gritty from the crying jag she'd indulged in. Silly to have allowed emotion to overwhelm her simply because she'd woken to find Leo's side of the bed empty and cold. He'd left a note, at least. A bold, handwritten scrawl advising her that he'd gone to a meeting and would be back by noon.

She looked around for her pyjamas, frowned when she couldn't see them, then remembered and went through to the lounge.

Yes—there. On the floor by the sofa, where she had discarded them so brazenly in the night.

She reached for them and a sudden powerful sob of emotion rushed up her throat. On shaky legs she sank to the sofa, hating it that she felt so off-balance, so raw and exposed.

But how could she not?

She wasn't the same woman who had left London a week ago. She felt different—more aware of herself. As if someone—no, not 'someone', *Leo*—had shone a great floodlight inside her and illuminated all the parts of herself she'd ignored for too long.

He made her feel desired. Wanted.

Worth something.

Made her want to rip down the safe, boring black and white walls she'd erected like a concrete tower around herself.

She rubbed her chest as if she could banish the ache within.

She loved Leo, but what future could they hope for? One in which he spent his days trying to forgive her and she spent hers trying to earn back his trust?

A shudder rippled through her. Her mother had endured a miserable marriage and she didn't want that for herself. She wanted a partnership based on honesty and respect. On *love*. That last especially. Because if two people loved each other they could overcome anything, surely?

She forced herself to her feet, returned to the bedroom to finish her packing.

She didn't know if Leo loved her—didn't know if what he felt for her ran any deeper than lust—but she would not play the desperate, needy lover. She would not pout and demand that he declare his feelings for her. *No*. She would do this with dignity and strength. With self-respect. The kind she had often wished over the years her mother possessed.

And if Leo chose to let her walk away…if he was content to see the back of her…she would have her answer.

Relief. That was what Leo told himself he was feeling. When he walked into the suite and saw Helena sitting on the sofa, her bags packed beside her, he felt relief. She had come to her senses. Realised in the cold light of day that she could do better. Better than a man who had let her down when she'd needed him most.

'You're leaving.' He kept his voice flat. Neutral. As if those words *hadn't* stripped the lining from his stomach.

She rose, her expression serious and her eyes, he realised on closer inspection, bloodshot and puffy. Self-loathing roiled in his stomach. No doubt *he* was the cause of her misery. He thrust his hands into his trouser pockets before he did something selfish, like haul her into his arms and beg her not to leave.

'I think that's wise,' he said.

'Do you?' She looked at him, her gaze wide, unblinking.

'*Si.* Of course.'

He strode to the wet bar, pulled a soda from the fridge. Later he'd need something stronger. For now he just needed something to do—an excuse not to look at her. Not to drown in those enormous pools of blue.

'Our seven days are up, are they not?'

Silence behind him. He popped the tab on the can, quashed the temptation to crush the aluminium in his fist. Instead he took a casual swig and turned.

She took a step towards him, her clasped hands twisting in front of her. 'Yes,' she said. 'And I know you can't stay here for ever. Neither can I—which is why I'm going back to my flat…' Her voice trailed off, an awkward silence descending.

'I video-conferenced with my board this morning, regarding my acquisition of ShawCorp.' He kept his delivery brisk. Businesslike. 'They've agreed to a delay on the asset divestment.'

'Oh?' Her eyebrows lifted. 'How long?'

'Nine months, initially—provided costs can be restricted and profits improved.' He put the soda down. 'Time to see how the company performs and consider options for its future.'

She blinked. 'I...thank you.'

'Don't thank me, Helena.' A bitter edge crept into his voice. 'We both know you don't owe me any gratitude.'

Something flashed in her eyes. An emotion he couldn't decipher. Her hands continued to fidget and he fought not to reach out and still them.

'When will you return to Rome?'

'Tonight.' A decision he had just now made. Why stay? He couldn't sleep here. Not knowing she was in the same city, close and yet untouchable. He needed land, water, miles between them.

'I see. Will you—?'

His mobile chimed and he pulled it from his pocket, saw it was his PA calling and answered with a clipped greeting. He listened to Gina relay an urgent message from his second-in-command, then asked her to hold.

He glanced at Helena. 'I need to take this,' he said, and without waiting for an acknowledgement he moved through the French doors onto the balcony.

Ten minutes later Leo ended his call and turned away from the view. Instinctively, before he even stepped into the room, he knew Helena was gone.

Inside, the fragrance of her perfume lingered in the air—a bittersweet echo of her presence.

Relief, he reminded himself, but the cold, heavy weight pressing on his chest didn't feel like relief. Nor did the sudden insane urge to run after her.

He flung himself into a recliner and closed his eyes. When he opened them long minutes later his gaze landed on a small unsealed envelope on the coffee table. Frowning, he reached for it, lifted the flap and removed the single item from within.

A photo of their son.

The one he had studied so intently the night before.

He turned it over, and as he read the neat lines of hand-writing on the back his eyes started to burn.

He was special because we made him.
Carry him in your heart, as I do in mine.
I love you—and I'm sorry.
H.

CHAPTER TWELVE

'Leonardo Vincenti, are you listening to me?'

Marietta's voice, sharp with exasperation, jerked Leo from his thoughts. He looked up from the dregs of his espresso, guilt pricking him. 'Sorry, *carina.*'

His sister's expression softened. 'You were miles away.'

He pushed his empty cup aside and cursed himself. This was Marietta's night. He'd brought her to her favourite restaurant in the upmarket Parioli district of Rome to celebrate the lucrative sale of two of her paintings, and yet all he'd managed to do was put a dampener on the occasion.

'What's wrong?' she said.

'Nothing is wrong.' If he didn't count the fact that he hadn't slept in weeks. Or eaten properly. Or achieved anything more productive than pushing paperwork from one side of his desk to the other.

'*Something* is going on with you.' She leaned in, elbows propped on the table, eyes searching his. 'Talk to me.'

Marietta's sweet-natured concern only amplified his guilt. He forced a smile. 'Tell me about this loft you found.'

She frowned at him, but she didn't push. Instead she said, 'It's perfect. Lots of natural light and open space.' A spark of excitement lit her eyes. 'And there's a car park and a lift, so access isn't a problem.'

His sister had searched for months for a space she could purchase and convert into a dedicated art studio. The need for wheelchair access had made the search more difficult, but she'd tackled the challenge with the same determination she applied to everything in her life.

Pride swelled. 'How much do you need for it?'

Her frown reappeared. She sat back. 'I have money saved for a deposit. I don't need a loan, Leo.'

'Of course not.' As if he'd ever *loan* his sister money and expect her to repay him. He could afford to buy her ten studios—one was hardly an imposition. 'You'll need a notary for the purchase contract. I'll call Alex in the morning.'

She threw her hands in the air. 'You're doing it *again*.'

'Doing what?'

'Taking over. Going all Big Brother on me. I can do this on my own—without your help.'

Leo stared at her, his jaw clenching, a stab of intense emotion—the kind he'd been feeling too much of lately—lancing his chest. He tried to smooth his expression, but Marietta knew him too well.

She reached for his hand. 'You know I love you?'

A fist-sized lump formed in his throat. '*Si*. I love you, too.'

'I know.' Her fingers squeezed his. 'And that's all I need.'

Leo swallowed. That damned lump was making it difficult to speak. 'It doesn't feel like enough,' he admitted, and realised he had never said those words out loud before.

Marietta's eyes grew misty. 'Enough for what? For this?' She tapped the arm of her wheelchair. When her question met with silence, she shook her head. 'Oh, Leo. This isn't your fault and you know it.'

'The surgery—'

'Wasn't successful,' she cut in. 'Maybe we waited too long, or maybe the delay made no difference—we'll never know for sure. But I've made peace with it and you must, too. My life is good. I have my job, my art, *you*.' She sat forward, her dark eyes glistening. 'I'm happy, Leo. Yes, my life has challenges, but I'm strong and I don't need you to prop me up or catch me every time I fall. All I need is for you to be the one person in the world I can rely on to love me—no matter what.'

Her fingers wrapped more tightly around his.

'There's one other thing I need, and that's to know my brother is happy, too.' She gave him a watery smile. 'Maybe you could start by sorting out whatever has turned you into such a grouch these last few weeks?'

Leo scowled, but underneath his mock affront his sister's words were looping on a fast-moving cycle through his head, their impact more profound than he cared to admit. He felt something loosen inside his chest. Felt the heavy shroud of darkness that had weighted his every thought and action for almost a month start to lift.

He reached across and tweaked her chin. 'I do love you, *piccola*. Even when you are giving me lip.'

She grinned. 'I know. Now, stop scowling. You're scaring off the waiter and I want my dessert.'

An hour later, after seeing Marietta safely home, Leo ignored the lift in his building and bounded up the seven flights of stairs, a burst of energy he hadn't experienced in weeks powering his legs.

He loved Helena. He had reached that conclusion within days of returning to Rome. Within minutes of walking into his apartment and realising how empty it felt—how empty *he* felt—with her gone.

For more than three weeks he'd clung to the belief that she deserved better than him.

But how could she do better than a man who would love her with everything he had for the rest of his life?

Paris, eight days later...

Helena pulled off her strappy sandals and took the stairs two at a time inside the old building near the bustling promenades of Les Grands Boulevards.

The apartment she and her mother had rented for the week was small but charming, with shiny wooden floors, decorative finishes, and a sunny balcony where each morning they soaked up the beauty of Paris over coffee and croissants.

It was a girls' holiday. A chance for mother and daughter to reconnect and a celebration of sorts. For Helena because she'd worked out her notice at the bank, and for Miriam because, following her discharge from hospital, she had walked out of the home she'd shared with her husband of twenty-nine years and retained one of London's most successful divorce lawyers.

The weeks since had been challenging—tongues had wagged and Douglas had refused to 'play nice'—but Miriam was holding strong and Helena was proud of her.

Warm from her stroll and the three-storey climb, she reached the landing, glad she'd worn her new dress today instead of shorts or jeans. With its camisole bodice and little flared skirt the yellow sundress was cute and bright, and she'd worn it to buoy her spirits as much as anything. She was doing her best to move on, to live the life she should have lived these last seven years, but still she had plenty of dark, desolate moments when all she wanted to do was curl into a ball and cry. When it seemed she would never excise Leo from her thoughts or her heart no matter how hard she tried.

It didn't help that he'd called her mobile several times this past week. She hadn't answered and he hadn't left any messages—which was good, because she wouldn't cope with hearing his voice. And, really, what could he say that she wanted to hear? Or vice versa? That last day at the hotel his lack of interest couldn't have been any clearer. The man who'd held her with such heartbreaking tenderness in the aftermath of their lovemaking had, in those final stilted moments, barely forced himself to look at her.

Sighing, she fished her key from her tote and ousted Leo from her thoughts. She was in Paris and the sun was shining—good reasons to smile. And she couldn't wait to tell her mother, who'd opted for an afternoon of lounging in the sun with a book, about the incredible street art she'd found nearby.

Helena pushed open the door. 'Mum!' she called. 'I found the most amazing—' She stopped short. Her mother had been outside on the balcony when she'd left but now Miriam sat in the cosy sun-filled lounge. And with her, looking utterly incongruous in an easy chair covered in pink floral upholstery, sat the man Helena decided some wistful part of her imagination must have conjured.

Her key and tote dangled from her fingers, forgotten. 'Leo?'

He rose and he looked…magnificent. Big and dark and sexy in faded jeans and a snug-fitting black tee shirt.

'*Ciao*, Helena.'

The deep baritone fired a zing of awareness through her she didn't welcome. Questions crowded her mind until one emerged from the jumble. 'How did you find me?'

His gaze roamed her face, her bare shoulders. For a second she thought she saw a flicker of heat in his eyes.

'When I couldn't reach you I contacted David. He told me you'd resigned.' His voice carried a note of surprise. 'He also said you'd planned a trip to Paris. The rest—' He shrugged. 'Let's just say I know someone who's good at tracking people down.'

She wanted to be annoyed. She wanted to be so very, *very* annoyed. But all she could focus on was fighting the desire to reach out and touch him.

She pulled in a breath and realised her mother was by her side, bag in hand.

'I want to check out that little bookstore and café we spotted yesterday.' Miriam touched Helena's cheek, her smile tender, then gave her daughter a quick hug. 'Hear him out,' she whispered, and then she was gone.

On rubbery legs, Helena went and perched her tote on the end of the small breakfast bar.

'I like this,' Leo said behind her, and she turned, ready to agree that the apartment was indeed likable.

But he wasn't looking at the chic decor, or the quintessentially Parisian views. He was staring at *her*—or, more specifically, at her dress.

He stepped closer and slid his finger under a thin daffodil-yellow strap. 'It's pretty.'

'And it's not black,' she quipped, nerves—and something else—jumping in her belly.

One corner of his mouth kicked up. 'It's certainly not that.' He fingered one of her curls, bleached amber by the sun, and let it spring free. 'So...no more black?'

'Well...*less* black.' She couldn't afford to ditch half her wardrobe. She'd made no definite decisions about her future, but whether she chose art school or simply a job that offered scope for creativity she'd need to stretch her savings. She shrugged. 'I guess I'm rediscovering my love of colour.'

'And what brought that about?'

'You did.' Her candour made her blush but she couldn't regret the words. She wanted to be truthful with him, even though it wouldn't change anything. 'You challenged me. Made me think twice about what I'd chosen to give up.'

He had reawakened her passion for art and life. For that, among other things, she would always love him.

She moved away, sat in a comfy chair, needing to escape the heat his close proximity generated.

'What do you want, Leo?' The question came out sharper than she intended, but that was all right. She needed to keep her barriers up. Already the sight of him was spreading unwanted warmth. Making her forget how cold and remote he'd been during their last encounter.

He reached for a jacket she hadn't noticed over the arm of a chair. He pulled an envelope from a pocket, tossed the jacket back down and dropped to his haunches in front of her. When he slid the photo out and handed it to her, back side up, a thick wad of emotion clogged her throat.

'Read it to me,' he said.

She glanced up, opened her mouth to refuse, but the firm set of his jaw made her reconsider. She looked down again, studying the words even though she didn't need to. They were carved for eternity on her heart.

She prayed her voice wouldn't wobble. '"He was special because we made him. Carry him in your heart...as I do in mine."'

The next line blurred in front of her eyes.

'Read the rest.'

Her throat thickened. 'Why?'

'Because I need to hear you say it.'

'Why?' she repeated, fighting back stupid tears. 'So you can watch me humiliate myself?'

He placed his hands on the arms of her chair. 'Why would those words humiliate you?'

'Because!'

She glared at him, discomfort turning to anger. Anger to resentment. He would do *this* to her? Make her pour out her wretched feelings? Confess her love in person to satisfy his ego? She should never have never written those words. *Never.*

'Because it *hurts*!' she cried, thumping the heel of her hand against his chest. 'It hurts to love someone and know they don't love you back.' She thumped again, her palm bouncing off a wall of immovable muscle. 'It hurts to know you've lost any chance with that person. It hurts, Leo—' She hiccupped on a stifled sob and whacked his chest a third time. 'Because I do, damn it. I love you!'

The silence that fell in the wake of her outburst threatened to suffocate her. As did her surge of outrage when she glimpsed the satisfaction on Leo's face. With a shriek of fury she shoved at his chest and tried to rise, but he seized her wrists, his grip strong. Unyielding. Instead of standing she fell on his lap, straddling his thighs, trapped against the chair with her dress hiked around her hips.

Her chest heaved, another mortifying sob rattling through her. She couldn't fight him any more than she could fight the hot stab of need in her belly. Being this close to his big, powerful body was agony. She writhed, helpless, conscious of her sprawled legs, her exposed panties.

'*Tesoro mio...*'

She stilled, but she had no time to wonder at the rawness in Leo's voice. He released her wrists, folded his arms around her and buried his face in her neck. His scent engulfed her. His body, so warm and strong, sent her pulse into overdrive. She couldn't move, could barely breathe he held her so tight.

'Leo...?'

Finally he pulled back. His hands cupped her face. 'I love you, *cara*,' he said, and Helena didn't know if it was the intensity in his dark eyes or his words that stole her breath. 'I loved you seven years ago and I love you now. And, like a fool, I let you get away from me—not once, or even twice, but three times. Believe me when I tell you—' his voice roughened '—it will not happen again.'

Shock. Disbelief. Hope. Too many emotions to process at once rushed through her. Her body shook. Her brain, too—or at least that was how it felt. As if her mind couldn't contain the enormity of what he'd just said.

She studied his face, unwilling to let hope take hold too soon. 'What makes you so sure you love me?'

Leo stared at the strong, stubborn, beautiful woman who had ignored every one of his calls these last eight days and driven him to the brink of despair. The smile he gave was tortured.

'Aside from spending every waking hour wanting to know where you are, who you're with, what you're doing... and whether or not you are thinking of me?' He brushed away the lone tear that rolled down her cheek. 'I've been a fool and a coward, *cara*. Paralysed by fear.'

'Fear?'

He touched his forehead to hers. 'Fear that I couldn't be the man you deserve. The kind of man you can depend on.' He lifted his head. 'I failed you, *cara*.'

Her brow pleated. 'How?'

'Seven years ago I sent you away because I was angry and hurt, my pride wounded. I refused to give you a second chance, and because of that I wasn't there when you needed me.'

'Oh, Leo…' She laid her palm along his jaw. 'That's not on you. I should have found you and told you I was pregnant but I wasn't brave enough—and that was *my* bad, not yours. You deserved to know and I denied you that.' Her mouth trembled, her eyes searching his. 'Can you ever forgive me?'

He shook his head. 'There is nothing to forgive. We have both made mistakes.' He offered up another smile, this one crooked. Rueful. 'I believe it is called being human.'

Two more tears slipped down her cheeks. He brushed each one away.

'We can't change our history,' she said. 'Undo our mistakes. What if you can't trust—?'

He laid his finger over her lips, then took her hand and pressed her palm to his chest. '*Il mio cuore è solo tuo.*' When she blinked, he translated. 'My heart is yours.' He punctuated the statement with a gentle kiss. 'There is nothing more valuable I can entrust to you. And I promise you this, *tesoro*. You will never have to fight for my love.'

The way she'd had to fight for her father's.

'It is yours. Unconditionally. Tell me it is enough,' he demanded. 'Tell me—'

His command went unfinished. Because Helena cut him off with a kiss. A sudden, fierce, full-on-the-mouth kiss that smashed the breath from his lungs and caused an explosion of heat in his blood. He groaned. She tasted of heaven. Warm, sweet—a taste he wouldn't tire of for as long as he lived.

When she finally pulled back they were both panting for breath. Her eyes were moist, her smile shaky but wide. 'It's enough, my darling,' she said. 'It's enough.'

She pressed her face into his throat and they stayed like that for long, contented minutes. Then he eased her back and let his gaze rove her face, her body. *Hell*. He loved the yellow dress. Bright. Bold. A little bit cheeky. It was the girl he remembered. The one he hoped was back for good. The one whose blue eyes sparkled now with a hint of mischief.

Her smile was coy. Sexy. 'I think my mother will be gone for at least an hour.'

Leo responded with a wolfish grin, sealed their future with a scorching kiss, and then set about demonstrating one of the many ways in which he planned to love his woman.

EPILOGUE

One year later...

HELENA PRISED THE lids off the two test pots of paint and smiled at the colours. The first, Sugar and Spice, was a gorgeous lilac with a pretty shimmer. The second, Surf's Up, was a deep purple-blue.

Neither colour was the one she'd originally planned for this sunny room on the second floor of the Tuscan villa, but when she'd started her flurry of redecorating she'd imagined the room as a studio. A dedicated space where she could work on her projects for the interior design course she'd undertaken and, in her downtime, dabble in creative pursuits.

She'd even thought she might try her hand at painting some landscapes under Marietta's expert tutelage. The Tuscan countryside, with its sun-drenched hills, fragrant orchards and acres of lush vegetation, offered no shortage of inspiration.

She and Leo spent most of their weekends here, escaping the bustle of London or Rome. It was calming, rejuvenating, and she wondered how he would feel about the villa becoming their more permanent home.

Her mobile whistled, indicating a text message, and she rose from the canvas sheet on the floor. Leo was en route from Rome, and he'd already texted to say he wanted her naked when he arrived. They'd been apart only two nights, but according to her husband of six months that was two nights too long.

She rarely came to the villa by herself, but she'd needed to organise some tradesmen and their short separation had given her some time alone. Time to absorb the news that made her tummy flutter with a mix of excitement and nerves every time she anticipated the moment she would tell Leo.

She swiped the screen of her phone. His message said he was thirty minutes out and— Heat flooded her as she read the rest.

She grinned, shaking her head. Her husband was wicked. And sexy. And she loved him with every atom of her being.

Half an hour later the crunch of gravel and the low purr of the Maserati's engine heralded his arrival.

Pulse leaping, Helena put down her brush and leaned out of the open window. Leo climbed from the car and she waved to him.

'Up here!'

He looked up, late-afternoon sunlight bathing his bronzed features, and she knew she'd never get used to him smiling at her like that. As if she was his favourite person in the entire world.

He disappeared into the house and she heard his footsteps thunder up the curved staircase.

She barely had time to run her fingers through her dishevelled hair before she was in his arms, her legs wrapped around his waist, her breath stolen by his ferocious kiss.

'*Dio*,' he growled when he broke for air. 'You are beautiful.'

She laughed. 'Hardly.' Her curls were a wild mess, not a trace of make-up adorned her face, and she wore the old short denim dungarees she kept for painting and decorating.

'Do not argue, *tesoro.*' Still holding her high, he started out of the room. 'And—speaking of disobedience—did I not request my wife be naked when I arrived?'

She giggled and squirmed. 'Leo, wait. Put me down. I have something to show you first.'

He stopped and gave a pained sigh, but did as she'd bade him. Heart thudding, she led him by the hand to the section of wall where she'd painted a large square of Sugar and Spice and another of Surf's Up.

'What do you think of these colours?'

He shrugged. 'You know I trust your choices...' He glanced around the room and frowned. 'But this is to be your studio, *si*? Had you not decided on orange?'

'I thought we might use this room for something else,' she said, and moved closer to the wall. She pointed to the shimmery lilac. 'I was thinking this might be nice for a...a girl. And this one...' She pointed to the other square, her hand trembling, her throat tightening on the words. 'This would be good for...for a boy.'

Her breath stopped as she watched the rapidly changing expressions on Leo's face. From bemusement to confusion and finally a dawning comprehension.

He stared at her, his jaw gone slack. 'Are you telling me...? Do you mean...? Are you...?'

'I'm pregnant,' she blurted, taking pity on her gorgeous tongue-tied husband. She blinked, her eyes growing hot and prickly. 'Seven weeks—'

She didn't get to finish her sentence. Leo pulled her into a hug so tight, so engulfing, she couldn't draw breath to speak. He broke into a string of Italian she partly followed, thanks to months of lessons. Mentally, she translated the words she understood.

Incredible...so happy... I love you.

At last he pulled back, his hands curling gently over her shoulders—as if she might suddenly break.

'How do you feel? Do you need to rest instead of...?' His voice trailed off, a deep furrow creasing his brow.

'I'm good,' she assured him.

'Are you sure—?'

'Leo.' She took his strong, familiar jaw between her hands and gave him a reassuring smile. 'I promise you I'm one hundred per cent healthy.'

But she understood his sudden caution, the dark glimmer of anxiety in his eyes. Beneath her own excitement lay a shadow of apprehension. A fear that she would lose this child as she had lost Lucas.

But even that flicker of fear could not eclipse her joy or hope for the future.

Because this time she was not alone. This time she had Leo by her side. This time, whatever ups and downs life had in store, they would face them as one.

He was perfect. Ten fingers, ten toes, a fine thatch of black hair and the loudest, gustiest cry the nurses said they'd ever heard from a newborn.

Not for the first time since his son's miraculous arrival into the world two hours ago, Leo thought his chest might explode from the torrent of emotions coursing through him. Pride. Elation. Relief. And, of course, love. So much love it threatened to overwhelm him.

It had certainly stolen his ability to find words for such a momentous occasion. To tell his beautiful, incredible wife in the wake of her ten-hour labour how proud he was of her. Of their son.

He looked up from the tiny bundle in his arms. Despite the rings of exhaustion around her eyes Helena was radiant, her glow of happiness reflecting his own. He shifted on the edge of the hospital bed and gently laid their son in her arms.

For a long moment he stared at the woman and child he would spend the rest of his days loving, supporting, protecting. 'I love you.' He dropped a kiss on her mouth, another on his son's downy head. 'I love you both.'

'I love you, too.' She smiled at him through her tears. 'No regrets?'

He looked at his sleeping son—the most amazing sight in the world—then back to his beautiful wife.

He smiled. 'None.'

* * * * *

THE ITALIAN'S
ONE-NIGHT BABY

LYNNE GRAHAM

My husband, Michael,
for his constant support and kindness over
the years.

CHAPTER ONE

RIO BENEDETTI SET his even, white teeth together hard and suppressed a very rude word as his godfather cheerfully chatted on about his plans to entertain his unexpected guest. Beppe Sorrentino was a naïve man, trusting and generous to a fault, not at all the sort of man to suspect his self-invited guest of a hidden agenda. Luckily he had a godson like Rio, determined to shield the older man from anyone trying to take him for a ride.

Rio, the billionaire veteran of many triumphant wins in the business world and a man cynically unimpressed by women, knew he had to proceed with discretion because Ellie Dixon had powerful, wealthy friends, and most important, she was the sister of Polly, the current queen of Dharia—a country which rejoiced in oil wealth. Even worse, on paper at least, Ellie was impressive. Nobody knew that better than Rio, who had met her at his friend Rashad's wedding to her sister Polly. She was a beautiful, intelligent and hard-working doctor. But saintly Dr Ellie's profile took a fast nosedive if you had her past history exhaustively checked. At best Rio knew her to be a thief and a gold-digger, at worst she could be the kind of doctor who befriended the elderly to persuade them to change their wills in her favour.

Ellie had had a disciplinary action brought against her at work after an elderly patient had died endowing Ellie with all her worldly goods. Not surprisingly, the old lady's nephew had filed a complaint. But then there had been indications that Ellie might have an unseemly lust for money earlier than that, Rio acknowledged, thinking of the section in the investigative report relating to her grandmother's diamond brooch. The valuable brooch should've gone to Ellie's uncle but Ellie had somehow acquired it instead, causing much family bitterness.

No, nothing about Ellie Dixon was straightforward, not least her surprising approach to his godfather in a letter in which she had asked to visit because Beppe had apparently once known her late mother.

Of course, it was equally possible that Rio himself was the actual target in Dr Ellie's sights, he conceded with a certain amount of cynical satisfaction at that idea. Perhaps Ellie hadn't realised just how very rich he was at the wedding and, knowing where he lived, had come up with this vague connection as an excuse to visit his godfather, Beppe. Women, after all, had often gone to quite extraordinary lengths to try to reel him in, and he was as slick as an eel when it came to avoiding commitment.

He refused to think about what had happened with Ellie at Rashad's wedding because Rio did not believe in reconstructing unpleasant past events. With women he was very much a 'hit it and quit it' kind of guy. He didn't do serious and he didn't do long-term. Why would he? He was thirty years old, rich as sin and very good-looking and his female options were so many and varied that, had he wanted to and without effort, he could have slept with a different woman every night of the year. So, if he was Dr Ellie's target she was in for a severe disillusionment. In any case, the woman was an absolute shrew with a streak of violence, he recalled sardonically.

'You're very quiet, Rio…' Beppe remarked. 'You don't approve of Annabel's daughter visiting, do you?'

'Why would you think that?' Rio parried, surprised that the older man had seen through his tolerant front.

Beppe simply grinned. He was a small man with greying hair and rather round in shape. Perched in his favourite armchair, he had the cheerful air of a playful gnome and Rio's shrewd dark eyes softened the instant they settled on him because Beppe Sorrentino was as dear to Rio as any father could have been.

'I saw you wince when I mentioned how disappointed I was that Ellie wouldn't agree to stay here in my home as my guest. She's a very frank young lady. She said she wouldn't be comfortable because she doesn't know me and would prefer to stay at the hotel.'

'It wouldn't be comfortable for you either to have her here. You're not used to having guests,' Rio pointed out, for Beppe had been a childless widower for almost twenty years and lived a very quiet and peaceful life in his family *palazzo* a few miles outside Florence.

'I know but I get bored,' Beppe admitted abruptly. 'Bored and lonely. No, don't look at me like that, Rio. You visit plenty. But, Ellie's visit will be stimulating. A fresh face, different company.'

'*Dio mio…*' Rio rhymed thoughtfully. 'Why are you

so reluctant to tell me anything about Ellie's mother and yet so excited about her daughter coming here?'

Beppe's rounded face locked down so fast it was like a vault sliding shut and his dark eyes evaded his godson's. 'It's not something I can discuss with you, Rio. Please don't take that the wrong way.'

Rio's even, white teeth gritted again. He had even considered the idea that in some way Ellie could be engaged in an attempt to blackmail his godfather about some dark secret, but even optimistic Beppe would hardly look forward so happily to the visit of a blackmailer. Furthermore Rio couldn't imagine that Beppe *had* any dark secrets because he was the most open, transparent personality Rio had ever known. Yet Beppe had known great unhappiness and loss in his private life. His delightful wife, Amalia, had given birth to a stillborn son and had then suffered a severe stroke. From then on right up until her death, Beppe's wife had endured precarious health and the confinement of a wheelchair. Beppe, however, had remained utterly devoted to his beloved Amalia and, although now pushing sixty, had evinced not the smallest desire to meet another woman.

Rio, in strong comparison, had never been open or trusting with other human beings. He was naturally suspicious and naturally complex. He had been abandoned in a dumpster at birth, born to a heroin-addicted mother and an unknown father and he had spent his formative years in an orphanage until Amalia Sorrentino took an interest in him. Through Amalia he had met her kindly husband, his benefactor. He knew very well that he owed almost everything he had become and everything he had achieved to the man seated by the fireside who had first recognised his intelligence and there was little he would not have done to protect Beppe from any potential harm. And Rio was absolutely convinced that in some way Ellie Dixon was a harmful threat.

Evil temptress? Gold-digging harpy? Hard-nosed feminist? Thief? Scam artist with the elderly? At Rashad's wedding, he had been treated to giggly, amusing Ellie and enraged Ellie. He had also been led down the garden path right to the door of his hotel room and then assaulted. He hadn't forgotten the experience. He hadn't forgiven it either. Insults lingered with Rio. For too many years of his life he had been a nameless orphan, bullied and abused and dismissed as unimportant. And Ellie Dixon had cut him down to size as effectively as the most terrifying nun at the orphanage, Sister Teresa, who had struggled to overcome Rio's stormy and essentially vengeful temperament.

No, Rio wasn't the forgiving and forgetting sort. He still occasionally dreamt about Ellie twirling on the dance floor in her diaphanous green dress, her glorious mane of red curls tumbling round her animated face, and he would remember how he had felt and it stung him like salt in an open wound. He had felt that night that he would die if he didn't have her. Lust multiplied by wine and wedding fervour, he dismissed now with still-gritted teeth. Now all he had to do was sit back and wait for Ellie and her character of many divergent colours to emerge into the unforgiving glare of daylight…

So, would she be the temptress, the prim doctor, the clever academic or the friendly, casual tourist? And just how long would it take for Rio to find out what her game was?

Whatever, it was still game on…

* * *

Ellie surveyed the vast cache of clothing in sheer wonderment.

'Yes, your pressie has arrived,' she confirmed to her sister Polly, with the phone tucked in her nape. 'What on earth were you thinking of?'

'I know you don't do shopping, so I did it for you,' Polly responded cheerfully. 'You need a holiday wardrobe for Italy and I bet you haven't had the time to buy anything… Am I right?'

On that score, Polly was right but Ellie, picking up a floaty white sundress with a designer label, was gobsmacked by her sister's generosity. Correction, her sister's embarrassingly *endless* generosity. 'Well, I'm really more of a "jeans and tee" sort of girl,' she reminded her sibling. 'In fact, I think the last time I put on a sundress was when I was visiting you. You know I'm very, very grateful, Polly, but I wish you wouldn't spend so much money on me. I'm a junior doctor, I'm not living on the breadline—'

'I'm your big sister and it gives me a lot of pleasure to buy you things,' Polly told her unanswerably. 'Come on, Ellie… Don't be stiff and stuffy about this. We never got much in the way of pressies and treats growing up and I want to share my good fortune with you. It's only money. Don't make it change things between us—'

But it *was* changing things, Ellie thought, suppressing a sigh. She might always have been the kid sister in their duo but she had also always been the leader and she couldn't help missing that familiarity and her sister, who now lived half the world away in Dharia. Polly didn't turn to her for advice any more. Polly no longer needed her in the same way. Polly had Rashad now, and a gorgeous little son, and unless Ellie was very much mistaken there would soon be another little royal prince or princess on the horizon. Her sister also had a pair of adoring grandparents in Dharia, who had welcomed her into her late father's side of the family with loving enthusiasm.

And that was why Ellie was travelling out to Italy clutching the emerald ring gifted to their by her late mother, Annabel, whom she had never known. Annabel had died in a hospice after a long illness while her daughters were raised by their grandmother. Ellie's mother had left behind three rings in separate envelopes for her daughters.

That there were *three* envelopes had been the first shock because until that moment Ellie and Polly had not realised that they had another sister, younger than they were, raised apart from them and most probably in council care. A sister, Lucy, completely unknown to them. In each envelope their mother had written the name of each girl's father.

Polly had flown out to Dharia to research her background in the hope of finding her father, only to discover that he had died before she was even born, but she had been compensated for that loss by the existence of welcoming, loving grandparents. In the midst of that family reunion, Polly had married Rashad, the king of Dharia, and become a queen. As soon as she had married she and Rashad had hired a private detective to try to locate Lucy but the search had been hampered by officialdom's rules of confidentiality.

Ellie had received an emerald ring along with two male names on a scrap of writing paper… Beppe and Vincenzo Sorrentino. She assumed that one of those men was her father and she already knew that one of them was dead. She knew absolutely nothing else and wasn't even sure she really *wanted* to know what kind of entanglement her mother had contrived to have with two men, who were brothers. If that made her a prude, too bad, she thought ruefully. She couldn't help her own nature, could she? And she didn't have unrealistic expectations about what she might discover about her paternity in Italy. Neither man might have been her father, in which case she would simply have to accept living with her ignorance. But the discovery of *any* kind of relative would be welcome, she conceded sadly, because since Polly's marriage she had missed having a family within reach.

At the same time she asked herself why she still cherished that idealistic image of 'family,' because the grandmother who had raised her and Polly had not been a warm or loving person and her mother's brother, her uncle Jim, had been downright horrible even when they were children. In fact, recalling how the older man had treated her in the aftermath of his own mother's death made Ellie flame up with angry resentment, which made her wonder if she would *ever* share that sad story with Polly. Probably not, because Polly preferred only to see the good in people.

In the same way Polly had blithely declared that her marriage would change nothing between the sisters but, in fact, it had changed *everything*. Ellie didn't even like to phone her sister too often because she was very aware that Polly had far more pressing and important commitments as a wife, a mother and a queen. Ellie loved to visit Dharia, as well, but the long flights would eat up a weekend off and she often spent her leave simply catching up on sleep because junior doctors routinely had to work very long hours. At her most recent training rotation she had been working at a hospice and her duties and her patients had drained her both mentally and emotionally.

Indeed as she packed the new wardrobe Polly had had delivered to her into a pair of suitcases Ellie was too weary even to examine the garments and belatedly very grateful that her sister had saved her from an exhaustive shopping trip. No doubt she would look a lot fancier and more feminine in clothing Polly had picked than she would in anything she would have chosen for herself, she thought ruefully, because she had never been interested in fashion.

Far more importantly, Ellie was much more excited about even the slight prospect that she might find her father in Italy. Even Polly, with whom Ellie had played it very cool and cynical on that topic, had no real idea how much Ellie longed to find a father at the end of the Italian trail.

Two days later, Ellie walked down the stairs of the small rural hotel she had chosen and was shown out to a delightful three-sided patio, which was festooned with flowers and overlooked a rolling section of the green, vine-covered Tuscan landscape. She breathed in the fresh air with a smile of pure pleasure and relaxed for the first time in many weeks.

Tomorrow she had an appointment to meet Beppe Sorrentino at his home, but today she was free to explore her surroundings and that lack of an actual to-do list was an unadulterated luxury. She settled down at her solo table, smoothing down the light cotton skirt and top she wore in mint green, only momentarily thinking that the uneven handkerchief hems Polly loved were very impractical. *Fashion isn't about practicality,* she could hear her sister telling her squarely, and she smiled fondly as a brimming cup of cappuccino coffee arrived along with a basket of pastries.

Ellie powered through her usual work schedule on snatched coffee pick-me-ups and the fresh cappuccino was glorious, as was the croissant, which melted in her appreciative mouth. Indeed it was as she was brushing tiny flakes of pastry from her lips that a tall, dark silhouette blotted out her wonderful view. She blinked behind her sunglasses, supposing it was too much to have hoped that she would be allowed to have the patio and the view all to herself. After all, it was a very small hotel but still a hotel and naturally there would be other guests.

A liquid burst of Italian greeted the new arrival, whom Ellie could not yet see because of the sunlight. The waiter seemed to be falling over himself in his eagerness to greet the man, which probably meant he was a regular or a local, she thought idly. He responded in equally fast and fluent Italian and there was something about that voice, that dark chocolate honeyed drawl, that struck a dauntingly familiar note with Ellie and she paled, dismissing that jolt of familiarity with brisk common sense. After all, it couldn't be the same man, simply couldn't be! *He* lived in the city of Florence and she was miles outside the city, staying in a village hotel convenient to Beppe Sorrentino's home. No, it absolutely couldn't be the male who had totally destroyed her enjoyment of her sister's wedding festivities and left her filled with self-loathing and regret.

Even fate couldn't be cruel enough to sentence her to a second meeting with Rio Benedetti, her worst nightmare cloaked in male flesh.

'*Buongiorno*, Ellie…' Rio murmured silkily as he yanked out the vacant chair at her table and sat down.

Shock, mortification and anger seized Ellie all at once. 'What the heck are you doing here?' she demanded baldly before she could think better of such revealing aggression.

Rio Benedetti angled his handsome dark head back, his dazzling dark golden eyes veiled by his ridiculously long black lashes. He had blue-black hair that he wore cropped short but the strands still revealed a striking tendency to curl, which gave him a tousled, sexy aspect. He had beautiful eyes, a lean straight nose and bone structure that belonged in an oil painting of a dark angel. He smiled back at her in complete silence.

That fast, Ellie wanted to slap Rio all over again and tell him what she thought of him even though she had already done that two years earlier. He was gorgeous and he *knew* it, a hanging offence in her list of the attributes of a decent man. In reality she had never met such a stunningly good-looking male as Rio and when she had, she had caved as fast as a brick shed built on sand foundations, she recalled with an inner shudder of revulsion.

Why? she still asked herself occasionally, because that kind of impulsive recklessness was not Ellie, not her way with men, not her style, nor even how she was prepared to behave. Unfortunately she hadn't counted on meeting a Rio Benedetti blessed with such extreme magnetism, intelligence and charm. At least that was how she had excused herself for having very nearly succumbed to a one-night stand that had no prospect of any future but she was still ashamed of her misjudgement, still unable to forget that awful moment when that hotel bedroom door opened and she saw what was already waiting on his bed for him…

Rio didn't want to smile. He didn't want to fake it, he wanted to glower at her, and he hadn't planned to sit down either. No, standing over her, intimidating her with his much greater height had been his intention. But then he had seen her and all bets were suddenly off. Watching the tip of that little pink tongue chase stray flakes of pastry from her full pink lips had been more than his libido could bear. And his libido rode him like a runaway express train around Ellie Dixon, his arousal enforcing the necessity of sitting down to conceal his condition. What was he? An uncontrollably horny fifteen-year-old again? Dark colour lined his hard cheekbones. Regardless of the fact that he disliked and distrusted Ellie, she was a real beauty with skin as translucent as creamy porcelain, luminous eyes as green as any emerald and a wealth of tumbling Titian curls. Although smaller than average height, she had stupendous sexy curves matched with a tiny waist. Her proportions were truly breathtaking.

Rio had been sexually entranced with Ellie Dixon from the instant he'd laid eyes on her and when he had been rejected for the first time in his adult life the bite of that experience had stayed with him. Ellie had returned to his hotel with him the night of her sister's wedding but, on the very brink of intimacy, it had all gone wrong. In departing, Ellie had slapped him and insulted him. Rio gritted his teeth at the recollection of that experience. Far too many people had treated Rio with contempt when he was younger for him to easily overlook that kind of slur.

'What do you think I'm doing here?' Rio enquired smoothly, turning her own question back on her.

Ellie shrugged a shoulder and concentrated on her cappuccino. She didn't even want to speak to him but could she be *that* rude? After all, he was her brother-in-law's best friend and she liked Polly's husband. 'Did Rashad tell you I was going to be here and ask you to check up on me?' she asked abruptly, thinking that that was just the sort of protective thing Rashad would do, believing that he was doing her a favour when she was staying in an unfamiliar place.

'No. I don't think Rashad knows you're in Italy,' Rio admitted.

'So, I don't need to be polite, then,' Ellie assumed with satisfaction, reaching out for another pastry.

A sizzling smile slashed Rio's wide, sensual mouth. 'No, neither of us need be polite.'

That smile of his engulfed Ellie like a blast of sun on a wintry day and she wanted to turn into it and smile back in reward. Suppressing that reaction took the exercising of several seconds of strained self-control. But Rio had still won in one sense because although she didn't return the smile her whole body was reacting to him in the most unnerving manner. Her teeth gritted as she recognised the stinging tightness of her nipples and the warm liquid feeling between her thighs. He could tempt her wretched hormones with just a glance and she hated him for having that much power over her treacherous body. Had she no pride? And after what he had done to her, had he not a single honourable streak in his character?

'So, if we don't need to be polite…' Ellie hesitated only for a second before giving him a very honest response. 'Go away, Rio.'

A very faint stab of bewilderment penetrated Rio's sharp-as-a-tack brain. He had decided in the absence of any other evidence that Ellie had most probably dreamt up some vague link between her late mother and his godfather purely to gain fresh access to *him*. And either she was now playing ridiculously hard to get in the hope of stoking his interest…*or*, he was actually nothing whatsoever to do with her reasons for visiting Tuscany.

'I don't believe in coincidences,' Rio asserted, his sculpted lips compressing as his coffee arrived along with the hotel owner, who lingered to exchange greetings both with Rio and Ellie.

'I don't believe in coincidences either,' Ellie told Rio with a freezing smile once they were alone again. 'I mean, it was bad enough meeting you at Polly's wedding…but *this*—this is overkill of the worst kind—'

'Is it really?' Rio was fearful of getting frostbite from that smile, marvelling that Ellie could dare to treat him with such disdain, and his strong and aggressive jawline clenched hard.

'Yes, I do appreciate that this is your home country but I can't believe we're running into each other again… accidentally,' she admitted.

'And you would be correct. My presence here is no accident,' Rio confirmed softly as he sipped his espresso, contriving to look relaxed.

But Ellie knew he wasn't relaxed. Rio had certain tells. She had picked up on them at Polly's wedding. His eyes were veiled, his jawline tight, his fingers too braced round the tiny cup he held. Rio was tense, *very* tense, and she wondered why and then she wondered why she would even care. He was the man whore she had almost slept with, and she was very grateful that she had found him out for what he was *before* she shared a bed with him. Having carefully ensured that she'd never visited Dharia when he was also visiting, there was no reason for her to waste further words or time on him.

'So, why are you calling on me? And how did you know where I was staying?'

'I want to know what you're doing here in Tuscany,' Rio informed her flatly without answering her questions.

'I'm on holiday,' Ellie told him with a roll of her fine eyes.

'I don't think that is the complete truth, Ellie,' Rio scoffed with a sardonic smile.

'Well, it's the only truth you're likely to get out of me,' Ellie responded as she stood up, her fine-boned features stiff with restraint and annoyance. 'It's not as though we're friends.'

Rio sprang upright with fluid grace. At her sister's wedding, his grace of movement had been one of the first things she'd noticed about him: he stalked like an animal on the hunt, all power and strength and purpose. 'Would you like to be friends?' he asked lethally.

Ellie stiffened where she stood, quick to pick up on the husky erotic note edging his enquiry. 'No. I'm very choosy about the men I call friends,' she declared with deliberate cool, not caring whether Rio assumed that she meant friends with benefits or not.

Heat flared like a storm warning in Rio's dark golden eyes. 'You chose me in Dharia,' he reminded her with satisfaction.

Ellie's hand tingled as she remembered slapping him hard that night. It occurred to her that a fist would have been better and less forgettable on his terms. She was outraged that he could remind her of that night when in her opinion, had he had any morals at all, he should've been thoroughly ashamed of how their short-lived flirtation had ended. But then Rio Benedetti was a shameless sort of guy, arrogant and selfish and promiscuous. That he should also be as hot as hellfire enraged her sense of justice.

'But I wouldn't touch you even with gloves on now,' Ellie traded without skipping a beat and, turning on her heel, she walked back into the hotel.

'Ellie… We will have this conversation whether you like it or not,' Rio ground out with a low-pitched derision that nonetheless cut through the sunlit silence like a knife. 'Walking away won't save you from it.'

'And you coming over all caveman and beating your chest won't get you anywhere,' Ellie murmured cuttingly over a slim shoulder. 'I've never been one of those women whose heart beats a little faster when a man turns domineering.'

'But then you hadn't met me,' Rio imparted in a raw undertone.

'And once met, never forgotten,' Ellie traded, saccharine sweet laced with acid. 'I live and learn, Rio… *Don't you?*'

With that final scornful comment, Ellie vanished into the cool gloom of the hotel. Rio wanted to smash something, break something, *shout*. It reminded him that that was yet another trait he loathed in his quarry. She got under his skin, set his teeth on edge, made him feel *violent*. And that wasn't him, had never been him around women, where he was usually the essence of complete cool and sophistication in his approach. At the same time Ellie sent disturbing cascades of sexual imagery tumbling through his brain. He would picture Ellie in his bed, all spread out and satisfied, Ellie on her knees, Ellie across the bonnet of his favourite sports car. *Troppa fantasia*...too much imagination, again a trait that only she awakened, and annoying. After all, he wasn't sex-starved, anything but. Possibly he had become a little bored with easily available women, who clung and flattered and pawed him like a trophy to be shown off, he reasoned impatiently.

But he didn't want Ellie Dixon except in the most basic male way and he had no intention of doing anything about the effect she had on him. And she might live and learn but she had still to learn that he didn't let *anyone* walk away from him before he had finished speaking. Without further hesitation, Rio strode indoors.

Ellie closed the door of her room behind her and leant back against it in a panic that nobody who knew her would ever have credited. Her heart was racing and she was sweating. She straightened her slim shoulders and stomped into the en-suite to wash her hands and put herself back into her usual calm, collected state of mind. She did not allow men to rattle her. She had never allowed men to rattle her.

But two years back, Rio Benedetti had pierced her shell and hurt her, she acknowledged grudgingly. He had contrived what no man before him had contrived and she had almost made a fool of herself over him. Wouldn't he just love to know that? Ellie grimaced. A man she had known for only a few hours had deprived her of her wits and defences and come close to ridding her of her virginity with her full collusion. And then he had unlocked his bedroom door and she had seen that his hotel bed was already occupied by not one, no, not one but *two* giggling naked women, twin sisters she had noticed at the wedding. Appalled, she had stepped back.

And Rio had smirked and laughed as if it was of no consequence that two other women were already waiting to entertain him. Even in retrospect she marvelled that she had slapped him instead of kicking him somewhere unforgivable because she had been devastated by that revealing glimpse of his lifestyle, his habits, his lack of scruple when it came to sex. The rose-tinted glasses had been cruelly wrenched off when she was least able to cope and vulnerable, forced to see with her own eyes how sleazy her chosen partner was. Awash with disgust, she had called him a man whore and stalked away with her head held high, concealing her agonised hurt. And it had been *agonised*, she conceded painfully. Rio Benedetti had knocked her for six and unravelled her emotionally for months after that night.

It had been too sordid a story to share with Polly, who would have been even more shocked to the extent that her sister might have discussed Ellie's experience with Rashad, and Ellie had not been able to bear the prospect of her humiliation being more widely known. At least what had happened had happened more or less in private.

Someone rapped on her bedroom door and she opened it, expecting it to be the maid because she had said she was going out after breakfast and the room would be free. She didn't use the peephole and was sharply disconcerted when she realised that Rio had followed her upstairs to her room.

Fixing her attention doggedly on his red silk tie, she said curtly, 'I don't want to speak to you... Leave me alone—'

'No can do, *principessa*. If only this living and learning life were so simple,' Rio intoned mockingly.

'Don't call me that!' she snapped. 'And you're not coming in—'

A brown lean-fingered hand curved round the door in silent threat and he moved forward but Ellie stood her ground. She had faced drunks in A & E, dealt with drug addicts and violent people, and she wasn't about to be intimidated by Rio Benedetti.

'I don't think you want me to say what I have to say out here where I could be overheard,' Rio murmured sibilantly. 'It won't embarrass me—'

'*Nothing* embarrasses you!' Ellie snapped with very real loathing.

'It's about Beppe... Beppe Sorrentino,' Rio extended, watching her face like a hawk.

And Ellie surprised herself by stepping back to let him into the room because she absolutely *had* to know what he had to say on that subject. She knew he didn't know the mission she was on in Italy and that she wanted to try to establish her father's identity. She was convinced that Rashad was far too reserved and protective of his own wife's privacy to have shared anything but the sketchiest details about Ellie and Polly's background. But that Rio should even know Beppe's name disturbed her.

'You can come in for five minutes...five minutes

only,' Ellie negotiated thinly. 'And then I want you to go away and forget you ever knew me.'

Rio's beautiful mouth curled, his whole carriage screaming that he wasn't convinced by that claim.

'And I warn you... If you smirk, I will slap you again.'

CHAPTER TWO

'I DO NOT SMIRK,' Rio retorted very drily.

'Oh, yes, you do… You always look awfully pleased with yourself!' Ellie snapped back, her nerves all of a quiver and her brain no longer in control of her tongue because Rio in a confined space was too much for her.

It wasn't a large room. She had gone for cheap and cheerful in the accommodation stakes because she was planning to stay for an entire month in Italy and a classier room would have swallowed her budget within two weeks. But in a room already crowded with a double bed and a big wardrobe, Rio stole all the available space because he was very tall, at least six foot three and large from his broad shoulders to his lean hips and long, powerful legs. Her momentarily distracted gaze ran over the entirety of his sculpted physique, outlined as it was by a wickedly tailored suit that was sufficiently sophisticated to strike a formal note, but which also sensually delineated his muscular strength with fidelity. Colour flared in her pale face as she suddenly realised what she was doing and glanced away, her mouth running dry, her breathing disrupted and her thoughts overpowered by the stricken fear that he could somehow guess what she felt by the way she looked at him. Guess that she hated him but *still* thought he was gorgeous and incredibly tempting and incredibly bad for her like too much ice cream…

'Let's cut to the chase. What are you *doing* in Tuscany?' Rio demanded and it was a demand as only Rio could make it, every accented vowel laced with command and hostility.

'That's none of your business,' Ellie told him flatly.

'Beppe's my business… He's my godfather.' Lustrous dark eyes landed on her like laser beams, watching her face, keen to construe her expression.

Ellie froze in receipt of the very bad news he had just dropped on her from a height and in a defensive move she lowered her eyes. Rio actually *knew* Beppe Sorrentino and, even worse, had a familial relationship with the older man.

'You wrote to him looking for information about some woman he met well over twenty years ago,' he prompted doggedly, his dismissal of the likelihood of such a request clear in every word.

'Not some woman, my mother,' Ellie corrected, seeing no harm in confirming a truth he was already acquainted with. It was quite probable that Rio had already read her very carefully constructed letter to his godfather. Naturally she had mentioned nothing about boyfriends, pregnancies or putative fathers in it. She had been discreet, fearful of ruffling feathers and causing offence, but she did plan to question the older man to establish whether or not he knew anything about her paternity. It might be a long shot but it was the *only* shot she had. Beppe's friendly response to her letter had encouraged her and lightened her heart but the discovery that Rio Benedetti could be involved in any way in her very private quest for information infuriated her. Was she never to escape the shadow of that misguided night in Dharia?

'A mother whom you somehow know nothing about?' Rio pressed in a disbelieving tone.

'I was a newborn when my mother placed me in my grandmother's care. I never knew her,' Ellie admitted grudgingly, throwing him a look of hatred because she deeply resented being forced to tell him anything personal.

'Don't look at me like that when it's a lie,' Rio urged with staggering abruptness, fiery sparks illuminating his stunning eyes to smouldering gold.

The sudden apparent change of subject disconcerted Ellie. 'What's a lie?'

'You looking at me with dislike when you would really much prefer to rip my clothes off me!' Rio contended without an ounce of doubt in his dark deep drawl.

'Is that how you get women?' Ellie asked drily even while the betraying colour of mortification was creeping up her throat in a hot, seething tide. 'You tell *them* that they want you?'

'No, I only need to see you blush like a tomato to know I've hit pay dirt,' Rio countered with satisfaction. 'I don't do pretences, *principessa.*'

Even while betraying red climbed her face, the absolute curse of her fair colouring, Ellie stared back at him in genuine fascination. 'You honestly think I'm here for you and that my letter to your godfather is just some silly excuse to see you again? Oh, my word, Rio, how did you get through the door with an ego that big?'

'I hate the way you beat all around the bush instead

of just coming to the point. It is a very *simple* point, after all,' Rio told her impatiently, wondering how the hell his dialogue with her had suddenly turned personal but somehow unable to stop it in its tracks.

'We're not having this conversation,' Ellie responded icily.

'You're not my teacher or my doctor, so you can drop the haughty chilling tone,' Rio advised, lounging back against the bedroom door, his sudden slumberous relaxation screaming sex and the kind of bad-boy attitude that set Ellie on fire with fury and curled her fingers into claws.

'We were talking about Beppe,' she reminded him in desperation.

'No. I was talking about us having angry sex—'

Ellie reddened again, her green eyes luminous with disbelief. 'You did *not* just say that to me—'

Rio laughed with unholy amusement. 'I did. Why wrap it up like a dirty secret? We may not like each other but, *per meraviglia*, with the chemistry we've got we would set the bed on fire—'

Ellie focussed on him because she refused to let her gaze drop, lest he take it as a coy invitation. But it *was* a mistake to meet those stunning dark golden eyes of his, a mistake to be close enough to note the luxuriant curling length of his black lashes and the hint of stubble accentuating the shape of his full-modelled mouth. Rio Benedetti made her think of sex. It was instinctual, utterly brazen and when she collided with his eyes it was as if he were operating a gravitational pull on her. Ellie's body turned so rigid that her muscles hurt but even that reality couldn't block the tide of physical awareness flooding her every skin cell. With deep bitter chagrin, she felt the pulse at the aching heart of her thighs and the swollen sensitivity of her breasts.

'Angry sex could be a lot of fun, *principessa*. It would loosen you up. You are very, *very* tense and I know exactly how to take care of that,' Rio purred, cool as ice water, his pride soothed by her dilated pupils and revealing flush. After all, if he had to tolerate being constantly aroused around her, why shouldn't she have to suffer the same? But in contrast to him why couldn't she be practical and honest about it? Did she still expect and demand the fake flowers-and-diamonds approach from the men in her life?

'That's enough.' Ellie lifted her chin and closed a hand into his sleeve to yank him off the door so that she could reach for the handle, but it was like trying to move a very large and heavy boulder and he didn't budge an inch.

'You really do enjoy getting physical with me in other ways, don't you?' Rio derided huskily, looking down at her from his intimidating height, wicked amusement dancing in his beautiful dark eyes. 'Is that a hint about your preferences? I'm not into bondage but I can definitely picture you in one of those dominatrix outfits, twirling a whip—'

And that was it for Ellie. He wouldn't move from the door and he wouldn't shut up and frustration made her temper spontaneously combust inside her and shoot up through her like a rocket. 'If you don't get out of here, I'm going to call the police!' she screamed at him.

Rio flicked an imaginary speck of fluff from the sleeve her tight grip had creased infinitesimally. 'Fortunately the *polizia locale* are unlikely to arrest a native for making a pass at a beautiful woman—'

'I don't care!' Ellie lashed back at him, all patience and restraint stripped from her. 'I hate you…I want you out of my room…*now*!'

'When you tell me what you *really* want from Beppe I'll leave,' Rio bargained softly. 'I want the truth.'

'It's private and it's none of your business and I won't allow you to bully me!' Ellie retorted angrily. 'Does your godfather even know that you're here torment-ing me?'

Rio fell very still, reluctantly recognising that he was dealing with a quarry worthy of his mettle. Beppe was an old-fashioned gentleman and particularly pro-tective of the female sex and he would be shocked by Rio's interference.

'I didn't think he did,' Ellie declared in the telling silence. 'The letter he sent me was kind and friendly. So back off, Rio, or I'll—'

'Or you'll what?' Rio growled in raw interruption. 'You think that you can threaten *me*?'

'Unlike you I'm not in the habit of threatening peo-ple,' Ellie countered, lifting her chin, her green eyes deeply troubled.

'Well, then let us reach an agreement here and now,' Rio suggested silkily. 'I could approach Beppe with the results of the investigative report I've had done on you and, if I did so, you would be turned away from the door tomorrow because there are enough dynamite allega-tions against you in that report to make him very wary.'

Ellie took an uncertain step backwards, hugely dis-concerted by that accusation coming out of nowhere at her. 'I haven't done anything wrong, so I can't imagine what you're talking about—'

'Of course you're going to say that,' Rio parried, unimpressed. 'But the point is that serious allegations have been made against you and by more than one person.'

Ellie fell silent because, although she was innocent of any wrongdoing and had been cleared during an internal enquiry, a serious allegation *had* been lodged against her, which could have had a most negative impact on her career as a doctor. Fortunately for her, she was protected by National Health Service rules there to safeguard staff in such situations and the allegation had been withdrawn and the complaint dismissed. Tears stung the backs of her eyes because that same allegation had caused Ellie a great deal of stress and many sleepless nights before it had been settled and she had viewed her Italian holiday as a much-needed period of rest and recuperation. To have that unpleasant business, in which she had been truly blameless, flung in her teeth by Rio Benedetti was seriously offensive.

'Those allegations were dismissed a week before I flew out here,' she spelt out curtly, struggling to control the wobble in her voice. 'And what were you doing getting an investigative report done on me, for goodness' sake?'

'I will always protect Beppe from anyone who could take advantage of him and I don't trust you or the coincidence that brings you here,' Rio stated grimly, noting the sheen in her eyes, wondering if it was fake, deciding not to be impressed because tears in a woman's eyes were nothing new to his experience. Virtually every woman he had ever been with had done the crying thing at some stage and all it had ever done was chase him off faster.

'That's not my problem,' Ellie traded with an unapologetic little sniff that strangely enough impressed

Rio much more than the hint of tears. 'And why would it even occur to you that I would *try* to take advantage of Beppe? Obviously you don't believe it but I'm not a dishonest person—'

At that claim, Rio quirked a sardonic ebony brow and thought about the diamond brooch she had somehow prevented her uncle from inheriting. 'Aren't you? Even though you can't even bring yourself to admit that you want me—'

'You know why—because nothing is going to happen between us,' Ellie told him piously, superiority ringing in every syllable. 'Why acknowledge it?'

And there it was again, that intonation that made Rio want to do or say something totally outrageous. It shot him straight back to his misspent youth when he had been regularly carpeted for his sins in Sister Teresa's school office. There was something so incredibly frustrating about Ellie's blanket ban on normal sexual behaviour, he reasoned angrily. He could not understand why a woman with so much pent-up passion should repeatedly strive to ignore the sizzle in the air between them. As if attraction was a weakness? Or a risk she wasn't prepared to take?

His own convoluted and uncharacteristic thoughts on that score exasperated him as much as they had in Dharia. The evening of her sister's wedding had been a washout but that hadn't been his fault, had it been? Ellie had been totally unreasonable and unjust when she'd blamed him for that episode. He had been honest with her, as well, *too* honest, and where had that got him? A slap on the face and a shedload of insults. They would never have worked anyway, he told himself impatiently, not with a woman seemingly hardwired to be touchy, angry and super judgemental.

'*Non c'è problema...* Don't worry about it,' Rio advised drily as he swung round and pulled open the door. 'But when you fall, I'll still be the one to catch you.'

'I won't be falling. Can I hope this is the last I'll be seeing of you?' Ellie dared as he strode out into the corridor and involuntarily she too stepped over the threshold.

'You have nothing to fear from me unless you distress or damage Beppe in some way,' Rio warned, his voice roughening at the mere thought of any harm coming to the older man. 'I don't know why you're being so secretive anyway. Beppe will eventually tell me what this was all about.'

Pretending sublime indifference to that prospect, Ellie shrugged a slight shoulder. 'Why would I care?' she said breezily, keen to discourage his suspicions that she was hiding anything of a serious nature.

But she *did* care. Rio could see it in her unusually expressive and anxious gaze. He realised that there was definitely a secret of some sort that connected Ellie to his godfather and that disturbed him because for the life of him he could not imagine any likely connection. Beppe, for one thing, had never travelled outside Italy and was very much a home bird. It occurred to him for the first time that perhaps he should have investigated the mother rather than the daughter, but unwisely he had overlooked that option because Ellie inspired greater curiosity.

'You *do* care,' Rio traded softly, moving slightly closer.

In a skittish move, Ellie backed up against the door

of her room. 'I'm a very private person,' she stated in a stubborn refusal to admit even the smallest weakness, because Rio was 100 per cent shark and she knew the blood in the water would be hers if she gave so much as an inch.

'Not always,' Rio disagreed, suddenly right there in front of her, eating her alive with his black-lashed smouldering eyes. A lean brown forefinger trailed gently down the side of her hot face.

She felt every tiny second of that fleeting caress like a brand burning right through to the centre of her body. She wasn't used to being touched, she told herself bracingly, should've been dating more, should've been less of a perfectionist, should've been less sensible. His eyes above hers flamed gold and she recalled a moment exactly like that on the dance floor in Dharia, and in a clumsy movement she tried to peel herself off the door into her room and safety but it was too late, way too late when Rio's beautifully shaped mouth came crashing down on hers.

And that kiss was something between a car crash and a shot of adrenalin in her veins. Her body came alive with a great whoosh of physical response and her hands flew up into his hair, touching, shaping, *clutching* the springy strands. And she wanted him as a dehydrated woman wanted water, as if he were the only thing that stood between her and death. That ferocious, screaming shout of need that instantly controlled her absolutely terrified her. The spear of his tongue in her mouth electrified her beyond all thought and the flick against the roof of her mouth was pure licking temptation by a maestro of sensation. He knew how to kiss, he knew how to do all the stuff she didn't and that drew her helplessly, that and the merciless craving making her heart beat too fast, making her body tremble and her legs weak.

'*Inferno*, Ellie…' Rio growled against her swollen mouth, rocking his hips ever so slightly against her.

And she could feel him through their clothing, long and hard and urgent with the same need that had already overwhelmed her and she shuddered, fighting for control against all the odds and without words, knowing that no, whatever happened, she just couldn't do this with him.

But Rio, womaniser that he was, kissed her again and again; being Rio, he had upped his game. Slow and tormenting had become rawly passionate and demanding and every skin cell in her body lit up in neon as if she had met her perfect match. The pulsing damp heat between her thighs was coalescing into a generalised burning ache that tortured and tempted and screamed. The sound of a metal bucket scraping across tiles was almost deafening and Rio sprang back from her at the same instant that Ellie literally forced her hands down to his shoulders to push him away.

And for once, Rio didn't have anything super smart to say, she noted with only the smallest amount of satisfaction because she had nothing to boast about either. Rio dealt her a scorchingly angry glance and swung away.

'I'll be in touch,' he said grittily.

'Not if I see you coming first,' Ellie quipped weakly, ducking back into her room under the curious appraisal of the cleaner and closing the door on legs that felt as limp as cotton wool. But *no*, she was not going to do that thing she usually did when she did something wrong.

She wasn't going to dwell on it and go over it endlessly. She had made a mistake and it was already behind her and that was all the brooding Rio Benedetti deserved. No more self-loathing, no more regret, she told herself squarely. He was like a cup of poison that tasted sweet, created only to tempt and destroy. Paranoiac…much, she asked herself then.

CHAPTER THREE

THAT MORNING, ELLIE explored the village, bought a small gift for a colleague and walked in the glorious sunshine through the *piazza* to the café to take a seat. She was beginning to enjoy herself, starting to recognise that beating herself up about Rio was counterproductive because it kept him in the forefront of her mind. One kiss... What was a kiss? *Nothing!* Well, unless it made your knees go weak and threw your brain into la-la land—then it was a threat.

While she sipped her coffee, crossly policing her thoughts, she watched an opulent cream sports car park. The driver, who had a little dog with him, hailed several locals seated outside the café and his attention lingered on Ellie before he strode across the *piazza* to enter the shop there. The dog, however, a bouncy little Yorkshire terrier, hurtled straight across to Ellie and bounced up against her legs, craving attention.

The dog's owner shouted what sounded like, 'Bambi!' in an exasperated voice but the dog wouldn't budge from Ellie's feet and, with an audible groan and a wave that promised his return, the young man went on ahead into the shop.

'You're not the most obedient dog,' Ellie scolded

softly a few minutes later as pleading little round eyes appealed to her from knee height. 'No, you can't get up on my lap. I'm not a doggy person—'

'You could've fooled me,' the owner remarked from beside her and she glanced up and laughed.

'Well, I suspect your dog's not very fussy,' she teased.

'Bambi belongs to my mother and I'm looking after the dog all week.' He rolled his eyes in speaking suffering. 'She hasn't been trained and prefers women.'

'But that's not her fault,' Ellie pointed out, scratching a blissed-out Bambi behind one flyaway ear.

'I'm Bruno Nigrelli.' He extended a friendly hand. 'Join me for a glass of wine—'

'A little early,' Ellie began before she recalled that she was on holiday and not on duty. 'No, that's a good idea,' she told him with a sudden smile. Loosen up, she told herself irritably.

Bruno stayed with her for about half an hour, making easy comfortable conversation, and it was so relaxing after the emotional angst of dealing with Rio, Ellie acknowledged ruefully. Bruno was a contracts lawyer based in Florence and he was currently staying at his mother's home to look after it while she was away. When he asked her to dine with him the following evening, Ellie agreed. Polly's voice was ringing loudly in her ears. 'Attractive man—tick. Employed—tick. Good manners—tick. Stop looking for what's wrong with every man you meet!' Polly had told her that the reason she rarely dated was that she was far too fussy. But Ellie didn't think that was fair because when it came to men, Polly had proved equally hard to impress.

The following morning, Ellie drove her little hire car

to Beppe's impressive *palazzo*. The huge gates stood wide in readiness for her arrival. She drove slowly through the elaborate gravelled gardens that fronted the big house and parked, climbing out, smoothing damp palms down over the casual white skirt she had teamed with a navy-and-white tee and canvas espadrilles. She walked up the shallow steps to the front door and a youthful manservant in a very correct black jacket opened it before she could even reach for the bell.

'Ellie Dixon for Mr Sorrentino,' she said helpfully.

'Yes,' he said gruffly in English. 'He waits for you.'

Ellie was a mass of nerves and trying not to show it. Could Beppe *be* her…? No, she refused to think about that because it wasn't very likely when Beppe had been married at the time. The more likely scenario would be Beppe telling her that he hadn't known her mother well enough to give her any useful information as to who her father might be.

'Miss Dixon…' A small man near her own height greeted her at the door of a book-lined room with a warm smile. 'Come in and sit down. Adriano will bring us morning coffee.'

With a soft sound of pleasure she sat down in the chair overlooking the beautiful garden. 'This is such a comfortable room,' she told him cheerfully. 'All these books and bits and pieces are fascinating and when you throw the view in, as well—'

'I'm a lifelong collector and passionate gardener,' Beppe admitted as he sat down opposite her.

'Thank you for being willing to see me like this,' Ellie said a little awkwardly. 'I can only hope that I'm not about to say anything that may make you regret it—'

'I don't take offence easily,' Beppe reassured her.

'But I confess that I'm very curious about your mother. What happened to her after she left Italy?'

'I didn't even know for sure that she *had* been in Italy, although it was a fairly obvious assumption,' Ellie admitted, opting for complete honesty as she dug into her bag and extracted the emerald ring. 'My mother left me this ring…'

Beppe paled, his easy smile slipping for an instant. He scooped up the ring at the same time as the door opened and Adriano brought in a tray. He spoke to the young man with a couple of hand signals. 'Adriano's deaf,' he muttered absently, his attention still fixedly focussed on the emerald.

'He's a great lip-reader,' Ellie remarked.

'He's had a lot of training over the years. Once he's acquired the necessary experience working here, he hopes to find a more exciting position abroad,' Beppe told her and he leant forward to deposit the ring back on the table beside her cup. '*I* gave your mother this ring. It once belonged to my mother,' he added heavily.

'Okay.' Taken aback by that admission, Ellie nodded acceptance. 'So you knew her well?'

'Better than I should have done in the circumstances,' Beppe confided in a weighted undertone of discomfiture. 'Annabel spent that summer working for an English family who had a holiday home not far from here. My brother, Vincenzo, met her first and they got engaged before I even met her. I think you would call it a whirlwind romance because they had only known each other for a few weeks.'

Ellie sighed, thinking of what she had learned about her mother from her sister Polly. 'What year was that?'

Beppe told her and the timing dovetailed in Ellie's

mind. Her older sister would only have been a toddler when Annabel came to work in Italy.

'How do I describe Annabel to you…her daughter?' Beppe sighed. 'She was full of life and tremendous fun to be with but she was a little impulsive when it came to love.'

'Yes,' Ellie agreed, wondering what was coming next.

'I was married to a wife who was disabled. That is *not* an excuse. There can be no excuse for what happened,' Beppe continued with unconcealed regret. 'I learned that I was not the man I believed I was. I fell head over heels in love with your mother and it was the same for her. I was thirty-five then, hardly an impressionable boy, and I fully believed that I loved my wife. Amalia was a wonderful wife. It was not an unhappy marriage yet I broke her heart and my brother's. But mercifully, *generously* my brother did not choose to publicly accuse me of what I had done and my wife was not humiliated. Together, Amalia and I concentrated on restoring our marriage, locked away that secret affair and moved on.'

'I honestly don't know what I can say to what you've just told me because I know none of the people involved,' Ellie said carefully. 'But I am sorry to hear that other people were injured by my mother's actions.'

'Annabel injured herself most of all. She could've had a good life with my brother but she gave him up because she met me,' Beppe admitted with remorse. 'Vincenzo was still estranged from me when he died. It was a horrible mess for all of us—'

'I'm very sorry,' Ellie breathed, feeling inadequate in the face of such honesty and a very personal story, which she had never expected to hear told.

'The last time I saw your mother she was very angry with me,' Beppe confessed unhappily. 'I had told her from the outset of our affair that I would not leave my wife but she refused to accept that. My love for my wife was a different kind of love but no less real to me. Although I was an unfaithful husband, Amalia forgave me and we stayed together and we were blessed by many more happy years before she passed away...'

'My goodness...I genuinely didn't come here to cause you distress, but I can see that I've done nothing but rake up disastrous memories!' Ellie exclaimed guiltily, seeing the tears that shone in Beppe's dark eyes. 'Unfortunately, I came here with a very different angle, Beppe. I'm trying to find out who my father is—'

'In Italy?' he cut in, his surprise unconcealed. 'Surely you are far too young to believe you were conceived *here*? When were you born?'

And she told him and his face became very sombre. 'I believed you were several years younger, but it is certainly a possibility that I could be the man you seek. *Dio mio*, that could explain why your mother told me that I would live to regret not leaving my wife for her.'

Ellie fell silent, disturbed by the harsh nature of what she was learning about the mother she had never known.

'*We* will have to look into this more. With tests? That is how it is done, is it not?'

'Are you willing to do that?'

'*Certamente*... Of course,' Beppe responded. 'Now perhaps we should discuss something less challenging while we consider what we have both learned.'

Ellie's hand shook a little as she lifted her cup because she was marvelling at his calm manner.

Beppe chuckled. 'I must be on my very best behaviour now in case you turn out to be a relative.'

And Ellie's hopes soared, that he was the man, that he would turn out to be her father and that a lifetime of frustrating speculation would be ended. They parted an hour later with Beppe promising to contact a doctor he was friendly with, who would advise them discreetly on their quest. Tears rolled down Ellie's cheeks as she drove back to her hotel. She was in a daze and she was praying that Beppe would be the man she sought because she had really, *really* liked him and it would be beyond wonderful to discover a father she could actually connect with as a person.

Rio, however, had a very different experience when he joined his godfather for lunch. After what transpired there, bitter anger consumed him and when he left he headed straight to Ellie's hotel, determined to confront her. Learning that she had gone for a walk to a local landmark, he set off to follow her in his car.

Ellie paused halfway up the very steep hill and wiped the perspiration from her brow, registering that in such sultry heat, she had tackled a challenge too great for her fitness level. Hearing the sound of an approaching vehicle, she stepped back onto the verge. She was disconcerted to see Rio at the wheel of a very racy scarlet sports car. He braked and leant across to open the passenger door. 'Get in!' he told her uninvitingly.

'No, thanks,' Ellie responded. Her day had been demanding enough without adding him into it.

Without a word, Rio shot her an intimidating glance from molten gold eyes and sprang out of the car, stalked round the bonnet, and before she could even guess his intention he had scooped her off her startled feet and dropped her into the passenger seat, slamming the door after her.

'What the heck do you think you're playing at?' Ellie yelled at him in disbelief as she struggled to open the door to get out again and failed because he had already engaged the child lock to prevent her from doing exactly that.

Rio shot back behind the wheel, his lean, darkly handsome face granite hard. 'We have to talk—'

'No, we don't. I have *nothing* to say to you!' Ellie proclaimed vehemently. 'Let me out of this car—'

'Put your seat belt on!' Rio growled at her as if she hadn't spoken.

'No, I won't. I refuse to go anywhere with you!' Ellie yelled back at him.

Rio leant across her to wrench the seat belt round her and she was so taken aback by the second act enforced against her wishes that she studied him in shock. 'This is kidnapping and assault,' she informed him furiously. 'I will go to the police and make an official complaint about you!'

'Go ahead!' Rio bit out rawly.

'You are out of control,' Ellie informed him. 'You're not thinking about what you're doing!'

'Sì... If I'd thought about it, I would have come armed with a gag!' Rio slung at her wrathfully.

'Much good that would do you. I'm a judo black belt,' Ellie countered. 'Had I known you were planning to kidnap me, I would have defended myself to stop you grabbing me.'

'Don't kid yourself,' Rio practically spat at her as he raked the car on up the hill she had been struggling to climb. 'If you were assaulted, you would be far too busy assessing the pros and cons of acting aggressively to take action quickly enough to defend yourself!'

And Ellie was stunned by that eerily accurate reading of her character. Rio was the single exception to her abhorrence of violence in all its forms and even when it came to him she didn't want to actually *hurt* him, just hold him at bay or make him go away. 'Where are you taking me?'

'Somewhere we can talk in peace,' he grated.

Ellie skimmed an infuriated glance at his set profile, noting the classic slope of his nose, the definition lent by his perfect cheekbones, the outrageous sweep of his black lashes. 'You're driving too fast—'

'I am within the speed limit.'

Ellie flung her head back with a sigh of frustration, her wild mane of hair blowing in the wind. She would look like a rag doll with corkscrew curls by the time she got out of the car but what did that matter? The breeze against her overheated skin was wonderfully cooling. Kidnapping and assault? Rio had a temper worse than her own and that was a revelation that had a surprisingly cooling effect on Ellie's own temper. She had learned young that she had to learn to control and contain the ferocity of her feelings. Rio, evidently, had not. The oddest sense of compassion flooded her because she had not a doubt that he would be very embarrassed when he looked back and fully thought through what he had done to her.

Rio, however, was in a rage to surpass all rages and he was well aware of it. Beppe's distress had provoked a visceral reaction in him that he could not deny or fight. He *loved* that man, would have done anything for him! That he had failed to shield Beppe from whatever nasty business Ellie had somehow involved him in slashed Rio's proud protective spirit to the bone. He was going to get the truth out of Ellie if it killed him. *Inferno...* This mysterious nonsense everybody was refusing to discuss had to end right now because his patience was at an end!

Rio turned the car off the road down a long track. Dense clusters of ancient oak trees prevented Ellie from seeing more than a few yards ahead and when the car rounded the final bend she had no inkling that they were heading for a house until she saw it right there in front of her. It was a breathtaking *palazzo*, with a remarkable resemblance to an elaborate dolls' house, and it fitted into the landscape where it had clearly held its commanding position for centuries. It was built on a hill and undoubtedly had views that stretched for miles. She unclasped her seat belt and climbed out with a look of exasperated tolerance in Rio's direction once the child lock was finally disengaged.

'You can apologise now,' Ellie said.

'Apologise?' Rio practically roared at her in disbelief. 'Beppe was in *tears* over lunch! I haven't seen him in such a state since his wife died. What did you do to him?'

Ellie froze beside the car, her fine-boned features locking tight, her pallor noticeable. Clearly she had upset Beppe Sorrentino and yet she had never wanted to do that. Had she ever truly considered what her quest to discover her father would do to the man involved? No, she hadn't, she conceded guiltily. In fact, she had believed that it would be *safe* to approach Beppe because he was a childless widower who seemed to have no close relatives. Of course, she hadn't known about

Rio's connection to the older man then and, seeing the intensity of Rio's fury, she instantly recognised that he was attached to Beppe and it hit her hard. Rio might not be a blood relative but the way he was reacting he might as well have been.

'I didn't do anything to Beppe. I simply gave him some information he wasn't expecting to hear,' Ellie countered uncomfortably, because what on earth was she supposed to say to Rio?

If Beppe hadn't told his godson the truth, it was certainly not her place to do so. And she quite understood the older man's reasoning. He had had an affair while he was married, an affair that more than twenty years on he still obviously regretted. He was ashamed of his affair with her mother and Ellie had to respect that reality. It hurt to appreciate that, even if tests were done and Beppe did prove to be her father, he might well want the existence of an illegitimate daughter to remain a secret. She couldn't fairly complain about that, couldn't possibly resent it because Beppe had the right to guard his privacy and make his own choices. That he had agreed to DNA testing was more than enough, she told herself doggedly, scolding herself for the fantasy of having a *real* father, which she had rather naively begun to entertain. Really, how likely was it that Beppe would seek an ongoing relationship with her now that she was an adult and fully independent?

'*Ellie!*' Rio raked back impatiently at her as he stalked back from the front door he had unlocked. She had once watched a tiger pace a cage in the same way and it was distinctly unnerving. For the first time it dawned on her that so volatile a personality should have frightened her and she was even more surprised to acknowledge that, not only was she unafraid, but also ridiculously attracted by Rio's sheer sizzling intensity. Even so, she wished that like a difficult piece of technology Rio came with a useful book of instructions because she didn't know how she was supposed to calm him down when she wasn't in a position to give him the explanation he so plainly wanted.

'The raised voice is getting really *old*,' Ellie told him drily instead.

Dark colour scored his razor-sharp cheekbones. 'Come inside—'

'Said the kidnapper to his victim,' Ellie added.

Rio swore in a flood of Italian.

'Yes, I give as good as I get,' Ellie pointed out, moving out of the sunshine into the shadow of the building because calling Rio's bluff was one thing, but baking alive while doing it would be foolish.

'I brought you to my home because I desired privacy in which to speak to you,' Rio framed with obvious difficulty in being that polite.

Ellie pondered her options, which were few. She had neither her phone nor any money on her person. Rio had stranded her in the Tuscan countryside. 'I'll come inside but there will be no more shouting and you will not put your hands on me again,' she warned him.

'I can't promise that I won't shout because I am very angry with you,' Rio admitted in a low-pitched growl as he watched her move towards him, her skirt fluttering above her slender knees, making him very aware of the long shapely legs beneath. His gaze filtered involuntarily upward, lingering on the soft fullness of her pink lips, and shifted with a jerk as she moved, the luscious sway of her full breasts below her top making his mouth run dry. 'And I wouldn't promise to keep my hands off you because I'm not sure I could ever deliver on that one, *principessa*.'

That honest response and possibly the reuse of that mocking label worked for Ellie and released a little of her nervous tension. In fact, she went pink while inwardly admitting that she wasn't that much better at keeping her hands off him, regardless of whether she was slapping him or kissing him. Rio awakened very strong reactions inside her. The usual barriers that she employed to keep a careful distance from people were shockingly absent with Rio Benedetti and that awareness rattled her nerves.

Ellie followed Rio into a cool, tiled hallway that was strikingly contemporary and into a vast reception room furnished with pale leather sofas and several dramatic modern paintings. The gorgeous house might be ancient but the cool interior decor and modern furnishings were in stark contrast.

Rio spun round to face her again, a dark shadow of stubble accentuating his beautifully shaped mouth and the raw tension etched in the hard line of his lips. And she found herself wondering for the first time if he was ever gentle or tender, traits that seemed far removed from his aggressive, competitive nature. And did it even matter, another voice mocked, when he looked the way he did? That mocking inner voice shocked her because it steamrollered over everything she believed she knew about herself, for since when had she been impressed by appearances? Yet when she looked at Rio, everything sane and sensible vanished from her brain as if it had been wiped. And then there was only room for glorying in his tempestuous male magnificence, room to marvel at the precise arrangement of his lean, darkly charismatic features and the stunning clarity of his smouldering golden eyes. She sucked in a startled breath to fill her deprived lungs.

'All I'm asking you to do is come clean with me,' Rio murmured lightly, as though what he was asking should be easy for her to do. 'Tell me what's going on...'

Ellie's slim figure tensed. 'It's not that simple, Rio.'

An ebony brow quirked in disagreement. 'It is a very simple matter that you are making difficult out of sheer stubbornness.'

'No, it is a private matter between Beppe and me,' she countered. 'Ask *him* to explain things.'

His intent gaze narrowed. 'You must know that I will not do anything more to upset him.'

'And I will not break his confidence without his permission, so we're at an impasse—'

'Have some wine,' Rio suggested wryly, strolling over to the drinks cabinet and giving her a choice.

'Rosé, but it won't loosen my tongue,' she warned him doggedly, but the extreme tension in her knees holding her stiff gave way a tad, reminding her that her meeting with Beppe and the walk had exhausted her.

'Help me out here... I am *trying* to be civilised,' Rio informed her.

'There was nothing civilised about the way you stuffed me in your car,' Ellie reminded him drily as she settled down on a sofa.

'*Per l'amor di Dio*, I never said I was perfect, *principessa.*'

'Why do you call me that?' she demanded abruptly as he settled a moisture-beaded wine glass into her hand, momentarily standing so close to her that the scent of him assailed her: hot, musky male laced with a hint of spicy cologne. A very faint shiver ricocheted through her.

Rio grinned and it was an unexpectedly boyish grin of keen amusement. 'Because the way you walk with your little superior nose in the air gives you that look. You remind me of the rich girls I used to watch when I was a penniless teenager. Oh, they looked at me, but they wouldn't have dirtied their lily-white hands by *touching* me.'

'I was never a rich girl,' Ellie parried uncomfortably, studying him with grass-green eyes that were luminous in the filtered sunshine and alive with curiosity. 'I grew up in my grandmother's working-class home and there were no airs or graces there.'

'*Cio nonostante...* Nonetheless you ooze that rich-girl quality of disdain,' Rio told her with assurance. 'And it sets my teeth on edge—'

'Everything about me sets your teeth on edge,' Ellie pointed out wryly while she wondered about his background, because she was surprised that he had ever been penniless and on the outside looking in at the more prosperous. '*We* annoy each other.'

'Beppe,' he reminded her darkly. 'Talk.'

In a sudden movement, Ellie stood up again because he was making her feel trapped. She understood exactly where he was coming from but she couldn't answer his questions. His godfather *could* have enlightened him and had chosen not to. Beppe's silence spoke for him. Clearly he had no desire to admit to Rio that he had had an extramarital affair or that that liaison could have led to the conception of a child.

'I don't back down, Ellie,' Rio murmured from close

by and every skin cell in her body jumped at the knock-on effect of that deep accented drawl of his, goose-bumps rising on her bare arms. 'I won't let you go until you fill in the blanks—'

'Well, then, you're going to be stuck with me!' Ellie exclaimed in growing frustration. 'Because I'm not going to talk—'

Rio removed the glass from her fingers and set it aside. 'Maybe talking's a total waste of time for us, *principessa*.'

'And what's that supposed to mean?' Ellie demanded thinly even though she had a very good idea.

Rio scored a light forefinger across her compressed lower lip. 'You're pushing it defying me. I don't have your patience—'

Ellie threw her head back, corkscrew curls tumbling across her pale brow, green eyes sharp with frustration and defensiveness. 'Don't touch me!' she warned him curtly.

'No, not a shred of patience,' Rio asserted with hypnotic quietness, reaching for her with scorching dark golden eyes of sensual threat.

CHAPTER FOUR

'I CAME INTO this house with you because I trusted you,' Ellie declared starkly, twisting away.

'No, you don't. You don't trust me,' Rio assured her with grim amusement. 'You most probably came into the house because you don't like arguments in public and you are nervous of how far I would go to win.'

'Well, doesn't that just say it all about you?' Ellie quipped.

'You know nothing about me yet you still judge,' Rio condemned.

Ellie stilled, disconcerted by that criticism, and Rio took advantage of her momentary abstraction. His arm curved to her spine and he yanked her close, bringing her up against the hard, unyielding strength of his lean, powerful body, and her hormones leapt as though he had electrified her. His mouth nibbled along the plump fullness of her lower lip and all of a sudden she couldn't breathe for anticipation. Her lips parted for him, letting his tongue plunge deep, and an aching sweetness that drowned every thought rose from the very heart of her. Something in the furthest reaches of her brain was saying no, no, *no*, but all the rest of her was in open rebellion.

It was the kiss to end all kisses, fit to eradicate any previous kiss because no man had ever made Ellie's head swim with a kiss before. She felt dizzy and delirious, utterly unlike herself, adrenalin charging through her veins and lighting her up as though she had crossed the finishing line of a race. Her fingers delved freely into his springy black hair, sheer delight at the freedom to touch him consuming her.

Overwhelmed by her response, Rio tensed, wondering when it would end and abandoning any plan to stage a slow seduction scene. He had never wanted any woman as he wanted Ellie Dixon. Need was already flaming through him like a burning torch. One hand at the shallow indentation of her spine, he ground against her, so hard, so ready, so overpoweringly hungry for the damp release of her body that he trembled. It didn't make sense to him. Yes, she was a challenge, but no woman had ever come between Rio and his wits. He was in control, he was always in control, but this one time, he *wasn't*. Shouldn't that worry him? He shelved the question, too much lost in the moment to waste time considering the drawbacks and inconsistencies. He brought Ellie down on the sofa and kissed her with unashamed passion.

'What are we…doing?' Ellie mumbled through swollen lips as Rio whipped off her top, exposing the heavy-duty white lace confection she wore to confine the breasts that she considered to be too large. It was a stupid question and she knew it and the sight of her own almost bare flesh unnerved her and filled her with discomfiture.

'*Sta' zitto*… Shut up!' Rio urged, burying his face between those utterly magnificent breasts while wrestling with a bra that had more restrictive hooks than a corset. If she talked, she would talk herself out of it, he thought in consternation, and he looked down into her beautiful eyes, emerald as the most precious of jewels, and told her to close them.

'You are incredible' was wrenched from him, breaking his self-imposed silence as he studied the lush creamy swell of her glorious breasts. An awed fingertip brushed a large pink nipple already pouting for his attention. He wanted to carry her up to his bedroom, spread her out and enjoy her as she should be enjoyed but he didn't want to break the spell.

Instead he bent his dark head and succumbed to the considerable allure of her breasts. He whisked his tongue over a rigid bud the colour of a tea rose and teased the tortured peak, loving the way she shifted under him, instantly responsive to his every caress.

Ellie had fallen so deep that she was drowning in the world of sensation she had always denied herself. The hunger in her for *more* was unbearable. Her breasts throbbed, sending messages to the lush damp place between her shifting thighs. Her hips lifted in frustration. She wanted Rio everywhere at once. She wanted the impossible. She also wanted his clothes off with a strength of craving that shook her because it was not as though she was a stranger to the male anatomy. In frustration, she hauled at the shoulders of his jacket and he reared back from her with a sudden surprised laugh and peeled it off to pitch it on the floor.

'And the shirt,' Ellie instructed him shakily, scarcely believing what she was doing, what she was participating in, and unable to dwell on it lest her caution yank her back from the edge. And she wanted Rio, she wanted him so much that she was weak from the wanting and the never-ending wondering and longing that had dogged her since the day they had first met.

A couple of shirt buttons came loose of their stitching as Rio ripped off the shirt with an almost joyful air of abandonment. He was all lean muscle sheathed in sleek bronzed skin from his wide shoulders to his narrow waist and she stared helplessly entranced and surprised at her visceral reaction to his masculinity. As the shirt dropped, he smiled at her in a way he had never smiled before and that slanting, teasing grin was purebred enticement on his darkly beautiful face. Indeed that smile had so much appeal that she sat up and hauled him down towards her to claim his devastating mouth for herself again.

He lay on his side, kissing her breathless and she revelled in every kiss and the brush of his skilled fingers over her wildly sensitised breasts. He pushed up her skirt and traced the edges of her panties, teasing, tormenting, making her agonisingly aware of just how desperate she was to be touched. A finger slid beneath the lace and stroked her swollen folds. She was wet, so wet she was embarrassed by her body and its screaming eagerness. A fingertip circled her and suddenly there was no room for embarrassment, no room for anything but her own gasping, jerking response. He took away that final barrier and explored her.

He shimmied down the sofa and used his mouth on that tender place between her thighs and if lying still had been a challenge before it soon became an impossible challenge for Ellie. Her fingers clawed into his luxuriant black hair, her body dancing and twisting to the powerful drumbeat of desire. The sensations he evoked were excruciatingly intense and only heightened the tormenting ache of need building deep in her pelvis. Heat gathered and mounted uncontrollably at the heart of her and then, taking her entirely by surprise, exploded outwards in a violent climax of sweet, shattering pleasure.

'*Madre di Dio...* I can't wait to be inside you, *bella mia*,' Rio said huskily, rearranging her and sliding fluidly between her parted thighs. 'I am so hungry for you.'

Do I want this? Ellie asked herself and she knew she didn't need to ask that question because when she looked up into Rio's gorgeous dark eyes she was ready to agree to do anything he wanted to do. It was as though she were in a dream without a past or a future or even a present. She felt as though there was nothing but that moment and she liked it that way.

Rio tilted her back and drove into her with a single powerful thrust. And Ellie twisted her head to one side and bit her lip because it hurt, it hurt much more than she had expected, and that burning sting of pain wrenched a muffled little moan of discomfort from between her gritted teeth.

'Something wrong?' Rio rasped, lifting his tousled dark head. '*Dio mio*, you are so tight you feel like a virgin!'

'I *am*!' Ellie gasped before she could think better of making that admission.

Rio had already sunk as deep as he could get into her tiny body and he froze in shock to gaze down at her. 'A virgin?' he echoed in ringing disbelief. 'How can you be a virgin?'

Ellie wrinkled her nose. 'Oh, just get it over with, for goodness' sake,' she told him in desperation.

Stunned by that irreverent urging, Rio took several seconds to absorb what had happened. She was a virgin? How was that possible? And why hadn't he noticed anything different about her? He shifted position, withdrawing and then slowly gliding back. *Get it over with?* What was he? An ordeal to be endured?

The friction of his movement created a little hum of pulsing sensation low in Ellie's body. She shut her eyes tight, refusing to think, indeed terrified to allow herself to think about what she had just done, what she had just allowed him to do. And while she was battening down her mental hatches, Rio was putting every atom of skill he possessed into rescuing the situation. But he was hugely aroused and working alone because Ellie lay there under him like a little felled tree.

He pushed her knees up and ground down into her, delving deeper, setting an insistent rhythm that she couldn't ignore. Her hips lifted but much against her will because she was set on simply tolerating him. A frenzied heat began to build and she fought it off as though it were a forest fire. Her hips rose involuntarily and he slammed down into her, sending a startling pulse of pleasure through her. Her heart thumped like crazy, the ability to breathe stolen from her as he picked up speed and force and dominated her. Wild excitement surged and gripped her but much against her will. Her hands bit into his shoulders and then slid caressingly down his muscular back as this time she sensed the peak she was reaching towards.

A chain reaction of convulsions claimed her and she cried out as the ripples of ecstasy spread in a blinding moment of release that consumed her. Rio shuddered and held her tight and bit out something raw and rough in Italian, his powerful body surging into hers. Within seconds, however, she was free again, watching in a daze as Rio sprang off the sofa to fix his trousers and reach for his shirt.

'You were a virgin?' Rio repeated incredulously, because innocence and Ellie were a combination that refused to compute in his brain.

Wincing, Ellie sat up and pushed down her skirt. Her panties were lying on the tiles but she had no intention of trying to reclaim them in front of him. She was shell-shocked and shattered by what had taken place. She couldn't believe she had had sex with Rio. Just then in the aftermath it looked like the worst decision ever after a lifetime of vigilant caution.

'A virgin?' Rio prompted again as if a virgin were as improbable as a glimpse of a unicorn. 'So, why give it up to me?'

'Maybe I wanted to lose it with someone who would put me off further experimentation,' Ellie suggested with honeyed derision. 'Stop acting as if you've been grievously assaulted by a virgin, Rio. I can't be the first you've been with—'

'You *are*!' Rio contradicted accusingly, taken aback by her gutsy attitude.

Ellie stood up, very discreetly retrieved her underwear and, quite deliberately ignoring him, went off in search of a cloakroom. It actually hurt to walk, she acknowledged in shock. She ached as though they had had sex for hours. The experience felt less like an introduction and more like a lesson. Be careful of what you wish for, she told herself unhappily. He had leapt off that sofa as though he had been electrocuted. Innocence was clearly a hanging offence in Rio's book.

Another much more worrying fact was screaming along the edge of Rio's ragged nerves while he paced the hall, waiting impatiently for Ellie to reappear. He had never met a woman like Ellie and he was very certain that he never wanted to meet another. She drove him crazy. She made him do and say things he never did or said with anyone else. She screwed with his brain, unleashed his temper and sent him racing off the edge of sanity. She had the seductive powers of a temptress and yet how could that be when she had self-evidently had no sexual experience whatsoever? He was terrific in bed and he knew that but she had behaved as though he were useless. So, why did he want her to stay the night? Simply to rescue his ego? And what about Beppe? *And what about the lack of a condom?* He groaned out loud in frustration and raked his fingers through his cropped black curls. Rio felt *raw*.

Only innate courage persuaded Ellie out of the sanctuary of the cloakroom because in reality she wanted to curl up and die somewhere well out of Rio's sight and reach. She didn't want to see him again; she didn't want to have to speak to him again either. She simply wanted to forget what had happened and continue her holiday.

'Please drive me back to my hotel,' she said woodenly, refusing to look directly at him.

'Are you on the pill? Or any other form of contraception?' Rio asked her with startling abruptness.

Ellie almost flinched. She had spent a year taking contraceptive pills after her sobering experience with Rio at her sister's wedding. She had feared meeting that level of temptation again and as a result had taken sensible precautions to protect herself in the future. Sadly, however, she had suffered side effects from the medication and had stopped taking the pills.

'No. I'm not.' Ellie shook her head slowly and walked back into the reception room to sit down again, because she felt literally weak with shock and anxiety. 'How could we both be so stupid?'

'There are still…options,' Rio selected in a grim undertone.

Ellie's head reared up, fiery corkscrew curls tumbling back from her white forehead, accentuating her bright green eyes. 'Don't you dare suggest options to me! I'm a doctor, sworn to protect life,' she shot back at him.

'I didn't say that *that* was what I wanted. *Accidenti!* We are not reckless teenagers but we behaved as though we were,' Rio intoned in open exasperation. 'When we get together it is as though we are cursed. Let us hope there are no consequences…'

CHAPTER FIVE

ELLIE BREATHED IN deeply and slowly released her breath in the hope of chasing away the brain fog afflicting her ability to think. She was struggling to perform little mental calculations around her menstrual cycle, very quickly realising that their timing had been little short of catastrophic. She had chosen the worst possible moment to abandon her usual caution, she recognised in steadily deepening dismay.

What if Rio made her pregnant? The consequences of unprotected sex were not something she wanted to contemplate, particularly when she had a very poor relationship with the potential father. She suppressed a fearful shudder and told herself to be strong. Whatever happened, it would happen and she couldn't change that. In the meantime it would be best to go on as though nothing had changed.

'Please take me back to my hotel or call me a taxi or something,' Ellie muttered in desperation.

'You still haven't told me what you've done to Beppe—'

'I haven't done anything to him!' Ellie proclaimed in a sudden fury roused by the stabbing of her conscience. After all, if Beppe Sorrentino was troubled, it *was* her fault because she had told him something that had upset him. She had been selfish and thoughtless, dwelling only on her right to know who her father was without ever considering the cost that that information might inflict on anyone else. Even worse, Rio was Beppe's godson and Beppe had no idea that Ellie had already met Rio and was currently involved with the younger man. But *was* she involved with him?

Ellie grimaced at the concept because that word, *involved*, lent a gravitas to their entanglement that it didn't deserve. They had engaged in a foolish and irresponsible sexual encounter, nothing more. They weren't in a relationship, nor were they likely to be. And how did she feel about that reality? And the answer was that that reality saddened and wounded her heart and her pride. With Rio, she was slowly and painfully learning that she was more vulnerable than she had ever appreciated. She had made a mistake with him two years earlier and almost unbelievably had made an even bigger mistake this time around. Sex might be a field that Rio played in but Ellie didn't play at anything she did. She didn't do casual either.

'Ellie...' Rio breathed impatiently.

Ellie rose from her seat to move back out to the hall. 'I can't discuss Beppe with you. I'm sorry but that's how it is—'

'What are you hiding from me?' Glittering dark eyes full of suspicion locked to the pale triangle of Ellie's face.

Ellie lifted her chin. 'People have secrets, Rio. Secrets they don't want to share. Dragging them out into the light of day isn't always the right thing to do,' she reasoned uneasily.

'Beppe has no secrets… He's not that kind of man,' Rio argued with sublime assurance. 'So, if you're not judging, you're preaching. Are you so perfect?'

'No, I know I'm far from perfect and I wasn't preaching. I was just speaking my thoughts out loud. I'm a little confused right now,' Ellie admitted tightly, her eyes suddenly stinging while she wondered if her entire trip to Italy had been an outsize blunder. Maybe she should have left the past buried, maybe she should've tried harder to suppress her curiosity. All she knew was that she felt very guilty at the knowledge that Beppe had been distressed by her visit. He had dealt with her kindly but perhaps she hadn't deserved that kindness.

'I'll take you back to the hotel,' Rio murmured without any expression at all. He had reached the conclusion that it would take a hacksaw to extract anything from Ellie that she did not want to share. What secrets was she concealing? What he had read in that investigative report? Or was there more?

'Yes, thank you. I have a da—' Ellie bit off the word before it could reach the tip of her tongue but she saw Rio's dark gaze switch fast to her face and she felt her cheeks burn.

'You have a date?' Rio pressed in growling disbelief, staring at her as she stood there in the comparative dimness of the hall, a glowing beauty with a sexily tousled mane of vibrant coppery curls, translucent skin and a mouth that would've tempted a saint. And he had never been a saint. Even less was he known as a possessive lover, because he didn't allow himself to become attached: once bitten, twice shy. So why did the very thought of Ellie becoming intimate with another man infuriate him? Disconcerted by that rush of anger, he tamped it down hard and gritted his teeth.

'A guy I met in the village invited me out to dinner tonight,' Ellie confided in a rush.

'His name?' Rio demanded.

'Bruno Nigrelli.'

Rio's nostrils flared. 'I think he did some work for Beppe once. Lawyer?'

Ellie nodded uncomfortably.

Rio gritted his teeth even harder in the smouldering silence. Was she expecting him to object? Even waiting for him to do so? Wasn't that how women sucked a man in, by assigning strings and conditions and making him want and demand more?

'I'm not much in the mood for dinner now, but I don't like letting people down—'

Rio's dark eyes flared golden as the sunset. 'Then cancel him and spend the night here with me instead.'

Ellie froze in bewilderment, green eyes flying over his lean, darkly handsome features. 'Spend the night?' she repeated shakily.

'It would make more sense—'

Ellie dropped her gaze defensively. 'Nothing about us makes sense—'

'We make perfect sense. You decided I was a *bastardo* two years ago and even if I saved the world you wouldn't budge an inch from that conviction,' Rio derided.

'I think a lot of women would think the same after that night at the wedding, but let's not get into that,' Ellie counselled heavily as she yanked open the hefty front door. 'We have enough differences without raking up the past. I can't stay, Rio—'

'Ellie… When will you know?'

Ellie dropped her head as she settled into the passenger seat of his sports car. 'In ten days to two weeks,' she framed jaggedly. 'I'll do a test as soon as I can.'

In the sunlight, Rio stood very still. What would he do if Ellie conceived his child? He recalled his own sordid origins with an inner shudder of recoil, knowing in that instant that there would be no sacrifice too great were it to mean that his child could look back with pride and contentment on his or her early years. Only when Beppe and Amalia took an interest in him had Rio learned what it was to have self-respect. Being cleverer than everyone around him had only attracted the bullies. Being prettier as a boy had also drawn the abusers. His lean, strong face was stamped by the grim lines and hollows of bitter recollection and experience. As an adult, Rio Benedetti might be as rich as the fabled Croesus but he had never forgotten his humble beginnings in that dumpster.

Ellie glanced up to see what was preventing Rio from joining her in the car and ended up staring, because it was a revelation to see that Rio, all lean, mean and magnificent six-foot-plus of him, could look haunted and almost vulnerable. She scolded herself for that imaginative flight as soon as he started up the car but his rebuke about her tendency to judge was still nagging at the back of her mind. Sometimes she was kind of black-and-white about situations, she acknowledged uneasily, but just as she had learned all her life to follow rules she *had* learned to compromise and understand what motivated people to do the things they did, as well. She supposed she *was* still holding the events of two years earlier against Rio because his colourful sex life had shocked her. As someone who had never pushed against conventional boundaries, possibly she *was* a little too conservative for a passionate free spirit like Rio.

Rio pulled the car to a halt in the hotel car park. He shot Ellie a glance, noting the fineness of her delicate bone structure and how clearly it showed beneath her pale skin. She was exhausted and he could see it and he compressed his mouth on the urge to make another comment about Beppe. He refused to think about the dinner date she had. He refused to admit that the idea annoyed him. After all, he wasn't possessive and he wasn't jealous. He didn't *ever* get attached to a woman—well, at least he hadn't in almost ten years.

And when Rio *had* got attached—to Franca—it had been a disaster, he recalled grimly. Treachery laced with infidelity and a woman's greed. Rio had learned the hard way that loving could be a one-way ticket to hell.

No, he definitely wasn't jealous. He already knew that Ellie was a gold-digger, he reminded himself resolutely. He would only care about Ellie Dixon's future if she became pregnant with his child. In the short term his *sole* interest in her lay in uncovering her mysterious connection to Beppe.

Rio sprang out of the car and strode round to open the passenger door. Disconcerted by that unexpected attention, Ellie climbed out and as she looked up warily into his glitteringly beautiful dark golden eyes, the sunlight hot on her skin, her conscience screamed like a fire alarm. She had been downright nasty about the sex even though he had been considerate and concerned and, bearing in mind that he had given her two climaxes, she had been unjust. Her skin flushed beet red.

'*Che cosa...* What?' Rio pressed in the strained silence.

'I shouldn't have said what I said back at your house,' Ellie gabbled before she could lose her nerve. 'It was a train wreck... Us, I mean, and me being...well, you know what. But you were good, I mean—'

Rio wanted to laugh but he fought the urge because she was so embarrassed, so utterly different from him in her attitude to sex. 'Okay...'

'I'm sorry,' Ellie said curtly. 'I was... I was upset.'

And with that apology she spun on her heel and walked into the hotel. Her head had a natural tilt, her hips a shapely sway, the skirt dancing above her long slender legs and, that fast, Rio was hard as a rock again, his hands clenching into fists by his sides. She drove him crazy, he reminded himself unnecessarily. But he had had her now and that should be that, game over. Hit it and quit it, he repeated to himself. He didn't *still* want her. Of course he didn't, so walk away, a little voice in his brain instructed.

Rio swung back into his car. The sound of Ellie moaning as he kissed her engulfed him, the surprised look of ecstasy on her face when she came, the exquisite feel of her soft, satiny skin. He swore vehemently, emptied his mind and dug out his phone. He needed a woman, *any* woman just as long as she wasn't Ellie.

In a daze, Ellie went for a shower. She still ached. There would be no forgetting what she had done. And the incredulous way Rio had looked at her in the car park would stay with her until the day she died. Her face burned afresh. She should have kept quiet, she shouldn't have said anything, should have left that short-lived intimacy and all memory of it back in his house in the hills where it belonged. A mistaken moment and not an important one in her scheme of things. Only sex. Although it would not be *only* sex if she fell pregnant, she conceded wretchedly, and refused to think about that angle on the grounds that it was stupid to worry before she knew she actually had something to worry about.

Although for the first time ever, Ellie desperately wanted to confide in someone and she thought about phoning Polly. She didn't think Polly would tell her husband, Rashad, about *that*. But how did she know for sure? She covered her face with wet hands, all the stress of the past forty-eight hours piling up on her along with every doubt and insecurity she possessed. She still didn't know how she had ended up having sex with Rio, but she knew she had wanted it to happen as much as he had. Being unable to put the blame on him stung, as well. He hadn't sweet-talked her, filled her up with booze or seduced her—*my goodness, anything but*, she conceded ruefully.

Beppe called her on her mobile and asked her to meet him at a doctor's surgery on the outskirts of Florence the next day. She refused the lift he offered her and assured him that she had satellite navigation and was happy to drive herself there. He invited her to dine at his home in the evening and she agreed, keen to take the opportunity to get to know him a little better, regardless of how Rio might feel about it. Should she tell Beppe that she knew Rio? Or would it be wiser to remain tactfully silent? She brooded about that while she got dressed to dine with Bruno.

It was a long evening. Bruno might have ticked all

the basic boxes in the tally of what made a man attractive but he bored on about his work ambitions while asking little about Ellie. He kissed her on the cheek outside her hotel. He invited her out again and she made a polite excuse and she didn't linger, speeding indoors, keen to get to bed.

Opening the door of her hotel room, she drew back with a sound of consternation when she saw the light burning beside her bed and the male reclining there. 'How on earth did you get in here?' she demanded.

Rio uncoiled fluidly off the bed and stretched with lazy assurance, not one whit perturbed by her attitude. 'It wasn't difficult. The staff know we're…close,' he selected with precision and the angry flush on her cheeks bloomed hotter still with chagrin. 'I also own a large stake in the hotel.'

'We are *not* close!' Ellie contradicted, tossing her bag down on the chair in the corner.

Rio shrugged a broad shoulder, gracefully and silently evasive. He was as effortlessly beautiful as a dark angel sent to tempt even with his black hair tousled, his jawline shadowed and his tie missing. Her heartbeat had picked up speed. Her tiredness had taken a mysterious step back and she was already breathing as if she had run up a hill. And there was the craziest melting sensation in that place where she still ached from his sheer sexual energy. Yet she didn't want *that* again, did she? It was a badly timed thought to have in Rio's presence because her entire body quickened as if she had punched a button to switch it on to supersensitivity. Her nipples stung and her thighs pressed together as if to silence the squirming readiness low in her pelvis.

'Are you planning to tell me what you're doing here?' Ellie enquired stiffly, tamping down all those disobedient thoughts and responses.

'I wanted to be sure you came back alone,' Rio told her.

'And how is that your business?'

'You were with me today,' Rio murmured.

Ellie tilted her chin, emerald eyes gleaming like chips of ice. 'Doesn't mean you own me.'

Rio shrugged again. 'I'd still have beaten the hell out of him had you brought him upstairs.'

Ellie's lips parted and then closed again because there really wasn't much she could say to that. 'You do a lot of that sort of thing?' she prompted a split second later, honest curiosity gripping her.

'Get physical? Once it was a regular activity.' Dark eyes spilling a glittering gleam of gold from below lush curling black lashes, Rio strode past her to the door. 'I had to, to protect myself. I grew up in a tough environment.'

'You're leaving?' Ellie framed in disconcertion and then could have bitten her tongue out because she was making it sound as though she wanted him to stay. And she didn't.

'*Sì...*' Rio treated her to a slow burning appraisal. 'Somehow I doubt that you'd be up for anything else tonight, *principessa*.'

Fury splintered through Ellie. Leave it to Rio to tell it as it is. He would stay for sex but not to chat or share a drink or supper or anything more civilised. The claustrophobic silence of the room enclosed her, increasing her nervous tension. The tip of her tongue stole out to moisten her dry lower lip.

'I *love* your mouth,' Rio husked soft and low, his attention locking to the sultry fullness of her pink lips.

Gooseflesh pebbled Ellie's arms and a wicked little quiver snaked down her taut spinal cord. She was so aware of him that her very skin prickled and tingled with it. For an insane moment she imagined pushing him backwards down on the bed and teaching him that he didn't know everything about her. And then she blinked, sane Ellie swimming back to the fore, and she spun and opened the door for him so that he would leave more quickly.

'Sometimes you crack me up, *bella mia*,' Rio confided with unholy amusement, recognising her defensiveness in that almost desperate pulling open of the door to hasten his departure. 'When you're thinking about me in bed tonight, will you be kissing me or thumping me?'

Ellie breathed in so deep she almost spontaneously combusted while she watched Rio clatter down the stairs without an ounce of discomfiture in his bearing. She had never met anyone quite like Rio Benedetti before and that was probably why he knocked her for six every time she saw him, she told herself soothingly. He was bad, he was brash, he was incredibly sexy and insolent and he had the kind of charismatic confidence that burned like a solar flare. She was too polite and inhibited to deal with him as he *should* be dealt with. Her hands clenched into fists.

He embarrassed her too. The staff had seen her going out with Bruno Nigrelli and now knew she had returned to find Rio waiting in her bedroom. Ought she to complain about that invasion? Or, having already been seen in Rio's company and kissing him, perhaps it was wiser to ignore the situation lest she end up even more embarrassed. Had Rio made her look slutty? Or like a femme fatale? She went to bed on that thought, deciding that Rio's pursuit, if she could label it with that word, made her look like a much more exciting woman than she actually was. But she still wanted to kill him for being so careless of appearances, so arrogant and incomprehensible.

Why would he have beaten up Bruno had she brought the other man back to her room? Presumably that had been a joke, although she had not seen the humour in it. She could not credit that Rio could be jealous or staking some sort of male claim to her. He wasn't the type. And instead of finding the sleep she badly needed the riddle of his complex personality ensured that she couldn't stop her brain running on and actually relax enough to drift off.

The following morning she met up with Beppe outside a smart suburban surgery near Florence. The older man looked perfectly calm and collected and there was no sign of strain or distress in either his expression or his friendly, easy manner. Had Rio exaggerated? Overreacted? They went inside the surgery and swabs were taken. Beppe passed over a tiny gold locket, which he quietly admitted contained a lock of his brother's hair. Ellie flushed and made no comment. After all, her mother, Annabel, had named both brothers as her daughter's possible father, and to do so, she had presumably been uncertain as to which had fathered her child.

'We will know within twenty-four hours,' Beppe assured her with quiet satisfaction. 'And now that I have you here in my beloved Firenze, I will play tourist with you and show you the sights as they should be seen.'

Relieved by his mood and the welcome offer of his company, Ellie relaxed and over a cup of coffee and a pastry in a sun-drenched square found herself admitting that she knew Rio and had first met him at her sister's wedding.

The older man did not hide his astonishment. 'He should've told me that—'

'To be honest,' Ellie added hurriedly, 'Rio and I didn't get on very well, so it wasn't an acquaintance either of us was likely to pursue.'

Beppe sighed. 'You surprise me. Women are drawn to my godson. Obviously you've seen him since your arrival—'

'He called in at the hotel on my first day. I didn't tell him anything,' Ellie assured him, her cheeks colouring when she was forced to think of what else she had done with Rio since that day, but it was a major relief for her to admit simply that she knew Rio.

'Rio put me on a pedestal a very long time ago,' Beppe confided wryly. 'If you and I discover that we are related by blood, it will be a huge shock for him and that is why I have told him nothing as yet.'

'Were you friends with his parents? I know he's your godson.'

'No, my wife and I never knew his parents,' Beppe admitted dismissively and changed the subject to ask her to choose where she would like to go first with him.

Beppe took her to see Michelangelo's sculptures in the Galleria dell'Academia before showing her his favourite paintings in the Uffizi. Her frank admission that she knew nothing whatsoever about art did her no

disservice in his eyes and when she liked something
he asked her *why* she liked it, evidently set on forming
her taste. He also told her a little about his own family
background. The *palazzo* had been in his family for
several generations and the Sorrentino prosperity had
originally been built on the production of internation-
ally acclaimed wines. His younger brother, Vincenzo,
had once managed the vineyards. Beppe had always
been academic and had worked as a university profes-
sor before his wife's ill health had forced him to take a
step back from his career. From that point on, he had
become more involved in his wife's charitable endeav-
ours, which had been very much focussed on the needs
of disabled and disadvantaged children.

'What time is dinner this evening?' Ellie asked when
Beppe had finally returned her to her car. She noted that
he was out of breath and perspiring and she scolded herself for letting him do so much on a hot day when he
was clearly by his girth and indoor habits not usually a
physically active man.

'Nine o'clock. And it will be formal,' Beppe warned
her. 'But don't worry about that if you have no formal
wear with you. Everyone will understand that you are
on holiday.'

Ellie smiled at that recollection as she returned to her
hotel. Thanks to Polly's holiday shop, Ellie had a dream
of a dress hanging in the wardrobe. In fact, uninterested
though she had always been in fashion, it was the sort
of dress that brought stars to her eyes because it was
wonderfully feminine and flowing. Fashioned of peach
lace, it was a daring colour for a redhead, but remark-
ably flattering against her pale skin and bright hair. She
showered and paid more heed than usual to the mini-

mal make-up she wore while wondering if Rio would be at the dinner. Would he be annoyed that she had gone ahead and told his godfather that they already knew each other? Staying silent on that score had become impossible for her because Beppe was so very straight-forward and plain-spoken and she did not want to risk losing his good opinion by keeping secrets from him.

The gravel in front of Beppe's home was a sea of luxury-model cars, which disconcerted Ellie because evidently the dinner party was a much bigger, fancier event than she had assumed it would be. Her fear that she would prove to be overdressed receded as soon as she was shown into a crowded salon filled with clusters of very elegant laughing and chattering guests. Beppe hurried straight over to welcome her and tucked her hand over his arm protectively as he took her to join the group he was with. Within a few minutes, Ellie had relaxed.

And then the door opened again and she glanced across the room to see the new arrivals and saw Rio entering with a tall willowy blonde clinging to his arm. Her heart sank and she couldn't stop it from doing that. Her pleasant smile lurched and her tummy flipped and all of a sudden she felt ridiculously sick and shaky. What the heck was the matter with her? She was not in a re-lationship with Rio, was she? Why should it bother her that he was already showing off another woman? After all, she had known from the outset that he was a noto-rious womaniser with few moral scruples.

Rio was taken aback by Ellie's presence because Beppe hadn't mentioned that his visitor would be at-tending. Nor did it help that Ellie looked stupendous in an apricot dress that smoothly shaped her lush curves at breast and hip while highlighting her porcelain-pale skin and the sheer vibrancy of her coppery tumbling mane of hair. His physical response was swift and urgent, the swelling at his groin an unwelcome reminder that 'hit it and quit it' hadn't worked for him where she was concerned. Above her breast, she had fastened a diamond brooch in the shape of a star and it was the only jewellery she wore. So, she *did* have the diamond brooch her uncle had accused her of stealing, Rio recognised in sudden disgust, the brooch she had denied all knowledge of after her grandmother's death. For Rio, it was a timely reminder of the kind of woman he was dealing with in Ellie Dixon. At heart she had to be a greedy, gold-digging liar who had learned how to put on a good show as a caring, compassionate doctor.

Rio strode straight up to Beppe and introduced his gorgeous companion, who seemed unable to take her eyes off Ellie's dress. The blonde's name was Carmela and she was unquestionably beautiful and very different in style from Ellie. She was taller, thinner, blue-eyed and possessed enviably straight, long silky blond hair. Her dress was much more revealing than Ellie's but then she had a perfect body to reveal. A long slender leg showed through the side slit in the dress while the plunging neckline showed a great deal of her improbably large, high breasts. Gorgeous but kind of slutty, Ellie decided, discomfited by the speed with which that shrewish opinion came to her mind.

'Of course, Ellie needs no introduction to you, Rio,' his godfather, Beppe, pointed out smoothly as an opening salvo. 'Since you first met at her sister's wedding.'

Rio was transfixed by that bombshell reminder coming at him out of nowhere and unadulterated rage roared through his big powerful frame as his attention shot to Ellie, who evaded his gaze while slowly turning as red as a tomato, her guilt writ large in her face. Ellie had chosen to come clean with Beppe and had dropped him in it without conscience, Rio registered grimly. A power play? Or was it a warning? What else might she choose to tell his godfather about him? Shot through with anger and frustration at his inability to respond with the truth, Rio was incapable of even forcing a smile.

'We didn't hit it off,' Ellie said abruptly. 'That's why he didn't mention it.'

Shot from rage to wonderment at that apparent intervention on his behalf, Rio dealt Ellie a suspicious look from glittering dark-as-jet eyes semiveiled by his lush lashes and shrugged. 'First impressions are rarely reliable,' he quipped as he turned away to address someone else who had spoken to him.

Ellie was appalled that something she had revealed had caused tension between Rio and Beppe. Her trip to Italy and her search for her father were definitely beginning to feel like a minefield she was trying to pick her way across.

As Rio moved to grasp a glass from a tray and pass it to her, Carmela hissed, 'That redhead's wearing a Lavroff!'

Rio shot the fashion model on his arm a blank appraisal.

'That dress was the star of the Lavroff show I walked for in the spring.'

A designer gown, surely a little rich for a junior doctor's salary? Although perhaps not too expensive for a doctor whose dying patient had left her everything she possessed, Rio reflected sombrely. It was starting to occur to him that he had underestimated Ellie and how much trouble she was capable of causing. He could see at a glance that she already had Beppe wrapped round her little finger. In fact, her hand was resting comfortably on the older man's arm. Rio dragged in a sudden breath, his lean, darkly handsome features tensing into tough lines of restraint. Was *that* what he had to fear?

Ironically that risk hadn't even crossed his mind because Beppe lived a celibate life and had never been known to seek out female companionship. But Beppe had been acquainted with Ellie's mother, and if Ellie's mother had been even half as beautiful as her daughter, she would hardly have been forgettable. Back then, however, Beppe had been safely married and now he was not and he was making no attempt to hide his delight in Ellie's company. Rio stationed himself where he could watch his godfather and he was sharply disconcerted by the level of familiarity he could already see developing between the pair. Ellie whispered something in Beppe's ear and he chuckled and patted her hand fondly. He moved her on with him to another group of guests, giving her no opportunity to stray.

At his elbow, Carmela was still whinging on enviously about the Lavroff gown. Rio wasn't interested. He often paid for the designer clothes his lovers wore but he took no interest in the names or the cost, writing the expenses off as the cost of maintaining a reasonable sex life. His entire focus remained on Ellie. He listened to her making intelligent conversation, heard her laugh several times and learned that she had toured the Uffizi gallery with Beppe. *Inferno*, she certainly didn't need to be taught how to best please a much older, lonely man with a lifelong love of art. But she would soon learn her mistake if she persisted on her current ambitious trajectory. Rio would destroy her before he would allow her to hurt Beppe Sorrentino.

And what if she's pregnant? Rio backed away a step as Carmela tried to get closer to him. He studied Ellie as they were seated at the dining table and strove to imagine that shapely body swollen with his child. The idea unnerved him but it also excited him in a peculiar way, which only had the effect of unnerving him even more.

Ellie barely touched the food on her plate. She eavesdropped on Carmela's airheaded views on suntans as affected by climate change. She noticed that Rio didn't listen to a word his companion said and appeared to be tuning her out like an irritating noise. She watched him, as well, catching the downward slant of his beautifully shaped mouth, the tension in his exquisite bone structure that hardened his exotic cheekbones and placed hollows beneath them. He was furious with her, she *knew* he was. Rio had a temper like a flamethrower and he was boiling like a cauldron of oil.

But Ellie was angry too. Only the day before he had been with her and last night he had been waiting for her in her hotel room. And now he was with a beautiful blonde model, who operated off one very talkative brain cell. Why was she hurt? Why the hell was she hurting over his rejection of her as a woman? Time after time over the years Ellie had learned that men didn't really want career-driven, independent women. She wasn't feminine enough, she wasn't *soft* enough, she could deal with a spider just fine but a mouse sent her screaming. She was stubborn and contrary and choosy and he didn't fit the bill for her either, so why was she agonising? Why would she want a gorgeous, arrogant, shameless man whore in her life anyway? She was far too sensible and strait-laced for a male of his ilk. Sheer lust had put her in his arms and she had got what she deserved, she told herself repressively.

Beppe took her and several other guests to admire his latest painting acquisition in the hall. Rio and Carmela joined them. Carmela wondered out loud if the seventeenth-century subject of the portrait was wearing hair extensions. Ellie whispered a polite, 'Excuse me...' in Beppe's ear as he guided the group into his library to show them something else and she walked down the corridor to the cloakroom instead. Freshening up, she grimaced at her anxious reflection in the mirror. Why was it that when Rio was around he dominated everything? Including her thoughts?

When she emerged, Rio was standing waiting for her, his lean, dark face stormy and tense. 'I want a word,' he told her grimly.

'But I *don't*,' Ellie told him as he snapped a hand round her wrist and pulled her outdoors onto the cool, formal *loggia* with pillars that ran along that side of the house.

'You're such a bully, Rio!' Ellie objected, rubbing her wrist the instant he released it as though he had bruised her.

Rio backed her up against the stone wall behind her by the simple expedient of moving forward, shutting out any view of the gardens and forcing her to tip her head back to look up at him. 'What did you tell Beppe about us?' he demanded in a raw undertone.

'Very little. That we met at the wedding and that you called on me at the hotel the day I arrived,' Ellie proffered. 'I didn't tell him what you said or threatened or anything of that nature. I simply wanted to clear the air. Pretending we were strangers…I mean, why would I mislead Beppe like that? I've got nothing to hide—'

'Not according to the report I had done on you,' Rio reminded her darkly.

Ellie bridled at that reference, fully convinced that any close and proper check on her background would reveal that she was innocent of any wrongdoing. 'I didn't intend to cause friction between you and Beppe. I didn't think of that angle,' she admitted guiltily. 'But I'm sorry that I embarrassed you like that—'

'Are you really?' Rio lifted a sardonic ebony brow, staring down at her, noting the mere hint at her neckline of the pale valley between her full breasts and entranced by the new discovery that showing so little could actually be sexier than showing a lot. As he tensed, inescapably recalling his own response to those luscious curves the day before, he whipped his gaze up to her face in the hope of lowering his temperature. 'I think you dropped me in it deliberately to cause trouble,' he contended.

'But then you would think that because you always think the worst of me,' Ellie shot back at him in exasperation. 'Exactly what is your problem, Rio?'

Rio ran his fingertip along the succulent curve of her lower lip and watched a tiny pulse flicker fast at the base of her elegant white throat. 'You're my only problem, *principessa*,' he told her huskily. 'We had our moment and that was supposed to be it—'

'It *is* it!' Ellie seethed, furious that he was cornering her when he had brought another woman to dinner.

'Not for me,' Rio confided, letting a coppery corkscrew curl coil round his finger like a vine, his stunning dark golden eyes hot and hungrily gripping hers by sheer force of will. 'I'm not done yet—'

'But I *am*,' Ellie spelled out thinly. 'You're ruining my holiday—'

'When we're done, I'll *tell* you,' Rio asserted, bending down to nip at her full lower lip with the edge of his teeth.

A violent shiver ran down through her taut body, that tiny sting of pain somehow setting off a chain reaction of electrified awareness and sensitivity. He lowered his head and he took her mouth with a raw sexual demand that momentarily stole Ellie's wits. She fell back against the wall, knees weak, melting heat surging in her pelvis.

'*Rio!*' a voice interposed curtly, and both of them froze.

Rio lifted his dark head and stepped back to study his godfather, keen to interpret his expression. Beppe looked angry and protective. Ellie straightened, her face flushing as mortification consumed her.

'Carmela's looking for you,' Beppe murmured flatly. 'I suggest that you take her home. I would also suggest that you stay away from Ellie.'

Rio released his breath in an audible hiss. 'Although I'm always ready to listen to suggestions, Beppe,' he conceded, 'I've always forged my own path.'

With a nod of acknowledgement to Ellie and the older man, Rio strode back indoors, not one whit perturbed by the scene Beppe had interrupted. Or, at least, if he was bothered, he wasn't showing it, Ellie acknowledged.

'I have no right to interfere,' Beppe said uncomfortably to Ellie. 'I love Rio like a son but I also know him.

He had some unfortunate experiences with women in his youth and I would advise you to keep your distance. He plays with women. He doesn't take them seriously. He would hurt you and I would hate to see that happen. Furthermore, if you prove to be either my niece or even my daughter, you will often meet Rio and that—'

'Could get very awkward,' Ellie filled in ruefully for herself. 'It's all right, Beppe. I kind of worked out that stuff about Rio anyway, so don't worry about me. I'm a big girl and I can look after myself.'

Rio and Carmela were nowhere to be seen when they rejoined the rest of the guests. Ellie stayed quite late but insisted on returning to her hotel when Beppe offered her the use of a guest room. She drove back in a contemplative state of mind and wondered if she would find Rio in her room again. Not this time however.

Soberly she lay in bed, wondering about the results of the DNA test. Would she prove to be half-Sorrentino? Or was she in for a shock on that score? It was perfectly possible, after all, that some time after Beppe's rejection her mother had spent a night with some other man. Well, at least she would soon know one way or another, even if she didn't actually manage to identify her father, she told herself soothingly.

But how would Rio react if she was a Sorrentino? Ironically she didn't want to upset him but nor was she willing to apologise for an act of fate. She was already wondering what Beppe's mention of Rio's 'unfortunate youthful experiences' with women had entailed. But then surely no intelligent male could be so innately distrustful and cynical about her sex without cause?

And what did it matter? She relived the teasing sting of his teeth on her lip and a forbidden little quiver

snaked through her. With a groan she rolled over and
pressed her offending mouth into the pillow. Rio was
as potent as poison and equally toxic and Beppe was
right, she *needed* to keep her distance. To do anything
else would be to court disaster because Rio had no off
switch, no respect for boundaries…and probably even
less respect for her, she conceded unhappily.

CHAPTER SIX

BEPPE CALLED ELLIE bright and early and asked her to come to his home. Ellie surmised that he had bad news and she took her time over her breakfast in the hotel courtyard, trying not to stress over what could not be changed. Beppe had been wonderfully approachable and kind and helpful and she wanted to thank him for that. He could've denied any knowledge of her late mother but instead he had told her the unvarnished truth, even though doing so had raked up guilty memories and regrets.

Ellie drove over to the *palazzo* and Adriano showed her out to the shaded *loggia*, quickly reappearing with a tray of coffee and biscuits. Beppe appeared then, rather flushed in appearance and with eyes that were a little shiny.

He studied her and he then smiled widely, a smile brimming with happiness and appreciation. 'Ellie,' he began emotively as he handed her a sheet of paper to study. 'You *are* my daughter and I cannot begin to describe how much that discovery means to me.'

Lively with excitement, Beppe could hardly be persuaded to drink his coffee as he ignored her medical training to explain rather unnecessarily the 99.99 recurring percentage of accuracy established by the success-ful DNA test. 'I would've been delighted to discover that you were my niece but to discover a daughter, a first child after all these years, is an unimaginable joy!'

Ellie reached across the small circular table and grasped his hand to squeeze it. 'Thank you for say-ing that.'

'It comes from the centre of my heart,' Beppe told her warmly. 'Amalia give birth to a stillborn son just weeks before she suffered her stroke. We were devas-tated. I don't believe, though, that I could have told her about you were she still alive. It would have hurt her too much and my affair had already caused her enor-mous grief.'

'How do you think Rio will take this news?' Ellie asked, dry-mouthed.

Beppe emitted a heavy sigh. 'He will be here for lunch and I will tell him then. He will be happy that I am happy but very disappointed to hear that I once be-trayed Amalia. If only we had adopted him as I wished, he would have been more certain of his place in the family.'

Ellie sat forward, brow furrowed, her curiosity en-gaged. 'You wanted to *adopt* Rio?'

'*Sì*. I will respect his privacy by not giving you de-tails but he had neither parents nor a home and I wanted to take him in, but Amalia refused to set another child in what she always viewed as our stillborn son's place,' he confided heavily. 'There were also elements of Rio's background which disturbed her and she could not be persuaded to change her mind. He never knew that I wanted to adopt him though. Our contribution to his life became less direct as he grew up. We advised him, ensured he got a good education and supported him when he needed us but we could have protected him a great deal more had we adopted him and brought him up here.'

'That's unfortunate but Rio has still done very well for himself, hasn't he?'

'If you measure success by prosperity, his wealth reached stratospheric proportions after he won the oil contracts in Dharia. He is very much a self-made man,' Beppe declared with pride. 'But he is also a man damaged by a traumatic childhood and a tough adolescence. I should've done more for him.'

'By the sound of it, you did the best you could in the circumstances,' Ellie remarked soothingly, troubled more than she liked by the reference to Rio's traumatic childhood and troubled adolescence. Yes, she could imagine how such experiences would have hardened him and what a difference a loving, supportive home background could have made. After all, she knew that she too was marked by the lack of love in her childhood. Her grandmother hadn't wanted to raise her daughter's two illegitimate children and had only done so because Annabel had paid her handsomely to take on that responsibility. When that flow of money had stopped, presumably because Annabel had suffered bankruptcy and ill health, her grandmother had complained bitterly about how much of a burden her granddaughters were. Polly's affection had provided the only love Ellie had experienced during those years.

'I think I'll go back to the hotel now,' Ellie announced, hardening herself to Beppe's look of disappointment. 'Rio will be arriving soon and we both need some time to think. This is a lot to take on board and so much more than I ever expected to learn.'

'I hope you will pack and come here to stay with me for what remains of your holiday,' Beppe admitted. 'And perhaps someday you will feel comfortable enough to call me *Papà*.'

Ellie's eyes prickled with tears as she left. She felt ridiculously emotional and when Beppe gave her a small, almost daring hug on the doorstep it almost made the pent-up tears spill down her cheeks. He was willing to be her father and she was in a daze of shock and happiness. It bothered her to appreciate that Rio was unlikely to celebrate the same news. Rio didn't like her and didn't trust her and the revelation that she was his precious godfather's daughter would hit him hard. Would it hurt him that she had the blood tie with Beppe that he had been denied? She flinched from the thought, marvelling at how oversensitive she was to any thought of Rio being hurt.

It was so ridiculous, she thought ruefully. Big, tough, angry, hostile Rio would not be so easily hurt. Why was she even considering how he would feel about her parentage? What business was it of his? After all, the scene had been set before she was even born by Beppe's affair with her unhappy mother. By the sound of it that extra-marital affair had caused tremendous unhappiness for all the parties involved, but surely after so many years Beppe could begin to forgive himself and both of them could now concentrate on forming a relationship? That conviction at the forefront of her mind, Ellie packed her case and then walked down to the village to kill some time and allow Beppe to speak to Rio in peace.

Rio departed from Beppe's home reeling from what his godfather had dropped on him. An adulterous affair and a daughter? No, he had certainly not seen that possibility on the horizon and it changed everything, his own position most of all. Ellie had played a blinder of a game by concealing her true motivation for being in Italy right to the very end, Rio acknowledged bitterly. In fact, she had trussed him up like a chicken ready for the roasting pot. Beppe had openly voiced his concern that Rio nourished dishonourable intentions towards his newfound daughter. Beppe had no idea that Rio had already gone much further than that and if he found out it would destroy his relationship with Rio. Worse still, if she was pregnant, Beppe would be digging out a shotgun.

It was time to take the initiative, not a time to sit back and vacillate over what-ifs and maybes, Rio reflected sardonically. Left in ignorance, he had dug himself into a deep hole and he had to dig himself out of it again and to do that he needed Ellie's help whether he liked it or not. Raging resentment surged up through the cracks inside him and there was no healing balm of acceptance to soothe it. Beppe was, after all, the only true family Rio had ever had, the only adult who had ever shown him love, consideration and understanding while he was still a child. And now Beppe had a daughter, whom Rio had wronged. That she could well be a money-grabbing young woman keen to feather her own nest scarcely counted now that she was about to become Beppe's heir. Furthermore, Beppe would never believe the allegations made against Ellie for there was virtually no proof of misconduct on her part.

Rio had hired a second agency to check and update the evidence he had originally been given. The hospice enquiry *had* cleared Ellie of any wrongdoing and she *had* refused the inheritance left to her by one of her patients. The only dirt left in the first investigative report relied heavily on her embittered uncle's tale about the diamond brooch and, as the police had refused to prosecute, the whole story could easily be written off as being more rumour and backstabbing than actual fact. And furthermore, if Ellie *was* a gold-digger, Rio was about to make her feel as if she'd won the lottery.

When he learned that she had checked out of the hotel he was taken aback until he noticed that her hire car was still parked outside. The receptionist told him that Ellie had walked down into the village. He found her in the cool of the ancient stone church, studying a much-admired triptych of the Madonna and Child.

When he spoke her name, she whirled round, a figure of light and movement in the dim, dark interior. Her dress was the ice blue of diamonds and the sunlight cascading through a stained-glass window high up the wall showered her in a dancing rainbow of colour that only emphasised the vibrant copper of her tumbling hair. She wasn't quick enough to hide the dismay and anxiety that crossed her face when she saw him and the tense expression and attitude that took over to stiffen her into stillness was no more welcoming.

Welcome to your biggest challenge yet, Rio thought grimly, trying not to notice how beautiful she was in that naturally beautiful way that so many women tried and failed to achieve. He froze there, suppressing his body's equally natural instincts, none of which felt appropriate in the House of God.

'Rio…' Ellie whispered uncertainly, mortified by the nerves that had stolen the volume from her voice.

He could have been carved from stone as he stood

there, still and quiet as a predator, sheathed in a light grey designer suit. He resembled a stone angel with cutting cheekbones, a hard-hewn jawline and a mouth as wilful, stubborn and passionate as sin. His eyes were a pure dazzling gold in the light and she blinked rapidly, striving to shut the sheer intensity of him out and to be polite but distant, treating him the same way she usually treated men. But how could she achieve that when she knew in her heart that he had sought her out because he was shocked and agitated by what Beppe had shared with him?

'Are you a believer?' he prompted lightly.

'Yes. Are you?'

'I was raised by nuns in an orphanage and spent more time on my knees than in school. Of course I am,' Rio told her wryly.

And it was as though he had squeezed her heart at the same time as he filled in some of the blanks in her repeated attempts to understand what made him what he was. An orphanage, she thought sadly.

'I bet you were always in trouble,' Ellie remarked without thinking.

'Pretty much. Beppe and his wife raised funds for the home and did a lot to help the children, particularly the disabled ones amongst us,' Rio admitted. 'Although that home is closed now and conditions are greatly improved in its replacement. Beppe is still very much involved in finding employment and educational opportunities for the less fortunate. He is a good man.'

'Yes,' Ellie agreed tightly.

'And you are his daughter,' Rio declared without any perceptible emotion at all. 'I must assume you take after your mother since you don't look much like your father.'

'She was tall, red-haired and pale-skinned like me. I think I get my lack of height from Beppe,' Ellie breathed uncomfortably. 'You're angry that I didn't tell you why I so particularly wanted to meet Beppe.'

'It wasn't your secret to share,' Rio conceded, surprising her. 'But I must confess that I was completely unprepared for what he admitted to me. I shouldn't have been. There must have been times when he felt trapped in his marriage. He is only human.'

'Let's not talk about that,' Ellie advised. 'I don't think we can ever understand that sort of situation unless we've actually lived the same experience—'

'*Porca miseria!* That's a very compassionate comment from judgemental Ellie!' Rio commented, an ebony brow slanting up in apparent wonderment.

'Let's also try not to argue.' Ellie sent him a rueful look of appeal. 'You're shocked right now, of course you're shocked. You thought you knew everything there was to know about Beppe—'

'I don't want judgemental Ellie *or* Dr Ellie right at this moment,' Rio interposed.

The pale triangle of her face flushed as though he had slapped her. 'I'm not sure I know how to be anything else—'

'We'll have coffee…and talk,' Rio framed, extending a lean, long-fingered hand to her in invitation.

Ellie hesitated as if a shark had bared its teeth at her. And then she forced her arm to lift and she grasped his hand, a frisson of quivering awareness shimmying down her spine. He was trying to accept her and because he was making the effort, she had to make it too. His attitude thoroughly disconcerted her because she had expected only anger, condemnation and suspicion from Rio and he had just as swiftly proven her expectations wrong.

She had expected Rio to walk her across the square to the local café but instead he tucked her into the car illegally parked outside. Belatedly it occurred to her that the busy little café would scarcely be a good choice for a private chat.

'Where are we going?' she asked.

'My home. Have you had lunch?'

'No, but I'm not really hungry… Too much excitement today,' she extended wryly.

His long brown fingers flexed smoothly round the steering wheel and she remembered those fingers skimming across her body, expert and deliberate. She dragged in a short sustaining breath but she could still feel the tingling in her swelling breasts and the pulse of damp heat between her thighs. He had stripped her bare of every conviction she had once had about herself, she acknowledged reluctantly. She was a much more sexual being than she had ever dreamt but it had taken Rio to awaken and set free that side of her nature. It was terrifying to feel so vulnerable and yet Rio was currently on his very best behaviour, she recognised suddenly. Why was that? What was he planning? Why had he not yet said a single angry or insulting word to her?

'Who did this house belong to before you bought it?' she asked to break the silence as he steered the Ferrari down the long drive.

'An ancestor of Beppe's, who kept his mistress here—'

'How novel,' Ellie said drily.

'Yes, he was considered the rotten apple in the very respectable family barrel and after he died the house was left to go to rack and ruin because no one in the family thought it acceptable to live in what had once been the mistress's home. I bought it at auction and restored it. It's convenient to have somewhere close when I visit…*your father.*'

He voiced the designation with cool clarity. *Your father.* It shook her to accept that she finally had a father and that the ancestor who had kept a mistress had actually been one of her ancestors, as well. It was as though a family tree had suddenly unfolded in front of her and she smiled at the wonderful sense of security that gave her. 'I thought you would've stayed with Beppe when you visited—'

'Not if I wanted female companionship. You may not have noticed it but Beppe is rather old-fashioned in spite of his liaison with your mother,' Rio commented. 'It's simply easier to keep that side of my life away from him.'

Ellie climbed out of the car in the sunlight, grateful to have movement to distract her from thoughts of Rio's chequered past. None of her business, she reminded herself doggedly as he led the way into the big house. A housekeeper greeted them at the door and Rio addressed her in Italian.

'I ordered a light lunch for you,' Rio told her. 'You shouldn't be skipping meals.'

Ellie compressed her lips on a hasty reply.

'And you know I'm right,' Rio added with unblemished assurance.

He guided her out to a shaded terrace and pulled out a comfortable padded chair for her. 'Sit down…'

'You're so bossy,' Ellie complained, settling down and kicking off her canvas shoes to flex her overheated bare feet on the cold stone.

His housekeeper arrived with freshly squeezed orange juice for her and a glass of wine for Rio. She wondered if she was being deprived of the alcohol option because she could be pregnant but said nothing because she had been avoiding alcohol since their moment of madness. She liked that label. A moment of madness suggested a crazy once-only impulse that was out of character, but then everything that had happened with Rio had been out of character.

'What did you want us to talk about?' she pressed boldly, not wanting him to think she was tongue-tied in his presence.

'I brought you here to propose to you but I'm not quite sure how to go about it,' Rio murmured lazily. 'If I got down on one knee, you would laugh. If I told you how much I'm worth, you would accuse me of being boorish—'

Her lashes lifted high on her bright green eyes as she stared at him fixedly. His lean, darkly handsome features were sardonic and she frowned in bewilderment. 'Propose…propose what exactly?'

Rio gazed steadily back at her, dark eyes glittering like black diamonds. 'Marriage…obviously.'

'Are you out of your mind?' Ellie gasped sharply.

'No, possibly I'm foreseeing Beppe's reaction if he discovers that I've got his wonderful new daughter pregnant,' Rio extended quietly. 'And, yes, I'm aware that we don't know as yet whether you have conceived but it would be much worse to wait and see in the current climate.'

'You *are* insane,' Ellie exclaimed, gulping down a reviving swallow of orange juice.

'Not at all. I know that Beppe will never forgive

me if I've got you pregnant. He will blame me entirely for it because I have a rather raunchy reputation with women—'

'Raunchy?' Ellie rested her head to one side as if she was considering that word. 'Do you think rumours of your three-in-a-bed sexcapades have spread?'

Rio groaned out loud and sprang upright while shooting her a reproachful look. 'Can't you please put judgemental Ellie away for a while and have a serious conversation with me?'

Ellie winced. 'Not really. I can't take a marriage proposal from you seriously.'

Rio backed up against a stone pillar like a cornered lion and studied her with scorching golden eyes. 'That night in Dharia, I did not invite those women to my hotel room. They bribed their way in—'

Ellie pushed her stiff shoulders back into her comfortable seat and inclined her head. 'Oh, I guessed that,' she admitted. 'I assumed you wouldn't have double-booked yourself.'

The faintest colour scored Rio's hard cheekbones. 'You can't blame me for what *they* chose to do—'

'No, but what they did and what they assumed was acceptable said a great deal about the nature of your prior relationship with them,' Ellie pointed out with hot cheeks.

Rio swore long and low in Italian and finished his wine to set the glass down with a jarring snap on the table. 'I didn't have a *relationship* with either of them!' he fired back. 'I had sex with them on one drunken night years before the wedding. I admit that I did stuff when I was younger that I wouldn't do now—'

Her face stiff as she struggled not to betray any reaction, Ellie nodded.

'Just because you never felt the urge to experiment doesn't mean we're all the same…or that you're better than me!' Rio raked back at her.

'I don't think I'm better than you in any way. But that kind of experimentation doesn't appeal to me,' she confided.

'I can't lie and say I'm surprised,' Rio breathed, watching her like a hawk. 'Now we've got that out of the way and I can disclose that I have no plans to involve you in any form of sexual deviancy, can we concentrate on the marriage proposal?'

Ellie stiffened. 'Why would you want me to marry you?'

'If you do turn out to be pregnant I would have been asking you anyway,' Rio advanced. 'There is no way I would allow any woman to raise my child without me—'

'Rio… These days, single and separated parents are common—'

'I want my child to have everything I *didn't* have. A home, a solid background, two caring parents, security,' Rio extended almost argumentatively. 'It's only when you don't have those advantages that you realise how very important they are.'

'I understand that and I understand how you feel,' Ellie assured him, relieved that she knew more about his background than she had. 'But there's a reasonable chance that I *won't* be pregnant—'

'I don't want to wait and take the risk that you are because Beppe will judge me for that, as well, and regard me as an unwilling husband and a very bad bet.

It would be much easier just to tell him that we have fallen in love and wish to get married as soon as possible,' Rio argued. 'He will understand that and he will see nothing wrong with it.'

'I'm here on holiday,' Ellie reminded him helplessly. 'In a little over three weeks, I have to go home and return to work—'

'I will not come between you and your medical career. I own property in England and if you have to be there to complete your training, I will make that possible, whether you are pregnant or not,' he asserted.

That argument taken from her, Ellie slowly shook her buzzing head because he had taken her so much by surprise that she could barely think straight. 'So, you want to marry me to help take care of any child we might have and to keep Beppe content... Am I correct?'

'Sometimes you have the tongue of a viper,' Rio condemned in a harsh undertone. 'I want you for myself and for my own reasons and you know that! You know it every time you see me look at you, every time I touch you and struggle to *stop* touching you...'

Her pale skin flamed red at the dark liquid intensity of his deep voice. She lowered her head, finally acknowledging that she was equally out of control around him. In that they were equals. One kiss, one touch, one moment of madness wasn't enough to sate the craving. But marriage, marriage was something else entirely, wasn't it? It was forging a future together as partners, trusting each other.

'You don't trust me,' she reminded him. 'How can you marry a woman you don't trust?'

'With care,' Rio fielded. 'You don't trust me either. Time and better understanding would take care of that.

I'm sure we would both try to make the marriage a success—'

'People try that all the time with marriage and fail.'

'But there is honour in the trying,' Rio declared without hesitation. 'At least we would be doing the best we could to give our child a brighter future.'

'What if there is no child?'

'Then we eventually divorce and blame your long hours as a doctor and my business trips for keeping us apart too much,' Rio told her smoothly. 'Getting married now is a precaution for our potential child's benefit. The right start, the right environment—'

Ellie held up a hand to silence him. 'Yes, I get it but living with you would be a little like living on the side of a volcano waiting on the next eruption. You're very volatile—'

'And you're *not*?' Rio tossed back, watching her closely as her fine-boned hand closed round her orange juice to raise it to her peach-coloured mouth. 'If I had you in my bed every night I would be a lot less volatile—'

Ellie almost choked on her drink and, spluttering, set it down, her face flushing.

Rio shrugged and dealt her an amused look. 'Well, it's true. Having Beppe warn me off you doesn't improve my mood and makes it almost impossible for me to be with you.'

'We don't even have a relationship—'

'Then what *do* we have? You're splitting hairs, being too cautious. Take a risk on me,' Rio invited.

And she so *wanted* to do that, Ellie realised in astonishment. She had never done a reckless thing in her life but Rio tempted her to the edge of foolishness. What if she *was* pregnant? It would upset Beppe and mess up his relationship with Rio. It would be virtually impossible for her to manage to work and care properly for a child without a partner and a settled home. But to make that decision now when she had no idea whether or not she had conceived? She glanced up at him, at the strong face that sent her heart racing and turned her resolve to mush. Was it wise to give into that side of herself? Or would she live to regret it?

'Ellie…' Rio prodded impatiently.

'I don't rush major decisions!' Ellie responded.

Rio shot her a wicked smile. 'We could go to bed and think about it—'

'Another version of angry sex?'

'But you're not angry with me right now. You're attempting to work me out,' Rio surmised, uncoiling with fluid grace from the pillar he had been lounging back up against. 'But I'm really quite basic. If I didn't want you I wouldn't be suggesting this.'

The silence smouldered with unspoken undertones. In the interim, Rio's housekeeper reappeared with a tray. A plate of delicate and ridiculously enticing little sandwiches and a pot of tea were set down in front of Ellie.

'Think of how simple all this could be…if we do it my way,' Rio urged silkily. 'We say we're in love. We marry in haste. Beppe tries to dissuade us but is secretly delighted… And a baby, if there is one…would be the icing on the cake for him.'

Ellie snatched up another sandwich, registering that listening to Rio weave his arguments with such panache and conviction improved her appetite. He had drawn an attractive picture. If she didn't marry him and then discovered she was pregnant, how much damage would she do to her new relationship with Beppe? And could she really stand by while Rio took the blame when she knew she was just as much to blame? In addition, if she was pregnant, she would definitely be seriously considering Rio's marriage proposal because no one knew better than Ellie that raising a child alone was hard. In the course of her work she had met a lot of exhausted single parents struggling to keep work and family afloat. Her grandmother had struggled with that burden, as well, and both Polly and Ellie had been made thoroughly aware of that fact.

'I'm thinking about it,' she told Rio, who was emanating a wave of silent impatience. 'I won't give up work, you know. I'll never be a trophy wife. I don't like shopping or fussing with my appearance either,' she warned him.

'I'll shop for you,' Rio countered smoothly.

'Stop being so reasonable!' Ellie exclaimed in frustration. 'I'm not used to it—'

Rio stole the last sandwich and grinned at her. 'Stop being so sensible and so negative in your outlook.'

Ellie breathed in slow and deep. 'All right… I'll do it. I'll marry you. Are you happy now?'

Rio treated her to an approving appraisal. '*Finally.* We'll go and tell Beppe straight away and I'll get my staff on to organising the wedding—'

'I have to phone my sister first…and I want to do it in private,' Ellie told him squarely, sounding a great deal more sure of herself than she actually felt.

'And then we go and buy a ring,' Rio informed her. 'We'll go the traditional route—'

'Will we?' Ellie looked at him uncertainly, for she

certainly hadn't expected to be offered what she as-sumed to be the equivalent of an engagement ring.

Was the ring to impress Beppe with the reality of them as a couple? Or was it supposed to please her? And what was she going to say to Beppe? And how was she going to explain to Polly that she was suddenly rush-ing into marriage with a guy she had said she loathed?

CHAPTER SEVEN

'I JUST NEVER thought I'd see the day,' Polly carolled with a misty smile as she stepped back to scrutinise Ellie's appearance. 'You're getting married. I thought you were all set to be a spinster with a string of important letters after your name and a cat.'

Ellie had thought that too but she didn't admit it. She had never compromised on what she wanted from a man until Rio had literally crashed into her life at Polly's wedding. And that encounter had altered her image of herself and softened her rigid views. She had gradually begun to appreciate that she was lonely and that there was something hollow about achievements and more painful about trials when she had nobody to share those experiences with. Only now she was putting herself out there in a way she never had before, taking a risk on getting attached to a male who against all the odds appealed to her more than any other for no sane reason that she could find.

For Rio, she had lied for the first time in her life. She had told her father that she loved Rio but in actuality she had no idea what she felt for him. At first she had thought it was a mad infatuation but her thirst for information about him and her craving when he was absent had not faded. Surely an infatuation would have long since died from lack of fuel? All she really knew for certain was that Rio absolutely fascinated her, drew her and compelled her. And he made her feel more with him than she had felt in a lifetime of sensibly repressing strong emotions that unsettled her. And Rio had always specialised in seriously unsettling her.

She had been impressed even more when Rio had accurately forecast her father's every reaction to their marital plans and the stages of it. Beppe had initially been taken aback and had urged her not to rush into anything, but then Beppe had also confided that had he been free when he had met Ellie's mother he would have rushed to marry her. He had also admitted that he thoroughly understood the powerful life-enhancing effect of falling madly in love. And ultimately he had decided that as far as family growth went he could wish for no more than to see his daughter married to a young man he had always valued.

'Rio will grow with you by his side,' Beppe had forecast loftily. 'You make him think, you make him question what he truly wants from life. And what he has always wanted most of all is a family.'

Ellie gazed into the mirror and wondered if she was pregnant, if she could give Rio what he supposedly most wanted. But *was* that what Rio most wanted? Cavorting with all those women seemed a funny way of going about attaining a stable family life. Tomorrow morning, however, she would carry out the pregnancy test she had already purchased. She was both excited and scared by the idea. But most of all she was wondering how Rio would feel, regardless of what the result was.

She had naively assumed that she would see a great

deal more of Rio once their relationship was out in the open, but Rio had flown out to Dharia to settle some complicated dispute about oil well rights and although he had urged her to accompany him and she would've loved to see her sister sooner, she had refused. Why? Girly though it was, she had wanted to work with the wedding planner Beppe had hired and make her individual choices while also being available to ensure her gown fitted perfectly. After all, she was only planning to marry once.

And her dress fitted like a dream. The corset top had been chosen with Rio in mind. She just knew Rio would revel in hooks and laces and cleavage. The long skirt skimmed down in a flattering cut over her curvy hips and fanned out below the knee. Her feet were shod in Polly's gift, a pair of enchanting high-heeled sandals studded with pearls.

'Rashad really likes Rio and the men will be able to go off together when you visit and give us peace to gossip,' Polly remarked happily.

Ellie hid a smile because Polly was sometimes so innocent. The very last thing Ellie could imagine wanting just then was to be deprived of Rio's company. After all, he had been more absent than present since the wedding fervour kicked off. Beppe had held a series of social evenings to introduce his long-lost daughter to friends and relatives. Rio had dutifully attended those evenings before he flew out to Dharia, but Ellie's need to respect Beppe's boundaries had ensured that the bridal couple had little time alone together. Predictably, Rio had been much less accepting about the simple reality that she did not feel free to leave the *palazzo* to spend the night with him and possibly Ellie's insistence on restraint had kept him from hurrying back to Tuscany.

'When you have me wondering if we could contrive to have sex in my car without being picked up on a charge of public indecency, we have a problem, *principessa*,' Rio had complained the night before when he had joined them with Polly and Rashad for a quiet prewedding dinner. 'You need to learn to be more selfish and put us first.'

'No,' she had said. 'You need to learn that anticipation can act as an aphrodisiac.'

'But I don't need one of those,' Rio had responded with sardonic bite.

An abstracted smile tilted Ellie's lips now.

'You're nuts about him. I don't know how I didn't spot it at my wedding—'

'Your attention was elsewhere…on your bridegroom? And I'm not what you call "nuts" about him—'

'Oh, you so *are*,' Polly contradicted. 'Everything you've done just screams it, Ellie. You are not the sort of woman who meets a man and marries him within a couple of weeks unless he rocks your world…'

'People change,' Ellie argued and, eager to change the subject, added, 'isn't it really sad that we still haven't managed to find our missing sister? She could have been with us here today…'

Tracking down Lucy had so far proved difficult because she lived a travelling life, moving around a lot and surviving on casual jobs.

'We'll find her eventually,' Polly said soothingly. 'And it'll be very exciting when we do. Haven't you been tempted to look in her envelope and see what ring she was left and what name is attached to it? It could possibly help us to locate her.'

'No, I was trusted with that envelope and I wouldn't open it,' Ellie swore. 'How would you ever explain that to her when we finally met?'

'We could use steam to open it,' Polly suggested, colouring lightly at Ellie's raised brows.

'No, we should respect her privacy,' Ellie decreed.

Ellie descended the stairs smiling at her father, who stood at the foot beaming with pride. Beppe could not compliment her on her appearance enough. They travelled to the church in a limousine. She paused on the steps in the morning sunshine and she breathed in deep and slow, recognising that the elation she was feeling was happiness and marvelling at it while also fearing the undeniable storms ahead. She knew that she and Rio would argue and tussle and that there would be many times when she wanted to strangle him. That was normal life, she told herself prosaically, but true happiness was so rare a sensation for her that she wanted to make the most of it while she was feeling it.

Rio turned from the altar to get the full effect of his bride. And Ellie was stunning with her coppery hair swept up and her green eyes gleaming with intelligence above her sultry mouth. As for the dress, well, he was extremely impressed by that surprisingly sexy corset, which defined his bride's splendid curves to perfection. No, getting married didn't feel half as bad as he had dimly expected. He had thought he might feel trapped but the prospect of peeling Ellie out of that corset was more than equal to the challenge of surrendering his freedom.

Her hand trembled in his when he grasped it to

thread on the wedding ring. She had worn her engagement ring on her other hand. And like Beppe's family
emerald, which she had brought out to Italy with her,
it was another emerald to reflect the colour of her eyes,
an emerald teamed with white diamonds but not over
large because Ellie didn't like flashy jewellery and had
wanted something she could occasionally wear to work.
So sensible, his Ellie, Rio thought wryly, wondering
just when he had started thinking of her as *his*. When
he'd imagined her pregnant with his child and liked the
idea? When he saw her walking down the aisle towards
him? Or when he realised that he was her first lover and
strangely determined to be her *last*?

Of course, he knew why he was marrying her. With
Ellie, the sex was on another level even though it had
gone wrong the one and only time it had happened. She
stood up to him, she talked back, she was his equal in
every way. But more importantly she had signed a pre-
nup contract ringed with so many iron hoops of protection that an escape artist couldn't have undermined
it. If Ellie liked money, he had plenty of it and there
were worse weaknesses for a woman to have, he reasoned. She could have been the unfaithful type, forever
in search of the next big thrill. She could've been the
uncaring, uncommitted type but he'd already seen her
bonding happily with Beppe and witnessed just how
close she was to her sister. And if there was to be a baby
Rio was convinced that she would always and without
hesitation do right by their child. The ability and the
desire to be a good mother was the most imperative
trait of all that a woman could have, he reflected with
sombre conviction.

Ellie emerged from the church on Rio's arm. A crowd

of people were crushed into the street outside. Fleeting introductions were made while the photographer fluttered around. They were congratulated and showered with rice.

In the midst of the noise and excitement, Ellie suddenly noticed two blondes wielding their camera phones and giggling like drains as they urged Rio to look at them and smile. And it was *them*, unmistakably the identical twins who had gambolled naked on Rio's bed in that Dharian hotel two years earlier. Ellie's throat convulsed. She couldn't have been mistaken, she thought angrily. They were highly noticeable women, blonde, beautiful twins, whippet thin and impossibly sparkly and effervescent in a way that was seen as ultrafeminine. Rio had actually *invited* the twins to their wedding. Ellie paled and compressed bloodless lips while the perplexed photographer urged her to smile.

She settled almost dizzily into the limousine beside Rio and looked at him. How could he do this to her? How could he be so insensitive to her feelings? Those blondes reminded her of the most humiliating moment of her life. Before Rio had opened the door to that hotel room she had been on a high, feeling like a sexy, attractive woman for the first time ever and ready to move forward, no longer feeling like the drab, clever redhead whom few men approached. And her first glimpse of the giggly twins on his bed had cut her like a knife, making her feel ridiculous and pathetic and useless.

'*Cosa c'e di sbagliato?* What's wrong?' Rio asked as the car moved off to whisk them back to the *palazzo* where the reception was being held.

And Ellie didn't know what to say. After all, he was

entitled to a sexual past and in marrying him she had accepted that past. Exes at a wedding, well, not exactly what you wanted but not always avoidable either. But did the twins recognise her as the shocked woman in that doorway two years back? And would they mention that to anyone? Have a good giggle about it? She cringed inside herself and said nothing.

'Nothing's wrong,' she assured him quietly. 'It's just all the wedding hullabaloo. When it comes all together, it leaves you feeling shell-shocked.'

'I didn't invite Becky and Roz,' Rio breathed impatiently, cutting through her pretence.

So, he had noticed the twins. Well, really, how could he have missed them bouncing up and down with excitement only a few feet from him, determined to be noticed by him? Yet he had somehow contrived not to look once in their direction, nor had he shown the smallest hint of self-consciousness. But then why would he?

'Is that their names?' Ellie queried with a wooden lack of expression.

'I told the wedding planner to contact Rashad for the list of our university friends because I haven't kept up with their addresses,' Rio explained. 'They were invited to your sister's wedding and that's probably how they ended up at ours. If I'd taken a greater personal interest, I would've left them off the list.'

If anything, Ellie had grown even stiffer. 'Of course, if they're uni friends, why would you leave them out?'

'Ellie, you're putting out more sub-zero chills than a freezer,' Rio said with sardonic bite. 'But I can't change the past and neither can you.'

'I didn't realise the twins had ever been actual friends of yours,' Ellie admitted stonily, not best pleased to hear that information. 'Probably because I've never slept with any of my male friends.'

'Sadly, I wasn't quite so particular,' Rio countered in the same measured tone. 'And neither were they. In those days I could only cope with casual—'

Her smooth brow indented. 'And why was that?'

Rio squared his broad shoulders and settled back with a sigh. 'I set up a property venture when I was nineteen. Beppe was pressuring me to go to university to study business but I thought I could take a shortcut to success,' he admitted wryly. 'My business partner, Jax, had the security of a wealthy background. The property market was booming and we were doing very well, which is when I met a gorgeous brunette. I fell in love with Franca, asked her to marry me and we moved in together.'

Ellie dragged in a startled breath, for what he had just admitted was the very last thing she had expected to hear from him. After all, she had simply assumed that Rio had *always* played the field without ever pausing to settle on one particular woman. Learning different shook her up, learning that he had found that one particular woman years earlier and presumably lost her again filled her with insecurity.

Rio skimmed narrowed dark eyes over the pale, still triangle of her face and his shapely mouth twisted. 'The property market stalled and I was overstretched. I still believe I could have made it through but Jax pulled out and hung me out to dry…and Franca, who had been screwing him behind my back and who very much liked the luxuries of life, ran off with him.'

Ellie winced and dropped her gaze, imagining the sting of that double blow of financial loss and treachery. 'I'm really sorry that that happened to you,' she murmured ruefully. 'It must've been very hard to pick yourself up after that experience.'

'It taught me a valuable lesson. At university I learned enough to ensure that I would never leave myself that vulnerable in business again,' he confided. 'I succeeded but after Franca, I avoided any kind of serious involvement with women. What the twins offered suited me at the time. No strings.'

'I can understand that,' she conceded reluctantly. 'You know…er…that night at Polly's wedding, after we parted…I've always wondered what happened—'

'You don't want to know,' Rio cut in succinctly, his tone cold as ice water.

And in telling her that he had told her everything there *was* to know, she acknowledged in consternation, just as suddenly furious with him. She had rejected him that night and had raced back to her room at the palace to take refuge in time-honoured tears and self-recriminations. But Rio had taken solace where he could find it and what right had she to object? Finding that out annoyed and disturbed her though. Rio could divide sex from emotion and treat sex like an athletic pursuit and he had done so for years before he met her. Could Rio really change? Could he switch back to the young, optimistic male he must once have been when he fell in love with Franca? And what exactly did it take to make Rio fall in love?

Rio was watching Ellie as the limo drove through the *palazzo* gates. Her delicate little profile was set, her brain running at a mile a minute on thoughts he didn't want to share. Maybe he should have lied. But lies would catch up with him sooner or later. Did she realise that she really wanted him to be perfect? Prince Charming straight out of a fairy story? And that he could never be perfect? Frustration and growing anger raged through his lean, powerful frame. He could not pretend to be something he was not in an attempt to impress her. And why would he want to anyway? Ellie would smell a rat sooner than most women because she was always looking below the surface, weighing pros and cons, picking up on inconsistencies, seeking out flaws. And he had still to confess his biggest flaw of all to a woman who had chattered animatedly about how her discovery of Beppe would now enable her to chart the previously unknown paternal half of her medical history.

In the greeting line, Becky and Roz made much of Rio and their previous acquaintance while acting as if they had never laid eyes on Ellie before. They didn't recognise her, she registered with relief, didn't remember her at all from that fleeting glimpse of her in the hotel doorway that night. But instead of being relieved at that realisation, Ellie was angry with Rio and angry with herself. She had agonised so much over that night and she had been so hurt but their backfired encounter had not had a similar effect on Rio's tough hide. She needed to guard herself from being too emotional and vulnerable around him. She had to toughen up, she told herself urgently.

Polly whisked her off after the meal. 'What on earth's wrong between you and Rio?' she demanded.

'There's nothing wrong—'

'Even Rashad's noticed the atmosphere and to be honest he's not usually that quick to notice that sort of stuff,' her sister admitted.

And Ellie spilled the whole story from its start two years earlier to the presence of the twins at the wedding. She was too upset to hold it all in any longer and Polly's shocked face spoke for her. It was several minutes before she could even move her sister on from repeatedly saying '*Both* of them?' as if she had never heard or dreamt of such behaviour before. Her attitude did nothing to improve Ellie's mood.

'And that night you met…?' Polly pressed. 'He told you that?'

'Yes, Polly,' Ellie confirmed wearily. 'I've married an unashamed man whore.'

'If Rashad had ever done anything like that, nothing would persuade him to admit it to me,' Polly declared wryly. 'But at least Rio is honest, well, brutally so.'

'I think he was just thoroughly fed up with me asking awkward questions.'

'I suspect he's already heard more than enough about that night and you shot him down in flames, which is not the sort of treatment he's used to receiving from women,' Polly pointed out grudgingly in Rio's defence. 'Let it go, Ellie. It's in the past and you weren't dating him or anything, so you can't fairly hold it against him. He didn't cheat on you. As for those blondes, ignore them, forget they're here!'

Ellie knew that was sensible advice but something stubborn in her refused to back down. Hard reality was steadily taking the bloom off her wedding day.

Rio tugged her stiff, resisting body close as he swept her out onto the floor to open the dancing. He bent his arrogant dark head and whispered, 'Do you know just how annoyed I'm getting with you?'

'Do you know how annoyed I am with you?' Ellie whispered back, unimpressed.

'Are you always going to be this jealous and possessive of me?' Rio enquired silkily.

A current of rage travelled through Ellie as hotly as a flame. 'Are you? I seem to remember you threatening to beat up Bruno for buying me dinner—'

'That was different,' Rio asserted without hesitation. 'We were already involved.'

Angry tears prickled behind Ellie's lowered eyelids and she finally knew what was really wrong with her. She had got involved with Rio on an emotional level the very first night she met him. But he hadn't got involved with her until she entered Beppe's life and became what he initially saw as a threat to someone he cared about. Was he even involved with her now that he had married her? Or had he only married her to please Beppe and because she might be pregnant? And why was she only asking herself that now and worrying about the answer?

Rio caught her hand firmly in his as they left the floor, deftly weaving them through the clusters of guests addressing them, never pausing longer than a few polite seconds. Only when they reached the foot of the main staircase did Ellie question where he was taking her and she tried to wrench her hand free.

'We're going to sort this out in private,' Rio delivered in a driven undertone.

'There's nothing to be sorted out,' Ellie protested, trying once again and failing to free her fingers from his.

Determined not to be sidetracked, Rio headed for the opulent guest suite where Ellie had dressed for the wedding. He thrust the door shut behind him in a movement that sent dismay skimming through Ellie. She had not expected Rio to turn confrontational because she had assumed that the presence of their guests would control and inhibit him. The message she was getting now was that Rio's temper was rarely repressed.

He dropped her hand and Ellie immediately made for the door. 'We can't do this in the middle of our wedding,' she argued.

Rio cut off her escape by stepping in front of the door, which in turn sent Ellie stalking and rustling angrily in all her finery across the room towards the window. She flipped round, colour accentuating her cheekbones, green eyes very bright and defiant.

'It's our wedding and it's almost over and we can do whatever we like,' he told her grittily.

'Do you have an off button?' Ellie asked helplessly. 'Because I think it's time to hit it. Yes, this is our wedding and we have had a slight difference of opinion but I have done and said nothing anyone could criticise—'

'I'm criticising you!' Rio bit out harshly.

Ellie stared at him in shock, her lips falling open, because once again, Rio was blindsiding her and catching her unprepared. He had the most amazing eyes, stunning dark gold fringed with black curling lashes, and for a split second she was held fast by them while noting the aggressive angle of his strong jaw line, the faint black stubble already shadowing his bronzed skin and, finally, the ferocious determination stamped into his amazing bone structure.

'I'm not perfect, Ellie, and I'm never going to be but I was prepared to give this my best shot—'

'I never expected you to be perfect, for goodness' sake!' Ellie spluttered uncertainly as she moved warily back towards him. 'Look, maybe I was a bit oversensitive but there's absolutely no need for us to start having this out now! Let me go back downstairs before anyone notices we're missing—'

'No,' Rio breathed with finality.

'You don't just tell me no like that and expect me to take it!' Ellie argued furiously, trying to push him away from the door.

'I keep on hoping that you'll learn from experience,' Rio growled, scooping her up, nudging a giant vase of flowers out of his path and planting her down squarely on the marble-topped side table behind her. 'But you never do.'

'This is getting ridiculous. Let me down,' Ellie told him forcefully.

Rio pinned her in place even more effectively by pushing her knees apart and stepping between them to wedge himself even closer.

'You may be physically stronger but you can't bully me,' Ellie informed him tartly.

'I don't want to bully you, *principessa*. I want you to start using your brain,' Rio bit out impatiently, settling his big hands down on her bare shoulders. 'It's time to put sulky, moody Ellie away, ditch the negativity and look forward.'

'I am neither sulky nor moody,' Ellie pronounced with as much dignity as she could summon while seated as she was on a table, being held still. His hands were hot on her bare skin, sending odd little prickles of awareness travelling through her.

'Bear in mind the fact that I'm not sulking about having had to marry a woman who *could* be a scheming little gold-digger,' Rio urged, stunning her with that statement as his long fingers flexed expressively over her shoulders.

Her lips opened. 'A...a *gold*—'

'But I gave *you* the benefit of the doubt. When do you extend the same privilege to me?' he demanded grimly.

Ellie tried to slide off the table but he forestalled her. Flushed by the undignified struggle and enraged by the label of gold-digger, she snapped, 'Let me go!'

'No. I'm keeping you right where I can see you and we're having this out right now,' Rio decreed.

'How *dare* you call me a gold-digger?' Ellie slung at him an octave higher.

'What else am I going to call you when you still haven't explained yourself? You see, I may not be perfect, Ellie but the news is that *you're* not perfect either. You've had serious allegations made against you and although I'm now aware that an enquiry dismissed one set, there are still others in your background made by a family member,' Rio reminded her caustically. 'But I was prepared to overlook that history to marry you and give you a fair chance.'

Ellie had frozen where she sat and she didn't know what to say or even where to begin. 'You said you'd *had* to marry me,' she said, instead of tackling his accusations head-on. 'But you didn't have to. I didn't demand it. I wouldn't have allowed my father to demand it either. It wasn't necessary—'

'It was necessary to me,' Rio cut in ruthlessly. 'I could not live with the chance that you could be pregnant. I had to ensure that we were a couple and that if there is a child, he or she will not grow up without me.'

'So, this really is a shotgun marriage,' Ellie breathed painfully.

'No, it's what we make of it and so far you're doing your best to undermine us,' Rio condemned.

'You know the enquiry cleared my name,' Ellie reminded him sharply. 'How can you still think I could be a gold-digger?'

'It's all those shades of grey that lie between black and white,' Rio commented reflectively. 'What was your true intent when you befriended that old lady at the hospice where you were working?'

'I didn't befriend her. I was doing my job, acting as a sympathetic listener when there was nobody else available!' Ellie told him angrily.

'Maybe you would've got away with that inheritance had a complaint not been lodged against you and maybe you thought you could get away with it. Maybe you only looked up your father after you found out that he was a reasonably affluent man,' Rio murmured lethally. 'Who can tell? That's what I mean about shades of grey. How can I know either way? But I still took a chance on you—'

Ellie relived the stress and worry she had endured when quite out of the blue, one of the patients she had been tending had altered her will and left her estate to Ellie instead. It had been wholly unexpected and she had not felt in any way that she deserved that bequest. She had reported it immediately but naturally the old lady's nephew had lodged a complaint. It had been a nasty business and there had been nothing she could have done to avoid the ordeal. Rage and distress over Rio's suggestions roared through her taut body. 'I hate you!' she gasped chokily.

'No, you don't. You just don't like being questioned

and judged without a fair trial but it's exactly what you do to me,' Rio condemned levelly.

'I don't want to be married to you!' Ellie slung at him wildly.

'You don't mean that,' Rio assured her, the hands on her shoulders smoothing her delicate skin as he bent his head. 'You want me as much as I want you.'

'Stop telling me what I want, what I think!' Ellie exclaimed in seething frustration.

'Maybe I'm talking too much… Maybe I should be *showing* you,' Rio husked, tipping her back a little and burying his mouth hotly in the smooth slope of her neck while his hands delved beneath her skirt and swept up over her thighs.

'Stop it!' Ellie hissed, struggling against the great wave of quivering weakness that assailed her as the heat of his lips and the teasing nip of his teeth grazed her sensitised flesh. 'You're not allowed to do this when we're fighting!'

In answer, Rio crushed her angrily parted lips beneath his own, his tongue flicking the roof of her mouth and tangling with her own. The forbidden pulse at the heart of her pounded faster and hotter while honeyed liquidity pooled in her pelvis. His hands firm on her thighs, she squirmed on the table.

'Rio!' she cried in frustration.

He ripped the delicate panties out of his path and traced the damp wet folds between her parted thighs, and so much excitement surged up inside Ellie that she feared she might go up in flames. He had distracted her, she knew he had distracted her with sex and she knew she had to defend herself but in that instant nothing was more important to Ellie than the fierce, urgent demands of her own body.

'We *can't*...' she moaned for her own benefit as much as his.

Rio sank his hands below her hips and lifted her to him as though she were a doll. He sank into her hard and fast and the sudden fullness of him boldly stretching her made her shudder and gasp. And then he moved with brutal efficiency, hitting some magical spot inside her that knew no shame and the treacherous excitement came in a drowning, remorseless flood that overwhelmed her. Her teeth dug into the shoulder of his jacket, her hands clawed any part of him she could reach. The pleasure was unbearable, pushing her relentlessly to the edge. Her body careened into a teeth-clenching climax that left her bereft of breath and he freed her as the final convulsions trammelled through her weakened body.

He disappeared off to the bathroom leaving her sagging on the table. He had taken precautions this time around, she registered in surprise. So, he was no longer willing to take that risk of conception with her, even though they were now married. Did Rio *still* want an escape route? Was he hoping she wasn't pregnant? That he could still walk away?

And why wouldn't he when he was convinced that she was a shameless gold-digger? Anger sizzled through Ellie. She had lost another battle with Rio. She slid, almost limp with satiation, off the table and retrieved one of her shoes, which had fallen off. Her torn underwear was nowhere to be seen and she had no spare clothing in the room since her suitcase had already been removed. With a grimace she smoothed down her dress and staggered slightly on cotton-wool legs in front of a mirror to check her hair.

'You look fantastic, *principessa*,' Rio said huskily, lazily, catching her hand in his. 'And you're my wife now—'

'Not sure I want reminding of that right now—'

'I *like* reminding you,' Rio murmured, studying her with hungry dark golden eyes. 'Smile, Ellie—'

'No, Rio—'

'Smile,' Rio insisted. 'It's our wedding day and we should be making the most of it—'

'Oh, I think you've already done that,' Ellie told him before she could think better of that comment.

And Rio laughed with unholy amusement. 'You're mine. I needed the proof of it.'

All shaken up and fizzing with conflicting feelings and emotions, Ellie returned to the wedding festivities. Rio kept a hold of her, not letting her stray far from his side. Her body still felt hot and alien, the aftershock of forbidden pleasure and excitement still trapped inside her like a shameful secret. There was wanting and then there was wanting Rio, and he had just taught her that she was the one without the off switch when she needed it. That knowledge made her feel achingly vulnerable.

CHAPTER EIGHT

Rɪᴏ sᴄᴏᴏᴘᴇᴅ ʜᴇʀ out of the helicopter with precision. The flight had taken less than an hour.

'Why won't you tell me where we're going?' Ellie demanded.

'In a few minutes you'll know exactly where we are—'

'I wouldn't bet on that. I haven't travelled much,' Ellie admitted as he walked her a few steps down a quay and assisted her into a motorboat.

But as he had forecast, Ellie recognised where she was even though it was a place she had only previously seen in pictures. The view of Venice as the boat sped across the lagoon was breathtakingly beautiful. 'It's just like the paintings Beppe showed me,' she whispered, entranced.

On the Grand Canal, the boat slowed amidst the busy water traffic and nosed in at a smartly decorated landing stage. Climbing out, she accompanied Rio into a magnificent foyer ornamented with huge Venetian glass chandeliers. 'Welcome to the Hotel Palazzo Sorrentino,' Rio murmured. 'The jewel in the crown of my hotel chain.'

'Sorrentino?' she queried in surprise.

'Yes, it once belonged to your family but it was last used as a home by your great-grandfather and even he only lived in a tiny corner of it. Beppe was quoted millions for the repairs that were needed and he sold it to me,' Rio explained. 'It was being used as a warehouse by then because it wasn't fit for habitation. Converting it into an exclusive hotel took years but it was a worthwhile investment. Now it's fully booked years in advance.'

Recognising that almost every eye in the reception area was on them, Ellie went pink, suddenly conscious of her wedding finery. A little man in a smart suit approached to welcome them and handed her a beautiful bouquet with the compliments of the staff. Rio accepted a key from him and guided her across the foyer and down a corridor.

'We're staying here?' she asked.

'Not in the hotel. The *palazzo* came with a couple of attached buildings and I retained one of them for personal use. Beppe uses it regularly. He loves Venice, particularly in the winter when it's quiet,' Rio told her, leading her outside and along a wisteria-clad walled alley to a narrow door flanked by Venetian gothic windows. 'It's very private here and the staff service it so we don't have to worry about housekeeping or cooking.'

Ellie walked into a charming wood-panelled reception room that overlooked a tiny lush green garden at the rear. Beyond the garden, a gondola sailed past on a narrow waterway. It was a magical scene.

Rio removed the bouquet from her hold. 'I'll stick the flowers in the sink.'

Ellie knew she should go with him and deal with

the flowers but the diverse traffic flowing past on the canal commanded her attention and she stayed where she was.

'I'll show you round now,' Rio said lightly, and in a great gilded antique mirror she caught a glimpse of her answering smile that softened her face, and looked away again, dismayed that she could look happy in the company of a man who had implied that she could be a gold-digger.

'I need to tell you about Violet… The lady in the hospice, who changed her will in my favour,' she said tightly.

'Not now, we've had enough stress. Leave it until later,' Rio urged as he opened the door on a dining room where food already awaited them on the table, fearful that any sudden revelations from Ellie would set them at odds again on a night that he very much wanted to be special and all about 'them.' 'We should eat first. You didn't have much earlier.'

'I wasn't hungry,' she admitted as he pulled out a chair for her. 'I didn't think you'd notice—'

'I notice everything about you,' Rio incised drily.

'If that was true, you'd know I'd never have sought out Beppe simply because he was well off,' Ellie contended uncomfortably. 'It didn't matter who or what he was. I just wanted to fill in the blank I've lived with all my life and know what happened between my parents. You couldn't possibly understand how much it means to me to know who my father is and to actually feel a sense of connection with him. It's so much more than I ever hoped to have.'

'I understand a lot more than you appreciate,' Rio countered, his lean dark face setting into grim lines. 'I will never know who my father is and, frankly, I don't *want* to know. I met my mother as an adult and that killed off any sentimental delusions I might have had. My mother and I didn't have a single thought or feeling in common.'

Ellie studied him in shock at that revelation.

'You were very lucky to find a man like Beppe waiting at the end of your identity trail,' Rio remarked wryly.

He had met his mother and it hadn't worked out? But he had grown up in an orphanage. Where had his mother been when he was a child? And why didn't he know who had fathered him? Consternation gripped Ellie and she veiled her eyes. Rio managed to be incredibly sanguine about realities that would have seriously disturbed her and it made her all the more aware of how very little she knew about him and how unwittingly tactless she must have been while she was happily rambling on about what finding Beppe had meant to her. Of course, what had she ever personally shared with Rio? Discomfiture filled her. As a rule, Ellie was reserved and she kept her secrets close. She didn't share personal stuff except with Polly but that had to change now that she was married. Didn't it? It wouldn't be fair to expect more from Rio than she was prepared to give herself.

'Yes, I was incredibly fortunate,' Ellie agreed ruefully as she took another appreciative bite of her delicious pasta salad. 'Can I ask you about something?'

'Anything…'

'Earlier when we were together, you…you used a condom,' Ellie reminded him.

'Isn't that what you wanted?' Rio responded, his

ebony brows drawing together in a frown. 'If you are pregnant, we'll make the best of it but if you're not, well…it gives us more options.'

'You mean, we wouldn't have to stay together,' Ellie framed, her heart suddenly beating with a dulled thunderous thud against her breastbone.

Rio lounged back in his chair with his wine glass and settled frowning dark golden eyes on her. 'Don't put words in my mouth. I said options and I *meant* options. I believe that babies should be planned and greeted with joy on their arrival.'

Ellie nodded woodenly, thinking about the pregnancy test waiting in her case. 'I agree. The circumstances weren't ideal.'

'Ideal isn't everything, *principessa*.' A slow-burning, wicked smile slanted Rio's beautiful mouth. 'But I did notice that day at my house that the idea of getting pregnant turned you as white as a sheet. It's not a risk I'll run with you unless you ask me to…'

And how likely was that? Yet that unexpected offer soothed her in some strange way. He wasn't slamming the door in her face. He had not said that if she wasn't pregnant they would eventually separate and divorce. His outlook wasn't that simple or that final. So why was she relieved? What had she feared? She searched his lean, darkly handsome features, her mouth running dry as she struggled to look beyond the sleek dark beauty of him into her appalled reaction to the threat of being parted from him. Polly had seen what she had hidden even from herself: she had got attached, dangerously attached to Rio Benedetti. Recognising that reality hollowed her out with fear. She was afraid of getting hurt and very reluctant to want more from Rio than he was likely to give.

She went upstairs to explore and discovered a dreamy spacious bedroom swathed in opulent fabrics and a divine four-poster bed. Their luggage had arrived in advance and had been unpacked for them. Off the bedroom there was a splendid marble bathroom with sumptuous heated towels and very fancy fittings. Champagne and flowers awaited them. She filched a chocolate off the silver dish beside the champagne flutes and bit into it with so much pleasure that she closed her eyes.

'You like chocolate,' Rio said huskily from the doorway.

'Correction—I would *kill* for chocolate,' Ellie admitted with a sudden laugh.

His amusement ebbed as he looked at her, the sheer stunning elegance of her in her gown, stray copper curls showing round her hairline now, the heavier make-up she had worn for the wedding faded, a faint streak of eyeliner at the side of one eye where she had rubbed. And yet she was still so beautiful with her clear green eyes and lush pink mouth. 'I think I would kill for you,' he breathed, stunned and unsettled both by the thought and the feeling.

Unfortunately Rio was being forced to work without a script. He was out of his comfort zone. Hit it and quit it was no blueprint for a marriage or a woman like Ellie. If she was pregnant, she would be with him for a long time, he reminded himself darkly. She would make demands, the sort of demands he had never had to deal with before. She would restrict him. She would also probably and regularly drive him nuts. But on the other hand, every pleasure came with a price tag and she was clever, amusing, passionate and ridiculously sexy.

Ellie plucked the pins from hair and let the thick mass fall to her shoulders. Then she spun round. 'I need your help to get out of this,' she admitted, turning and indicating the lace ties. 'It's beginning to feel very tight.'

Rio removed his jacket and cravat and unbuttoned his shirt. He was thinking about the curves inside that corset, the wondrous curves that bad timing had forced him to neglect that afternoon. Raw hunger roared through him afresh. 'I love corsets,' he confided.

'Thought you would,' Ellie murmured a tad smugly.

He released the ties and the hooks and let the garment drop to the floor while she exhaled in relief that the constriction had gone. He kept his arms round her, dipped his mouth to the smooth slope between her neck and shoulder and dallied there, lifting his head to nip teasingly at her earlobe at the same time as he raised his hands to cup her full breasts.

Ellie rested her head back against him, tiny flames of arousal dancing over her skin as long fingers tugged and teased at her swollen nipples. She was so sensitive there that she pressed her thighs together as if she could contain the rush of damp heat at her core. He backed her down on the bed but she demurred, pausing to unzip her skirt and let it fall, momentarily forgetting that she was bare beneath.

'Memories,' Rio teased with a wicked grin, disposing of his shirt to reveal a corrugated abdomen, hard with lean muscle.

'You work out,' Ellie guessed, studying him closely, faint colour feathering into her cheeks.

'Every day. I'm at a desk too much. Ah…is that a look of approval from Dr Ellie?'

Ellie scrambled onto the bed and beneath the smooth white linen sheet and immediately felt better about hiding her overlarge behind and sturdy thighs. She didn't think there was anything wrong with her body, she simply wished that when she had been blessed with curves she had also been blessed with more height to carry them. Rio undressed, dropping everything in a heap while Ellie watched him like a hawk, thinking that it had never occurred to her to wonder what it would be like to have her own male stripper. He had a really great body. Broad shoulders, lean hips, the inverted V of muscle running down to…*that*! Ellie stared, reddened, no longer marvelling that she had been sore in the aftermath of her introduction to sex. He wasn't small anywhere and, being Rio, he was already primed for action.

'We can do without this,' he told her, yanking the sheet back. 'I plan to make you very hot, *principessa*.'

Ellie rested back on the pillows. 'And I plan to make you equally hot,' she warned him.

Grinning, Rio came down on the bed beside her. 'You've already achieved that…or didn't you notice?'

Ellie stroked the velvet-smooth thrust of him with wondering fingers. 'I noticed—'

'A little less of that,' he censured as she explored him.

'No, you don't get to hand out orders in bed,' Ellie told him.

And Rio laughed with startled appreciation and looked at her, the humour slowly draining from his lean dark face to accentuate the black diamond glitter of his slumberous eyes and the feverish colour lacing his exotic cheekbones. 'Am I being treated to bossy Ellie now?'

'I have more than one setting. I can't have you getting bored,' Ellie murmured intently as her hand spread over his chest. 'My goodness, I'm so pale I must look like a milk bottle beside you—'

Rio rolled over and pinned her half beneath him. 'A very, very sexy, curvy milk bottle—'

'In the mood you're in you'd find anything female sexy,' Ellie protested.

'No, you really don't get it, do you? Growing up, you were probably too busy polishing your brain cells to look in the mirror,' Rio quipped, running a fingertip along the peach-soft curve of her lower lip. 'You have the body of a goddess and a very beautiful face. Did I mention the gorgeous hair…?'

'I hate the hair. I went through school being called "ginger,"' Ellie muttered. 'And "clever clogs."'

'But you still triumphed, *bella mia*. Passed all your exams, married me—'

'Marrying you counts as a triumph?' Ellie gasped.

'See how you feel about me in the morning,' Rio murmured with lashings of sexual assurance.

'That you're tiring me out?' Ellie teased, her fingers dancing over a smooth bronzed shoulder, enjoyment lighting her eyes for such intimacy was very new to her and unexpectedly wonderful to find.

And then he leant down and he kissed her and it was exactly what he had promised, hot and hungry and wildly intoxicating. The heat of his long, lean, powerful frame against hers sent a current of prickling awareness flying across her entire skin surface. The plunge of his tongue electrified her, sending tiny shivers darting through every pleasure receptor. Her breasts tingled and swelled, the tips straining.

His mouth roamed over her, tugging at the sensitive buds, seeking out delicate spots and lingering. He worked his way down her body to explore the most responsive place of all and her hips writhed and her lips parted on tiny cries. She had never felt so much pleasure or such a relentless drive for release. It was as if something deep within her were screaming impatiently for satisfaction. She twisted and turned, drowning in sensation, her body programmed to leap and rise to fever point at his every caress. Slowly she could feel her control being torn away from her but this time it didn't frighten her. She didn't fight, she let go, rejoicing in the strong waves of pleasure convulsing her and thrumming like a euphoric song through every skin cell.

'You're really, really good at that,' Ellie whispered, limp and breathless in the aftermath.

'I'm good at a lot of things,' Rio husked, all sexual promise and dominance as he rose over her, rearranging her singing body to his satisfaction.

And if he was set on proving the fact, he proved it as he plunged into her tender depths with passionate force, reawakening her to arousal. Her heart hammered, her adrenalin kicking in as she arched beneath him, deepening his penetration, and suddenly she was greedy to experience every thrilling sensation. He moved faster, lithe and potent. Her excitement climbed with every compelling thrust. Perspiration dampened her skin, a furnace-like heat rising from the heart of her as the desire for fulfilment clawed at her. And then she was there at the summit and the blinding surge of heart-stopping pleasure seized her body and soul. She jerked and shuddered and cried out, thrown over the boundary between reality and fantasy.

Afterwards, Ellie wrapped her arms tight round Rio, feeling madly affectionate and happy.

'What are you doing?' Rio asked, tensing.

CHAPTER NINE

'I'M HUGGING YOU,' Ellie said witheringly.

'I don't do hugs.'

'I do a lot of hugging. You'll have to get used to it.' She sighed, blissfully unconcerned by his objection. She loved the hot, damp heaviness of him against her and smoothed her fingers gently down the long line of his spine. 'If I'm pregnant, you'll have a child to hug.'

She felt the charge of tension that stiffened him in her arms.

'That day...you went pale at the prospect too,' she pointed out sleepily, exhaustion weighing heavily on her.

'Of course I did. I haven't a clue how to be a parent,' Rio pointed out feelingly. 'How could I? I never had one—'

'Just like me. You'll learn as you go along,' Ellie told him drowsily, the words slurring slightly.

Rio lifted his tousled dark head. 'You can't go to sleep yet... It's our wedding night.'

But Ellie was already sound asleep. He went for a shower and eventually climbed back into bed.

Ellie wakened while it was still dark and suppressed a sigh. Her sleeping pattern had been disrupted by ever-changing shifts and a regular shortage of sufficient rest while she worked. Knowing that she was unlikely to drift off again, she got up and put on a comfy dress while scrutinising Rio as he lay sprawled in bed. He was taking up more than his share of the space, she noted without surprise. It was as well for him that he could look so good doing it, she acknowledged with tender amusement, noting the black hair curling against the pillow, the angular bone structure shaded in by stubble, the relaxed line of his mouth. Asleep he looked younger than his thirty years.

Dragging her attention from him, she went downstairs and the first thing she noticed in the sink of the elegant little kitchen was the bouquet of flowers, and guilt shot through her. A trawl through the cupboards produced a vase and she settled the blooms into water and put them on display in the sitting room. A search of the fridge revealed bottled water and savoury pastries and she ate standing up, watching the dawn light rise over the building on the other side of the canal and slowly illuminate the little garden.

'What are you thinking about?' Rio asked from behind her.

Ellie turned her head to take in Rio clad only in a pair of ripped blue jeans, his feet bare. 'Violet,' she mused wryly. 'The old lady who died in the hospice. She loved to see the dawn. If I was on duty I'd open the curtains early for her. I was thinking of how much she would have loved Venice but she never got to travel because her husband liked home best and in her day husbands ruled the roost—'

Rio grinned. 'Dare I hope it'll be the same for us?'

'Wouldn't hold my breath on that one,' Ellie advised.

'Why are you out of bed so early?'

'I've always been an early riser,' she confided. 'But then I'm not used to having the freedom to sleep in. If I wasn't working the past few years, I was studying for exams. The pressure is constant.'

Rio groaned out loud. 'Tell me about Violet while I order breakfast.'

'She was lonely. She'd outlived everyone who mattered to her,' Ellie told him. 'She had no visitors. Her nephew came once when she first entered the facility but he didn't come back. Some relatives can't handle the last stages of a terminal illness. You can't judge them for it. We're supposed to stay detached…and I never thought I'd have a problem with that.'

'Sometimes you get involved whether you want to or not.'

Ellie squared her slight shoulders. 'When I had a few minutes free I kept Violet company. That was all. She reminisced about her past and I would listen and it made her happy. Once she was asleep I would tip-toe out again. I knew nothing about her changing her will until her solicitor contacted me after her death,' she admitted. 'I couldn't have accepted anything from her anyway because it's against the rules of the trust that employed me for medical staff to make a financial gain from patients. Even though I'd turned it down, the nephew made an official complaint against me and the whole business dragged on for months before it got to the enquiry stage and I was officially cleared. Why would I have wanted her money anyway?'

'What do you mean?'

'Rashad and Polly insisted on paying off my student loans but they also tried to persuade me to accept a large lump sum off them to buy a property. It was very generous of them but I turned it down because, while I can deal with the extravagant gifts they insist on giving me, I don't want to be the family charity case,' Ellie admitted ruefully. 'Polly buys all my clothes as it is, but she's married to Rashad and I'm not. That's *her* life, not mine.'

'And now you've got a life with me,' Rio murmured, tugging her backwards into the circle of his arms.

'I'm not sure how much of a life I can have with a man who thinks I'm after his money.' Ellie sighed just as a loud knock sounded on the front door.

Without responding to that leading comment, Rio went to answer it.

It was a waiter with a covered trolley and at Ellie's instigation it was wheeled out to the small patio, which was now bathed in early morning sunshine. The screening shrubs in the garden gave it all the charm of a forest glade.

Ellie poured the coffee. 'So now you know about Violet. It was a storm in a teacup but it had long-lasting repercussions. Mud sticks. People I trusted made nasty comments. I was worried it would damage my career and I got very stressed.'

'Naturally,' Rio conceded, wondering why it hadn't occurred to him that, had she been mercenary, Ellie could have chosen to rely on her seriously rich brother-in-law for financial support. Rashad was very generous and very family-orientated. Had she so desired, Ellie could have given up work and lived the life of a rich socialite. Why had that very obvious fact never crossed his mind at any stage? Had he preferred to think of Ellie as a gold-digger? And if so, why was that?

'That's why this break in Italy was so important to me. I needed a holiday—'

'And instead you got me—'

A natural smile tilted Ellie's lips as she looked at him, lounging back shirtless in his seat, a beautiful, self-assured and ruthless work of art, who continually surprised her. 'Yes, I got you.'

'When do we find out whether or not you're pregnant?' he prompted without warning.

'I was planning to do a test now,' she confided.

'For *yourself*?' Rio queried in visible consternation. 'No, that won't do at all. We'll go and see a doctor, get it done properly—'

'I am a doctor—'

'*Sì...*' Rio gave a fluid, very Italian shrug '...but this is an occasion and it requires special treatment.'

Midmorning, following their visit to a very charming private doctor, they sat down to coffee and pastries in the atmospheric Piazza San Marco. Both of them were shell-shocked, Ellie most of all, because she had believed she would recognise some tiny sign and somehow *know*. But she hadn't known, hadn't recognised anything that different with the exception of being more tired than usual, and with all the fuss of the wedding that hadn't seemed worthy of note.

'So, now we know,' Rio pronounced without any expression at all.

And Ellie recognised the dazed light in his eyes and knew that he was just as stunned as she was to learn that he was going to become a parent in a few months.

'I just didn't really think it could happen that... *easily*,' he admitted in an almost embarrassed undertone.

'I've met a few distressed teenagers who made the same assumption,' Ellie admitted, smiling to herself, quietly pleased with the knowledge that she was carrying her first child. And no, their baby hadn't been planned and was likely to drive a horse and cart through her career choices, but neither of those facts mattered when set beside the wonder of conception, which she had watched give such great joy to Polly and Rashad. She would gladly make space in her life for her child, she acknowledged, recognising that in the blink of an eye after hearing that news that her goals had changed.

'Saying we would make the best of this development if it happened wasn't the most supportive or sensitive approach,' Rio conceded belatedly. 'I want to celebrate now but not only can you not drink, you've even been warned off coffee.'

There it was again, that ability to surprise her that made her love Rio all the more, Ellie reflected. In fact, loving Rio seemed to have been stamped into her genes like a no-escape clause because, of course, she loved him, didn't know quite when it had happened and certainly not *how*. She smiled, happiness bubbling through her that he was so flexible, so willing to happily embrace their unplanned baby. 'I'll drink decaf—'

Rio grimaced at the idea for he had a true Italian love of unadulterated coffee.

'There are other ways of celebrating,' Ellie pointed out, lashes screening her eyes as she covertly studied him, recognising that she would never tire of this particular view. Rio, hair blue-black and gleaming in the sunshine, stunning dark golden eyes welded to her with an intensity she could feel, sprawled back with indolent grace in his seat, his shirt pulled taut across his broad chest, his trousers straining over his powerful thighs. Her mouth ran dry.

'Eat your ice cream, Signora Benedetti. I love your curves—'

'Just as well. My curves will be expanding—'

A slashing grin curved his sculpted mouth. 'I can only look forward to it, *principessa*. But when it comes to celebrating—'

'You could take me out on a gondola,' Ellie suggested with enthusiasm.

Rio looked pained. 'Seriously uncool. That's a touristy thing—'

'Please...' Ellie urged.

And she got her gondola ride the whole length of the Grand Canal. Rio had caved and she was touched. He was much more comfortable sweeping her into a fancy jeweller's store afterwards, where he insisted on buying her an emerald pendant to mark the occasion. They lunched back at the house and he watched her smother a yawn.

'You should lie down for a while—'

'Only if you lie down with me,' Ellie murmured softly.

Disconcerted, Rio flashed her a glance as if he couldn't quite credit the invitation. But without hesitation he lifted her up out of her seat and crushed her ripe mouth under his own, all the seething passion of his intense sexuality rising to the fore.

He tumbled her down on the bed but he unwrapped her from her clothes like a precious parcel, pausing to admire and tease what he exposed, and she writhed like a wanton on top of the silk bedspread in the full glare of the Venetian sunlight, utterly lost in passion and equally lost to all shame. He took her from behind then, hands firm on her overheated body as he drove into her with a roughened growl of satisfaction. His urgent rhythm was wildly exciting. Heart pounding, breathing forgotten, Ellie reached a peak and her body detonated in an explosive charge of pleasure. She slumped down winded on the bed with Rio on top of her.

He released her from his weight and settled down beside her, reaching for her to pull her into his arms.

'Thought you didn't do hugs,' Ellie commented.

Rio splayed a large hand across her flat stomach and said piously, 'I'm hugging my child.'

Ellie laughed, feeling amazingly relaxed and at peace. Her fingers lifted and fiddled absently with the emerald she still wore round her neck.

'You can tell me about your uncle now,' Rio informed her in the tone of someone doing her a favour.

Ellie wrinkled her nose. 'Jim Dixon? My mother's brother? I guessed he would be the family member you mentioned. I take it he's still peddling his sob story about how I ripped him off?'

'You're not surprised?'

'Jim's vilified me everywhere and no matter what I said to him, he refused to listen. He doesn't *want* the truth. He didn't get on with my mother and he never liked Polly and me, but my grandmother was living on the poverty line when she agreed to raise us. Our mother gave her a lot of money to take care of us and the arrangement suited them both from that point of view. Unfortunately my uncle always resented us being there.'

'Tell me about the brooch,' Rio urged with typical impatience.

'Oh, the *famous* diamond brooch, the family heirloom for several generations and the only item of worth the Dixons ever owned,' Ellie recounted ruefully. 'My grandmother sent me a letter during my first term at medical school. In it she told me she wanted me to have the brooch because she was so proud that I was going to be a doctor. She gave it to me the first weekend I was home after that. I didn't tell Polly, well, I couldn't *bear* to—'

Rio had sat up, glorious dark eyes locked to her expressive face and narrowing. 'Why not? I thought you and your sister were really close.'

'Oh, come on, Rio, think about it! Polly was the eldest and the brooch should have gone to her if it had gone to anyone!' Ellie argued. 'Polly sacrificed her chance to go to art college to get a job and help out financially and when Gran developed dementia, it was Polly who looked after her. She deserved the brooch, *not* me, and I was astonished enough to get it because our grandmother wasn't a warm woman. She didn't neglect or abuse us but she didn't love us either. Polly would've been hurt by me getting the brooch, so I decided to sell it and split the proceeds with her and make up some story about where I got the money from.'

'Women… Why do you always complicate things?' Rio groaned. 'A man would just have told the truth. It wasn't your fault that your grandmother chose to give it to you.'

Ellie rolled her eyes, unimpressed. 'But when I tried to sell the brooch, I discovered it was only paste, not real diamonds, which made better sense to me. I mean, why *would* a poor family have held on to a valuable diamond brooch all those years? It was worth so little that I didn't bother selling it but I still haven't told Polly about it,' she completed guiltily.

'Where does your uncle come into this?'

'Our grandmother left her son the contents of her house when she died and, of course, he assumed that the brooch would be there and when I told him she'd given it to me a couple of years earlier, Jim accused me of being a thief. While Polly was out applying for the death certificate and making burial arrangements, I was wrangling with Jim. I told him the brooch was only a costume piece but he wouldn't believe me and he stomped off and wouldn't speak to us at the funeral. A few weeks later he got the police involved,' she revealed wryly. 'They came to see me at university. I showed them the letter. They were satisfied—'

'But your uncle wasn't?'

'No, he'll probably go to his grave convinced that I deprived him of his prized inheritance. I tried to sort it out with him and he wouldn't listen and by that stage I was past caring. I was sick and tired of the whole stupid business,' she confessed.

Rio traced a fingertip over the shadows below her eyes. 'You look tired, *principessa*. Have a nap.'

He owed her an apology for having entertained the ridiculous idea that she could be a gold-digger, Ellie thought in annoyance, but she was *still* waiting for that apology. He was far from perfect, she mused, and he was too strong to find it easy to own up to being in the wrong. On the other hand, he had wonderful taste in emeralds, had endured a gondola ride at her behest, was learning to hug and he was happy about the baby, she reasoned with sneaking contentment while swallowing another yawn.

Rio watched Ellie sleep and heaved a sigh. Had she noticed his moment of sheer panic when her pregnancy was confirmed? His blood had run cold. He had asked himself how he could possibly be a decent parent when his own parents had had more in common with the dregs of humanity. He didn't know what was in his genes, never would know, but that sort of stuff was important to Ellie. Was that why he *still* hadn't told her about the dumpster? Pride? He had always told himself that where he started out didn't matter; indeed that all that really mattered was where he ended up.

And where had he ended up? Married to a woman he had treated badly! His sins had come back to find him out and haunt him. So, he had to reinvent himself again, just as he had as a boy, as a young failed businessman, a student and, finally, a success story. He would change and adapt to his new lifestyle. He would be *the perfect husband*. That was what Ellie deserved. He owed her that. All her life, Ellie had only had her sister Polly to rely on but now she had him. He smoothed a corkscrew curl back from her pale brow, careful not to wake her, and abstractedly wondered if it would be too soon to visit a toy shop. Probably as uncool as that awful gondola ride, he conceded ruefully. But then wasn't he supposed to be reinventing himself?

'So how do you think my Italian is coming on?' Ellie enquired in the language.

'You are learning quickly and the accent, it is good,' Beppe told her cheerfully. 'Rio must be a better and more patient teacher than I expected.'

'He's been very patient but we only talk in Italian for a couple of hours a day. I find it exhausting,' she admitted. 'But I have a good memory. Outside of maths and science, languages were my best subject.'

'When will you be home?' Beppe asked plaintively. 'I miss you both.'

'Tomorrow. We'll join you for dinner,' Ellie promised and she finished the call because Polly had already texted her twice asking her to ring.

'What's happened?' she asked her sister worriedly minutes later.

'You *have* to open Lucy's envelope,' Polly told her and then she explained why and Ellie came off the phone again looking worried.

'What's wrong?' Rio pressed, lifting his handsome dark head from his laptop.

'Well, that kid sister we've been trying to find?' She sighed. 'It turns out that we didn't really think things through properly at the start. Because we didn't know who our fathers were, we assumed Lucy would be in the same boat. But Lucy's had access to her original birth certificate since she was eighteen and her father's name is probably on it. After all, he was living in London with our mother when she was conceived. All the investigator has been able to discover from enquiries is that Lucy's father is Greek and he thinks it's possible that the reason we can't trace her is that she could be in Greece.'

'That's reasonable, so stop fussing and open the envelope. It's only a name and a ring, nothing more important.'

'It just feels wrong,' Ellie muttered, going upstairs to extract the envelope from her case and clattering back down into the sitting room. She opened the envelope and extracted a ruby ring and read the name. 'Kreon Thiarkis,' she sounded out uncertainly.

'I think I've heard that surname before. I'll look into it. Text the name to Polly so that she can pass it straight on to the investigator,' he urged unnecessarily because she was already doing exactly that.

'Stop with the bossy stuff,' she warned him.

'Have you ever listened to yourself talking to Beppe? Telling him to eat more vegetables and drink less wine? Urging a man, who is physically very lazy, to go for walks? It's not going to kill him to be a little overweight at this stage of his life,' Rio opined. 'You climb on your healthy-living soapbox every time you're on the phone.'

Ellie winced. 'Have I been overdoing it?'

'No. Beppe enjoys being fussed over. He's never had that before. And if it's any consolation, you're giving him very good advice but he's very set in his ways.'

Afternoon tea was served to them out in the little garden and Ellie sat watching the canal traffic wend past in all its tremendous variety while she ate a divine slice of blackberry-limoncello tart. She was thinking about how very happy she was and that it seemed downright incredible to her that she had only been married for four short weeks.

After all, she had made some very major decisions during those four weeks. Finding Beppe, marrying Rio and discovering she was pregnant had forced her to have a serious rethink about her future. She had withdrawn at the last minute from her scheduled placement in London and was officially unemployed. But she was learning Italian as fast as she could and with Rio's assistance had already collected up the documents required for her to register as a doctor in Italy. Her career wasn't taking a back seat, she reasoned, she was simply on a go-slow diversion for a few months. Obviously, her priorities had changed.

She didn't want to leave Italy now that she had found her father. With Polly married to Rashad and living in Dharia, she had no family waiting for her back in London. She wanted the time and the space to get to know Beppe, as well. And she loved Italy and saw no reason to demand that Rio live in the UK when it was perfectly possible for her to work in Italy. That decision had removed much of the stress and the fear of the future weighing her down.

And she was so happy with Rio, even though he was the sort of near-workaholic who brought his tablet out even for afternoon tea in the sunshine. They had still contrived to enjoy the most incredible honeymoon exploring Venice. Well, she had explored and he had guided, occasionally complaining bitterly when she dragged him into old buildings or shot what she thought were interesting historical facts at him. They had wandered hand in hand off the beaten track and eaten wonderful food at little restaurants known only to the locals.

Many a morning had drifted long past noon before they got dressed. He was insatiable or maybe she was, she reflected ruefully, but they at least seemed well matched in that field. For the first time ever Ellie was learning what it was to have time to waste, to be indolent, to read a something that wasn't a textbook or a research paper.

And throughout every step of that most entertaining renaissance of hers, Rio had encouraged her and supported her. He made her happy: it was that simple and that was probably why she loved him. They still argued though. After she had told him the story of her grandmother's brooch, Rio had made the very extravagant gesture of buying her a star-shaped brooch studded with enough diamonds to sink the Titanic. 'You *deserve* it,' he had told her while she was trying to remonstrate with him over the expensive jewellery he kept on buying for her even though she rarely wore jewellery because she had never had much to wear. Stone Age man went hunting and dragged a carcass home to his cave to feed his woman. Rio's equivalent was inviting exclusive jewellers to visit the house to show her an array of fabulous gems worth a small fortune. And if she said no, he looked frustrated and hurt, and it was the hurt she couldn't bear to see.

If she made any sort of comment relating to golddiggers, he froze and changed the subject. No, he still hadn't apologised but she was bright enough to know that the flood of expensive jewels was Rio's way of telling her that he no longer nourished such insulting suspicions about her. And the one thing he wouldn't talk about was his time in the orphanage and his dealings with his mother as an adult. For some reason the story of his early years was a complete conversation killer.

Ellie stirred that night soon after she heard the phone ring, for working in the medical field had wired her to take greater note of alarms and phone calls. Coming sleepily awake, she sat up and watched Rio pace the floor naked. He was speaking in Italian and far too fast for her to follow, shooting urgent questions to whoever was on the other end of the call. And he was upset, lines grooved into his lean dark features, mouth a thinned tense line. Disturbed by what she was seeing, Ellie breathed in deep, bracing herself for trouble of some kind.

Rio made another call and then looked across at her with unconcealed anxiety. 'We need to go home. Beppe's in hospital. He had a heart attack while one of his friends was dining with him. He received immediate attention…which is good. *Isn't it?*' he demanded jerkily, seeking reassurance.

Ellie braced herself, fighting the strong emotions tearing at her at the very thought of losing the father she had only recently found. 'Yes, it will greatly improve his chances of making a full recovery,' she muttered hollowly, striving and failing to be more upbeat.

CHAPTER TEN

'SILLY FUSS,' BEPPE said again as Ellie gripped his hand. 'No reason to come back early.'

Even though Ellie was no stranger to the environment of an Intensive Care Unit, she was having a first-hand experience of how very intimidating it could be to see someone she loved lying in a railed bed, and Beppe looked so small and shrunken. She breathed in deep and slow, composing herself, because she was determined not to inflict more pressure on her father by overreacting.

Beppe had had an emergency angioplasty to clear a blocked artery soon after his arrival at the hospital and his prognosis was good if he followed the rules on how best to maximise his recuperation. But her father's heart attack had given him a terrible fright because he had not spent even a day in hospital before and had enjoyed excellent health.

Rio, however, had suffered an even worse fright, Ellie acknowledged. For during the flight that had whisked them back to Florence in time to see the dawn, Rio, sky-high on anxiety, had sat lost in his thoughts and barely speaking. Right at that moment he was poised at the foot of Beppe's hospital bed trying to act strong and optimistic for Beppe's benefit but Ellie could spot a pretence when she could see one. One of Rio's hands was clenching and repeatedly unclenching in a betrayal of stress that could not be hidden. And for the first time—and she scolded herself thoroughly for it being the first time—she finally recognised that Rio loved Beppe as much as she did, indeed probably more because Beppe Sorrentino had been a part of Rio's life since he was a child.

'Want to live to see grandchildren,' Beppe told them apologetically, his speech abbreviated and slurred by the medication. 'Never had family, want that now.'

'And you'll have that family,' Ellie assured him soothingly.

'Maybe sooner than you think,' Rio slotted in, ready, Ellie could see, to expose her there and then as a pregnant bride if it helped his godfather to look forward and raised his spirits.

'Hopefully we'll have news of that nature sometime soon,' Ellie delivered to silence Rio.

A nurse adjusted the machinery surrounding Beppe and a more senior nurse with a clipboard questioned her quietly from the doorway.

'Franca…' Beppe murmured with a weak smile in the direction of the woman in the doorway. 'Wondered when you'd visit.'

Ellie watched Rio freeze in patent disbelief and then slowly turn round. Her own brain, drained by the sleepless night and the stress, seemed to be refusing to function. The nurse in the doorway was Rio's ex? Or another Franca entirely? Could she possibly be the woman Rio had once planned to marry? The same one who had run off with his one-time business partner, Jax, when

Rio's property venture failed? It was a moment when Ellie would happily have given ten years of her life to be seated in the right place to actually see Rio's face and interpret his reaction.

'Franca…' he acknowledged after a noticeable pause and he addressed her in quiet Italian, moving forward and indeed stepping outside into the corridor to speak to her at length. She was a small, fragile brunette with big dark eyes and ridiculously pretty and right at that moment she was gazing soulfully up at Rio as though he had hung the moon for her.

Beppe squeezed Ellie's limp fingers to attract her attention and her shaken eyes darted back to him. 'She's been working here for years,' he whispered. 'I knew and never said. He didn't know.'

'They're old friends though,' Ellie pointed out with forced casualness, deliberately avoiding any hint of discomfiture for the older man's benefit.

Beppe patted her hand. 'Good girl,' he mumbled. 'Sensible girl.'

Ellie watched his eyes drift shut and slowly breathed in again, feeling almost giddy as the oxygen hit her lungs. Switching her attention back to Rio and Franca, she saw a doctor joining them and she rose from her chair quickly, keen to join the medical discussion clearly taking place in the corridor. But as she straightened she lurched and stumbled, a sudden wall of blackness closing in around her. And her last thought was, *How could you be so stupid?*

Rio scooped up Ellie at such speed that he almost tripped over Beppe's bed in his haste to reach his wife. 'She's pregnant,' he announced in a panic to anyone who cared to listen.

Guilt slashed at Rio as he carted Ellie out to the waiting limousine. He had dragged her out of bed in the middle of the night and she hadn't eaten in hours. That combined with the stress of Beppe's condition had been too much for a newly pregnant woman. Why hadn't he paid more attention to Ellie's needs? As Franca had explained, Ellie was probably experiencing low blood pressure and low blood sugar at this stage.

Ellie began to try to sit up in the car, saying limply, 'What are you doing? I don't want to leave the hospital—'

'Beppe is asleep. For the moment, the crisis is over and there's no reason for you to stay by his bedside,' Rio argued forcefully. 'Right now, you need to eat and rest. And *no*,' he instructed, actually daring to rest two long fingers against her parted lips in reproof. 'Don't bother reminding me that you're a doctor when you can't remember to look after yourself.'

A furious flush mantled Ellie's cheeks. She felt the sting of his censure all the more because it was warranted. But there had been no food on the private jet because there had not been time to restock it for the emergency flight from Venice, so eating had not been an option during the flight, and since their arrival she had only seen the inside of the ICU.

'Beppe didn't see me faint, did he?' she pressed worriedly.

'No, he was fast asleep—'

'What did his doctor tell you?'

'That he's on the mend but that he needs to make the changes you mentioned.' Rio swore under his breath in driven Italian. 'I feel guilty now. I should've tried to talk to him too—'

'At the end of the day, it's his life and his decision,' she said tiredly. 'I think he'll be practical, especially once he realises the next generation is on the way, although how he didn't guess from the way you were talking I'll never know!'

'*Dio mio...*' Rio growled out of patience. 'We *are* talking about a man who had an adulterous affair with your mother! Beppe wasn't perfect. Why would he expect us to be?'

Ellie sniffed, still reluctant to be exposed as the loose woman who had ended up on a sofa with Rio within days of her arrival in Italy. Not even in a bed, her censorious alter ego reminded her darkly. Rio made her reckless but he also made her happy...well, when he wasn't annoying her or worrying her.

'So was that the same Franca you once planned to marry?' she simply shot at him, going straight for the jugular, in no mood to contrive a subtle approach.

Rio flexed his broad shoulders and sprawled back in his corner. 'That was a surprise but I gather Beppe knew and never mentioned it.'

'I didn't know she worked in the medical field—'

'How would you?' Rio parried. 'It's not relevant in any way.'

Ellie pursed her lips. No, it might not be relevant on his terms, she was thinking grimly, but that one little fact of Franca's nursing profession and her treatment of him could certainly shed some light on Rio's reluctance to view medical staff as being 'caring' and the suspicious reception he had given Ellie.

'How did you feel seeing her again?' Ellie asked baldly, knowing it was intrusive but unable to kill the question before it leapt off her tongue. Because, in truth, the answer to that one little question was literally *all* she wanted to know.

Rio treated her to an incredulous appraisal. 'I'm not going to answer that. It's a stupid question.'

Ellie nodded, mouth compressing harder than ever.

And Rio thought quite spontaneously that Beppe would never have got the chance to stray from his marital vows with a wife like Ellie around. Ellie picked up on every nuance, dissected it, stressed about it and absolutely had to *talk* about it immediately. And sometimes it drove Rio crazy because his brain didn't work like hers. Why would he even *want* to talk about Franca? Aside from the reality that that liaison had happened what felt like half a lifetime ago? Women discussed feelings but he had never felt that need, had he? He very shrewdly kept that kind of nonsense to himself. Why did Ellie always want something from him that he couldn't deliver? Time and time again she showed him that he was failing to meet her expectations.

His jawline setting like granite, Rio brooded about yet another major flaw in his character. He didn't know how to talk about feelings, where even to begin, never mind end. He had had lots and lots of feelings when he was a boy, but he had learned through hard experience that it was wiser and safer to suppress them. He was resolutely practical and always had been. There was no point wanting what you couldn't have and even less point in wasting energy agonising over life's misfortunes. That creed had served him faithfully for thirty years. So, how *had* he felt seeing Franca without warning? Surprise and curiosity. Nothing wrong with those reactions, was there?

'You go to bed while I make you something to eat. What would you like?'

'You can cook?' Ellie gasped.

'Proficiently,' Rio assured her with satisfaction.

'Could you manage an omelette? Omelettes are kind of complicated, aren't they?' Ellie said in the tone of a woman who lived off salads and ready meals.

'Not that complicated,' Rio told her.

He led Ellie up to the master bedroom in his house and her luggage was brought up. She studied her surroundings with tired interest. Luxury fabrics and pale oak furniture lent the bedroom a traditional, almost feminine opulence that disconcerted her because it was very far from what she had expected to find in a rampant womaniser's intimate lair. Had she been less tired she might have noticed that Rio was scanning the bedroom, as well, in a manner that suggested he was equally unfamiliar with it.

And so he was, having hired a decorator to chuck out his man cave accoutrements and decor while they were in Venice. Everything was new, fresh and Ellie approved even though she didn't know it because he had made note of her favourite colours and the style of furniture she liked. She didn't like cutting-edge contemporary and she didn't like flashy and his former bedroom decor would have qualified in both categories. There had also been the serious risk of inadvertently encouraging Ellie to think about how many other women could have visited his home and slept in that bed. No, Rio was convinced that keeping Ellie happy meant acting as if that past of his didn't exist. He understood her passionate possessiveness, in fact, it warmed him as much as the hottest day, but he didn't want any element of his libidinous past coming between them.

And that included Franca. If he talked about Franca, he would be clumsy and he might well say the wrong thing. For that reason it was much better not to discuss Franca at all. Thinking that that was the troublesome topic of Franca now as done and dusted as a gravestone in a cemetery, Rio went downstairs to make an omelette worthy of a cordon bleu chef because he never missed out on an opportunity to impress Ellie and he had just realised that she couldn't cook.

As removed from the real world as a zombie, Ellie opened her case, extracted the necessities and went into the bathroom. She had a quick shower, discovered she had left her toothbrush behind in Venice and searched the drawers in the storage units. She found several new toothbrushes, a giant box of condoms, a choice of several different lipsticks and make-up containers and two unmatched earrings. All had clearly been left behind by previous visitors. Tomorrow she would dump them. Right at that moment, she was reminding herself that Rio was her husband, that, yes, he had had a past with other women, but that that was nothing to do with her, certainly not something she should be worrying about.

Rio presented her with a perfect golden omelette and she was undeniably as impressed as though he had owned up to being a rocket scientist. Washed and fed, she was taken over by exhaustion again and she slid down in the blissfully comfortable bed, quite unaware that Rio went for a shower and then slid in beside her.

When she wakened it was afternoon the next day and she was alone. She was shocked that she had slept so long and anxious to get to the hospital and see how her father was doing. When she came downstairs, Rio's housekeeper appeared, introduced herself as Sofia and brought her lunch on the terrace. Marooned without transport, she went into the large garage off the rear courtyard and discovered a stable of vehicles. Rio liked sports cars, she thought with amusement. *Boy*, did Rio like sports cars. Sofia showed her where the keys were and she picked a car in fire-engine red that appealed to her mood.

Navigating the many turns in the sweeping road that led down to the main route was more of a challenge than she had expected because she had never driven such a powerful car before but she made it to the hospital in good time and went straight to the ICU. Beppe, however, had been moved out of intensive care to his own room, a sign that he was making good progress, and she greeted him with a smile when she found him sitting up in bed and much more able to talk than he had been in the early hours of the morning.

'Rio's gone for coffee in the canteen,' he explained. 'You've just missed him.'

After she had been with him about thirty minutes, Beppe began to flag and she suggested he have a nap, reminding him when he argued that he was recovering from surgery and that it would take a few days for him to regain his strength. Ellie went straight down to the canteen in the basement to find Rio but it was very busy and she bought herself a cup of hot chocolate as a treat, while she queued and scanned the crowded tables.

When she finally located him, she stopped midway on her path to joining him because he was not alone, he was sitting with Franca. Reluctant to interrupt out of the fear that Rio would deem it jealous and possessive behaviour on her part, Ellie slid into a corner table nicely shielded by a tall fake potted plant and waited for his companion to leave. She barely sipped her hot chocolate while she watched the pair of them, former lovers, looking much more friendly than anyone would have expected in the circumstances as they sat opposite each other, both leaning forward to get closer and talking intently.

In not treating Franca like an enemy, Rio was acting like an adult, she told herself soothingly. It was downright nasty of her to think that Franca was looking at him with much more appreciation than the occasion could surely require. Slowly it sank in that they appeared to be having a quite emotional conversation and that unnerved her, but all the signs were there. Franca reached across the table and gripped one of Rio's hands at one point and then brushed away tears. Rio did not go into retreat. In fact, none of the barriers that most would expect to be present between lovers who had parted on very bad terms were to be seen.

Stop being so blasted jealous and suspicious, Ellie urged herself in exasperation. Obviously Rio and Franca were catching up on the past and had discovered that at heart they were still friends. But it really, *really* bothered Ellie that Rio was clearly having the sort of emotional chat with his ex-girlfriend that he refused to have with his wife. And for how long had he been chatting to Franca? All that time she had been upstairs sitting with Beppe? And he was *still* with her?

Ellie drank her hot chocolate, refusing to allow herself to watch Rio and Franca any more since she was obviously too susceptible to paranoia. She had fallen insanely in love with Rio, married him and turned into a maniac she didn't recognise. Every hour of the day she wanted Rio *so* much. It was frightening, mortifying, but she had to get control of her craving, her suspicions, her insecurity. One last look at them and then she would go and check on Beppe again, she bargained with herself.

And Ellie glanced, only allowed herself that one glance, and she saw Rio reach over the table to grip Franca's hand in a heartfelt gesture that felt like a knife plunging into her own heart. Franca put one of her hands on top of his and gave him a wobbly, tearful smile full of warmth and admiration. Ellie's glance became a stare and then she literally tore her gaze away at the same time as she stood up, abandoning her drink, and walked out of the canteen to wait for the lift.

Right, so, Rio had some weird new connection with his ex, not necessarily a sexual or romantic connection. Who was she trying to kid? She had sat watching a woman crying and smiling and holding hands with her husband. What was she supposed to think? A woman he had once loved enough to want to marry. But he had never loved or wanted to marry Ellie, had he? And now he was stuck in a marriage with a woman he didn't love, who was pregnant.

Ellie's eyes prickled like mad. She hardly ever cried and right at that moment she had a crazy urge to howl and sob, and holding all that pent-up emotion in was a challenge. Rio was so intense in everything he did and yet, unless he lost his temper, he didn't let that emotion escape, at least not around Ellie. But what had really seriously hurt was seeing Rio demonstrate unashamed emotion with Franca, Rio taking part in the kind of emotional exchange he had denied Ellie. So what had they been talking about?

Had they discovered that they both still had feelings for each other? Franca must have been Rio's first love and first loves, with all the memories involved, were notoriously hard attachments to shake. Ellie breathed in slow and deep to calm herself and checked on Beppe, but he was sound asleep and, according to the nurse she spoke to, likely to be for some time. There was no reason for Ellie to remain at the hospital, particularly not when she wanted to avoid Rio, who she knew very well wouldn't tell her anything about his encounter with Franca. If she taxed him he would think she was a jealous, suspicious cow and he would be right. She *was*…

As she drove off from the hospital she struggled to calm down. Only a couple of hours earlier, aside of her ongoing concern for her father, she had been blissfully happy and Beppe did seem to be improving. She was making a mountain out of a molehill, she told herself soothingly. She would say nothing, do nothing, wait and see how matters went.

But inside herself, Ellie felt as though her heart were breaking. She kept on getting a flashback of Rio holding hands with Franca, Franca staring back at him with so much brimming emotion. Was that love she had seen between them? Why not? Why shouldn't he love Franca? Seeing his former love in such a crisis as Beppe's illness had created when Rio had been in a very emotional state of mind, even though he wouldn't ever admit the fact? Had Franca and Rio recognised that they both still had feelings for each other?

And, yes, she had believed that Rio was happy with her in Venice, but what if all along from the very outset of their marriage Rio had only been making the best of things? The best of a bad job? He found her sexually attractive but was there any more to their connection on his side than that? Meeting Franca again could well have made Rio appreciate the difference between love and sex. Her stomach turned over sickly.

So *why* should she keep quiet about what she had seen? an angry voice inside her demanded.

After all, how would Rio have reacted to seeing her holding hands with another man? Rio would have gone up in flames, created a scene and demanded an immediate explanation. That was the truth of it. Rio was as hot-headed and impulsive as she was invariably sensible and cautious. So, if Rio wouldn't swallow that kind of behaviour, why should she?

Ellie drove back to the house, steadily getting more and more upset and tearful. Whatever she did, she had to make a statement. She had to make it clear that she would not tolerate any kind of flirtation because if she didn't Rio might go on doing it. He needed boundaries, no, he needed a giant wall built round him to keep him within acceptable behaviour limits, she decided furiously. So, it was better to overreact now in the hope that the fallout from her anger ensured that there would not be a *next* time, she reasoned in growing desperation.

A preventative gesture in mind, Ellie began to pack her cases again. She would move into Beppe's house for a few days and Rio would appreciate that she was seriously annoyed with him. But was that the right thing to do? What if Rio had realised he was still in love with Franca? A terrible frightening sensation of emptiness spread inside Ellie, because if she lost Rio, she felt as if she would lose everything.

And that was sad, really, *really* sad, she told herself bracingly. She loved him but that didn't mean that she intended to be a doormat or throw wild, volatile scenes whenever he did something she disliked. Walking out on him for a couple of days was a better, quieter option and he would realise that she was serious. Screaming at Rio would be unproductive because he was as stubborn as a mule.

Rio drove back to his house, still surprised that he had somehow missed Ellie at the hospital. He was in an extraordinarily good mood. Beppe was on the mend, Ellie was pregnant and certain misconceptions he had once held had been cleared up and had left him feeling more in tune with the world than he had felt in a long time. He was in the wrong place mentally to reach home and have a troubled Sofia indicate the envelope left on a coffee table while learning that his wife had departed with cases.

He tore open the envelope. It was an Ellie letter, very succinct and to the point. There was only one sentence, telling him that he had failed to demonstrate the commitment she required from a husband. What the hell was that supposed to mean? Rio swore and then he swore again. It was as if electric shocks were going off in his brain. Ellie had walked out on him and moved into Beppe's *palazzo*. Outrage roared through him. He had made a huge effort to meet Ellie's high standards and yet now she was trying to ditch him like an old shoe.

Rio reacted by doing something that Ellie had not foreseen. He phoned Rashad and asked to speak to Polly. But within a minute of speaking to Ellie's sister, he realised that she was as shocked as he was and had no idea what could have fired Ellie up to that extent.

'Ellie's really not the dramatic type,' Polly told him

unreassuringly, because that only suggested that he must have been guilty of some giant sin that had provoked sudden and uncharacteristic behaviour.

'But I haven't *done* anything!' Rio raged, pacing round the hall in sizzling frustration. 'Do you think it could be pregnancy hormones or something weird?'

Polly's astonishment at that news only convinced Rio that phoning your wife's sister for insight into an unfathomable development could be a seriously bad and undiplomatic move. But then it had never occurred to him that Ellie could have kept quiet about the baby even with her sibling. After all, she and Polly talked most days! It finally dawned on him that Ellie was a much more private person in nature than he had appreciated—someone who didn't share personal stuff unless forced, as he had had to almost force her to tell him about the diamond brooch and the old lady at the hospice. She held all her distress in, *hid* it, trying to stay strong. Until that moment he hadn't recognised just how similar they were in that category and he suppressed a groan because it only complicated his situation more. Maybe she was deeply unhappy living with him. How was he to know? She wasn't a talker or an emoter... *Per l'amor di Dio*, he was *so* grateful for her restraint in that line. After all, Franca had almost talked him into a trance.

Initially, powered on anger, fear and a desperate need to take a stance, Ellie had expected Rio to rush straight to Beppe's home to confront her, but as time wore on into the afternoon she started to worry that he wouldn't even *try* to get her back. In fact, maybe she had played right into his hands by leaving, maybe he had reached the conclusion that he didn't want to be married any longer. For a male as rich and gorgeous as Rio the grass always had to look greener on the *single* side of the fence.

What had she done in walking out like that? What way was that to save a marriage?

She *loved* him, for goodness' sake, even if it turned out that he was the biggest flirt imaginable!

Suddenly feeling distinctly nauseous for the first time in her pregnancy, and shaky and damp with nerves, Ellie went upstairs to lie down. She knew the stress was bad for her and her baby and she beat herself up more for the decision she had made. Since when had she been a drama queen? And walking out on the assumption that the man you were leaving would follow to beg you to return was almost suicidal if he didn't love you. Tears prickled and stung behind Ellie's lowered eyelids. What had persuaded her that she had to make such a theatrical challenge to Rio of all people? A fit of temporary insanity?

Rio walked through the bedroom door and surveyed his wife. She was fast asleep and his keen gaze could detect the faint redness round her eyes that suggested tears had been shed. His confidence rose. If his unemotional Ellie had been crying, that was a healthy sign. He sat down on the side of the bed and gently shook her shoulder.

Luminous green eyes flew open and settled on him in strained silence. Her lush lips parted and closed again as she regrouped and sat up to hug her knees. 'What are you doing here?' she asked coolly.

'You're here,' Rio said simply.

'You can't stay here,' Ellie argued, thoroughly disconcerted by that declaration. 'It's Beppe's house.'

'It's not. I bought it from him years ago when the upkeep was becoming too much for him. I begged him to stay on and look after it,' he explained with a casual shrug. 'It was a property investment for me—'

'You're such a liar!' Ellie told him helplessly. 'You did it because you love him!'

'That too.' Rio looked uncomfortable. 'Can we get to the point of what that stupid note you left behind meant? One sentence? I get *one* sentence of explanation?'

Ellie stiffened, more challenged than she had expected because Rio wasn't shouting or raging, giving her the fight she had subconsciously craved and yet feared with every atom of her being, lest it lead to the end of their relationship. She lowered her legs and slid off the other side of the bed. 'After the way you spent your morning, I should think the note was self-explanatory...'

'After the way I spent... Franca? You *saw* me with Franca?' Rio thundered without warning as he finally made the connection. 'Why the hell didn't you rescue me?'

Taken aback, Ellie froze. '*Rescue* you?'

'*Sì*... I'm sitting in a public place while a woman weeps and sobs and talks about the kind of stuff I really don't want to know and I can't *decently* escape!' Rio recounted wrathfully. 'You think I was enjoying that? Are you out of your mind?'

It began to sink in on Ellie that she could have made a huge error of judgement.

'I can't believe this is all about Franca!' Rio exclaimed with rampant incredulity.

'You were holding hands. I thought you were flirting with her—'

'You need to learn what flirting entails, *principessa*. I assure you that there was no flirting whatsoever. Franca lost her eldest daughter to leukaemia only weeks ago and has only recently returned to work after compassionate leave.'

'Oh, my goodness…' Ellie whispered in shock. 'That poor, poor woman.'

'Yes, even Rio with the heart of a stone was not going to get up and walk away from that!' Rio grated. 'And that was only a part of the doom and gloom rehash of the previous nine years that took place. She said it did her good to get it off her conscience but it only made me realise that my sense of moral superiority over events back then was entirely unmerited.'

Ellie nodded. 'Okay. You contributed to the breakup and her going off with your business partner. I assumed that some of it must've been your fault.'

Rio dealt her an exasperated look. 'I *didn't*. I blamed Franca and Jax, but then I didn't know what was going on behind the scenes. Her fling with Jax only lasted about five minutes, and at her lowest ebb she ended up homeless.'

Feeling guiltier than ever for her wrong assumptions, Ellie backed down into a corner armchair and sighed. 'That can't have been easy for you to hear—'

Rio's gaze was sombre. 'No, even at the time I never wished harm on her, but then she lived with me and I didn't even realise I was living with an alcoholic—'

Ellie's brows lifted in wonderment.

Rio grimaced. 'That tells you how much attention I gave Franca. My sole interest back then was really the business of making money. But to some extent that wasn't *all* my fault. I was driven by the need to show

Franca's family that I could provide well for her. They had done everything they could to try to separate us—'

Ellie was now genuinely interested in what he was telling her and some of her stress had ebbed because she had recognised that her worst fears had been groundless. 'But why?'

'Primarily my background,' Rio divulged stiffly.

'That you grew up as an orphan?' Ellie exclaimed. 'But that's so unfair!'

Rio braced himself to tell the truth and he paled and gritted his teeth. 'It was more sordid than that. I was an abandoned baby, born addicted to heroin. I was left in a cardboard box in a dumpster and found by street cleaners,' he admitted very stiffly. 'The manufacturer's name on the box was Rio. The nuns christened me Jerome after St Jerome but I was always known as Rio.'

Ellie was so appalled that she couldn't speak. She glanced away to get herself back under control but her eyes shone with shocked tears. To think of Rio as a defenceless baby thrown out like so much rubbish absolutely broke her heart. 'Why…a dumpster? Why not somewhere safer?'

'I asked my mother when I met her. She said she didn't want to get in trouble or be asked questions. It was nothing to do with my safety—it was *all* to do with her. I meant nothing to her. She was an addict and a whore,' he confessed grimly. 'Franca's family were convinced that I had to have evil genes. Some people *do* think like that, Ellie, which is why I've always kept the circumstances of my birth a secret. It is not that I am ashamed but that I do not wish to be pitied or thought of as being a lesser person because of those circumstances.'

Fierce protectiveness slivered through Ellie as she looked back at him, all the love she had for him enveloping her. 'I love you no matter what you came from. I love you more than I've ever loved anyone or anything and I *like* Rio as a name. And only now understanding why it was so important for you to give our child a safer, happier start in life…well, it only makes me love you even more!'

Rio was transfixed. He had been prepared for Ellie to flinch and be repulsed by the sleazy facts of his birth and ancestry and then pretend that they didn't matter even when it was obvious that they did. He certainly hadn't expected her to tell him that she loved him without reservation.

'Don't you realise,' she murmured gruffly, her throat thickening, so great was her emotion, 'that you should be *proud* of what you've achieved from such a tough beginning in life? It genuinely makes me feel incredibly proud of you.'

Rio studied her, lustrous dark golden eyes with a suspicious shine, lean, darkly handsome face clenched hard. 'You mean…all that?'

Ellie rose from her seat, empowered by his stillness, his uncharacteristic uncertainty. Never had she loved him more or understood him better. Franca and her family had taught him to be ashamed of his birth and background and she marvelled at their unwitting cruelty over something that he could not have influenced as she crossed the room and wrapped both arms tightly round him.

'Hug time?' Rio interpreted shakily, hoping she didn't catch the break in his voice, because in his whole life he had never known such a relief as the moment when Ellie told him that she *loved* him no matter what. It was the unconditional love he had sought without ever knowing it and suddenly he didn't feel alone and pitched against the world any longer.

'Hug time,' Ellie confirmed unevenly, winding round him like a vine. 'I'm really sorry I misunderstood what I saw with you and Franca. I sort of went haywire. I knew she was your first love and I thought maybe—'

'No.' Rio shuddered at the thought. 'She's happily married to a radiographer at the hospital and has two other children. But she developed a guilt complex about me when she finally got into rehab and started to rebuild her life. She says part of the recovery therapy was the need to mend fences with those she had wronged while she was still drinking but she could never face getting in touch with me after what she had done.'

'So, when she met you again—'

'It all came spilling out.' Rio sighed heavily. 'And I *had* to listen. It would have been cruel to tell her that it was very old history for me and that I no longer cared. I kept on saying that we had both made mistakes and weren't suited in any case but she kept on and on and on talking and crying—'

'I'm glad I didn't interrupt. Listening was the right thing to do. That was kind because I'm sure you were very uncomfortable and if I could've seen your face, I would've known that, but I could only see *her* face. When did you become that sensitive without me noticing?' Ellie asked in honest surprise.

'Oh, that probably happened when I realised I was in love with you. I then decided that I wanted to be the perfect husband—'

'You are…but I'm a very imperfect, distrustful wife,'

Ellie mumbled in shame, burying her hot face in his shoulder, drinking in the familiar scent of him with an enormous sense of relief combined with sheer wonderment. He *loved* her? Her gorgeous, passion-filled, outrageously exciting husband loved her? He didn't find her too boring or sensible? Jealous and possessive? She was ecstatic with wondering happiness. 'So what happened with your mother when you did meet her?'

'There was a piece in the newspaper about me being found when I was abandoned and she always knew where I was. When I began to make money she looked me up,' he confided grimly. 'And that's all she wanted… Money. She told me a lot of lies. I found out that although she had weaned herself off her own addiction, she made a living by dealing drugs to others. I had nothing more to do with her—'

'That must have hurt.' Ellie sighed in sympathy.

'It is what it is. Getting off drugs didn't magically turn her into a nice or caring woman.' Rio shrugged. 'As to my potential father? I was an accident. Probably one of her customers. She had no idea.'

'It really doesn't matter to me,' Ellie emphasised. 'I wasn't only saying that. What matters to me is the man you are now and I love him. I even love you a little more for being kind to Franca, which you must've found trying.'

Rio tilted up her face, dark golden eyes adoring. 'There could never be another woman for me, Ellie. I've never loved like this. I didn't know I even *could* love like this but you're everything I ever wanted in a woman…even if I didn't realise that until I met you the second time.'

'We just fought,' Ellie groaned.

'And I got more of a kick out of fighting with you than I got out of any affair I've ever had,' Rio confessed. 'But the hunger for you was overwhelming…I couldn't fight that—'

Ellie lifted warm eyes to his lean, strong face, glorying in his scorching appraisal. 'I couldn't either. I always keep my feet firmly on the ground and then I met you and everything, including me, went crazy—'

'But we've had so much enjoyment out of each other,' Rio commented with appreciation. 'On levels I didn't even know there could be between a man and a woman. Before you, it was all about sex for me—'

'Oh, I know that.' Ellie flushed. 'In Dharia—'

Rio winced. 'I was a jerk…but I had never wanted any woman the way I wanted you that night and I was on a high and then it all went pear-shaped, thanks to the twins—'

'Perhaps we both needed another couple of years to be ready for something more serious,' Ellie suggested forgivingly.

'*Dio mio*, I love you!' Rio swore passionately in receipt of the face-saving, utterly unearned excuse she was giving him and appreciating her generosity. He gathered her into his arms and almost squeezed her with his enthusiasm into suffocation. 'Really, *really* love you and I can't wait for the baby now that I know for sure that I have you by my side…'

'Well, when you ordered that giant train set in Venice and told me there was no reason why a little girl shouldn't enjoy it as much as a little boy I kind of guessed that our baby would be welcomed,' Ellie confided as he smoothly edged her down onto the bed. 'Nap time for pregnant Ellie, is it?'

'No. No rest for the imperfect wife,' Rio teased with a charismatic slashing grin as he looked down at her flushed, smiling face. 'Adriano was so relieved when you and then I showed up. He hates the house being empty because he has nothing to do and he's been fretting about Beppe. He's making dinner for seven, which gives us a few hours to fill—'

Ellie's eyes widened at that implication. 'You mean, you were so sure of yourself when you arrived here that you just went ahead and ordered dinner?' she exclaimed in disbelief.

'I wasn't prepared to leave here without you and if you refused to leave I had a case out in the car to enable me to stay here with you,' Rio explained without hesitation. 'When I want something, *principessa*…I don't quit and I don't surrender and I do believe that I would fight to the death to keep you in my life.'

'At heart you're a romantic,' Ellie told him with satisfaction and approval. 'When I came here, I was fighting for you too—'

Rio interrupted her in Italian to tell her argumentatively that walking out of their marital home had been a dreadful, shocking action to take.

Ellie refused to apologise. 'I was trying to make a statement, draw a line for you. Maybe it was a little extreme but I was hurting so badly—'

'I don't need a damn line, woman…I've got you in the flesh!' Rio told her aggressively. 'And it was not only extreme but also forbidden. You are not allowed to walk out on me ever again in this lifetime!'

'Is that a fact?'

'*Sì*… You're my wife, the centre of my world, my everything. You don't walk out. You stay and *shout*.'

Ellie breathed in deep, helplessly touched by that instruction. 'I'll shout the next time,' she promised.

'There won't *be* a next time!' Rio spelled out feelingly. 'Promise me—'

'*Sì*... I can promise that,' Ellie whispered, running adoring fingers through his cropped black hair and down one proud cheekbone to rest against his wilful lower lip. 'You're mine. I'm never going to walk away from you again.'

'Or drive off in my sports car,' Rio instructed. 'It's far too fast and powerful on these roads when you're not used to it.'

'I liked it—'

'No. I want you safe, *bella mia*.'

And before Ellie could demand that she had the right to influence what *he* drove in the interests of *his* safety, Rio kissed her with all the passion of his relief, love and desire for her and her impressionable toes curled. *Take that, sensible Dr Ellie*, she thought in wonderment that he truly was hers after all her anxiety and distrust, and then a thought occurred and she wrenched her mouth free...

'You never apologised for calling me a gold-digger!' she reminded him hotly.

'Of course I didn't.' Rio slowly shook his handsome dark head in apparent amazement at that reminder. 'That would have been owning up to flawed judgement or stupidity and it would've made you think less of me, so I decided to tough it out because I was trying to win you over to wanting to keep me by that stage.'

'*Nothing* would make me think less of you, you stupid man,' Ellie mumbled before she locked her lips to his again, his instant forgiveness procured, and there was no further conversation or indeed argument for quite some time. The excitement of their reconciliation powered the passion and the promises with buoyant happiness and fresh appreciation of the love they had found where they least expected it.

EPILOGUE

POLLY GROANED. 'I'M OUT of my depth here. What *do* we do about this situation?'

Ellie groaned too. 'Mind our own business for now. If the sister we haven't even met has a thoroughly wicked and dishonest father, it's not our place to tell her so. Lucy doesn't know us or trust us yet. She's found her dad and, at the very least, probably thinks very highly of him and, at worst, really loves him because he's been kind to her—'

'But what if he's just using her for some reason?' Polly proclaimed emotively. 'Doesn't she deserve to know he went to prison for fraud?'

'We need to establish a relationship with her as sisters first,' Ellie opined, crossing the terrace of her Italian home to prevent her fiery little daughter from striking the younger prince of Dharia, tall, sturdy Hassan, aged two, for taking one of her dolls and wheeling his toy tractor over the top of it with little-boy glee.

Across the terrace, his older brother, Karim, the crown prince of Dharia, shouted at his little brother in Arabic.

'He's telling him off,' Polly translated. 'He's so like Rashad, very well behaved.'

'That's never going to be my problem with Teresina,' Ellie whispered. 'She's always ready to fight for what she wants. It's a continual battle.'

'Well, you mix two pretty opinionated people like you and Rio and that's what you get,' Polly pointed out cheerfully. 'She's gorgeous with that hair though.'

Ellie smiled at her daughter, who was two years old now. Born of parents who both had curly hair, Teresina had miraculously straight shoulder-length black hair and eyes that were a lighter green than her mother's. She was small and slight in build and had learned to walk at nine months old. She was lively and quick-tempered and the greatest joy in Ellie's world, for she had never realised just how much she would love her child.

In the three years that Ellie had been married, her whole life had changed and she had not a single regret. She spoke fluent Italian and had secured her dream job in the hospital where Beppe had been treated and where she was now continuing her training as a doctor specialising in children's ailments. Beppe had made an excellent recovery and had, under considerable protest, begun walking to take exercise. She had grown very close to her father and was profoundly grateful to have found him in time to get to know him.

They had finally contrived to trace their long-lost sister to Greece, where she was living with her birth father, who appeared to be a most unsavoury man. But Ellie was convinced that considerable tact had to be utilised where their unknown sister was concerned and Polly and Ellie had yet to work out how to best approach Lucy without frightening her off. Ellie was in favour of sending the ruby ring with a letter introducing themselves and inviting contact. How that would go down was anyone's guess but at least it couldn't be seen as threatening or interfering.

Ellie had grown no keener on shopping in recent years, because if she wasn't at work she was exulting in precious *family* time and certainly didn't want to waste that time shopping and preening. Ellie had always dressed for comfort and she was still doing it. For that reason, Polly was still buying her clothes and now Rio was doing it too and her wardrobe was bursting at the seams with designer garments she only wore at the occasional swanky event Rio attended. On the jewellery front, however, her collection could almost have rivalled the jewellery of Dharia's royal family. Rio never went anywhere and came back without gifts for her and Teresina, and soon he would have a third little person to buy for, Ellie thought with quiet contentment. And she had finally told her sister the story of their grandmother's diamond brooch and Polly had simply laughed and dismissed the matter without concern, more worried that Ellie had had to deal with their uncle's spite without support.

The sound of a car coming down the drive sent Ellie leaping upright.

'I'll watch the kids,' Polly proffered. 'Go on…greet him and make his day! Rio's so romantic.'

Rashad climbed out of the passenger seat. The friendship he and Rio had formed while at university had only deepened when the men married sisters who liked to see each other regularly.

Rio's sizzling smile broke out as Ellie threw herself at him and wrapped her arms round his neck as if she hadn't seen him in a week. He was a little disconcerted because he had only left her early that morning and she wasn't usually given to any public displays of affection.

'You missed me?' he whispered, wondering if something was worrying her.

'A little. I've got news,' Ellie murmured soft and low. 'Let's go upstairs.'

'Is this about your sister Lucy?'

'No, nothing new there. Polly still wants to jump in the royal jet and land on Lucy's doorstep and explode into her life,' Ellie told him ruefully. 'But I think she's beginning to come round to a more diplomatic approach.'

As Rashad, the king of Dharia, strolled past them to join his wife and two sons Ellie gripped Rio's hand and practically dragged him up to their bedroom.

'You're beginning to worry me,' Rio confided, shooting a glance at Ellie's glowing face and registering that whatever had happened, it couldn't be anything bad.

'We're pregnant again!' Ellie announced with delight.

Rio blinked and nodded very slowly. 'I wasn't aware we were even *trying*…'

'I didn't want to put pressure on you so I didn't mention that I wasn't taking anything,' Ellie revealed cheerfully.

Rio almost laughed out loud. *Put pressure on him?* Nothing could keep him away from Ellie. He adored her. But he still compressed his lips and said, 'It might have been nice to be asked…to have discussed this as a couple,' he remarked, rather woodenly because he still wanted to laugh.

Ellie's face fell as if he'd slapped it. 'I didn't think of that. I know how much you love having Teresina and I want to have my family while I'm still young and I would like them close together in age.' She chewed uncomfortably at her lower lip. 'I suppose I should've said something—'

Rio grinned. 'I was only joking. I'm delighted,' he assured her with heartfelt enthusiasm. 'The more the merrier—'

'Polly's pregnant again too. She's very keen to have a daughter,' she confided. 'I'll tell her about me over dinner, so don't go breaking my news ahead of me like you did the last time with that phone call.'

Rio linked his arms round her slim waist. 'It's my news too, *principessa*. I did figure in the conception.'

Ellie beamed up at him approvingly. 'Yes, you're wonderfully fertile—'

'Good to know I'm useful for something—'

'*And* spectacularly good at the action part,' Ellie whispered lovingly, hands running below his jacket to skate possessively over his hard muscled chest and then lowering in a much more intimate caress.

Rio shed his jacket and his shirt in record time. 'I won't sulk about not being consulted on the extending-the-family issue,' he admitted huskily. 'I know Dr Ellie was in the driving seat worrying that I might suffer from performance anxiety in bed for the first time in my life. In short, I'm perfectly happy to be used and useful.'

'I know you are,' Ellie told him cheerfully, shimmying out of her dress even faster, her eyes full of love and appreciation as she fasted her gaze on his lean, bronzed body, the passion that always simmered below the surface of their marriage gripping both of them with its scorching intensity. 'Did I ever tell you how much I love you?'

'Not since last night.' Rio studied his wife with wondering admiration and marvelled that he had found her, that she had married him, learned to love him and overlooked his every flaw. Loving Ellie had brought him untold riches in the happiness stakes and he would never ever take it for granted because he had lived too long without that security. 'But if you want to be competitive, you couldn't possibly love me as much as I love you…'

* * * * *